The Souls of Lost Lake

Books by Jaime Jo Wright

The Souls of Lost Lake

JAIME JO WRIGHT

BETHANYHOUSE
a division of Baker Publishing Group
Minneapolis, Minnesota

© 2022 by Jaime Sundsmo

Published by Bethany House Publishers
11400 Hampshire Avenue South
Minneapolis, Minnesota 55438
www.bethanyhouse.com

Bethany House Publishers is a division of
Baker Publishing Group, Grand Rapids, Michigan

Printed in the United States of America

Library of Congress Cataloging-in-Publication Data
Names: Wright, Jaime Jo, author.
Title: The souls of Lost Lake / Jaime Jo Wright.
Description: Minneapolis, Minnesota : Bethany House, a division of Baker
    Publishing Group, [2022]
Identifiers: LCCN 2021047418 | ISBN 9780764238321 (paperback) | ISBN
    9780764239861 (casebound) | ISBN 9781493436071 (ebook)
Subjects: LCGFT: Thrillers (Fiction)
Classification: LCC PS3623.R5388 S68 2022 | DDC 813/.6—dc23/eng/20211006
LC record available at https://lccn.loc.gov/2021047418

Scripture quotations are from the King James Version of the Bible.

Cover design by Jennifer Parker
Cover image © Drunaa / Trevillion Images

Author is represented by Books & Such Literary Agency.

Baker Publishing Group publications use paper produced from sustainable forestry practices and post-consumer waste whenever possible.

22 23 24 25 26 27 28   7 6 5 4 3 2 1

To Cap'n Hook
This story is yours.
You murderously minded, marvelous man.

And to Momma
You're with the Master Story-Teller.
But oh, how I miss you.

CAMPFIRE TALES

Campfires were meant to be places of shadows. In between the flickering light of orange-and-blue hues, raging white centers, and filmy smoke tendrils lingered the dark places. In these places hid the stories that flavored the tongue of every storyteller, tightened the chest of every listener, and perked the ears of the most afraid.

"This is the tale of Ava Coons," the story begins.

A marshmallow catches fire, flames into a gorge of sticky mess, and falls into the flame, consumed by the raw heat that shows mercy to none.

"In the days of prohibition, before the Depression was at its worst, and before Hitler became a household enemy, there lived in the Northwoods, in a place near Tempter's Creek, a backward family of questionable origin. Few in Tempter's Creek truly knew who the Coons family was, and the fact that they lived deep in the forest once inhabited by the Chippewa made them even more of a mystery. But they were a mystery few cared about, and few gave any thought to. Until that morning, the morning of July seventeenth, when a girl emerged from the woods, her flour-sack dress stained with the blood of her family."

A gasp follows.

A camper flicks on a flashlight for safety.

An adult waves it back into darkness.

Two girls huddle closer together.

The storyteller scans his listeners, identifying them all by the flickering glows against their faces. Their eyes whiter as they widen with fear.

"She limped forward, her right hand gripping the thick handle of a logger's ax, which she dragged behind her because of its weight. When she approached, the townsfolk noted the ax was bloodied, darkening the wood of the grip, dried to the tip of its blade."

The storyteller pauses.

The fire cracks its regrets and its conviction that the story has much yet to be told.

"It was murder. All of Tempter's Creek knew it. The Coons family's only daughter had brought the weapon to their doorsteps. Ava Coons, a thin, dirty backwoods girl, vowed she knew nothing of what had happened to her family. *Vanished* was the word Tempter's Creek applied to the Coonses. To the father, the mother, the two older boys, and even the family dog. A search party gathered, and into the woods they traipsed. Calling, looking, and very much afraid of the carnage they would uncover."

An owl warbles its night cry.

A camper yelps at the eerie sound.

The storyteller waits until all the attention is back on him, riveted to his next words.

"There was a lake hidden miles into the forest. Surrounded by oak and aspen. A haven for water birds like the wood duck, the loon, and a hiding place for the black bear, coyote, and the raccoon. Few knew of this lake, but that day the search party stumbled on it. Lost in the wilderness, they found its shoreline, and set away in the woods they uncovered its horror."

"What was it?" A camper breaks into the story.

The storyteller is not perturbed. Instead, he smiles. That sneaky, knowing smile that the story is only going to instill more delicious campfire fear.

"The Coons cabin was burned to the ground. Its charred remains left only a portion of its southern wall. There was no blood. There were no bodies. The only clues left behind from the horrific scene were a lone shoe that had dropped halfway between the cabin and the lake, and on the shoreline, long rivets in the wet earth, as though someone's fingers had raked into the soil trying to save their life before being swallowed by the lake itself."

Silence meets the storyteller.

The campers, enthralled and terrified, are exactly where the storyteller wishes them to be.

"And Ava Coons grew up with no memories. They called her the 'Wood Nymph' of Lost Lake. Until one day, years later, when she wandered back into the woods and vanished. Just as her family had. The only object she left behind was the logger's ax, leaning against the house that had given her shelter as an orphaned child. Bloodied once more with the stains of her guardian. Knowing she was a murderess, the town of Tempter's Creek argued over how a girl could wield a logger's ax and dispose of her entire family to the depths of Lost Lake. They argued how, years later, she could have hypnotized them all into believing her to be an innocent, only to be starved for more bloodlust. Assuaged now, Ava Coons was out there. In the woods. She wandered there. She wanders there still. Ava Coons and the souls she has buried there, and the souls she still takes from time to time. The souls of Lost Lake."

1

Ava Coons

If someone had asked what her earliest memory was—and if she had been truthful—Ava Coons would have described the metallic scent lingering in the air, a blackbird eyeing the grisly scene from its perch on a crooked fence post, and her bare toes curling into a pool of blood on the front porch of her family's cabin.

That was most of what she could remember. Odd, how a small memory could wipe all others from a person's mind. She'd been thirteen when they found her wandering the outskirts of the small logging town in northern Wisconsin. The "Wood Nymph," they'd called her—she supposed it was because she'd come from the woods. Deep in the woods. In the places where, hundreds of years ago, only the Indians knew how to maneuver through them, and now few white men bothered to inhabit. The forest was good for logging, and that was about it. There were even rumors that it was in danger of limitation because of a new government movement to turn the woods into national forestry. Habitation this far north was for the hardy, not the cultured—especially during these troubled times when the economy had gone bust and work in these parts was scarcer than a tick on the back of a coon dog.

Ava dangled her legs as she perched on a wood barrel, topped and sealed with its tin binding. Inside, the contents boasted a sort of liquid prohibitionists would be appalled to see out in the open. But again, this was up north. No one here cared about laws and rights, or anything American other than the freedom to exist. To remember. But she didn't even have that. It had been six years since they'd found her, covered head to toe in dried blood that wasn't her own. They said she'd kept muttering something about "they're all dead, they're all dead." Yet they never found anyone. No bodies. No family. Nothing. Except for blood, and an ax.

Even now, blades intrigued Ava, and she couldn't rightly explain why. But that ax had been heavy. A logger's ax. Too heavy for a slip of a girl to wield over her head and incite that much inferred carnage. Still, she was the only survivor. Assuming anyone was actually dead. Without bodies, there was no case, no broken laws, no ghastly crime scene. There was just Ava Coons, the Wood Nymph, and her empty memories. Her parents—her brothers? They were shadow people in her memory, or who she saw from time to time out of the corner of her eye. When she looked directly at them, they vanished. It was their thing, she supposed, the vanishing. Vanishing left the questions, and the questions, if Ava thought too long about them, made her think she was going crazy.

"Here." Ned Hampton jabbed a peppermint stick in her direction. When she took it, he left a dirty fingerprint on its sticky side.

Ava stuck it in the corner of her mouth anyway. Like a cigar. She'd admired men who smoked cigars. It made them look like one of them Chicago gangsters minus the Tommy gun.

"I'm not a kid, Ned. Don't need candy." She mouthed the peppermint stick. It was delicious, but she wasn't going to admit that to Ned.

The older man, who had to have twenty or so years on her, assessed her for a moment. It had been six years, after all. She was nineteen now—and she wasn't married or nothin'. She was still living with the Widower Frisk and his wife by common-law marriage, Jipsy. Funny how most girls her age had at least married with a kid on the way, but she was stuck. Stuck at age thirteen when time began and yet never progressed.

Ned spit on the ground, a long stream of yellow tobacco. "I know that. But your teeth need brushed."

"Don't got me a toothbrush." Ava slurped around the peppermint. She hiked a foot up on top of the barrel, her boot busting at the side seam, and her overalls leg lifting to reveal a sockless ankle.

"I can see that." Ned rolled his eyes, and his eyebrows, connected in the middle to make one long caterpillar, lifted. "What's with Jipsy anyway? She ain't never been no mama to you, that's for sure."

Ava gave Ned a crooked smile and a wave of her hand. "Frisk borrows me his from time to time. I'm fine."

Ned eyed her for a long second. "You sure?"

There was something gentlemanly about the logger. Ava knew if she gave him half a nod, he'd hoist her over his shoulder and haul her off to be his own common-law bride. And there was a preacher in town now! So there was no excuse for "loose livin'," as Jipsy called it—even though she was faithfully committed to Frisk with no intention of being anything but his wife, even if the state said it wasn't legal.

"Just goin' to sit there all day?" Ned asked. He seemed reluctant to take his leave, even though he'd finished his purchases in the small general store.

"On this delightful thing?" Ava patted the side of the barrel. "Someone's got to guard the moonshine, Ned, you know that."

He snickered so intensely it should have cleared out his sinuses altogether. "Ava Coons, you'd best figger out your life. It ain't pausin' for you."

She didn't allow Ned to see his comment spear into her soul and draw blood. Instead, she waved him off. "One of these days."

"Sure. Sure." He finally started off toward the camp, a burlap sack filled with goods slung over his shoulder. "One of these days," he repeated.

Ava watched him go, lanky, familiar, yet so superficial. He didn't really know her. She didn't really know him. But they'd known each other since the day she'd first wandered into Tempter's Creek. Still. Knowin' and *knowin'* weren't the same thing. And if she didn't know herself, well, how could anyone else figure out who she was? She had a name. She had a vague memory. A bloody one at that.

A blackbird cawed from across the dirt road, and Ava looked up to meet its beady black eye and caress its brilliant feathery coat of black.

Bloody memories weren't worth dredging up.

So here she sat. On a barrel of whiskey. Not even known to herself.

Arwen Blythe

PRESENT DAY

Even in sleep, the missing haunted her. Trailed behind her as if she'd somehow run out ahead of them and forgotten to wait up. It was these uninvited dreams—visions maybe?—that kept Arwen with questions lingering in the recesses of her mind. Why her? Why the missing? Why did they visit her, dead or alive, real or imagined, in her sleep? Sleep was meant to be peaceful. Restful. Renewing. Instead, since she was a child, sleep had played Russian roulette with her dreams. And like tonight, her dreams became real enough to be memories of something that never happened—or had it?

Even in her slumber, Arwen knew she was seeing something not tangible and yet it was remarkably real. The depths of the forest were like an unending grave, stretching for miles in shades of green that taunted the shadows with the hope of life, only to suffocate because of the heavy drapery of foliage. Her hiking boots crunched on the undergrowth. Undergrowth that didn't really exist, although in her vision she still heard the sticks snap. Leaves argued against the weight of her. A headlamp's ray bobbed in the far distance to her left, and an echo undulated through the night, laced with desperation.

"Jasmine!"

The call faded as the forest swallowed the sound waves. An echo, and nothing else, of a man's voice, followed by a woman's, and then another man's. The search party.

Jasmine.

Or was it in her mind, in her head? One of the moments when life became surreal and she questioned what was and what wasn't?

Arwen could hear her breath in her ears. Her heartbeat thrummed like a rhythmic pounding of hands on a cajón.

The night air, crisp for it being early summer, infiltrated her senses and put them on edge. She was alive. This was real. She was alive. This was real. Or so her mind tried to convince herself while her heart fought against it.

Another *snap!* as her foot crunched on a dry stick, this time sending a chip into a nearby tree trunk.

Arwen could smell something metallic. Ironlike. She'd smelled it before when she had helped her cousin butcher a deer during hunting season. It was the smell of death but with life still pulsating through the vessels, attempting to accomplish what the body had already decided against.

Her own headlamp swept the darkness in front of her. God help her if the scent lingering in the air was from a child. Six-year-old Jasmine Riviera had gone missing. The search party was refusing to give up, even though it was well past midnight. Somehow, Arwen had found herself separated from the searchers. Deviating from the search grid. Instinct—or maybe something else—taking her into the deeper places yet to be mapped. The deeper places of her mind.

Lost Lake's back in there somewhere. It's Ava Coons's place. The place where she wanders.

Arwen could hear the campfire storyteller's scratchy voice as he entertained with tales of the forest. Her hiking boot slipped off a rock buried beneath wet leaves. Arwen took another step, this time the voice growing louder in her mind, and the shouting for Jasmine elusive and far away.

"Ava Coons still haunts it—if you can find it. But anyone who gets near it disappears. Poof! Like a vanishing act. No one ever sees them again. Man went missing in 1967. Some hunters found his body in '93. Bones. That's all that was left. People say a soul loses their senses in these woods. They become turned around and they hear things. Drives them mad until . . . well, until all that's left of them are bones."

They were meant to scare, the stories, told around campfires during the summer. With s'mores. With hot cocoa. Exaggerated tales of the murderess Ava Coons and all the gory elements that came after them.

Arwen paused, realizing her breathing was coming so fast and so hard that her chest heaved as if she'd been sprinting. She palmed the rough bark of a tree, leaning against it. *Feeling* it. She shouldn't *feel* it. Not in a dream. Not in a vision. But her senses were sparked, as always, disguising reality.

Her headlamp flickered.

No. No, no no.

It went out.

The forest became a silent coffin, closing in around Arwen. Be it the memories of stories, the truth of the disorienting nature of the forest, or something else—something altogether different—Arwen didn't know. She didn't understand.

A child's giggle filtered through the pitch-black night and floated away across the leaves.

"Jasmine!" Arwen's voice was loud. An interruption in the unforgiving stillness.

Little girl missing. Only six. They'd been searching for hours now. Hours.

Could she hear the ticking of a clock?

Arwen closed her eyes, and when she opened them, it was there. In front of her. A lake pooling out of the darkness, fog floating above its lily pads. Several yards from shore was a dilapidated cabin. Its roof was half sunken, revealing a gaping hole. The front door-frame was empty, an open, doorless smile into unknown ruins.

The tree she leaned against grew cold beneath her touch. Arwen snatched her hand back, looking down at her palm. She could see its whiteness against the blue-black of the forest floor.

"Wren?" The voice was whisper-like. It drifted toward her just as another set of girlish giggles chimed behind her.

Arwen squinted into the darkness toward the lake, so strangely illuminated. Toward the cabin, so oddly juxtaposed with the serenity of the scene.

"Wren?" The voice came from the cabin.

Arwen could hear herself breathing.

"Wren?"

Her head snapped up at the voice by her shoulder. A branch from the tree snagged the stocking cap that covered her hair. She scrambled to free herself.

There was no one.

Arwen squeezed her eyes shut and then opened them again.

There she was.

The little girl.

Jasmine.

She lay on the cold shoreline of the lake. Lost Lake. White. Cold. Unmoving.

Arwen's scream sucked the last breath from her already horrified body, and then more than the forest went dark.

2

Ava

The town hall consisted of one room, with wood floors that re-
sounded with the hollow claps of footsteps. Agitated voices bounced
off the walls, which also were bare except for the fact that Mrs.
Sanderson had whitewashed them last year and insisted on install-
ing electric lights that didn't work—wouldn't work—not until electricity was run to the town hall. Which would probably be decades
from now.

Mrs. Sanderson stood next to her husband, the highfalutin
woman in her prissy dress with lace collar and pearl buttons, and
her brand-new saddle shoes that made Ava's shoes with the split
seams laughable. Mrs. Sanderson was only five years Ava's senior,
but she comported herself as though she were in her thirties with a
passel of children and years of wisdom and earthly culture. Her eyes
narrowed when they landed on Ava. She placed a gloved hand on
her handsome husband's arm. He was the man who ran the lumber
office. Son of the lumber baron Sanderson and heir to Sanderson
Lumber Mill. Now he exchanged looks with his wife and then
eyed Ava. The thinning of his lips that reminded Ava of flattened
worms surrounded by a beard told her all she needed to know. She
would somehow be tied to the events of last night—at least with
suspicion. It was inevitable.

As the Wood Nymph, Ava was also the town's pariah of sorts.

An enigma. For six years they'd been both enamored with and horrified by her. Her most pivotal years as she grew into womanhood, Ava could barely comprehend how to maneuver through the raw fascination and rude curiosity of the folks of Tempter's Creek. Their opinion of her had twisted her own opinion of herself, until Ava knew she couldn't stay in Tempter's Creek, but she couldn't leave either. The people here were her family, in a tangled way, and in another they were enemies waiting to pounce. Stalking her. Expecting that one day the bloodied girl would emerge into womanhood a violent, torturous mess of a soul. Ava wished she had mustered the courage to leave Tempter's Creek years ago, when she was of the mind enough to manage on her own. But she was tied to this place. In her soul. A depth of a bond she both hated and cherished simultaneously.

Ned edged his way toward her, amid the throng of townsfolk who had come out of their houses for the spectacle, if not for the justice of the event. Ava averted her eyes from Ned. She didn't need him. Not him, not nobody, if she was honest. Jipsy nudged her with a bony elbow, and her sharp black eyes drilled into Ava.

"You could fare worse than Ned," she hissed, reading Ava's reticence to acknowledge the older man's devotion.

Ava chose not to answer the woman who had taken her in the day she'd wandered from the woods covered in blood.

Town Councilman William Pitford raised beefy arms over his head and shouted for the room to still. The din silenced, and the thirty-plus people in attendance shifted their focus to the councilman and his balding head dotted with sweat. He swiped a bandanna over it as though he knew Ava was counting the droplets.

"Folks. Folks." His repetition only made Ava's nerves grate. "Folks, we need to settle down."

"Settle down?" someone shouted. "After Matthew Hubbard's been found with an ax to the head, you want us to all settle down?"

A few ladies gave a swooning moan. Ava noticed that Mrs. Sanderson maintained her ramrod-straight backbone and didn't flinch.

"Folks!" Councilman Pitford reinforced his moniker for them with a pronounced octave raise. "We don't know what's happened!"

"What's happened is someone done killed Hubbard with an ax!" Widower Frisk barked from beside Jipsy and Ava, his gray stubble around his mouth yellowed from his tobacco-chewing habit.

"Yeah, an' you probably know who done it too!" another man retorted, making Ava step behind Jipsy. Not because the shrewish woman would do anything to protect her, but because it felt better than standing out in the open.

"Folks!" Councilman Pitford shouted.

"Hold up now!" Another male voice split through the ruckus of mutters and rumbling. It was the lead lawman in Tempter's Creek, and he was, as Widower Frisk put it, no Wyatt Earp. He elbowed through a few men who were taller than him and rose up on the balls of his feet so his five-foot-four frame would appear as imposing as possible. Officer Floyd Larson hung his thumbs over his gun belt. At least his voice was baritone, and a deep one that bordered on being bass. It gave him the authority that his stature did not. "Here's what we know—and it's more than you should *need* to know!" He eyed everyone in the room, his blue eyes narrowed. They landed on Ava for a moment, paused, then moved along. "Matthew Hubbard was found earlier today by Sanderson Mill."

"My mill had nothing to do with this!" Mr. Sanderson inserted.

Officer Larson held up a hand. "No one is going to convict the scene of a crime, Sanderson."

"My employees weren't involved," Sanderson insisted.

Officer Larson's facial muscles tightened with annoyance. "What I was saying was that Mr. Hubbard's body was found today, and we have concluded it was a murder."

"What gave it away? The ax stickin' out of his head?" someone barked from the back of the room. They met the question with grumbles, murmurs, and a few chuckles.

Larson remained passive, though Ava noticed a twitch to the tip of his nose. He was perturbed. Hiding it well, but still perturbed. He raised his hands, palms forward. "Listen here, we've no reason to believe anyone is in immediate danger. But while we're investigating the situation, we are advising you all to take to locking your doors at night. Windows too, if you have locks on them."

Another round of murmurs.

Mrs. Sanderson blinked.

Ava met her gaze and dropped hers to the scuffed floor. There was something about Mrs. Sanderson that made her feel smaller than a drowning beetle in a barrel of water.

"Never mind her." Ned's whisper touched her ear.

Ava stepped away, instinctively raising her hand to tuck the tendrils of blond hair behind her ear that his breath had dislodged.

"Who's on the suspect list?" Mr. Sanderson's voice held a very distinct edge. As if he had already built his own list and wanted to make sure that Larson's matched.

Larson ran his tongue along the inside of his lower lip, tucking his tobacco chew and making the lump jut out from his cheek like a tumor. "Can't say. You know that."

"Is *she* on it?" Tipping his head in her direction, Sanderson's brown eyes—which should've been warm like coffee—skewered her like a hand-carved wooden spike.

The room fell quiet.

Larson exchanged glances with Councilman Pitford.

Widower Frisk spit a stream into the nearby corner, more out of boredom than irritation or concern. Jipsy stepped away from in front of Ava, so that Ava was forced to bear the full brunt of most of the town's leading citizens' gazes.

Ned was the only one who didn't move.

"Well?" Sanderson pressed.

The law-enforcement officer cleared his throat again. "I can't say."

"And that's a yes!" someone shouted from the far wall.

Rumbles began again. Everyone expressing their opinions. Ava shot a desperate look toward Ned, because he seemed to be the only person who cared at the moment. But the look on his face was distant. He seemed mesmerized by the power of suspicion when fed on by a crowd.

"I need to go," Ava muttered to no one in particular. She took a few steps toward the door. It had been foolish to come tonight. It would be best if she left Tempter's Creek now altogether. It'd never been an idea far from her mind, but her ties to this place—to her family—arrested her every time. Now? It seemed destiny was going to make her decision for her. Innocence was not a trait she could carry well.

"Don't let her go!" a man shouted.

Another stiff-armed her, planting his palm against the wall so her chest bumped into his arm as she tried to get to the door.

"She needs to be taken into custody!"

"What if she comes after our children?"

"We knew all along she wasn't as angelic as you all said she was!"

"Anyone check old Frisk's place to see if his ax is missin'? She probably swiped it from him!"

"My ax is right where it should be!" Widower Frisk shouted back into the rising fray, intent on keeping his name—and his ax—clear of suspicions.

"Folks!" Councilman Pitford tried to maintain control. He even pounded on the podium at the front of the town hall, demanding attention with more than just his voice. But the body was growing more restless and more exaggerated.

"Can't no one forget what happened six years ago!" a fresh voice added to the fray.

"Wood Nymph, my eye—she's a bad omen, that Ava Coons!"

"Matthew Hubbard was a good man. God-fearing too!" This time it was a woman, and Ava knew right then that any hope the fairer sex would come to the aid of their own was for naught.

She ducked under the arm that still blockaded her in the room. Her overalls bagged around her thin legs as Ava hurried toward the back of the room. Toward the door.

"Don't come home, now, hear?" Widower Frisk's voice broke over the din, and it was the only one Ava heard. Squashing her intent to take refuge in the small lean-to at Frisk's property that had been her alone spot since she first emerged from the forest, Ava ignored the tears that burned her eyes.

So quickly. So quickly a group of people, roused into chaos by lies and untruths, by fearmongering and assumptions, could turn on their own.

The cool night air slammed into Ava as she burst from the town hall. She drew in long gasps, willing away the tears of betrayal and summoning every stubborn ounce she had left in her willpower. Even in May, the chill of the Northwoods was enhanced by the sound of crickets, chirruping their own mockery. Mockery of her. Mockery of the mystery girl who had emerged from the woods, dragging a bloodied ax, bearing tales of ignorance and memory loss with a desperate need to belong. To anyone. Anywhere. Only Widower Frisk and Jipsy had stepped up then, until now. Now, Ava was alone. Once again, very much alone, in the shadow of a brutal slaying like the one her own past implied. A past bereft of facts, of crime, and of corpses.

3

Wren

"Hey. Hey. Wren, wake up."

Wren flung her arm out to push away the offending voice that carried into her dream like a wraith. She didn't trust it any more than she trusted the vision in her fitful sleep.

"Wren!"

Hands held her against her pillow, the grip on her shoulders gentle but firm. She managed to open her eyes. The room was dark, save the light casting from the hallway, stretching across the floor in a band of hope.

"You're having another dream."

The voice was husky. Warm. Familiar.

She blinked, clearing sleep from her eyes, willing away the fog, and the image of the child's body stretched on the bank of the lake like a discarded doll.

A hand chucked the bottom of her chin in a soft tap laced with camaraderie.

Eddie.

His ruffled honey-blond hair stood in random strands off his head. His face was shadowed, but Wren could still make out the outline of his broken nose, healed but never straightened, from an old hockey game scuffle. His T-shirt hung from his frame, and he wore basketball shorts. The bed dipped on the edge where he sat.

Wren pushed herself into a sitting position and glanced at the old radio clock with its red digital letters—2:00 a.m. She looked back at her friend."I had a nightmare."

"You okay?" Eddie never really minced words. He was straight to the point and a realist. She both liked and hated that about him. Her childhood friend who had collected her as his pet project when she'd arrived at Deer Lake Bible Camp, when she was eleven and her dad had taken on the role of head of ministry education. It wasn't a small Bible camp. Deer Lake was year-round with groups that came and went, so there was a need for full-time mission staff.

Wren pushed her hair back from her face. Her coppery straight hair looked more burnished red in the darkness. "Yeah. Yeah, I think so. Sorry to wake you up."

Eddie shrugged. "Not the first time."

No. It wasn't. Nightmares were a regular occurrence for Wren, ever since her mom had passed away not long after they came to camp. Mom had left her with her father and her older brother, Pippin, who topped her by twelve years. For all sakes and purposes, Mom had left her alone, and somehow left behind images that tumbled into her dreams those times Wren was the most anxious. Images of abandoned dead children. It didn't take much during the day to trigger the dreams at night. They were always associated with the lost. The missing. It was unsettling at best.

"I'll get you some water." Eddie eased off the bed. "Then I'm going to head back to bed."

Wren gave him a wordless nod.

These were the things Eddie Markham was made of. Sensible logic, consistent loyalty, respecter of personal privacy. He'd never inquire what her dream was about. He didn't dig. He was a lot like his mom, Patty Markham, who slept in the next room, under palliative care. End of life. Cancer. The C-word was as ominous as Wren's nightmares. It was little wonder her fitful sleeping habits had only increased in recent weeks.

Wren fell back into her pillows, waiting for Eddie to return with the water. Life sucked. Pure and simple. It was no wonder she dreamed of missing children—it was what she felt like inside. Wandering and lost. Aimless. It wasn't until Wren bonded with Patty, Eddie's mom, that she'd felt like she could hope again. That someone would understand her. It was Patty who had taught her how to take care of her first time of the month, how to maneuver her first boyfriend, how to handle annoying girls in high school, and how to function under her father's criticism of her decision not to attend the university.

The Markhams had filled an enormous gap in Wren's life. It was why she slept here more than she did at her dad's house. They were all a close community. Camp staff was like that. Their homes were within a mile or two of each other's. Staff kids growing up, drifting from house to house, but they typically wound up at their own by nighttime. Not Wren. She had become buddies with Eddie, and then her reliance on Patty had become so pivotal that Patty had even turned her sewing room into an extra bedroom—just for Wren.

Now Patty was dying. Wren's world was going to fall apart again. She would become that aimless child, lost and waiting to be found.

The hallway floor creaked as Eddie returned. He handed her the glass of lukewarm tap water.

"Thanks." Wren took a sip. This was the millionth time Eddie had rescued her from a nightmare. Her first had been when she was twelve and spending the night with the camp's middle school staff slumber party. Boys in one room, girls in the other. The girls had giggled until they'd fallen asleep, but when Wren woke up screaming, it was Eddie who had barreled into the girls' room without permission, and it was Eddie who had helped set Wren to rights. He set a lot of things to rights over the years, and he'd also followed in his father's steps and devoted himself to camp ministry.

"You going to be all right?" Eddie hadn't sat back down on the bed. Instead, he stood over her, staring down, assessing her.

Wren nodded and reached to set the glass of water on the nightstand. "Yeah. I'll be fine."

He searched her face for a moment, his expressionless. "The girl?" he finally asked.

Wren nodded. "I can't imagine . . ." She let her words drain away.

Eddie's response was matter-of-fact. "It's not the first time someone has gone missing in the woods. There are thousands of acres out there."

"That's what scares me." Wren thought of the little girl in her dreams, body sprawled like a dejected mass. She couldn't help the shiver that passed through her. "She's just a kid, Eddie."

"And she's not yours." Eddie squeezed the calf of her leg through the blanket.

To anyone listening, his words would sound cold and unfeeling, but Wren understood. Eddie didn't know how to polish the truth into something tolerable.

"I know she's not mine," Wren replied, "but her parents have to be going mad."

"And we can help in the morning." Eddie removed his hand from her leg. So platonic, but yet the loss of it made Wren want to snatch it back. "You won't do anyone any good by losing sleep over it. They have people looking tonight. You need to do your part and get some rest so you can help with the search in the morning."

Truth. Fact. Eddie was right.

"Okay." Wren nodded.

"K." Eddie nodded back. "Get some sleep now."

"I will." Wren watched Eddie as he headed out of the room. Snuggling back into her pillows, she pulled the sheet and blanket up until they were tucked under her chin. But she didn't close her eyes. She didn't want to close her eyes. The visions from her dream haunted her with eyes wide open and could only become worse again if she closed them.

Little girl dead.

The shoreline. Lost Lake. Wren knew it. The old lake that for decades had been rumored to exist. A few locals claimed they'd found it. Campfire stories made Lost Lake seem like a vortex of evil. Eddie's dad claimed to have rediscovered it with his buddies years before when they were in high school, before handheld GPS was a thing. They had returned Lost Lake to the map. It wasn't a lost lake anymore. GPS coordinates would make sure it never got lost again. Yet Lost Lake was a place of haunting, of almost mythical lore. Its aura, if nothing else, sucked people into the wilderness and tried to trap them.

Wren turned on her side and curled her knees up against her stomach.

People got lost in this wilderness. Just as they did in life. Lost in a vast acreage of hiding places that claimed souls like time claimed lives.

She stared at the wall, unwilling to close her eyes just yet. She should be thankful. She still had her dad and her brother. This internal feeling of restlessness had never made sense to her, and even here, at the Markhams', where she felt the most at peace, Wren still felt lost.

It would be even worse when Patty died.

———

"Here. Coffee." Eddie pushed a mug toward her as if it would magically solve the world's problems.

Wren sipped, considered, and swallowed. Perhaps it would.

"It's strong." There was a thank-you hidden in her complaint as she balanced on a barstool at the Markham kitchen bar, leaning on its cold granite top. It kissed the skin on her bare forearms.

"After that nightmare you had last night, I should've added whiskey." Eddie swept errant coffee grounds onto the floor with a callused hand, his back to her as he cleaned the French press. His morning hair was tousled, streaked with blond and light brown tones that would make any woman jealous of the natural ombré.

Wren stared at his back. So familiar. Eddie had always been there, changing the course of her life in little ways that had a large impact. When she'd first arrived at Deer Lake Bible Camp, her father had split his time between his role in developing educational courses for staff development and campers requesting camp-provided speakers and educators, along with teaching English literature courses at an extension of the University of Wisconsin.

Camp staff was a different type of life most didn't understand. Especially larger camps like Deer Lake. Because staff was needed year-round, mission support raising had become part and parcel with running the place. But Dad wasn't keen on fundraising or "living off someone else's dime." He'd never judged people like the Markhams, who were one hundred percent supported by mission funding—Eddie's dad being the camp's maintenance manager. Instead, Wren's father had maintained a frenetic pace of professorship and camp education, until finally he'd succumbed to the necessity to fully invest in his position at camp. When Wren was a freshman in high school, he'd resigned as professor, so that now he rarely left the camp's grounds. Royalties from books he'd published, reinforced by his PhD in literature, made up for what he needed financially.

His first love would always be literature. Specifically focused on Tolkien. Hence her name Arwen, which Eddie had immediately shortened to Wren. A slight gesture, yet it had instigated an entire Bible camp's worth of staff to call her the same, much to her Tolkien-loving father's chagrin. *"Arwen,"* he'd correct them. Even so, everyone seemed to prefer Wren. She wasn't a Tolkien fan herself. Not like her older brother, Pippin. Even her mother had adopted the family obsession, having a custom-made sign to hang over each doorway in their house.

Wren's bedroom had been dubbed *Rivendell*.

The Green Dragon Inn was the family kitchen.

Mordor—Wren's personal favorite for the humor in it—was her father's bathroom.

"So about that nightmare?" Eddie broke into her thoughts. He leaned against the kitchen sink, eyeing her. There wasn't anything remarkably handsome about his face. His eyes were a general brown. He was at ease, too, about his mom, her breast cancer, and that she was in hospice care. He had a quiet disposition that Wren envied. That sort of faith was rare. The accepting sort. The kind that honestly believed God was God, nothing was out of control, and life carried on far beyond the immediate one.

This was also why Wren had never dated Eddie. They were too different. He was too cavalier. *Unaffected* might be the better word. Instead, while she would always need Eddie in her life, Wren was three months into a relationship with Troy. He understood the emotional side of her faith, the side that struggled, and he shared it. Troy was an adult version of a Hemsworth brother, with his sensitive eyes, masculine brawn, and overall gentle-giant persona. But Troy was out in the wilderness. Searching for the missing girl. Like everyone else, except for her and Eddie.

Wren might not be attracted to her childhood pal, but she was nothing if not honest with him. "My dream sucked. I was searching for the missing girl and I found her body. On the shore of the lake by a cabin." She tried on Eddie's matter-of-fact approach to life. It was difficult. Especially when her dream saturated every corner of her soul, making her insides shiver and causing her to want to pinch herself to make sure she was now awake and it truly had been just a dream.

"Lost Lake?"

She widened her eyes. "Where else?"

Eddie chuckled and rubbed his chin. The scratching noise from the stubble against his callused palm drew her attention. "Nice" was all he said in contribution to the conversation.

"No word this morning about the little girl?" Wren swallowed back the urge to panic on behalf of the family of the missing girl.

Eddie palmed the counter and hoisted himself onto it, bending slightly so he didn't knock his head against the cupboard. "Nothing."

Wren took a sip of her coffee to still her insides. "She's only five." Her observation made her feel worse.

"Six."

Not any better. Five, six, either way it was a little girl against the elements.

Eddie continued, "Jasmine's family is from the Milwaukee area. I talked to my buddy Bruce—from the police force, remember?—and he said the Rivieras have their RV parked in one of the campsites off Highway 82. You know, the ones over by Deer Lake?"

One of the many lakes in the area, and a lake by which the Deer Lake Bible Camp owned most of the surrounding acres.

"And that's why the police got word to us at camp?" Wren thought of Bruce, Eddie's friend from high school who was new to the police force of the town of Tempter's Creek, population 6,090.

Eddie drummed his fingers as they curled around the countertop by his thighs. "Yeah. They asked us for resources to help with the search. Troy has had a search party out all night helping look, but no news yet."

Wren had meant to be with Troy, only the kitchen staff had the stomach flu rampaging through their ranks, and she'd had to stay behind to help feed the campers—120 ten- to twelve-year-olds. It was Classic Camp week number two, and they needed all the help they could get to wrangle that many kids into the dining hall and force-feed them a concoction of hamburgers, hash browns, cream of chicken soup, and some sort of cheese slathering on top. In her opinion, they needed a new kitchen manager. Someone who didn't believe in recycling the food from the day before into weird casseroles. That would mean Eddie would be out of a job. While he was no chef, Eddie knew how to prepare food that made sense for campers and for the camp's budget, and he ran the kitchen like a well-greased machine. The campers never complained. She shouldn't either. But a great meal like a juicy steak . . . now *that* was another matter altogether.

She slipped off the barstool and slid the coffee mug away from her. "I should go check my phone. See if Troy texted at all."

Eddie nodded. "Yeah. Do that. And, Wren?"

She paused as she moved to exit the kitchen. A glance over her shoulder at Eddie revealed a seriousness in his eyes she wasn't used to. "What is it?"

"Don't try to be tough. Dreams can be upsetting."

He knew her. All too well. While they'd skirted the topic of her dream, it still swirled inside her. Real. Very real. It was all so . . . well, if she believed in visions, it was more of a vision than a dream. That was why she'd flippantly avoided the depth of the conversation and instead settled for general details about the missing Jasmine Riviera. If it was a vision, then the search party would never find her. It wasn't the first time the wilderness here had cursed a person. If it was a vision, then the search party was a futile effort, and everything pointed to the fact that little Jasmine Riviera was already dead.

4

Ava

"Get back in here!"

Ava had aspired to leave the throng and escape, but a few of the men burst from the town hall, their boots clomping on the plank sidewalk. She didn't bother to run. She recognized them. Ned was with them—probably to help her. But Ava knew she had nowhere to run to, as Mr. Frisk's parting shout continued to hammer through her head, *"Don't come home. Don't come home."*

A rough hand encircled her upper arm, pinching her skin and yanking her back in the direction of the town hall.

"Easy there!" Ned argued.

Chuck Weber's hand tightened around her arm. He was a logger—with a family—and she was sure he had visions running through his head of her sneaking into their home in the dark of night and slaughtering them all in their beds.

Ava stumbled.

Chuck jerked her upright, bruising her arm further. Ava bit back a whimper.

"I said *easy!*" Ned contested.

One of the other men marching beside them shoved Ned so that he tripped off the sidewalk. Ned cursed. Chuck hauled Ava up the steps and slammed open the door to the town hall.

Reentering the building was like jumping into a hot oven. The

33

room was stifling with body heat, hot tempers, fear, and a very thin thread of control. Officer Larson had his hands up in the air demanding attention, while Chuck and his cronies shoved Ava forward until she was smack-dab in the middle of the gathering of concerned citizens. She searched the crowd for Ned. She could see the top of his head in the back of the room. For the first time, Ava would have run away with him if given half a chance. Ned was safer than anyone here, even if he couldn't actually save her.

"Enough!" Councilman Pitford shouted.

Chuck released Ava with another shove. She stumbled over her own feet and held her arm to her chest, rubbing it where the man's heavy grip had nigh on near bruised it permanently. She glared at him with a ferocity she felt but knew she couldn't possibly back up with any sort of action. Didn't they realize the only thing she'd ever killed was a wasp, or from time to time, a wolf spider in the outhouse?

"She's gotta be locked up!" Chuck demanded, waving his arm in a wild sweep.

The group nodded and cried out their agreement.

"Murder us all in our beds, she will!" Chuck shouted. "Wood Nymph wielding her ax—we all know what that means."

"People, I say—" Officer Larson was interrupted again.

Mr. Sanderson released an ear-piercing whistle. "Let Larson speak! For the sake of all that's holy!" His face was flushed. His pretty, thin-lipped wife was not. She eyed Ava with such condescension that Ava suddenly wondered if it'd be better if Officer Larson hauled her off to jail. At least then she'd be safe behind iron bars. She hoped anyway.

"Thank you." Larson cast Mr. Sanderson an exasperated nod. "Now listen here. We can't just go locking away Miss Coons with no proof or evidence that she had anything to do with Matthew's murder."

"Murder!" A woman gasped as though it was the first time she'd realized axes didn't embed themselves into skulls by accident.

"Shush now!" Sanderson barked.

Larson nodded. "Yes. No different'n I can't lock any one of you up either."

"She did it! It's in her blood!" Chuck spit.

Larson narrowed his eyes at the man. "On what grounds? That we found her as a young woman with an ax in hand? As if a girl could slaughter anyone with a logger's ax! Use reason, man. No one ever found no dead bodies anyway. It's all speculation."

"Speculation? That she killed her entire family?" Mrs. Sanderson's chilly modulated voice cut through the air. Her blue eyes flashed, and she ignored the light touch of her husband's fingertips. "We all know she's orphaned. For the last six years we have hypothesized upon it, so let us not mince our words now. The Coons family was never seen after we found Ava. They vanished. Barely a young woman, and covered in their blood? It stands to reason she played a part, doesn't it?"

"Theory—that's all it is! You were barely a woman yourself then, so how would you know?" Ned hollered from the back of the room. "You ever seen a gal, or a full-grown female, heft a logger's ax over her head? Let alone chop her family to bits and pieces?"

A *thud* sounded, and one of the women landed in a pile on the floor. The woman's husband kneeled beside her.

"Someone get her some water!" Councilman Pitford didn't even have the courtesy to hide the exasperated roll of his eyes.

"Take the Coons gal into custody, Larson. The town demands it. Leastways till all this gets sorted out." Chuck's mean glare bored into Ava. She glared back until she couldn't anymore. Ave dropped her gaze to the floor.

"I cannot keep the girl locked up!" Larson protested.

"Then someone's gotta keep watch on her!" Chuck said. "Day and night! Twenty-four hours!"

One of Chuck's pals added to the advice, "Put her in the icehouse and have somebody stand guard."

"I can't *do* that!" Larson cried. "She'll freeze to death—and we've no proof of her guilt! Are none of you listening?"

"Frisk? You up for it?" Chuck ignored the lawman, apparently betting on the fact that majority rule would override law and order.

Jipsy gave a curt shake of her head.

Widower Frisk grunted and cussed.

Chuck's laugh was downright mean. "Figured. Take care of her while she's worth somethin' to ya. Cheap maid service an' who knows what else, that's what." His lewd insinuation didn't miss its mark.

Ava instantly wrapped her arms around herself and shrank back against the wall. She wished she *did* have enough guts and glory to ram an ax into Chuck. He didn't know the many nights she'd listened for Frisk's footsteps outside her tiny room. How many nights she heard Jipsy in the hallway intervene, until Jipsy put a lock on the door for Ava. She wasn't Frisk's plaything, no matter what Frisk had wanted. The idea the town even thought that . . . well, it'd never crossed her mind, and now it slammed into her with a vengeance.

"That's enough!" Officer Larson tried to put an end to the growing frenzy.

Widower Frisk was glowering, his fists balled at his sides.

Jipsy caught Ava's eye and gave a quick shake of her head. Silence. It'd serve them all best. Jipsy may not be her friend, but she wasn't keen on Frisk's attention toward Ava. It was a jealous dislike, not a protective one. Either way, Ava had learned to listen to Jipsy. It'd saved her more than once.

"I'll watch her."

The voice was low. So low, it was a miracle anyone heard him. He took two steps toward Ava, toward Chuck, and toward the circle of fire that was the accusations of everyone in the room.

"Reverend Pritchard?" Even Chuck's voice rose an octave in surprise.

Pritchard was new to town and the reverend at its one and only church. The thrumming of voices lowered to nonexistence. Sheer respect and utter shock had lulled them to rest.

Ava didn't dare raise her eyes. She'd never even seen Preacher Pritchard before. He'd only been in Tempter's Creek for all of a month, and she wasn't keen on Jesus or God or Mother Mary or whatever saint he was pushing. She just thought his name was funny and had bantered wisecracks about him with Ned. *"Preacher Pritchard prayed a prayer to pitch apart a pulpit."* It made little sense, but it had been fun . . . at the moment.

"I said, I'll watch her."

He had an even voice. Confident but not harsh. Gentle but not weak.

"Reverend, can't let you do that." Officer Larson clicked his tongue. "It shouldn't be necessary"—he leveled a look on Chuck—"not to mention, you know how unseemly that'd be? She'd have to be under your roof, and you're not married yourself and . . . well, I don't need more women passing out on me for the sheer scandal of it."

"I have Hanny nearby," the preacher offered.

"Hanny?" Chuck shouted with laughter. "Old woman is as loony as a bird."

"She's my neighbor."

"Yeah, well, she ain't *under* your roof, now, is she?" Officer Larson shook his head. "Fact is, Miss Coons doesn't need watching out for. She *isn't* a suspect." He spit the last words at Chuck and the rest of the room.

"You willing to take the liability for her if something happens?" Mr. Sanderson inserted.

Officer Larson stiffened to attention and leveled a narrow-eyed glare at the man. "Are you threatening Miss Coons?"

"No." Mr. Sanderson remained placid. "But I'd place a hefty wager there's several in this room who aren't keen on the idea of her being free to roam, and they're willing to do something about it."

"Fine kettle of fish," Councilman Pitford muttered.

Ava tried to breathe through her nose, but her breaths were coming in shorter sniffs now. She could feel the panic rising in her.

There was no way out. None. She was trapped—in danger herself—and they thought *she* was capable of murder!

"I'll watch her," Preacher Pritchard stated again. "I'm sure Hanny will provide the proper *chaperoning* you're concerned about."

"I'm concerned for *you*," Officer Larson retorted. "Don't need the preacher gettin' the boot a month into his pulpit here just 'cause he housed a young woman with a questionable past and dubious intentions."

"Dubious intentions." There was a tiny laugh in the preacher's voice as he repeated the officer's big words. "I'm sure we'll manage, sir."

"Fine." Larson shook his head and blew out a sigh so large it was akin to the wolf trying to blow down the little pig's house. "It's your pile of—well, it's yours to manage. Hear that, y'all? Ava Coons is under the watchful guardianship of the Reverend Pritchard for now. Go home! Lock your doors if you feel the need. Heck, yeah, actually *do* that. 'Cause Matthew's killer is still out there, and I'm telling you all, you're off your rockers if you think Miss Coons hacked a man to death with a logger's ax."

Ava lifted her eyes then. She had to. The compulsion to look at her guardian was too strong. Especially with the shock of Officer Larson's verbal imagery. If the preacher was going to back out, now would be the time.

Her gaze slammed into his. Dark. Bottomless. Deep. The preacher was younger than she'd expected. But his eyes. His eyes told stories that rivaled her own and held secrets that could wound a thousand souls.

5

Wren

Deer Lake Bible Camp was nestled along Deer Lake in the middle of a large piece of acreage bought in 1952 by the camp's founders, Bill and Alice Westphal. It never failed to bring contentment to Wren when she pulled her pickup truck onto its mile-long entrance drive, bordered by thick woods that shut out the sky. In 1952, the camp had been lucky enough to welcome fifteen campers the first summer it opened, and now it hosted programs throughout the year that entertained thousands of guests. The farthest border of its property melded into 225,000 acres of federal land. The forest that had swallowed little Jasmine alive.

The suspension on her truck was nothing to envy as Wren hit a rut and bounced on the seat. The main lodge came into view, its log exterior boasting triangular windows and potted evergreens at the main entrance. The second-floor windows were the staff offices. Somewhere up there was her father. Tristan Blythe. She would avoid him today. Not because they didn't get along, but because a missing child would likely turn him into the wild version of *The Hobbit*'s Bilbo Baggins when he went all crazy-eyed under the influence of the Ring. He was absolutely right to be incensed about a missing child, but being the dry professor-type that he was, his reactions would be more eccentric than helpful.

Wren pulled the truck into a parking spot and wrestled the gear-shift into park. Shutting off the engine, she spotted Troy trudging up the path from the east side of camp, where the horse stables and mini farm sprawled across ten acres. He looked exhausted. His longish dark hair was shoved back under a stocking cap. His face looked drawn, tired, and while it was remarkably attractive, Wren didn't allow herself to even give that idea the time of day.

She hopped out of her truck and slammed the door. "Troy!"

He looked up from his zeroed-in focus on the lodge and swerved to head in her direction. When he approached her, he wasted no time in wrapping his arms around her and drawing her close. The outlook on little Jasmine was bad. She could tell by the way he breathed, the way his entire countenance put off an aura of failed efforts.

"We didn't find her," Troy mumbled into her hair, which was pulled up in a messy bun.

Wren drew back a bit to look up into his sky-blue eyes. "I know. But that's good, though—I mean, she's not . . . dead." There was no way to tiptoe around the darkest fear of the searchers.

Troy grimaced. "Who knows? At least it didn't get too cold last night, but still. A six-year-old kid lost in these woods? It's like a needle in a haystack." He released Wren and wrestled his way out of the well-used backpack on his back. His role at Deer Lake Bible Camp was as their wilderness guide, planning excursions for the campers plus other trips for families, men, and even including a se-niors' summer canoe trip. Troy was at home in the woods and on the lakes and rivers that stretched into ancient tribal lands and into the Upper Peninsula of Michigan and Lake Superior. It was ominous that, after one solid night of searching, Troy was already so pessimistic.

"They'll find her. They *will*." Wren opted for optimism, how-ever misguided it might be. She ignored her dream. She refused to remember its eerie premonition. "There are more search parties out today, right?"

Troy yawned, and as he did, he dragged his hat off his head. Black hair stuck out in multiple directions and flopped into his eyes. He raked it back with his fingers. "Yeah. The search-and-rescue teams have about five hundred acres divided up into grids."

"That's good!" Wren nodded affirmatively.

Troy sniffed. "Yeah. Only leaves two hundred and twenty-four thousand, five hundred acres left."

"You really think a six-year-old would have the stamina to go farther?"

"I don't know." It was obvious Troy was tired. Defeated. He yawned again, rubbing his face with his hand, the stubble of whiskers making a scratching sound against his callused palm. "Listen, I need to check in with the camp's director. Search and Rescue is going to need more help setting up a larger base camp than they currently have. I want to get as many camp staff as are available to pitch in. I also want to see if we can open up the kitchens and make meals for the searchers. It's been over twenty-four hours since Jasmine went missing. There's going to be a need for food."

"I'll call Eddie. I'm sure he'll help coordinate that." She didn't miss the hesitation before Troy nodded. She knew he wasn't always comfortable with her and Eddie's camaraderie. But he also understood that they'd been playmates and cohorts at the camp since her family first moved here when she was just a kid.

"Yeah. Do that." Troy squeezed her hand. "Thanks."

By noon, Search and Rescue had set up headquarters in the Rec Barn, a large metal structure in the maintenance section of the camp. Wren had assisted some summer camp staff volunteers in setting up folding tables and chairs. They ran orange extension cords to bring in electricity to power the ham radios. They set up a few laptops by the Search and Rescue team, along with a massive map stretched along the wall and adhered there with duct tape. Sticker flags marred the grid work that stretched over the plat map, outlining different search teams by color, completion, in progress, or searched.

Wren listened to the SAR manager brief them on how to search. There were more inexperienced searchers than there were trained SAR volunteers. Each search party was assigned a SAR leader, and they'd be taken to their allotted grid by truck or ATV, depending on the condition of any adjacent logging trails that may still be maneuverable.

An arm brushed hers, and she glanced to her right side. "Pippin!" Her brother stood beside her. Blue jeans, hiking boots, a baseball cap. He had the same green eyes she did, and the same coppery head of hair. That he was here and not working on his vlog channel and gaming development surprised her. Pippin was the opposite of Troy and far nerdier than Eddie. A Comic-Con junkie, a whiz at programming, and someone who stayed up into the wee hours of the morning playing video games. He might be her senior by twelve years, but unlike her, he hadn't moved out of their parents' basement. He was the proverbial adult child who never left home. He was also company for Dad. They got along well—in their mutual quirkiness.

"What are you doing here?" she whispered.

Pippin looked sideways at her with an expression that said the answer to her question should be obvious. "I'm here to help."

Wren smirked in spite of the circumstances. "And you're aware it requires physical exertion and potential encounters with trees and rocks?"

Pippin glowered at her from beneath the rim of his cap. "I'm not a moron."

"No, you're a thirty-eight-year-old teenage boy with daddy issues."

"Knock it off," he gritted between clenched teeth, trying to avoid a scene. Their banter since childhood had been a brutal mix of insult and affection.

Wren bit her lip to stifle a chuckle. She loved getting under Pippin's skin. He always took everything so seriously, so intensely. It made him good as a gaming app developer. It was also what made him difficult to get along with.

The SAR leader was finishing up. "Head over to the table in the corner there and grab your sack lunch, thanks to the camp here. I want you to work in pairs, so be sure you have a partner."

"You and me?" Wren tossed over her shoulder to Pippin, who was on her heels.

"Sure."

Wren snagged a white paper bag lunch Eddie had whipped together. Probably off-brand granola bars and PB and Js, if she knew him. He could get an assembly line of teenage summer staff organized for that menial task in a split second. She snatched one for Pippin and tossed it to him.

"Heads up!"

Pippin's hands smacked around the paper, and he jammed it into his pack with all the finesse of a man. The jelly would squish out before he even ate it. "This really isn't a laughing matter, Arwen." He scolded with the bossiness of an older brother and the wisdom of someone whose ability to deal with trauma was perpetually more advanced than her own. Wren laughed at funerals, not because she found them funny but because her nervous energy or grief was dealt with through humor—her coping mechanism.

"I know." She was gentler as she packed her sack lunch.

Pippin zipped his pack. "Let's hope the poor kid has avoided wolves."

The pit in her stomach grew. Wren had been trying to see this search mission as an adventure of sorts—through a heroic lens—one that would ultimately result in finding the dirty uninjured child curled at the base of a tree, sleeping. Or something like that. She hadn't allowed herself to go down the path of wolves, black bears, or coyotes. Hunting human prey wasn't high on the bear or coyote list, but still . . . Wren shuddered, remembering ghost stories from campfires and tales of lurking monsters in the woods.

"C'mon. Pull it together. We got this." Pippin's tone of voice had shifted into one of encouragement. She'd take any of that she could get.

6

Sticks crunched under their hiking shoes, interrupting the strain to hear for any sounds a little girl might make after hours alone in the forest. The trees and foliage were thick, an overhead canopy that all but excluded the daylight, plunging the woods into its own kind of bluish-green darkness.

"Just a sec." Pippin motioned for Wren to stop. Tugging his water bottle from his pack, he flipped the top and took a long draw. The day was warming up, and thankfully what was left of the night chill had now dissipated into a comfortable mid-seventies.

Wren battled discouragement. They'd been canvassing their assigned section for over an hour. Yet besides the occasional birdcall, squirrel scampering across their path, and the one white-tailed deer they'd frightened, all was silent. Her dream from the night before was becoming more vivid as they searched. Maybe the tentacles of fear it'd placed into her subconscious were stronger than she'd bargained for. Maybe she should have just blurted out the nightmare in all its haunting depths and allowed Eddie to debunk it for what it was. A dream. Not a vision. Not a premonition.

"Okay." Pippin's voice, coupled with the snap of his closing the water bottle, made Wren jump. The corner of his mouth tilted up in a slight grin. "Jumpy?"

"Shut up," Wren snapped, resorting to fourth-grade techniques for silence.

"Maybe Ava Coons got her." Pippin jammed his water bottle into the side pocket of his pack.

"Not funny." Wren bent and picked up a small stone. She launched it at a nearby tree, bouncing it off the trunk.

"You know how it goes. Ava Coons is always lurking—wanting her next victim."

Wren glared at her brother.

He wagged red eyebrows. "I saw her once."

"No, you didn't." Wren hooked her thumbs beneath her backpack straps and started forward. Her brother was annoying. Almost immature sometimes. She'd heard him claim this many times before. Ava Coons, the ghost story, the ax murderess who went Lizzie Borden on her family.

"No one believes me," he muttered.

Wren awarded him a sideways glance. "Yeah, well, most don't believe ghosts are real either."

"I do." Pippin stepped over a fallen rotted sapling.

"I know."

Pippin halted and studied her intently. Wren followed suit but squirmed. She hated it when her brother did that. He'd always been like that. Psychologically reading her as if she were some anime character in one of his cartoons, which always played in the background while he coded.

Pippin muttered, "We don't know what we cannot see."

"Don't be like Dad." Wren rolled her eyes. Their father's way of weaving bookish wisdom into everyday life had aged itself out of being tolerable by the time she was the missing girl Jasmine's age.

"Don't believe Ava Coons exists. That's fine. But don't put the entire responsibility of finding Jasmine Riviera on your shoulders either."

Wren avoided her brother's frank stare. "First I'm too flippant, and now I'm too serious? I'm never quite what you want me to be, is that it?"

Pippin cleared his throat and rubbed his hand over his goatee. "Don't start with that."

"You're always trying to influence how I think," she argued.

45

Now wasn't the time for this. She needed to focus on Jasmine, but she also got irritable anytime Pippin tried to program her thoughts the way he believed they should be. She wasn't a gaming app. She was his sister.

"Something has you out of sorts." He was also far too observant. It came with his intense nature.

"Yeah. A missing kid." Wren skewered him with a look.

"No." Pippin tilted his head and narrowed his eyes at her. "No, there's something else."

They engaged in a silent standoff, until Wren admitted defeat. There wasn't any point in hiding it from Pippin. He'd make it his mission to find out, and it would distract him from finding Jasmine. "I had a dream—more like a premonition. That's all. Last night when I stayed at the Markhams' house."

Pippin was laser-focused on her. "I'm sure Troy loves it when you stay there."

Wren reached out and snapped a dead stick off a branch from an oak tree. "I've stayed at Eddie's house since I was a kid. I don't have slumber parties with *him*. You know his mom has been there for me during—well, everything."

Pippin's expression remained passive. He had never been close to the Markhams, and Eddie's mom's fight with breast cancer was a vague concern to him, unlike how it was eating at Wren's insides.

"What was your dream about?" He skirted any further discussion about Wren's surrogate mom. She knew it was purposeful. Losing their own mother had crushed Pippin. In his early twenties at the time, Wren wondered now if that was why he'd never really come up out of the family basement. Coming up meant facing a loss. Pippin didn't face loss any better than she did. Not really.

Wren broke a three-inch section off the stick and flicked it at Pippin. "So, you know Lost Lake?"

Pippin nodded.

"I dreamed I went there searching for Jasmine and I found her. She was lying on the shoreline. Dead."

Pippin eyed her. "Dreams aren't real."

"But ghosts are?" Wren tossed the dead stick to the forest floor.

"Did anyone search Lost Lake?"

"I don't know." She looked up at her brother, who topped her by three inches.

"If they did, then you'd know your dream was just a dream and nothing more."

No dead little girl. He had a point.

"Lost Lake doesn't even fall within the search area. It's outside the grid. You know how deep in the wilderness preserve that lake is."

Pippin nodded. "Fair enough. Let's keep moving then?" He took a few steps, dismissing Lost Lake altogether. When Wren didn't follow, he stopped and looked over his shoulder. "You coming?"

Wren couldn't shake the feeling that had gnawed at her ever since she'd admitted her dream aloud. It must have shown on her face, because Pippin gave an exasperated cluck of his tongue.

"We're not going to Lost Lake *now*."

She lifted her eyes and met her brother's.

"They've assigned us this search area," he continued, "and it's our responsibility to make sure it's well covered. You could screw up the entire search and rescue by deviating off course, not to mention how it could have terrible ramifications for the girl. The odds that Jasmine is here and not at Lost Lake are much higher."

Wren covered the few steps between them. "We can finish searching this grid, but then later today we can just hike out on our own. I think we can find it. Lost Lake? Eddie can come with us. He's got the coordinates for it on his GPS."

"No."

"Why not?" Wren challenged him. "What if my dream was really a premonition? God's way of saying 'Look here'? What if we need to get there to save her before she dies?"

"You're being ridiculous."

"But thinking Ava Coons haunts these woods and steals people isn't?"

"Do what you want," Pippin said. "But our priority is to finish what we started here or we could sabotage the entire search and rescue."

He was right. Wren knew that. But she also knew she couldn't dismiss her dream that easily—that readily—and that she was going to have to find Lost Lake. Even if she went alone.

—————~~~

They hadn't found Jasmine. No one had. Not even a torn piece of her clothing, a shoe, a candy wrapper, nothing. The mood at the SAR base was somber. There was little to no socialization as search teams arrived shaking their heads. Another nine hours added to Jasmine's clock. And while this wasn't a kidnapping, that didn't mean the odds were any better after the first twenty-four hours gone missing.

Wren was thankful the parents hadn't been stationed at the SAR base. The idea of watching their desperation was horrific. She heard that Jasmine's father had demanded to join a search team but was finally convinced to stay behind after his wife collapsed. Wren couldn't fathom how torn he was. His wife versus his little girl.

"Hey." Eddie met Wren as she hiked toward the canteen. It was for campers, but all she could think about was a cherry slushie. It would be refreshing, and she could drown her own sense of failure in sugar.

"Thanks for whipping together those sack lunches." She gave him the side-eye as he matched her pace.

"I had the volunteers bag a bunch more for tomorrow. I'm glad we've got a good set of high-school camp staff this summer. They're eager to help out."

"Good." Wren nodded. They maneuvered the wooden steps onto the sprawling front porch of the canteen. Eddie opened the screen door, and they were met by an assault on the senses. Hot fudge smells mixed with popcorn, and someone had ordered a pizza.

One of the high-school summer staff bobbed to the counter, her ponytail wagging back and forth. She was too happy. Too perky. Wait. Wren reined in her emotions. No, the girl was exactly what she should be. Deer Lake Bible Camp hadn't closed just because Jasmine had gone missing. There were oodles of campers and camp counselors roaming around, and they needed a sense of normalcy.

"Hey, Eddie!" The girl had braces that spanned her teeth. Wren noted the sparkle in her brown eyes. Crushing on the kitchen manager. She wanted to chuckle. Camp was like that. First, there was summer fun, and second, there were summer crushes. And always for the older staff because, well, they were older.

"Hey, Abby. Wren needs a cherry slushie."

Wren hadn't told him. It was just Eddie's way. He knew.

"Okey-dokey!" Abby tossed Wren a toothy smile and spun around, her ponytail slapping her cheek. "Did you want anything, Ed?"

Ed?

He didn't seem to notice the little flirt. "No thanks." Ever polite. Unassuming. Really, Eddie was sort of boring, if Wren was being honest. His primary pastime, outside of mastering casserole concoctions out of leftovers, was reading exegetical books that rivaled the dictionary for length and for their interesting content. He was a thinker. Sort of like her own dad, only Eddie didn't live in the fictional world of Hobbiton, but in the spiritual world of Christendom.

"You're not going to Lost Lake." Eddie's words penetrated her thoughts, and Wren shot him an incredulous look.

"Wha—?"

"Pippin texted me."

"Snitch."

"You can't take on the responsibility of Jasmine's well-being by assuming your dream was a premonition." Eddie dragged a wooden picnic table–style bench from one of the canteen tables and plopped down on it. He didn't motion for Wren to join him, but she did anyway.

"So, no one in the Bible was told anything important through a dream?" Wren countered, knowing he'd bite.

Eddie's eyes narrowed. "Unfair."

"Why?"

"Fine." He smiled a little, but she noted the depth in the corners of his eyes. A sadness that had been there for months now. He was a mama's boy—in the best of ways—and his mama was dying.

"So maybe there *is* credence to my dream?" Wren ventured.

Eddie shrugged in his typical blasé way of dealing with serious issues. "I wouldn't discredit anything God might deem to use. All I'm saying is to be cautious that you don't put too much emphasis on emotional outputs versus factual ones."

Whatever that meant. "So then we *should* check it out."

"It's a two-and-a-half-hour hike."

"Then let's get going!" Wren leaned forward.

Eddie pulled away. He shook his head. "No go. It's already four p.m. By the time we get there—assuming the trail isn't all grown over—it'll be almost seven. We'd be hiking back in the dark."

"I'm not scared of the dark," Wren argued. "Not to mention, Jasmine is out there alone in it!"

"I have over a hundred campers to feed."

"Esther can do it." Wren's reference to Eddie's assistant brought a grin to his face.

"Yeah, she could manage the entire Marines if needed."

"I'm sure she'd be willing to." Wren knew Esther well enough—they'd been friends for the past two years, since the day Esther first came to camp as a member of the paid staff. Wren didn't make friends with females very well. Her upbringing at the camp, coupled with literary parents who ran in administrative circles, had made her socialization attempts awkward.

"Here you are!" Abby's chirpy voice interrupted them. The slushie looked fabulous and Wren told her so, and was rewarded with a beaming, metallic smile.

Eddie appeared to be caving. Wren could see it in his eyes.

"I could ask Troy to help us."

Eddie nodded, clearly thinking it through. "Not a bad idea. He'd have headlamps. Some extra gear if we need it."

"You will then?" Wren straightened in her seat, swallowing a gulp of the slushie. She couldn't help the smile that spread across her face at the anticipation. Somehow she knew—she just *knew*— the dream hadn't been a random subliminal story playing in her mind.

Eddie drummed his fingers on the table. "If Esther is okay with taking kitchen lead, then yeah. And—" he hesitated before finishing—"I need to check in on Mom."

Wren's smile faded. "Of course."

Why was it that during small victories, death hovered? Like a phantom in black, undulating above them with the threat of descending and cloaking them in its embrace. It was inevitable really. Patty Markham was dying. She'd been sent home to live out her last days with her husband and son. Eddie had moved out of staff housing to return home. And now? Jasmine. In Wren's mind, she was too quickly moving into position next to Patty. Imminent death, immediate loss, and the agonizing aftereffects.

"You okay?" Eddie's words pierced her spiraling thoughts.

"Hmm? Oh. Yeah," she answered. Watching her friend, she took a sip of her slushie. Ten years ago, they'd sat in this very spot, with ice cream cones, and dreams, and ideas that would take them far away from their camp roots. Instead, they were still here, more tied to the camp, to its story, and to the grief that seemed to lurk in the cracks of it all. A grief that was slowly seeping out and threatening to poison them.

7

Ava

She followed him silently. His strides weren't remarkably long, as he wasn't remarkably tall. In fact, he only topped her by an inch or two. Yet for a preacher, the other qualities made up for his lack of height. Ava made a promise to herself to avoid his eyes. They were haunting, and there was such depth in them, she was afraid a person could rightly crawl in and drown. His jawline was distinct but not harsh. Just strong enough to indicate he might get a stubborn set to it if pushed too far. She noticed his suit was worn, and he could use a haircut.

He led her to the parsonage, and when they arrived at the porch steps, he hesitated, turned, and eyed her. Ava looked at the toes of her very scuffed shoes. If nothing else, he should be able to figure out that she wasn't a murderess. She could hardly look a man in the eyes if he was good-looking. How then could anyone think she could hack a man to death and stare at the gore of it?

"I'm sorry you're in this predicament." Preacher Pritchard was soft-spoken. Ava had a hard time picturing him leveling fire and brimstone down, but she expected it. He'd probably jumped at the chance to take in a wayward sinner and have her completely under his soul-correcting influence.

She didn't reply.

He sighed. He didn't move to enter the parsonage, which was small and definitely not set up for a boardinghouse. The preacher took off his hat and ran fingers through his hair. He was agitated. Probably because she wasn't saved yet. Going to hell in a hand-basket.

"Miss Coons—"

"Ava." She hadn't meant to speak. It came out habit-like.

"Ava," he nodded. "Okay." The man was at a sheer loss. He cleared his throat. Put his foot on the first porch step as if he was going to step up it, but then he retracted it back to the earth. "I'm sorry. I didn't think this through as well as I should have."

She was sorry for him then, if she was honest. So, Ava lifted her eyes from her shoes and made sure her attention landed on his nose.

"You don't got a mama or a sister or nothin'?" She tried to offer him some justification for bringing a lone woman into the home of a single preacher.

"No." He sighed. "Not here." Now it was his turn for downcast eyes.

Ava crossed her arms over her thin form. "Looks like you've dug yourself a hole and crawled right in. Tell ya what, I can just haul myself off and you can be rid of me."

"No." He shook his head. "That will not be adequate for your safety."

"I'll be fine." She didn't believe the words herself, so it was obvious why he didn't believe her either.

Instead of climbing the porch steps, the minister lowered himself to sit on them. He leaned his elbows on his knees and stared past her, across the dirt road to the small clapboard church flanked by two saloons.

"I was so sure God called me here. To Tempter's Creek." His mumble might not have been meant for Ava, but she responded.

"What'd He do? Shout at ya?"

Preacher Pritchard raised his eyes, the first glimmer of a smile at the corners. He gave a little laugh. "No. No, He didn't shout."

"Seems like people sayin' 'God called me' is a piece of work, if you ask me." Which he hadn't, Ava realized. "If God can't talk, then He can't call. So then you're just going off into the wild blue on your own whims and fancies, not thinkin' 'bout no one you might've left behind."

He reddened.

Ava waited. It was awkward. Truly, it was. Her habit of over-talking was fast coming to the fore. She did that when she was nervous—which was all the time—talk. Talk like a chatter bug and hope no one could see inside of her.

"Preacher Pritchard—" she started.

"Noah," he retorted.

"I ain't callin' you by your first name!" Ava's voice squeaked. "Goin' to be bad enough, me livin' in your house! If'n I use your first name, then folks'll think we done common-law married up. All familiar like. You really want that?"

He paled this time. "God, what have I gotten myself into?" Noah Pritchard squeezed his eyes tight.

"You prayin' or swearin'?"

"Neither." His response was under his breath, but Ava heard it. A preacher who cussed? He shook his head quickly then. "No. No, it was a prayer."

Ava bit the inside of her bottom lip. She had a feeling he was lying now. Maybe not. But if he was, maybe he wasn't the Goody Two-shoes she thought preachers were. She shifted her weight to her other foot, and the movement grabbed Noah's attention.

"I'm so sorry, Miss Coons." Seemed he'd taken her comment about first-name familiarity to heart and reapplied it to her as well. He stood up, wiping his trouser legs as if the porch step were filthy. "Come inside." Seeming to arrive at some resigned acceptance of their situation, Noah hiked the three steps until his feet were planted on the porch. He reached for the front door and opened it.

She felt as though she was sinning just setting her backside on the bed in the parsonage's guest room. Of course, Preacher Pritchard—Noah, if she used his first name and to the devil what people thought—had already high-tailed it from the place like God himself were about to set foot there and utter all sorts of condemnation. So for now, Ava was alone, and God was really quiet.

She swept her gaze over the room. It was simple. Whitewashed walls made the room brighter. She wondered briefly what sucker of a church member had to mix the lime and salt and water and what-have-you to make this room as pretty as it was. Ava had figured the parsonage would be dull, uninviting, even dark. Dark like hell itself. That was what the church preached anyway. Seeing the bright walls and the patchwork quilt on the bed made of green and blue gave Ava pause.

"I ain't proper enough for this." Ava stood from the bed as if poked by a porcupine. She noted the bureau on the far side of the small room, which had a dresser scarf of embroidered cotton stretched atop it. A hand mirror lay facedown. It tempted her, so Ava gave in—which was what sinners did when tempted—and moved to pick it up. Turning the mirror, she stared at her image as it reflected back at her.

Ava knew that behind their hands, townsfolk tittered about her looks. She was on the thin side but had a "nice bosom," as Jipsy had once uncouthly declared. Her hair was blond like a hay bale, which made it *not* corn-silk yellow, a color Ava had always secretly wished for. Her eyes were blue like the sky, and someone told her once that the Coons family had been rumored to have Norway running in their blood. Maybe some Sweden. Ava hardly knew what that meant, except that they were other countries far away. She wasn't stupid, she reminded herself as she counted the tiny brown moles that dotted her face in various places like freckles. She was just uneducated. That meant she hadn't a clue where Norway or Sweden was, and what *were* moles on one's face for anyway? They sure weren't becoming like that porcelain doll complexion of Mrs. Sanderson's.

"Contemplating your next kill?"

The wizened voice of an old woman broke the silence.

Ava dropped the hand mirror, and it clattered onto the dresser.

"Easy there. A broken mirror is a mighty long streak of bad luck, you know?" She was short. Squat. Barely five-foot, if that, and her chin rested almost on her chest. Ava wasn't sure if the old woman really had a neck—oh yes, it was there—and her brown eyes swallowed her face that was otherwise as wrinkled as package paper balled up and tossed away. The woman hardly blinked as she eyed Ava with an intensity that was both curious and knowing.

"Did you know that about forty years ago a woman in Massachusetts hacked her parents to death in their bed with an ax?"

Ava wished she hadn't moved from the bed so she could let her knees buckle and flop down onto the mattress in shock at the woman's audacity.

The elderly lady didn't stop there. She took a few steps into the room and eyed the mirror for cracks. "She didn't go to prison for it either. Guess it's hard to prove a woman can wield an ax as well as a man." A little chuckle, and then the brown eyes rested on Ava again.

Ava squirmed. It'd be nice if the lady left her alone. In peace. But apparently the town's doubts had crept in through the parsonage door. Fine job Preacher Pritchard was doing of protecting her!

"I'm Ramona B. Hancock—not related to the late president—but I *am* the great-aunt of Mildred Hancock from Madison." She waited as though that would ring some bell of recognition in Ava's mind.

Ava stared blankly back at her.

"You can call me Hanny. Ramona was my mother's name, and God forbid I even try to follow in her footsteps, rest her soul. Hancock is just so plain lofty, it makes me sound like I'm running for office myself." Hanny patted the side of her hair, which was neatly pulled back into a knot at the nape. It was white, like snow, and spectacles perched on her nose. "Now, what's this I hear about Noah putting you in such a pickle?"

"I think I did that to him." Ava finally found her voice. Which was dangerous, 'cause once she found her voice, it rarely shut up. "He volunteered to take me in, and of course what was I to do? People think I killed that man, and I didn't, but no one will believe me."

"Except Noah," Hanny inserted.

"Except Noah," Ava nodded. "I think," she added. He'd never outright *said* he thought she was innocent.

Hanny walked past Ava to the lone window and peeked out. Her head didn't come up to the first trim piece that cut the window into a half pane. "Can't blame folk. They say Matthew was quite a sight after he was axed."

It didn't seem to faze Hanny—talking of murder.

"I didn't kill him, though." Ava couldn't help but insist once more.

Hanny turned, her eyes narrowed. "Are you sure?"

Ava didn't like the way dread coursed through her with the paralyzing effect that truth could be a fearsome thing, and she wanted to be sure she was on the right side of it.

Hanny waggled her index finger in the air. Its knuckle was swollen, the skin wrinkled from age. "I've seen a lot in my eighty-nine years, and one of them is that some people have wickedness deep inside, and it scares them so fiercely they choose not to remember it."

"I never killed no one," Ava insisted again, and she sure would not admit to Hanny that her observation was terribly correct. At least the not-remembering part.

Hanny huffed and shuffled past her. Ava trailed behind, mostly because she didn't really know what she was supposed to do. They entered the short hallway, with Noah's bedroom door down just a tad from her own, and then they entered the main living space, which had a sitting couch, a small woodstove, a bookshelf packed with books, and a small secretary where Noah must sit and prepare his sermons. In the room's corner by the front window was a stuffed chair covered in a goldenrod yellow velvet that had seen better days.

A sigh pushed through Hanny's pale lips. She clucked her tongue.

"I never thought—not once—I'd be living in a parsonage." Before Ava could respond, Hanny finished, "But I guess that boy Noah has no choice but to let me stay here too. Otherwise you'll both be gettin' married by morning's light or the town will chase you both out for sure and for certain."

Ava blanched.

Hanny's laugh was simple. Small. Resigned and a little overwhelmed. "A murderess, a coward, and an old widow with her own tales to tell. Aren't we the trio of sinners to congregate under a steeple?"

8

The ground felt cool beneath her bare feet, but not freezing. A small rock scored her flesh, and Ava stumbled, stretching out her arms to break her fall. Her palms skidded across the soil, the rough ground biting into her soft skin. Her knee cracked against a tree root that jutted up, and the momentum of the fall rolled her to her side, where she thudded into the base of a tree trunk.

Startled, Ava blinked rapidly to clear her vision. It was night. If stars twinkled, she couldn't see them. The forest was too thick overhead where the tree branches arched in a canopy of darkness. Crickets chirruped from the deep, and an owl's lonesome cry echoed the pounding of her heart.

"No. No, not again." Her whisper startled even herself as she twisted onto her backside and shoved her back against the tree. She held her hands out, palms upward, the stinging of torn skin making her eyes water. She couldn't tell in the darkness if her knee was bleeding, but it felt sticky when she touched it with the tip of her index finger. Her feet throbbed.

A bat swooped down in front of her, and Ava whimpered, shrinking back as though the oak tree would grow arms and embrace her, shielding her from the wretched evil darkness of the woods. She smelled that metallic scent again. It permeated her senses so much that she could taste it on her tongue. That familiar, pungent, ironlike flavor. Blood. It shouldn't be familiar to her. There was no reason it was familiar to her. But yet it was.

"Go away," she whispered. Her words carried through the black, winding around branches, cutting beneath the underbrush, and floating away into the depths that continued for miles beyond. "Go away," she whispered again as if the blood could hear her. As if it would draw back from her mouth, from her nostrils, shun her senses and return to wherever it had come from.

It had happened again. The last time had been over a year ago. The night wandering. The sleepwalking. The awaking to find herself deep in the forest, as if her body and subconscious were returning her somewhere she'd been before. Somewhere she couldn't remember. Or didn't want to remember. But always it came with the scent of blood. Always she ended up bruised, cut, or hurt. Widower Frisk had taken to locking the door to the room she slept in when she was younger. Locking it from the outside with a bolt lock, not knowing Jipsy had already taught Ava to lock it from the inside for other reasons. It made her feel extra safe instead of trapped. Until the night she was sixteen and had, in her stupor, shoved her arms through the window of the little room, ending her silent unexplained quest in blood.

Ava released a shuddering breath, squeezing her eyes closed against the willful threat of the woods. Of whatever lay inside of it. Lurking. Looming. Like a wolf that darted between trees. Just a shadowing glimpse now and then. Wisps of a tail, a fang . . . but never the full picture. Never the beast in its entirety.

The bobbing light from a flashlight startled her. Ava snapped her head in the direction from where she'd come. The light was circular, stretching out into the dark like a small beacon of hope, but Ava felt only dread. Dread that it chased her for no good reason but to condemn her. She stumbled to her feet. Her knee throbbed, and she was now very aware of the cut on her foot as she applied weight to it. She'd no intention of hanging around waiting for the light to discover her. To shed on her truth or reveal the reality of why she was here to begin with.

That she was crazy. Plumb lost her mind. And, that every so often, it came again—the craziness—and when it did, it came worse and angrier than before. Until one of these days when it finally ate her alive.

~~~~~~~

"Ava! Ava Coons!" It was more hushed than a shout. As if the man calling was afraid he'd wake someone.

Ava shrank into the underbrush, ignoring the thorns on the bush that ripped and poked into her cotton blouse.

Sticks cracked. Leaves rustled. Footsteps as shoes connected with the ground.

"Ava, where are you?"

A familiarity unraveled around her. The voice. She knew it. Still bewildered enough to be uncertain, she clapped a hand over her mouth, feeling the scrapes on her palm against her lips.

"You need to come home, Ava," the man insisted.

Home? For a moment, the vision of a rocking chair fluttered through her mind. It was rocking, but there was no one in it. It tipped backward, then forward, backward, forward, backward . . .

"Ava!" Louder now.

Where had she heard the voice before? She closed her eyes, trying to identify it. Friend or foe? Widower Frisk? No. And right now, that was the only man she could recall. The mind was as dark as the night around her. Suffocating with its stifling weight.

A shoe appeared in front of the bush she'd hidden under.

Ava muffled a yelp.

The man stopped.

She held her breath. *Keep on movin', mister.*

But he didn't. The body bent at the knees, and the man aimed the flashlight in her direction until its beam landed on her.

Ava squinted, blocking out the light by pressing her arm over her eyes.

"Ava?"

"Go away," she said. She tried to sound firm. Commanding even.

"Ava, please." The man's hand stretched out and scraped along the thorns that speared from the branches in front of her. "Come out of there."

She swatted at him. Her fingertips slapping his, sandwiching the thorns between them. Instinct made him snatch his hand back. Ava heard him suck at his finger. Must've gotten poked. Blood. Again.

"You need to come home."

You need to come home. The words echoed in her memory. Far in the distance. Someone yelling after her. Pulling her back with their words. *No. Don't go home.* Everything in Ava's body resisted, and she squirmed farther back into the brush.

"I'll sit then." The man laid the flashlight on the ground. He shut it off. They were plunged into the natural darkness of night. She heard him shuffle, his body shifting. She could sense him. Near. But he stayed away too. He left her alone. That was good. It was safer that way. For her, and for him.

———

A cool, wet cloth touched her face, stinging and startling Ava to her senses. Morning light cast its sunshine glow through the filmy white curtains. She quickly swept the room with her vision. The parsonage. Her bedroom. Hanny.

The elderly woman had positioned her petite body on the edge of the bed, and her hand had an old-age tremor to it as she moved the damp cloth to press it against Ava's forehead. Her brown eyes were dull, ringed with a foggy circle around the irises that bespoke her age. There was worry there.

"Lay still." Hanny lifted the cloth and leaned to dip it into a basin of water on the nightstand. Her movement made the white iron bed frame creak.

Ava looked down at her hands. Scratches covered them. Her knee was throbbing, but the green-and-blue patchwork quilt covered her body so she couldn't see if it was bruised or hurt worse than that.

The bedroom door was open halfway, and the creak of the hinges as it was pushed further open alerted both women to the added presence in the room. Noah filled the doorway. His shirtsleeves were rolled up to his elbows. Ava could see similar scratches on his arms. His eyes had shadows under them. There was a small twig stuck in his nut-brown hair that he must not realize was there.

"Hanny?" His even voice was soft, as if he didn't want to alert Ava even though she stared at him from her vantage point in the bed.

Hanny paused in her ministrations to Ava. "What is it, Noah?"

Noah hesitated, met Ava's eyes, then dropped his gaze back to Hanny. "There's been—I need to go out for a bit."

So much was unspoken in his words. Hanny must have sensed it. She gave Ava's blanket-covered leg a gentle pat and murmured, "I'll be right back, dear." She wobbled across the floor, reaching for the iron bedpost and the shepherd's crook cane she'd hooked there. Once stabilized, Hanny moved to meet Noah at the door, her cane thumping a cadence against the scuffed wood floor.

Ava strained to hear as they stepped into the hallway.

"Jipsy . . ."

A muffled sigh from Hanny.

Noah's voice again, a deep rumble. ". . . not looking good. She's lost a lot of blood."

"Who?" Hanny's voice was strained.

Noah's response, if there was one, was quiet enough that Ava couldn't hear it.

Tired of eavesdropping, Ava pushed the blanket back from her body, intent on joining them in the hallway. She swung her legs from the bed, and it was then she noticed herself. Her blouse was filthy, streaked with dirt and sticky with pine sap. The cotton skirt she'd been wearing was gone, and all that remained was her cotton drawers, falling loose around her thighs with no lace edging like the fancy ones she'd caught a glimpse of in the general store's catalog. Her left knee was skinned, the surface peeled back revealing dried blood, the edges of the wound bruised and scraped.

"Back to bed, dear." Hanny's cane pounded on the floor as she reentered the bedroom. Noah followed her. He ran his fingers through his hair in agitation, his eyes shifting between Ava and the window.

"What happened?" God knew the pit in her stomach was already giving her a premonition of the truth of the matter.

"You walked in your sleep last night, dear." Hanny tried to placate Ava while looking directly at Noah with a distinctly stern gaze. He avoided it and instead stuffed his hands in his trouser pockets.

"I brought you back this morning. You—were quite disoriented." He turned his attention to Hanny. "I need to go. Please, both of you stay here in the parsonage."

"They're not going to—" Hanny started.

"I don't know." Noah gave a quick jerk of his head. "Just stay put."

"Last thing I was planning to do was leave either of you alone with each other," Hanny asserted.

Noah's face colored, and he hustled from the room—a man with a mission and also what seemed like a very burdened soul.

Ava rubbed the top of her left thigh. The muscle was sore. "I don't remember much of anything."

"Of course you don't," Hanny muttered as she set about pushing Ava's shoulder gently to get her to lie back against the pillows. "I'm an old woman, and it's difficult to get through the night. Blessed be the parsonage has indoor plumbing. I was also bent on making sure you two were on the up and up. Sure enough, Preacher Pritchard was asleep in his long johns in bed like the reformed soul he is. But you? You were nowhere to be found."

Ava knew what had happened now. It'd been so long, she'd hoped they had passed for good. The blackouts. The long periods of time that went by when she sleepwalked, wandered, even held conversations without realizing it. Whenever she was upset, they would get worse. Ever since she was a child. Ever since . . .

Ava clutched the blanket. "Did the preacher come after me?"

"He did." Hanny nodded. She leaned forward and unbuttoned Ava's soiled blouse. "I awakened him, and he headed out to find you. And find you he did." Her swollen fingers stilled over the second button, and she studied Ava's face. "Where were you going out there in the woods?"

Ava reached up to place her hand over the old woman's and the button.

Hanny withdrew her hand. She clucked her tongue and shook her head. "I'm afraid you're in a heap of trouble, missy. It took Noah over an hour to find your trail heading off into the forest. Now?"

"Now what?" Ava held her blouse together, refusing to remove her last vestige of mustered-up pride.

Hanny sank onto the edge of the bed once more, leaning her cane against the mattress. She rested her hand on Ava's leg, careful not to touch her knee.

"What is it?" Ava insisted. The old dame might as well tell her, considerin' she'd know sooner than later in this small town of talkers.

"Jipsy. Woman who raised you with Widower Frisk."

Of course she knew who Jipsy was!

Hanny swallowed. Her wrinkled cheeks twitched as if she'd rather not say but knew she had to. "They found her this morning. Noah has been called out to be with the Widower Frisk. Someone killed her. They're saying—"

"It was me," Ava finished. The hollowness in her voice matching that in her soul.

"Tell me it wasn't, and I'll believe you." Hanny lifted her hand from Ava's leg and moved it to her cheek. The warm flesh of the fragile palm against Ava's face brought Ava's gaze up to meld with Hanny's. "Noah said he found you hiding in thornbushes. You had some blood on you, but we figured—well, it looks like you'd fallen a few times and it was from that. You had nothing to do with Jipsy dying," Hanny concluded with a vehemence that made Ava believe

65

the grandmotherly woman over her own betraying memory. "You didn't." Hanny patted her cheek.

Ava didn't answer. Couldn't answer. Because she simply didn't know. The town said killing was in her nature, and when she couldn't remember—couldn't account for where she'd been—there was the chance, of course, that they were right. Ava had always been close friends with death, though she could never explain why.

9

Wren

It was just as she had dreamed it was. The woods opened up and Lost Lake spread before them, looking more like a large pond nestled amid a forest of aspen and oak, poplar and cedar.

Wren charged forward, anxious to view the shoreline closer and to erase from her memory the vivid image of the body of a child. It had been just a dream after all. Nothing prophetic. Wren had been telling herself that over and over for the last couple of hours as Troy and Eddie bushwhacked ahead of her through the woods like two men in a wilderness competition.

Eddie's hand on her wrist stilled her.

"Hold up."

She exchanged glances with Troy, who shrugged, eyeing Eddie's hold on her. "Why are we stopping?"

Eddie released her wrist as he surveyed the scene ahead of them. "If your dream has any credibility, then Jasmine could be here. We don't want to startle her."

"Dreams aren't maps to the future," Troy muttered. Wren offered him an understanding smile, and he raised his brows. "We could barely find this lake, so I doubt Jasmine is even in the area. It's way outside of the search grid."

Eddie nodded. "You're probably right, but what's the harm in showing some caution?"

"Is she dangerous or something?" Troy snapped back.

"Guys!" Wren offered Troy an exasperated glare. "This isn't a competition as to who's right. I had a dream, okay? It's probably nothing but—"

"Don't discredit yourself," Eddie said.

"I'm not." Wren leveled a similar glare on her buddy, then pushed between them and into the clearing.

A crow, its glossy-black feathers outlining its shape, swept overhead from an aspen to the top of a cedar. Its *caw-caw* echoed through the clearing, and then a frog leaped from the rocky lakeshore, landing with a splash. Wren moved swiftly toward Lost Lake, noting its greenish water that looked almost navy blue in the quickening evening. A felled oak with the circumference of a beer barrel stretched out along the shore, and on the end a wood duck perched. Sighting Wren and the dueling males behind her, it too took flight, quacking its warning and swooping into the sky. A female wood duck then emerged from behind the log, following her mate in their wild flight escape.

Wren steadied her breath, scanning the shoreline. There was no body. No child. Relief infiltrated every pore in her body. She'd withheld that awful element of her dream—the fact that in it, Jasmine was dead. She wasn't certain what she'd have done had it been proven true.

"Over here!" Troy's voice had an entirely different tone to it than it had a few minutes prior. Wren spun to find him bent over a pile of dead branches and brush that had naturally collected over years of silent habitation. He was kicking at the brush, hooking his hand around what he had repositioned, and pulling it back.

"What is it?" Eddie jogged to his side, Wren close behind him.

Troy dragged more tangled brush away. "Looks like an old foundation is here."

Wren's heart sank. Disappointment merged with her determination to find Jasmine. A foundation wasn't a sign of a lost little girl. It was merely a ghost sighting of sorts. The ruins of a long-ago dwelling.

"Ever hear of an old house out by Lost Lake?" Troy tossed a small piece of broken-off tree trunk into the woods.

Eddie helped with clearing the section of foundation that was barely visible. Fieldstone, it appeared, covered in years of moss and lichen. "Yeah. The old Coons place."

"That old ghost tale?" Troy laughed.

"All ghost stories come with an element of truth," Eddie corrected, tugging at a mass of tangled vines.

Wren nosed her way in between them, dropping to all fours and trying to see under the branches and brambles. "Ava Coons is *not* the story I want to hear right now." It gave her the willies. A raving madwoman, ax-murdering her family. "Not when a little kid is missing in the very woods she roams."

Troy cleared more branches. "She roams? So, we're going to make it present tense, huh?" There was teasing in his voice. He knew the story and knew the shivers it caused campers.

"Thus is the tale of Ava Coons." Eddie picked up his hat from the ground where a resisting sapling had knocked it from his head. His voice had an overdramatic quaver to it. "She's never left Lost Lake or these woods. She's always searching for her next kill. The next bloodletting."

"Soul-stealer." Troy grinned and winked at Wren, who glanced in his direction.

"Body snatcher," Eddie jousted back.

"I heard one version that she threw her family's bodies into Lost Lake and that's why they vanished," Troy supplied.

"Ahhh," Eddie nodded, swiping at another branch. "Cement shoes, eh? All gangster style."

"Would you both knock it off?" She'd already had enough with Pippin's actual belief in the story earlier, and now with these two clowns hamming it up . . .

Wren squeezed through the opening the guys had cleared, crouching low and avoiding getting her hair stuck in the growth. "You're creeping me out." She paused at the corner of the foundation, only to feel Eddie squeeze in beside her.

"No one knows for sure, but this probably *was* the Coons homestead."

Wren pointed. "Is that part of a wall?" Through the web of branches and vines she could see the outline of what appeared to be boards, broken and sheared off yet still in a vertical position at the far wall.

"I think so," Eddie answered.

"You two going to make room?" Troy broke in behind them. Wren felt his hand on her back as he attempted to squeeze in.

"Hold on." Eddie moved forward, dropping to an army crawl. He twisted his cap around so the brim lay against the back of his neck and scooted forward on his belly. Leaning over the edge of the fieldstone, he peered down. "There's a basement. Or cellar maybe? It's a good seven feet or so down."

"I'll check it out." Troy eased past Wren.

"I got it." Eddie started shoving at vines.

"Seriously, dude, it'll just take me a second." Troy began his own battle against the growth.

"If this *is* the Coons homestead," Eddie grunted, "I want first dibs at the look."

"Don't count me out yet, Markham," Troy bantered back.

Wren was going to kill them both very, very soon, and Ava Coons could writhe in jealousy.

There was an *oomf* and then Eddie disappeared from sight, not waiting for Troy. Wren gave up. She wasn't about to be left behind. Copying Eddie, she crawled in after. Another few feet gave her access to squeeze her torso onto the cool stone of the foundation. She curled her fingertips around the edge and peered over.

By now, Troy had joined Eddie, and the men were toeing at the earth. Eddie bent and lifted an old glass bottle, the green a similar hue to the moss that spread across the back wall of the basement foundation.

"Old medicine bottle?"

"Could be." Troy reached for it, and Eddie relinquished it.

Wren twisted her body over the foundation wall and lowered herself, dropping the extra few feet. Her foot twisted upon landing, and a small pang shot through her ankle.

"You okay?" Eddie asked.

"I'm fine." Wren offered a smile. The basement floor was covered in layers of dirt and sticks. Fieldstone that had dropped from the foundation littered the area, and a maple sapling grew in the far west corner. "Is that an old woodstove?" She pointed at the base of the sapling, where a rusted metal box lay on its side. A door hung open on the front, its bottom hinge busted off.

"Looks like it." Troy trudged over to it and squatted down. He lifted the door, and the remaining hinge grated and squeaked its resistance. "An old one, probably the main source of heat for the winter."

"Had to be. There wasn't electricity or propane out here." Eddie picked up another bottle, this one with the neck broken off. He turned it toward Wren. "It still has part of its label."

"I'm surprised no one has ever mentioned this place." Wren nudged debris with the toe of her shoe.

"It's been mentioned," Eddie countered. He was pulling free a rusted piece of wire from beneath a rotted log. "Locals know about it. It's just not easy to get to, so is pretty much left alone."

"I guess I never paid attention," Wren admitted.

"So the Coonses really aren't just a ghost story?" Troy countered.

Eddie nodded, his cap still on backward. "The Coons family lived near Lost Lake back in the 1920s."

"Hey." Troy's boot thudded on the ground as he stomped on it. "Hear that?"

Both Eddie and Wren perked up to listen. Troy kicked at the ground again, his blue eyes alight with interest. "It's hollow." He kneeled and scraped at the dirt. "There's a hatch."

"Probably the cellar." Eddie bent next to Troy and helped clear away the earth. The evening light was draining away, so Wren dug into the backpack Troy had discarded to retrieve a headlamp.

"Here." Troy stretched out his hand for it.

"Ohhhh no." Wren smiled faintly. "Mine. You two have had your fun of being first in. If it's a cellar, I'm going first this time." Her senses fired like the engine on a race car. She flicked the light on and leaned over the men, eyeing the outline of a square hatch that looked as if, once open, it would swallow her whole.

"Let me go. No guessing what's down there." Eddie gave her a sideways look. Of course he would challenge her.

"Like Ava Coons's stockpile of murdered bodies? No way. I got to the headlamp first." Her retort sounded far from brave as she'd hoped, and Eddie knew it. While Troy was preoccupied with wedging a stick into the crack to pry open the hatch, Wren couldn't escape Eddie's furrowed-brow study of her.

"What?" The headlamp shone in his eyes.

Eddie held up a palm to block it. "You're spooked."

Wren challenged him back with a look that was meant to be confident, but even she knew it wavered. "I can't shake the idea of little Jasmine being out here all alone."

"Got it," Troy announced as the cellar trapdoor gave way.

"Fabulous," Wren muttered.

"Sure you want to go first?" Eddie pointed at the cellar. "Dark as Hades in there."

The black hole stared up at Wren with the ominous insinuation that not only was it dark, but it hid many untold secrets.

"I've got this." She noticed her voice had dropped to just above a whisper.

Still squatting next to the opening, Troy looked up at her and said, "Maybe Ava Coons is hiding down there."

"Stop it." Wren glowered at him.

"There's a lot of variables to a ghost story," Eddie interjected, "and not all of them are true. There *is* a possibility of finding a body."

"Eddie!" That was the last thing she needed to hear from him and his logical way of thinking. Especially with Ava Coons's spirit hovering over them like a horrid omen, and Jasmine Riviera having gone missing.

"My bad," he apologized.

Wren nodded while imagining the long, bony arm of a skeleton reaching out from the darkness and grabbing her ankle, pulling her down into the depths.

"Give me the lamp. I'll go." Eddie wagged his fingers toward Wren.

She scowled at her childhood pal. "Think again, Edward James Markham." Wren lowered herself so she sat on her backside, her legs hanging into the cavernous pit. There was a ladder, and she rested her feet on it.

"Careful. That thing is old," Troy warned.

Great. Now she was really freaked. "Here." Wren yanked the headlamp from her head and handed it to Eddie.

He laughed and pushed it back toward her. "Wren." Their eyes connected and spoke a thousand words without even verbalizing them.

Just go. You're fine.

I'm scared.

Sure. So was every explorer ever. It's just an old cellar. Go, Wren.

Eddie, I'm scared.

You're overreacting.

Say again?

I said you're overreacting, Wren.

"Fine!" Wren's exclamation of irritation toward Eddie startled Troy. She shot him an apologetic look and then lowered herself into the cellar.

The hole smelled of damp earth, undisturbed for years. As she swung her head around, the light shone against the cellar walls. Roots grew from the dirt. She noted a few boards acting as braces were still standing against the earth-carved walls.

"No body," she announced.

"Yet," Eddie teased back.

It was dark. So dark. A few spiderwebs swooped across the ladder and stuck to her hands as Wren gripped the rungs. Their sticky netting was disgusting, and she removed the hand with the most cobwebs on it and wiped it frantically against her jeans.

"You okay?" Troy stared down at her from above, but she couldn't look up for fear of blinding him with the headlamp.

"Yeah. The ladder seems strong."

"What do you see?" Eddie asked.

Wren paused a few feet from the floor and scanned the small cellar. The far wall held four shelves. On them were various old tin cans, a few bottles, and a couple of jars of who knew what. A barrel stood near the far wall. Wren stepped to the ground and eased her way toward the barrel. As she peeked in, the light revealed a mound of dirt at the bottom. Maybe old potatoes returned to the earth from whence they had come? There was also a glass bottle. She reached down, careful to avoid one large cobweb that spanned the bottom third of the barrel. Wrapping her fingers around the neck of the bottle, she lifted it.

"Rum." The world above her fell away. Troy and Eddie's voices became distant echoes. Rum from the 1920s. Prohibition era, if her history classes served her well. Which meant one of the Coonses had probably hidden this rum beneath all the potatoes. A lost bottle of illegal liquor, left behind after a murdering child hacked them all to death and threw their bodies into Lost Lake.

She set the rum bottle on the dirt floor and roved her gaze to the other wall. More wooden shelves, most of them broken now, with jars of food long since leaked and decayed, lying in pieces on the floor. Several shards of glass from Mason jars were piled in the corner. Wren could make out something beneath them.

Stepping toward the pile, she leaned over and carefully picked up one of the broken jars. Setting it to the side, she repeated the motion a few times until she could make out what was buried beneath.

A doll.

Wren mimed a gag even though no one could see her. Of course. Of course there would be an old cracked-faced porcelain doll in the cellar of the murder house of the Northwoods. She tentatively reached for the head of the doll, her fingers wrapping around its hair. She lifted it, bits of glass from the jars falling away.

"That's human hair."

"Gah!" Wren spun around and slapped her palm against Eddie's chest. He'd climbed down and had come up behind her without so much as a peep. Troy was halfway down the ladder behind him. The cellar was fast becoming very tiny.

"That's human hair," Eddie repeated.

Wren let go of the doll. Eddie's hand shot out and grabbed it by the foot before it descended onto its previous graveyard of shattered Mason jars.

"Careful." The doll now hung upside down, his hand wrapped around one of its legs. The hair was not synthetic and fine. It was coarse, half of it missing from the doll's head, the remaining hair tied by a ragged velvet string. The doll's face stared up at Wren from its upside-down position. Its eyes were rolled back into the doll's head, and its face had a gazillion tiny cracks in it. But the mouth was still pink, as if painted on only months before. The purple-flowered dress that covered the doll hung away from its body, revealing the cloth underside, stuffed with whatever dolls were stuffed with back in the day. The porcelain legs were somehow sewn into and attached to the cloth torso of the doll, and one of the legs was missing its leather bootie.

"Wren." Eddie's voice was grave, and it sent a chill through her. A chill that disturbed her worse than the doll hanging from his hand. He shifted his fingers, turning the bottom of the doll's foot toward her. "Look."

Wren studied the foot, then lifted her eyes to Eddie. "What?"

"Look." He said that awful lone word again.

So she looked closer. Wren read the name etched into the bottom of the doll's foot and then inked over so it was difficult to miss.

Arwen.

Arwen. A name synonymous with Tolkien. Was her name known even before the books had been written? Did the name exist in 1930 when the Coons family was murdered? When their cabin was burned to the foundation, and when their cellar was sealed like a tomb for the next ninety-plus years?

Arwen.

Her name was written on the foot of the old doll with the clarity of an omen that had risen from its historical grave. A soul that had returned to life, awakened, and was now ready to roam free and tell its true tale.

10

Ava

"Do not leave the parsonage." Noah's directive sliced through Ava with the swiftness of a well-sharpened blade.

Ava froze in her spot on the worn-out stuffed chair in the front room. Hanny was putzing in the kitchen making tea, and Noah had entered the front door in a hustle. He slammed it too. Which seemed out of sorts for the soft-spoken man. Now his eyes were sparking with that fire and brimstone Ava expected from a preacher. She shrank into the chair. Sure enough, he was going to level it on her, and here she was with nothing to defend herself with except the pillow she leaned against. And its tassels were already coming off, so they sure wouldn't be of any help!

"What if I have to use the outhouse?" She countered with the first thought that popped into her head.

Noah looked at her sharply, assessing whether she was joking. His brow furrowed. "We have indoor plumbing."

"Sure. You're right." And he was, Ava remembered. She also remembered how nice the indoor plumbing had been. No swatting mosquitoes away from your bare legs when you had to do your business in the middle of the night—or day. "I might need to take a walk, though," she added for the sake of defense.

Noah yanked his hat from his head and tossed it onto the desk by the window. He ran agitated fingers through his hair, mussing it and making Ava wonder when the last time was he'd had a haircut. Not that she minded. She was used to grubby-looking men who didn't pomade their hair into submission.

"Just—don't leave." His response was inadequate.

Ava wrestled the pillow into her lap and played with the half-worn-off tassels. "Why not? Outside of the fact that half the town wants to string me up by my toes." She avoided mentioning her midnight escapade into the darkness that had left her again with no memories, and for sure with a swollen knee. It wouldn't help her cause to bring that up. Her argument was already thinner than the ice on Deer Lake during a warm spring.

Noah rested his hands at his waist and eyed her. They barely knew each other and here they were habituating like man and wife. Ava felt warmth spread up her cheeks. Well, not *like* man and wife. Hanny might be their umbrella of redemption, but considering she was hard of hearing and moved with the speed of a snail, she wouldn't be much help if there was any hanky-panky going on.

"You need to trust me on this," Noah said with a sigh.

"I never trust no man," Ava retorted, suddenly feeling backward. Like her words jumbled, and she was shy a string of pearls of being worthy to even sit in the parsonage. Noah Pritchard was cultured. Maybe not rich, but he spoke fine. She was an orphaned child from the woods and had all the etiquette of a groundhog at an evening ball.

"Please." Much of the spark had dimmed in his eyes. Whatever hellfire he'd been wanting to rage had been put under control. Ava wished she could see the preacher lose his temper. At least then she'd know what to do with him. A small flicker in his eyes made her cheeks warm even more. Enough to make her irritated. Maybe more at herself, but she decided to take it out on him anyway.

Ava wanted to stand, but her knee was throbbing. "Ever seen a bird in a cage, Preacher Pritchard?"

"Noah."

"Ever seen a bird in a cage, *Noah*? Near on breaks their wings tryin' to bust free. Now, I'm no fancy bird, but even a sparrow wants to fly now and then."

"They think you killed Jipsy."

Ava stilled. "I didn't." She hadn't wanted to ruminate on the idea of Jipsy being dead. Being *murdered*. She hadn't been remarkably fond of the older woman, but she'd hardly wished harm on her.

"You sure?"

Her silence answered for her.

Noah blew another massive sigh from his mouth, and he plopped down across from her in a straight-back chair and leaned forward with his elbows on his knees. "The town thinks you've run off, Ava." Dark eyes lifted to meet hers. "Vanished, and you took Jipsy's body with you."

Ava reared back, her eyes widening. "I did no such thing!"

Noah continued as though she hadn't interrupted. "Let me lay out the facts for you as clear as I'm able."

"Please do, Preacher Pritchard." Ava crossed her arms over her chest.

Noah scowled at her. "Widower Frisk found blood this morning all over their front porch. Jipsy has disappeared—not unlike your family did, according to Deputy Larson. Mr. Sanderson states he saw you wandering last night—which you were."

"You were with me," Ava snapped.

"They don't know that."

"You didn't tell them? You didn't tell them you brought me back here?"

Noah held out his hands to slow her down. She sure wasn't keen on slowing down. Yesterday she'd wanted to run from the crowd of naysayers, but today she wanted to confront them all. How would they like it if they spent their childhood wonderin' what had happened to their family and why they disappeared and where all the blood came from? How would they like it if the entire town decided they were guilty of killin' just because their parents died in a similar way?

"Ava."

The way the preacher said her name brought her frenetic thoughts to a standstill. His voice mesmerized her for a long moment. Kind of like the time she'd seen Ned take a draw from his cigarette and then close his eyes as if some sort of calm had come over him.

Noah edged forward in his chair, nearing her. His nearness was like Ned's cigarette. Hypnotic in a curious sort of way. What would it taste like? Ava's eyes dropped to the preacher's mouth.

For Pete's sake, she was sure as shootin' going to hell in a handbasket now.

"Ava," he said again.

This time she bit her tongue and lifted her eyes to meet his.

"Listen to me really careful now, all right?"

She nodded.

"The townsfolk are suspicious you're behind all of this, even though no one has found Jipsy's body."

"Then how do they know she's dead?" Ava interrupted.

"Assumption based on the amount of blood."

"How do you know it wasn't no pig?"

"We'd see a dead pig."

"Unless a bear hauled off with it," Ava argued.

"It wasn't a pig."

"You know that, huh?" Ava raised an eyebrow.

Noah's lips pressed together. He was getting exasperated. That spark had come back into his eyes. "It wasn't a pig."

"Think you'd see a dead Jipsy too, based on your logic." Ava's mutter was rude, she knew it, and she really didn't care.

Noah looked to the ceiling as if praying to the good Lord for patience, and he must have gotten some too. He leveled a calm look on Ava, and she squirmed. Darned if he wasn't just the most handsome thing for a preacher, and that in and of itself was a sin akin to murder, wasn't it? Preachers weren't supposed to be good-lookin'.

"I was trying to spare you the details, but since you insist on pushing the matter . . ." Noah tapped his knees with his fingers.

"Jipsy's jacket was left behind. There were holes in it, like stab wounds from a knife, and it was drenched in blood."

Well, there was nothing to say to that, really and truly, except . . . "I didn't kill her and haul her body off nowhere. 'Sides, supposedly my weapon of choice is an ax, not a knife."

Ava's sarcasm wasn't lost on Noah.

"Stop that." Noah pushed to his feet and crossed the room. He moved the curtain back a tad and peered out into the street. "Now if you'll listen and let me finish, I will make my point. Can you do that, Ava?"

"Don't need to talk down to me." She didn't like his tone.

"My point is, the townsfolk think you have run off. Jipsy's body is missing. Mr. Sanderson saw you wandering last night, and I can't provide enough of a time covering to say I was with you the whole night. And even if I could, the story that you were sleepwalking and can't remember a thing you did—well, it will not sit well with anyone."

"So, you didn't tell them I came back to the parsonage after last night?"

"I started to . . ." Noah hesitated. "The fact is, they came to their own conclusions based on Sanderson seeing you, and Jipsy having vanished. When they asked me about you, I . . . well, I thought that it might be in your best interest to let the town think you actually *have* run off."

"You mean not let 'em know I'm still here with you?"

"Yes." Noah continued, "If you don't leave the parsonage *at all*, they won't know you're here. With me."

"And what good does that do?" She couldn't help the incredulous tone in her voice. The whole situation seemed like a game of cat and mouse.

Noah raked his fingers through his hair again, then dared another look out the front window. "They're fit to be tied to find you and place blame on your head. I'm not sure they'd even follow the law and not string you up like in some Wild West shantytown. Chuck Weber is putting together a search party."

"For Jipsy?" Ava asked. She'd just about worn the tassels right off the pillow.

"No." Noah faced her. "For *you*."

"And they didn't think to storm over to the parsonage where I'm *supposed* to be?" Ava raised a skeptical eyebrow.

Noah reddened. "They did not."

"Why?"

"Because I affirmed their assumptions and let them believe you *had* run off."

Ava shot to her feet, but the motion was so sudden it made the room spin. She grabbed for the chair, pushing off Noah's quick movement to help steady her. Regaining her balance, Ava glowered at the preacher. "You *lied*?"

"It's not the first time." Noah's expression dared her to ask more questions. Ava didn't rise to the challenge.

"But lettin' them think that will only prove to them they were right in thinkin' I *did* kill Hubbard! That's the whole reason why I'm here in the first place. So nothin' happens to an *innocent person*! You just made me look guiltier than sin, *Preacher*." Gosh almighty, she'd've thought the preacher was a heck of a lot smarter than herself. Guess she was wrong.

"If I let them know you were still here at the parsonage, then we'd have to explain why you were out last night. I already told you, there are too many holes in that story to adequately appease their suspicions."

"Truth don't lie, though, and truth usually is the best. I shouldn't have to tell you that. Tell 'em the truth!" Ava waved her hand in the air. "There's a thought, Preacher. Tell the truth that I was sleepwalkin'. Widower Frisk knows that's a fact about me. Heck, he's seen it happen."

Noah stilled, working his mouth from side to side, contemplating. His hands were at his waist. Ava noted the cords in the backs of them, the bronzed skin, the trimmed nails. They were strong hands. She averted her eyes.

"Ava . . ." Noah dared a step closer toward her.

She looked down and off to the side, away from him.

He stopped. "Are *we* sure you didn't do anything to Jipsy?"

And there it was. The reason he'd let the town believe and get in a fury that she'd up and left with Jipsy's body somehow in tow. The reason he was himself a liar. The reason he didn't want to let anyone know she was still under his roof.

Ava lifted accusing eyes. "You think I killed her, don't ya?"

Noah's eyes never flinched. Small embers brewed in them as he looked directly back at her. "I need to know."

"And Hanny?"

"What about Hanny?" Noah asked.

"Does she think maybe I killed Jipsy too? And Hubbard? What reason would I have? You all think I'm a monster?"

"Ava."

"No!" Ava raised her palms toward Noah. "Now you've got me in a fix and a fiddle. I look like I'm on the run and I done hacked away at two of the town's members. But I'm here. Here and right as rain. I didn't *do* nothin' to Jipsy!"

Noah evaded her proclamation of innocence and countered it with conversation, as if she'd not just ranted a few inches from his face. "Until we figure out how to prove you didn't kill Matthew Hubbard, or have anything to do with Jipsy, you're safer here with no one knowing your whereabouts. Otherwise you're going to get locked up with no proof of the crime, or worse, someone's going to enact their own justice."

"You're all heartless beasts," Ava mumbled. "And what makes you sure I won't kill you or Hanny?"

Noah didn't answer right away. Instead, he reached for a letter on the desk in front of him, lifted it, studied the writing, then set it back down. Finally he looked at her. This time, truly looked. Deep into her heart, she was sure of it, and that was troubling.

"I don't know, Ava, but I know everyone needs someone to believe in them."

"And you're sayin' that's you? That you're goin' to risk believin' in me? Risk your life even on the chance you're wrong and I'll sneak into your room tonight and chop you up like kindling?" Ava challenged.

Noah's laugh was sad and not at all laced with humor or even irony. It was just sad. Colorless. Hopeless, if Ava were to really try to pinpoint it. His smile was more of a wince.

"I owe it to God."

"Well, that's just heartwarmin'." Ava sank back into the chair. So, she was penance for Noah Pritchard. Which meant if she turned out to be a murdering vixen—as the town of Tempter's Creek thought her to be—then he'd done something so bad that his life was worth the risk to gain forgiveness. And was forgiveness even worth a person's life? Ava was hard-pressed to believe that it was.

If Ava was going to hide away in the parsonage, then Hanny had to go. At least that was Hanny's argument, which was now being vehemently protested against by Noah. Ava could hear the two through the open doorway of the front room. Their voices carried from the kitchen through the tiny dining area.

"If I stay, they'll all know there's a reason for me to still be here with you. Now, there's nothing untoward about that, but if they figure out the reason is that Ava is here, well then your secret is out and she's back on the chopping block."

"If you don't stay, then I'm a single man living alone with a single woman, and that scandal will ruin me."

"And you didn't think of that *before* you volunteered to watch over her?"

Noah's frustration dropped from his voice, and he almost sounded like a scolded schoolboy. "I banked on prayer you'd be willing to help me out."

"And I was. I *am*. Silly boy, you're a wretch."

"I am." A huge sigh.

"That's *not* what I meant." Hanny banged a pot.

Ava strained to hear over the clatter.

"You're in a pickle. What excuse will you give them when my little house stays dark at night, and you still have an eighty-two-year-old woman playing grandmother to you in the parsonage? Hmmm? No one is going to believe *I* need help."

Ava's hand clapped over her mouth to stifle a laugh.

"I'll tell them you fell and hurt yourself. That you need looking after." Noah's reasoning made sense. Ava nodded, even though no one was there to see her.

"So you'll lie?" Hanny retorted.

"I'll stretch the truth," Noah snapped.

"It's a lie," Hanny concluded. "I'd think you'd not want to add breaking a commandment to your list of regrets. Although it seems a mite too late for that."

They fell silent, and Ava snuck to the door. She peeked around it, past the small dining table with its lace runner down the middle, and through the kitchen doorway at the far end of the room. Noah sagged against the doorframe. Hanny, beyond him, was pouring tea into a china cup. She set the kettle back on the stove with another clatter.

"I won't stay. My house is right next door if you need me. But you've put yourself in a pickle, and whether you like it or not, my staying is going to create another batch of pickles."

Her statement brought an even lower sag to Noah's shoulders.

"You know as well as I do that there isn't one person in Tempter's Creek who will think it's normal for me to stay here after the girl has supposedly run off!" Hanny took a sip of her tea. She slurped it through her lips and it made a bubbling, sucking noise as the fiery liquid cooled before entering her mouth. "It's safer for you both if I go home and things go back to what everyone thinks is normal."

"I'm not convinced Ava will even play along with this," Noah muttered. "That she'll even stay put here like I've told her to."

"Well, lies have a way of creating deeper predicaments, don't they—*Preacher*? She isn't your prisoner any more than she was Larson's. You're supposed to look out for her, not create more problems for the girl." Hanny looked rather pleased with herself for besting the reverend. "The truth of things doesn't frighten me like it does you."

Now he colored. Ava wondered why.

"It's not my responsibility to smooth over your mishaps, Noah Pritchard, and I certainly will not add to further suspicion that might end up harming Ava."

"It will harm Ava if you leave!" Noah gritted through his teeth. He pointed behind him, toward the room where he thought Ava was quietly composed and sitting properly until she was bidden. Instead, she hid around the door, eavesdropping with absolutely no shame or regret. "If they catch wind that Ava is staying here with me, a single man . . ."

Hanny slapped her palms on the table. "Well then, for your sake they better not catch wind of it, because I highly doubt Ava Coons is concerned about that over everything else that haunts that poor child." The old woman pushed herself up from the table. "There's a thing called *wisdom*, Noah, and it may be time you used some of it. Seems to me that Bible you preach from has outlined it pretty clear. A lie is a lie, and you pay for it in the end."

"What was I supposed to do?" His voice rose in distress. "Tell the town Ava hadn't run off? That she's still here? They would have stormed the parsonage! They're in a mad frenzy, Hanny, and they think Ava is to blame for two very violent murders." Noah spit out the last words without censure.

He was met with silence.

Ava ached to peek around the corner to see the look on Hanny's face.

Instead, they all three seemed to pause to listen to the clock tick. Ten seconds . . . eighteen . . . twenty-two . . .

"You've made life messier, Preacher Pritchard," Hanny stated. "I suggest you start cleaning it up."

11

Wren

Campfire stories were *not* supposed to be real! Wren charged into the Markham home with the familiarity of someone who had earned the right to, after spending more hours here growing up than in her own home.

Eddie followed her but with far less dramatic flair. They had left Troy behind at the camp, and with night having fallen, it was easier to walk the half-mile trail through the woods to the Markham house than . . . well, Wren really had no excuse except that she felt more at home here. Safer. Not that she had any reason to feel unsafe. It was Jasmine Riviera who'd gone missing, not her. And she'd Web-searched her name, and Arwen *was* an older name than she'd thought, and not proprietary to Tolkien. So maybe—*maybe*—there was nothing to their finding that creepy ogle-eyed doll with her name on its foot.

Wren shuddered and flopped onto a recliner in the living room set just off the Markham kitchen. Eddie followed her into the room, and darn it if he wasn't cradling the evil doll in the crook of his arm.

"It's not a baby that needs loved," Wren tossed at him.

Eddie's mouth tilted in a sideways smile. "She needs some TLC."

"She needs to be installed in a house of horrors somewhere in Las Vegas and be put on show for being the creepiest thing to be found. Ever. She's probably possessed."

"I think opening Jeffrey Dahmer's freezer would be creepier," Eddie retorted.

Wren leveled him with a glare. "You need to stop watching stuff about serial killers. It's sick."

"*They're* sick. I just watch to learn."

"Learn what? How to disembowel someone?" Wren's irritation was coming to the fore. It was what happened when her anxiety rose. She got snippy. It was that or burst into tears, and her parents had taught her long ago that the quest to gain emotional stability was the avoidance of all eye leakage.

"Relax." Eddie dropped the doll onto the couch. "She's not possessed."

"How do you know?" Wren eyed the doll. "I mean, look at her!" The cracked face, the one eye that had rolled back into its head and stuck there, and the other eye that stared straight ahead. "Possession has to be considered," Wren determined.

They stared at each other for a long moment. Finally, Eddie reached out and flipped the doll over so at least her eyes were staring into the couch cushion and not at Wren.

"I need to check on Mom." Eddie's quiet statement jolted Wren back to the present and back under the other dark cloud hanging over them.

"I'll go with you." She stood from her sprawled position in the recliner and followed Eddie. He smelled like the woods, and she noticed the cuffs of his jeans had little burrs stuck to them from the underbrush.

The hallway to his mom's bedroom was dimly lit, and the carpet sank under their feet. Patty's bedroom door was slightly ajar. Eddie gave it a light rap with his knuckles, pushing it open.

Gary, Eddie's dad, looked up from his place in a chair by the bed. A book was open on his lap, his one leg crossed at the ankle on his opposite knee. His glasses were balanced on the tip of his nose, his beard hanging onto his chest. He was, after all, the epitome of a Northwoods man.

"Hey, kids." Gary's voice was soft, not unlike Eddie's, and level. There was kindness in his blue eyes as he closed his paperback, keeping his thumb in between the pages to mark his spot. "Any news?"

"Nothing." Eddie shook his head, and Wren knew Gary was referring to Jasmine—not the creepy doll on the living room couch. "How's Mom?"

"She's . . . hanging in there." Gary's gaze strayed to his wife. Patty lay in a quiet slumber, but even looking at her made Wren's heart ache. Patty had always been beautiful. Even now she was. But the sixty-year-old was gaunt, her sixty-two-pound weight loss from the battle with breast cancer leaving her almost skeletal. Her cheeks were sunken, and the rosy luster and twinkle that had always been the Patty Wren knew growing up were gone. Hospice was doing a good job caring for her. The last hospital stay had been a week ago, and then she'd been sent home, a sentence applied to her lifespan. Three months would be a miracle. A few weeks more likely.

Wren swallowed hard. She held her eyes shut against the burning and willed tears away. Life without Patty Markham was going to be empty. Void. She'd bonded with Patty since the day Eddie had hid earthworms in her chicken noodle soup. Patty had taken Wren's side and said if Eddie thought worms were so wonderful, he was welcome to finish Wren's for her. And she'd held her stance until Eddie lifted the spoon to his mouth, a squiggling worm dangling. Mercy had been shown. Eddie chastised. Wren had received a chocolate brownie for dessert, while Eddie had to settle for a carrot.

It wasn't the first time Patty had come to Wren's aid. When she'd broken up with her first boyfriend in middle school, Eddie had teased her mercilessly. Patty had held her and encouraged her to *maybe wait till you're older before you date again.* When Patty spoke, Wren listened. So she had waited. She'd brought her prom date home, and then they'd stopped at the Markham house to double date with Eddie and his then-girlfriend. Patty had made as big a deal over Wren as she had over Eddie. Wren was the daughter she'd never had, she always said. When Wren attended a community college in place of a university, her dad had been—*upset* might be a lackluster word for it. But Patty had encouraged Wren by saying the unpopular *"not everyone needs to have a four-year degree."*

It was Patty who'd changed over her sewing room and put in a twin-sized bed. *"Sometimes you need to get away from the family home."* Patty was right. It was easier to get away to the Markham home than to face all the questions at her own.

Wren knew she mocked the fact that Pippin was nearing forty and living in their dad's basement. But here she was, twenty-six years of age and working in the administration building at camp, doing admin work. A secretary, if an old-school term could be applied. Which meant she'd been saving to buy her own house now for a few years, but she too was in limbo. Tempter's Creek downtown was miles away from camp, so getting an apartment there had been impractical when she spent all but sleeping hours on the grounds.

The truth was, between Wren and Pippin, her dad didn't seem proud of their career successes—or failures. Pippin's programming work at least *sounded* smart. Wren knew her dad still waited for the moment she would leave for higher pursuits. She loved her dad. Wren never questioned that. And he loved her. They just didn't see eye to eye on a lot of things. Patty Markham, on the other hand, saw Wren's heart.

Pushing aside the disturbing thoughts, Wren joined the men by Patty's bedside. "Do you need me to sit with her awhile?" Wren offered.

Gary drew in a deep breath, weighted with the imminence of bidding his soulmate farewell, and shook his head. "No. No, I'll stay with her, but thanks, Wren. I've got the chair here—I'll catch some sleep later."

Wren didn't miss Eddie from the corner of her eye. He had rounded his mother's bed and now sat carefully on the edge. He looked so strong, so vibrant compared to Patty. Where they had once shared very similar features—the same eyes, the same cheeky grin, the same facial expressions—now it was just Eddie, looking down at the shell of the only woman he'd ever really adored. Wren knew this. Eddie was a mama's boy through and through, and in the best of ways. They were inseparable. They always had been.

Wren had to get away before she burst into inopportune tears. She gave Gary a quick nod and could tell he seemed to understand. One last glance at Eddie and Patty brought the first unwelcome tear rolling down her cheek. He had wrapped his hand around Patty's and was singing some silly song from the Lawrence Welk show. About pleasant dreams. Sleep tight. It was all so pithy and would've been comical had Wren not known that it was the song Patty had sung to Eddie since he was a baby. He was tucking her in for the night. A reversal of roles.

She hurried into the living room, leaned over the horrific doll, and snagged a tissue from a box on the end table. Wren wiped at her eyes, sniffed, and resorted to the one distraction that was sure to not fail.

Her phone screen blinked to life, and Wren scrolled through her notifications. Text message from Troy. She quickly responded.

> At Markhams' for the night.

His reply was swift.

> Got it. Everything is going to be all right. See you in the morning.

Troy. He was an optimist. Wren loved that about him. Right now she wished he'd also be heroic and show up at the door, wrap her in his arms, and let her hide her face in his chest. But coddling Wren over a weird scare about a doll and burned-out cabin remains was second priority to finding Jasmine. The little girl was going on her second night missing in the woods, and the longer it went without finding even a hint of her . . .

Wren's phone trilled in her hand, and she swiped to answer. "Hello?"

"Arwen." It was her dad.

"Hey, Dad."

"I thought you might stop by the house tonight."

Wren grimaced, glad he couldn't see her reaction. "Sorry. We've been out searching."

"Yes." His voice became grave. "I checked in at the SAR base here on the grounds. They've found absolutely no sign of her."

"I know." Wren waited. Her dad wasn't one to waste time with empty chatter. He had a reason for calling her.

"I ran into Troy—he said you were out looking in the Lost Lake area?"

"Yes." She didn't offer more information.

There was a pause. "Arwen, you *know* Ava Coons is a ghost story." Wren didn't answer.

"She's a campfire story. She didn't take the little girl," her father reiterated. "You can't let your dreams get to you like this."

Her dreams. She leaned her head back on the couch and closed her eyes. Dad knew about her dreams and the way that they ate at her as if they were premonitions. It didn't help that she'd had one right before Mom died. Years ago, as a little girl, she'd been afraid that Mom would leave. Where her sense of abandonment had come from, they had no idea, but it was there nonetheless. When she'd dreamt about Mom's death and then it had happened, it was like a nail in a coffin. Dreams had meaning. They were prophetic. But they weren't—at least that was Dad's argument. *Had been* Dad's argument. Yet Wren couldn't help but question—wonder—because weren't dreams typically the mental manifestation of some subliminal truth?

Wren bit her tongue. What really upset her sometimes was how her father could see right through her dreams to her deeper fears. The ones that lived in the irrational, fictionalized realm. The part of Wren that made her believe Mordor and the ring, and Gollum and Orcs actually *were* real evil lurking. Dad had probably read her too much Tolkien when she was a toddler. She remembered the board book of *The Hobbit* she'd had as a three-year-old. It had come with a plastic ring she'd insisted on wearing to church. Dad had been proud. But as she grew, he'd become wary.

"Don't turn fantasy into reality," he reminded her now. This from the man who'd encouraged his wife to name the rooms in their house after various locales in Tolkien's novel *The Lord of the Rings*.

"I'm not, Dad. You just—I've never liked the story of Ava Coons. The rumor that she snatches people and buries them in Lost Lake."

"It's just a story," he argued.

"You know people have claimed to still see her." Even as she said the words, Wren knew how silly they sounded. That Ava Coons—campfire terror—would return from the forest in which she'd disappeared to murder again. Besides, Jasmine hadn't been murdered—God forbid—or even kidnapped. She'd just gone missing.

Right?

"Arwen." Her dad's voice cut through her thoughts. "Come home."

"I am home" was all she could think to say in response.

12

"They found blood."

It was not the phrase Wren wanted to hear. Troy came up behind her, slipping his arms around her waist and pulling her back into him. He whispered in her ear as they stood off to the side of the bulk of the SAR volunteers.

"This morning, Group Six found Jasmine's hoodie. It had blood on it."

Wren twisted in his arms, not feeling affectionate, even though she knew Troy's way of dealing with emotion was to reach for her. She pulled away, a gripping fear tightening her middle. "What do you mean, blood? There shouldn't be blood if she just wandered off and got lost, right? Unless she was injured?" Wren searched his face. "She *is* just lost, right, she wasn't taken? Tell me they're not changing their assessment."

There was a flicker in Troy's eyes that spoke of more when a wail rent the air. Wren jumped at the sound and then clamped her hand over her mouth as she watched Jasmine's mother collapse into her husband's embrace. They had both come out this morning, intent on being part of the search, no longer willing to be coddled and mollified by the authorities. They wanted answers.

Now they had one—a very unsavory one.

"Friends. Volunteers," Sheriff Floyd called from across the machine barn, his voice echoing off the concrete floor and metal sides. "Over here, please."

They all gathered, including Jasmine's parents. Wren noticed

Eddie's pal Bruce standing off to the side in full police uniform. He met her eyes and looked away. That didn't bode well. The already ominous overtones in the room had turned heavier. Weightier. Suffocating.

Sheriff Floyd waited until they had all gathered around. He consulted in John Hipken's ear, the director of the SAR teams. John gave a curt nod, his mouth a tight firm line.

"All right," Sheriff Floyd began, scanning the group of volunteers. Bruce moved to stand beside him and John. "As you probably know by now, earlier this morning Group Six found Jasmine's sweatshirt. There was evidence of an injury, as we found some blood on the garment. Ben, Meghan"—he addressed Jasmine's parents—"and the rest of you"—his eyes once again scanned the group—"this is *still* an ongoing search and rescue. We have no reason to believe anything other than that Jasmine is alive, but we do have concerns for her welfare in the event she's suffering from an injury."

A hand shot up.

John pointed at it. "Yes?"

"Do we still believe she got lost?" one of the volunteers asked.

John deferred to the sheriff, whose expression remained passive. "We are still going under the theory that Jasmine is lost and cannot find her way back home. However, we aren't ruling out other possibilities."

"Abduction?" the volunteer asked.

Wren wanted to throttle the person for the insensitivity with the girl's parents being present.

Sheriff Floyd managed it well. "As I said, we're not ruling anything out at the moment. We're looking at this from all angles. For now, we need all of you to maintain strict adherence to the direction of John and his experienced SAR team." He held up his palms. "We don't need heroes. Stick to the search grid and the techniques you've been coached on. Thank you."

There was a general murmur that started up in the group. Jasmine's parents moved to a cluster of metal folding chairs. Bruce made his way toward Troy, and Wren held on to Troy's hand, squeezing it as the officer approached. His brown eyes were missing the customary sparkle Wren was used to, even though she didn't know Bruce nearly as well as Eddie did.

"Please pass our thanks on to the camp administration." Bruce shook Troy's hand, then Wren's.

Troy nodded. "Of course."

Bruce ran his fingers around the collar at his neck. "This is just—heavy."

"Not what you signed up for?" Troy tried to meet the officer in conversation halfway.

Bruce gave him a quick look. "Oh, I signed up for it. It just isn't easy. Not when it's a kid."

"Is there a possibility Jasmine was taken?" Wren inserted, not missing the way Sheriff Floyd had left that door open.

Bruce gave her a semi-apologetic smile. "You know I can't comment about that, Wren."

"But the fact you can't says there is that possibility," she surmised.

Bruce shrugged. "Interpret it however you want. Either way, she's missing. The investigation is ongoing."

Wren knew she shouldn't push further. Her gaze landed on the grieving parents, Ben and Meghan. "And the Rivieras? How are they holding up?"

Bruce barked a short, dry laugh. "Horrid." He sighed. "I have a daughter now, and man, if it were Clara out there, I'd . . . I don't know how the Rivieras are even keeping it together."

Wren's heart constricted at the idea. "I feel like I should talk to them. The camp should be offering them support beyond just a place to run SAR."

"They could use that," Bruce said before ducking his head and walking away.

Troy tugged at her hand, pulling her closer. Wren came but with barely concealed resistance. She peered over his shoulder at the grieving, desperate parents even as Troy held her.

Sensing the stiffness in her body, he drew back, searching her face. "You okay?"

Wren bit her lip. Troy's gaze followed the movement, and then he returned his attention to her, waiting for an answer.

"I'm just—" Wren hesitated. Somehow telling Eddie was easier than telling Troy. But it was Troy who held her, wanted her, who understood her in so many ways. "I've got a bad feeling. Ever since last night—when we were at the Coons cabin ruins and Lost Lake. Something isn't right."

"It's not." Troy reached up and pushed a tendril of her coppery hair from her face. "It's not all right. We've got a camp full of campers to run, a missing girl, and for what it's worth, that doll was creepy. It would've unnerved you on a good day."

"But it was just a doll," Wren affirmed, more for herself than for Troy.

He gripped her shoulders and stared into her eyes. "Yeah. Just a doll. It's not like Ava Coons wanders the woods and writes your name on an old doll's foot. She's not hunting you—or anyone."

Wren pulled away. "I'm not afraid of a ghost, Troy."

He frowned and rubbed the back of his neck. "I didn't mean that you were. I'm just saying—"

"Never mind." Wren waved his explanation off. It wasn't worth the tension. Jasmine was the focus—*should* be the focus. Not the doll, or the cabin, or Ava Coons.

"I get why she's on your mind." Troy didn't let it go.

Wren met his frank liquid-blue stare.

Troy continued, "Everyone is thinking it to a degree. Jasmine isn't the first to go missing around here."

Wren bit the inside of her cheek and looked away from him. No. No, she wasn't. There was that girl who disappeared when Wren was in high school. They never found her either. No one talked about it anymore, and the most accepted explanation was that the girl's father had kidnapped her. People liked to blame Ava Coons when bad things happened. Sometimes a ghost story was easier than the raw truth.

"But you know they're all explained. Hunting accident. That kid's dad taking her. It wasn't anything with these woods—or Lost Lake. Or you."

Wren jerked her head back and locked eyes with Troy. She didn't like the way he was searching her face, trying to impress some element of truth on her she didn't want to hear.

"I never said this was about me," she snapped. Why on earth would Troy think that, outside of the doll they'd found? A nagging feeling in her stomach worried Wren that somehow she was coming across narcissistic enough to turn Jasmine's disappearance into her issue. Her problem. Some plea for attention. "It's about Jasmine," she reaffirmed.

"I don't doubt your intentions." Troy offered her a gentle smile. God bless him. Wren allowed the strain to ebb from her body. Troy looked over to the Rivieras. "Go," he nudged her. "You said you wanted to reach out to Jasmine's parents. Go. Do it. It's a good idea. I'm not sure if camp has had the chance to yet, and Deer Lake Bible Camp *should* be more to them than just a base camp for their daughter's search."

Troy dropped a kiss on her cheek. Affectionate but understandably distant, considering Wren hadn't shown any particular warmth toward him that morning. She wrapped her arms around herself and nodded. He chucked her under the chin with his knuckle and moved away, heading toward John and the other SAR teams. He was going to lead Group Four today. Wren had chosen to stay behind. Something about the woods seemed darker this morning. More dangerous. She wasn't convinced she wanted to enter them.

"Ben? Meghan?" Wren approached the parents, who clutched Styrofoam cups of camp coffee. The two looked up, lost expressions on their faces. Wren eased onto a chair, the cold from the metal seeping through her shorts and cooling the backs of her bare legs.

Ben lifted dark eyes. He was handsome, his dark hair and olive skin a striking physical contrast next to his wife, Meghan, who was blond and even on a bad day could probably walk the runway as a model. But stress and trauma were taking a toll. Wren could see the remnants of hours of tears by the red-rimmed eyes, the puffiness, and the trembling in Meghan's hands.

Wren leaned forward and drew in a deep breath, praying for the right words.

"I'm Wren. Wren Blythe. I work here at Deer Lake Bible Camp. We just wanted to let you know we are praying, and hoping, and will do whatever we can to help."

"You will?" Meghan's head snapped up, her blue eyes intense.

Wren shot a hesitant look at Ben, who reached for his wife's hand.

"Meghan," he began.

"No." Meghan shook her head at her husband. "I know—I *know* Jasmine didn't just wander off!" Meghan swung her attention back to Wren. She leaned forward, matching Wren's stance of elbows on knees. She lowered her voice. "The day Jasmine disappeared, she told me about a woman she'd seen. In the woods."

"A woman?" Wren ignored the return of the tension in her stomach. The foreboding that she consistently stuffed away as ludicrous.

Meghan nodded, ignoring Ben's squeeze of his hand on her upper thigh. "Jasmine said it was a woman wearing overalls."

"There isn't anything suspicious about a woman in overalls." Ben's grave tone sliced through his wife's frantic words.

"See?" Meghan waved her hand at Ben, bitter desperation trailing across her features. "He doesn't believe me."

"*Por el amor de Dios!* I believe you." Ben blew out a breath. "I just don't see what is—"

"Overalls!" Meghan almost shrieked. A few of the people gathered not far away cast covert glances.

Ben squeezed Meghan's knee. Wren noticed it wasn't a tight squeeze but meant to be comforting, calming.

Meghan drew in a deep breath, pursing her lips together. "We may be from Milwaukee, but I grew up in this area, you know? Our family owned a cabin close to camp. We've come up every summer, sometimes for a week at a time. I *know* the story of Ava Coons in her overalls and her boots. I *know* she haunts the woods. I know she *hunts* in these woods."

Ben growled deep in his throat, hanging his head and shaking it back and forth. His black hair flipped forward, hiding his expression. Meghan side-eyed him as she addressed Wren. "He doesn't think it's true—the story of Ava Coons—but he didn't grow up around here. He's from Florida, where their biggest fear is alligators!"

Wren squelched all the various responses flying through her head. None of them were adequate. None of them helped her ease her own insecurities about the recent events, nor would they help Meghan.

"You believe in Ava Coons, don't you?" Meghan sniffed. The edge of anger in her voice was dissipating into a watery hope that someone wouldn't think she was crazy.

Wren tapped her fingers on her bare knees, feeling a rivulet of sweat trickle down her back. It wasn't *that* hot outside. But it didn't change the fact that she felt as though she were in the hot seat.

"Don't you?" Meghan insisted.

Even Ben lifted his head, awaiting Wren's reply.

Wren opened her mouth, started to answer, then paused. The wrong words right now could be catastrophic for Meghan Riviera's emotional state.

"I believe Jasmine probably saw a woman in overalls. I know Ava Coons's legend is all about her being in overalls and—"

"Carrying an ax." Meghan leveled a satisfied *someone believes me* look on her husband.

Wren cleared her throat. "Yes."

"See?" Meghan's voice filled with urgency. She scooted to the edge of her chair with intense concentration on Wren. "We need to figure out if Ava Coons is out there somewhere! People think my baby just wandered off!" Meghan waved her hand haphazardly. "Wandered off and somehow got lost in the woods! She's *six*! How far would she go? We should have found her by now. I know—I *know* something worse happened."

"Meghan," Ben started.

"No!" Meghan skewered her husband with a glare. "I am her *mother*. I feel it." She clapped her hands over her heart. "I feel it here. Someone took Jasmine. She didn't just get lost."

Wren had no words. Her mind had gone completely blank as she took in the anguished worry on Ben's face, and the fierce determination on Meghan's.

Ben twisted in his chair and reached for Meghan. Grasping her hands, he sagged toward her, every ounce of him reflecting the anxiety that was in Meghan's desperate grasp for answers. "*Cariño*, it is a ghost story. That's it. A story. If Jasmine saw a woman in overalls, it could have been anyone."

"Then we need to interview all the women in the area who wear overalls!" Meghan insisted.

"That's unreasonable," Ben snapped.

"*You* believe me, don't you?" Meghan pushed Ben's hand from her leg and edged closer to Wren. "That Jasmine has been taken?"

Crud.

"Meghan, I—I don't know." She never should have come over here. She'd intended to offer to pray with them. That felt pithy now, but this? She hadn't expected this. She was sure the authorities had already interrogated the parents for every minute detail that might help. Where had they last seen Jasmine? Was she alone? Why would she have wandered into the forest? Was she familiar with the area? And so on . . .

"The sweatshirt," Meghan pleaded. "Jasmine wouldn't have taken it off. It was her favorite. And if there was b-blood . . . that's Ava Coons's signature."

"Ava Coons is just a story. She doesn't have a signature," Ben interjected.

Wren saw the look of war on Meghan's face toward her husband, and she hurried to intervene and avoid a battle. "Ava Coons existed, yes, but no one knows what really happened to her. We don't know which parts of the story are true and which parts are not, and . . . she's been said to have roamed the forest for decades. Even before she was dead, they said she roamed the forest. She's . . . Ava Coons *is* the forest. But she's not capable of kidnapping a child."

Thank you. Ben mouthed his appreciation.

Wren shifted in her chair. She wished she'd sounded more convincing. But it must have been enough, because Meghan sniffed, wiped her nose with the back of her hand, and directed a dismissive look to Ben. "I need to go to the bathroom. I'm going to walk to the lodge."

"There's porta potties—"

"I'm going to walk to the lodge." Meghan's voice was sharp when she interrupted Wren's attempt to help. Meghan pushed her metal chair backward, and it scraped on the shed's concrete floor. She staggered for a moment, and Ben jumped to help her, but she shrugged him off and zeroed in on the exit.

Ben stood helplessly, his arms hanging at his sides. Wren noticed the gray hairs in his sideburns and goatee. She wondered if it was because he'd crossed the threshold of forty, or if it was because his daughter was missing and they'd sprung up overnight.

Wren stood awkwardly, wiping her damp palms on her shorts. "My wife isn't crazy."

"I know." Wren heard the empathy in her voice. "She's desperate—you're both desperate—for answers."

Ben shook his head and raked his fingers through his hair. "My little *chica* is out there. Whether she was lost or taken, she's out there. Alone. Without her *papi*."

Wren just listened. She wasn't sure what else to say.

"This story—the one my wife is hung up on—it *is* just a story? *Sí?*"

The image of the old doll, the burned-out cabin, the cellar with broken jars and cobwebs flashed through her memory. Wren swallowed her own doubts. "It's an old story from the 1930s."

"And there're no relatives of Ava Coons, no one around who could tell my wife that it's just a story? That the Coons family isn't a generational tree of raving lunatics running around the woods? Or ghosts?"

She'd never thought of that. "Um, I-I don't know. I don't know if there are any Coonses left in the area."

Ben's expression made Wren squirm. She looked everywhere but at him. She looked at Troy as he gave instructions to the people in his search party. She noted Sheriff Floyd at one of the folding tables, leaning over Officer Bruce's shoulder and his laptop. She saw Pippin enter the shed and head toward John, probably to get assigned to another search team. Eddie was absent. He was directing the kitchen staff to provide support for the camp and its campers.

"Let me help Meghan." Wren winced the moment the words escaped her lips.

Ben looked at her sharply. "We need to work with the authorities."

"But would it hurt?" Wren battled herself internally even as she responded to Ben. "If Jasmine did talk to a woman at the park, maybe she knows something. Maybe it's worth looking into?"

"And leading my wife on to believe there's a ghost woman in the woods snatching children?" Ben's dark eyes flashed.

Wren couldn't blame him. "I-I didn't mean that we look for a ghost. I just meant—"

"The police already looked into that angle." Ben ran his fingers through his hair. Agitated. "They didn't find anything."

"But would it hurt for us to look?" Wren bit her tongue. She really needed to back off. Leave it be. She was as bad as Meghan, but that twisting in her gut had only worsened. The vision of Jasmine lying dead on the shore of Lost Lake throbbed in her mind like a haunting that was far worse than Ava Coons.

Ben glanced over his shoulder to make sure Meghan hadn't returned. "I just want her to sleep. She hasn't slept. And she's not acting rationally. I need—I need her to rest, not chase a wild idea."

"Assuming she's wrong," Wren concluded.

Ben's mouth thinned. "Let the search parties look for my *niña*. Let the authorities do what they do best."

"Would you let me spend time with Meghan?" Wren hurried on. "Let me help her look into who Ava Coons was. What the real story is. If the Coons family has a reputation for doing bad things in these woods, it may help her feel like she's doing something to find Jasmine, even if she's—if *we* are wrong." It was a weak argument. Wren knew the camp would give her time off because it was what they did here. Helped people. And Lord knew Meghan needed the support. Yet Wren couldn't convince herself she was offering a disservice to Meghan. Helping Meghan chase after her own suspicions wasn't fair to her emotionally if there was evidence to conclude any legitimate suspicions.

Ben locked eyes with Wren. "Fine." His shoulders dropped in resignation. "Do whatever you need to. I can't fight her on this anymore."

Wren touched the man's elbow, hoping her sincerity seeped into her words. "I promise—we'll just explore the idea."

"Sure." Ben shrugged off her hand. He held up his palms. "I need to go look for my baby girl. You do whatever you and Meghan need to do."

Wren watched him stalk away, his shoulders ladened with a grief so thick, and an anxiety so heavy, she wouldn't have been surprised if he'd toppled over. She squeezed her eyes shut. What had she done? Offering to help Meghan explore her conviction that something more had happened to Jasmine? Wasn't that interfering with a police investigation? Or was it? There was just a missing child. Not an abduction.

Ava Coons was long dead.

The woods of Lost Lake weren't haunted.

Dreams weren't reality.

Even as she repeated the truths in her mind, Wren admitted she herself was not completely convinced.

13

Ava

"Dyin' of boredom ain't far off," Ava mumbled to herself as she paced the front room. She couldn't even look out the window. Noah had instructed strictly that window peeking was too high a risk, and then he'd hauled his merry self off to the church or some go-gettin'-saved mission. Of course, Ava had to admit he wasn't especially peppy in his step that morning. His fedora made him look distinguished, and his brooding eyes brought a sense of obligation to the preacher. Heck, she'd get saved just to spare herself from having him glower all over her like a sad puppy dog that had been separated from its mama.

Hanny had hustled, or waddled rather, her way next door to her own house, her bag of belongings in hand. She really *was* going through with her plan to move back home and leave Ava here alone with the preacher.

"Fine fix." Ava plopped onto a chair, hiking her right leg up to balance her foot on the seat cushion. The leg of her overalls was frayed, threads hanging around her calf. She wasn't wearing shoes or socks, and that at least was a bit freeing. "I didn't kill no one," she mumbled to herself. Maybe if she snuck out and found Ned, he would help her hide. Then she wouldn't be trapped here in the parsonage, staring at a painting of Jesus, who looked off to the side as if He were ashamed to match her stare.

"You of all people should know, the time I snared that rabbit and then broke its neck when Frisk told me to just about done me in." Ava jumped to her feet and stared up at Jesus. "How on your green earth could people think I'd hack a body to bits like a demon outta hell?" She paused. "Sorry 'bout that." She stared at the motionless painting. He didn't answer. Which wasn't uncommon. Jesus, God, the saints, they'd all been silent for as long as Ava could remember. But then she couldn't remember much, so that didn't say a whole lot about any of their existence.

"You know, you could say somethin'." Ava crossed her arms and leveled a final glare at Jesus. "Seems like you expect a lot of folks to talk to you, but you don't say much back." She waited. Silence.

Giving up on Jesus for the moment, Ava paced the room some more before stopping at Noah's desk. It was a small wooden secretary with its desk lowered on a hinge and a chair slid under it. The left side of the secretary had four shelves filled with books. She bent to peruse the titles. Nothing but preacher books. She could read. At least that was a bonus. Straightening, she observed the few items on the desktop. Pencils in a leather cup. A Bible tucked neatly off to the side. Its corners were worn, but the gold-embossed *Holy Bible* on the cover looked new still. An envelope lay underneath the book. Ava tugged it out and read it.

"Emmaline Radcliff," she whispered, rubbing her thumb over the return address with its flowery script. "Fancy name." Without regard to right or wrong, Ava opened the envelope and pulled out a single page of stationery. She skimmed it.

My dearest Noah,

I wished to write to you once more, if only to express my own deepest regrets for all that transpired between us. I realize we will never speak to each other again—at least in this lifetime— and while I have reconciled with that, I have also been overcome by the grief that only you can share with me. None other can comprehend the loss which knifes at my heart every waking moment. Would that I could have changed the outcome. As it is, such is our life now, and I can only pray that you, and God, will extend mercy and forgiveness in the midst of the sorrow. That God will see fit to bring beauty from the ruins of my soul. My wrongs against you have been great, and yet I will remember you with bittersweet love. Godspeed, dear Noah.

Yours in memory alone,

Emmaline

The words caused tears to spring unbidden to Ava's eyes. She swiped at them, not fully understanding why she felt the pang of sadness and why, in that moment, she felt as though Emmaline Radcliff had reached across the miles to *her*. Bring beauty from ruin . . . it was an image Ava had never before considered. It made her hesitate and made her settle on the chair at the desk and lay the letter out flat, running her fingers over the words as if they were as precious as Scripture itself.

What was beauty anyway? Ava wasn't sure she'd ever seen it. Not really. Her chest constricted as sadness—that deep, sucking sadness—washed over her again. It came often, if Ava was honest. It gnawed at the edges of her, leaving her heart in tattered fragments. Grief. Loss. That sense of aimless belonging. She belonged, but she didn't. Ava squeezed her eyes closed. The memories that were just out of reach. She could see them. Shadows of them. Her father— he'd smoked a pipe. She knew that. When she caught the scent of tobacco from another man's pipe, her body reacted with a start. Yet her father wasn't there. Nor was her mother. She remembered the butter churn and her mother's stained apron. Funny things to remember really. No lullabies or kisses. Just butter and an article of clothing that didn't exist anymore. Like her brothers didn't exist. Arnie and Ricky. Both of them older. Wild. She remembered they were wild. Wild like the woods they lived in. And then the memories disappeared into a void of blackness. Nothing but this hollow ache that made Ava feel as if she were outside her body and looking in, and that she was missing something of herself—something just out of reach of her fingertips.

Ava folded the letter and slipped it back into its envelope. Emmaline wished to have changed the outcome of whatever shared grief had weighted her words and remained harbored behind Noah's eyes.

Well, Ava *could* change *her* outcome. A sense of determination rose within her, running through her blood, reaching into the bowels of her spirit and screaming for vindication. It was there, pounding, like a heartbeat thudding against her chest cavity, pressing against her ribs with a ferocity to scream the truth. The truth of what had happened. The truth of who she was.

Who was Ava Coons?

A murderer?

It was her darkest fear. In the confinement of her soul and in the recesses of her being, Ava asked it of herself daily. Was she a killer? And now, had she killed again?

Ava looked down at her hands as if they were stained with blood, and bile rose in her throat. She knew something no one else did. She knew that betrayal caused a person to hate, and with hate the borders of morality were demolished with the power of vengeful need. A need to pay back evil for evil. Wickedness for wickedness. It was inside her. A bitter poison first planted as a child in the corners of her mind—corners hidden even to herself.

Noah Pritchard had missed something that morning when he'd told Ava to stay inside, to stay out of sight while Jipsy had vanished, with murder on the tongues of the townspeople. He had missed the lack of grief in Ava's expression. He had missed that she showed no surprise or shock. He had missed that Ava had felt nothing. Nothing at all on word of Jipsy's death.

It was the nothing she felt that scared Ava the most.

14

This time she was very much awake, her mind clear. The moon hid behind clouds and treetops, but Ava slipped into the night anyway. Ava waited for what seemed like hours until she heard Noah's bedroom door close. She'd heard him pacing like a madman. Heard him grumbling something about Hanny. About being alone in the house with a woman. Maybe he was arguing at a picture of Jesus too. Ava figured he'd find out soon enough that Jesus wasn't gonna say nothin'.

Ava gave him another hour to be sure he was asleep with no more wearing ruts into his bedroom floor. Now her feet landed on the earth outside her bedroom window. She glanced back, assured Noah hadn't sensed her absence from the parsonage. The lights remained off. Crickets chirruped their night song, and a bat wove in an undulating flight over her head. Mosquitoes on the menu. Blood-sucking insects that took from their prey until it satisfied their bloodlust.

Ava darted across the dirt road, ducking into the shadows of the church. If Mr. Sanderson had seen her the other night, she needed to be particularly aware that slinking about Tempter's Creek in the wee hours would only add suspicion, if not injury, to her already inflamed reputation of guilt. Sneaking along the side of the church, Ava looked over her shoulder before tiptoeing up the back steps of the building. She tried the rear door. Locked. Peering in the window to the right of the door, Ava could make out the back entrance of the church. A few boxes answered for the dark shadows in the far corner. A snow shovel leaned against a wall next to a broom. The frame of a cross was propped against the wall. She recognized it as the Easter cross, which was rammed into the ground in the front yard of the church every spring. Now it collected dust. Forgotten. Redemption usually was forgotten. The irony was not lost on Ava.

She rattled the doorknob again. Getting into the church would gain her access to the pastoral records. If she remembered anything, it was that her mama and daddy were married in this church. That being the case, Ava figured if she could find the records, it might tell her who was in attendance—if anyone—and then she could find those people. Ask questions. See if she could uncover more memories of her parents. Her brothers. Find out why they'd lived so deep in the woods alongside a lake no one seemed to talk about, and find out why, after all these years, the Coons family was a whisper on people's tongues. That mysterious awe of death and the lore of unsolved questions. Ava needed to find who in Tempter's Creek knew them—who knew the Coons family as people, not victims of violent assault. Maybe even people who knew Ava as a little girl, before she'd wandered from the woods after the bloodbath. Before she'd lost all recollection of who she was and what had happened. Ava needed to exonerate herself. If not for the folks of Tempter's Creek, then for herself. While they assumed she was Jipsy's killer and perhaps Matthew Hubbard's, Ava needed to prove to herself she wasn't. Or else uncover that she was and turn herself in before she caused more eternal harm.

Another sweep of her gaze into the night revealed nothing. Ava reached into the pocket of her overalls and tugged out a soiled handkerchief. Wrapping it around her knuckles like a bandage, she gripped the loose ends of it in her palm. Without hesitation, Ava punched the bottom corner of the window. The glass shattered, silencing the crickets and sending all night sounds into complete stillness. Ava held her breath. A light breeze blew tendrils of hair across her face. She stuck her arm through the hole in the glass, careful to avoid the sharp edges of the broken windowpane. Ava felt along the door until her hand connected with the knob. She turned the lock, then with her free hand twisted the doorknob from the outside. The door gave way, opening with an inevitable creak of its hinges to announce Ava's arrival.

Her shoes made small thuds against the floorboards as she moved. The smell of must and closed-up building met her senses. The back entryway had another closed door leading into the main room of the church. She turned its knob, relieved that it wasn't locked. Opening it, Ava peered into the darkness. The short hallway before her led straight into the sanctuary. She could see shadows dancing across the floor, the pews appearing as dark lines of predatory observers, hissing through the darkness into Ava's mind.

You never come.

You never come.

No. She had never been inside this building. Church was always something to be avoided, like its goers avoided hell. Ava steered away from the sanctuary and instead ducked into a small office off the hallway. This room smelled more familiar. Scents of coffee and old books, and the warm smell of Noah Pritchard's spicy cologne. She wished she had a flashlight. Should've thought to swipe one from the parsonage kitchen. Instead, here she was, in the pitch-black, looking to find church records that went back over three decades. And right here was where Ned would insert some off-the-cuff remark about how if she'd been educated, she'd have known to think through what she needed.

The crunch of a foot stepping on broken glass made Ava freeze. She caught her breath, standing motionless in the darkness of Noah's church office.

"Aaaaaava?" A singsongy whisper sent chills through her. She backed up a step, her hip colliding with the corner of Noah's desk. She couldn't tell if the voice was male or female.

"Aaaaaava Coons?"

Another footstep, only this time it was a thud against solid wood flooring.

Ava dropped to all fours and felt in front of her. The corner of the desk. The desk chair. There. The darker alcove beneath the desk. She slipped into it, huddling in the corner. It wasn't Noah out there, no sir. That much she knew. He didn't play hide-and-seek with her. She knew this after just two days in his home. Noah Pritchard was nothing if not straightforward.

The footsteps stopped in the office's doorway. There was a low chuckle. The kind that erupted in a person's throat and sounded more like a growl.

"Ava Coons took an ax and gave her mother forty whacks . . ." It was a whisper with just a slight undertone of song.

Ava's skin broke out in fleshy bumps. She took a breath, heard it shudder, and clamped her mouth tight.

Another footstep. This time closer.

"When she saw what she had done, she gave her father forty-one . . ."

Another throaty chuckle.

Ava's lungs burned. She dared to inhale the tiniest of breaths through her nose. She could smell something familiar, metallic. Like iron. Or blood.

"Whack, whack, whack," the voice taunted.

Silence followed. No footsteps. No breathing. No limerick. Just an ugly silence that convinced Ava of nothing but that she should remain huddled in her hiding spot. Beneath the preacher's desk. In the innards of the church. The place that doomed souls to the lake of fire for a thing like murder.

Morning light stretching from the doorway of the office alerted Ava to the fact that dawn had indeed come. She'd remained huddled under Noah's desk for far too long, afraid to make use of the time to search the office for fear that the person behind the taunting voice was lying in wait. Her legs cramped as she stretched them out. Peeking from the alcove beneath the desk, Ava blinked against the sandpapery sensation in her eyes. She'd not slept. Not a wink. Fear had always been a distant thrum in her body, there but not sharp or identifiable. Now it stabbed through her repeatedly. The voice from the night before played havoc with her determination to clear her name—the Coons name—and try to seek some sort of normalcy.

Whack, whack, whack.

The voice had been a cackle, a harsh whisper of sorts, as if the speaker attempted to disguise it from recognition. The words had replayed in her mind throughout the night, and now, even as she slipped from beneath the desk into the morning light, Ava shuddered. Someone knew she'd been here. Someone was goading her. Toying with her. Reminding her of the demons just out of reach.

Ava's hair had come unraveled from its braid. She rubbed sand from the corners of her eyes and willed her body to compose itself. Being on high alert all night had left her shaky. She looked around the small office, attempting to center herself. She didn't have time to search any church records. If the light was any sign of a clock, it had to be past seven in the morning. Noah would notice she hadn't come down for breakfast. Especially without Hanny in the house to distract him now. Ava needed to get back to the parsonage. A quick dart across the street . . . she should be able to do so without being seen.

She moved swiftly toward the office door that led into the hall. Looking down, she noticed a few clumps of mud and pine needles, as if whoever had stood in the doorway had traipsed through the woods and marsh. Skirting them, Ava hurried around the corner toward the rear door of the church.

A body slammed her against the wall, forearm under her chin and over her chest, pinning her there as another hand clamped around her wrist. She writhed against the grip, her scream slicing her throat as it echoed in the empty hallway. Ava hiked her knee up and was met with an *oompf*, a release of her body, and the bulk of the man curled on the floor, clutching what appeared to be his midsection. Yet it wasn't.

"Lord have mercy!" Ava exclaimed, dropping to the floor beside Noah, whose pained expression told her that, had he been an authentic threat, she had done a fair-to-middlin' job of incapacitating him.

"G-go-ahhhh!" Noah sputtered, and Ava couldn't tell if he was trying not to cuss or if he was gasping for air. ". . . the heck are you doing here, Ava Coons?" he barked.

"Can preachers say *heck*?" Ava didn't know what else to ask, so she asked the first thing that came to mind.

Noah glared at her, uncurling his body and scowling. His eyes were anything but brooding. Yes. There was fire in them. Coals like one might find in a woodstove. All that was needed was a tad bit of oxygen fanned on them and they'd break into flames.

"Did you bust out the church window?" He sounded incredulous as he eased himself into a sitting position.

Ava didn't move from her spot on the floor opposite him. She also didn't answer.

He shook his head and blew out a sigh. "You did."

"Just a tiny bit," Ava admitted. Better to be honest, she figured, than to lie to a preacher.

"A tiny bit," Noah repeated, as if her honesty didn't count for much. "Why in the name of all that is holy are you breaking into my church?" It was more of a supremely irritated hiss than a direct question.

"Thought this was Tempter's Creek's church, not your'n," Ava countered.

"Ava."

She shrugged, the clasps on her overall straps clanking at the movement.

"Fine then. *Why* did you break into *the* church?"

Ava pressed her lips together. Noah's eyes dropped to look at them, then flew back up to stare into hers. He was a stern one when he was boiling mad. Just under the surface. She could tell a man who was itching to lose it, and Noah Pritchard was one, if ever there was. Stubbornness made her stiffen her shoulders. She certainly would not tell him why she was here either. Not after he'd made things so much worse by lyin' to the folks of Tempter's Creek about her! And she sure as shootin' wasn't going to tell him about last night's visitor who hunted her like she hunted her past.

"I should be gettin' back" was Ava's only response.

Noah's eyes narrowed. "Getting back? To the parsonage? That you weren't supposed to leave in the first place?"

"I'm not a prisoner," she hissed.

"The entire town is ready to string you up for Hubbard's murder and Jipsy's disappearance," Noah spat back. He leaned forward.

Ava matched his stance. "But I didn't do it."

"We've established that is your claim, but you need evidence and—" He chopped off his words as enlightenment spread across his face, followed quickly by confusion. "What do you think is in the church that would clear you?"

Ava tilted her chin upward. She'd seen Mrs. Sanderson do it now and then, and it seemed to shut *her* husband up.

Noah's eyes darkened. He twisted onto his knees faster than she expected, and his face was very close to hers when he spoke. "Listen to me, Ava Coons, and listen very closely. I've stepped out on a dry, dead twig for you. One wrong move and it snaps and we both come crashing down. Do you hear me?"

"Ain't my fault you lied," she snapped.

Noah leaned even closer, his stare so intense it made her pause. She was drowning again. His eyes. Pools of chocolate. She'd seen melted chocolate once and—

"You don't *move* without telling me why you're moving. You don't leave the parsonage without my say-so. You don't scamper around town in the dark of night when most crimes are committed, and you don't break into my church *ever again*."

"Preacher Pritchard?" Ava leaned toward him, and for a moment her insides curled at the fact that just another inch or two, and in a different setting with a different mindset, the preacher could level a kiss on her like the kind some said you could see in the motion pictures.

"W-what?" He backed away a bit. Maybe he'd just had the same thought.

"I told you this ain't your church." Ava raised an eyebrow. "It's God's. And if it's God's, and if what you say about Him sayin' everyone is welcome is true, well, I guess I'm not breaking in if I pay Him a visit here, am I?"

Noah's jaw muscle twitched. He sniffed. He closed his eyes and drew in a leveling breath. Opening his eyes, Noah burrowed his authoritative glare into her. "Ava . . ."

She didn't answer. Couldn't answer. That fire was brewing again, and she could tell she'd pushed her limits with the good-lookin' preacher.

"I'm goin' home. I'm goin' home," Ava mumbled as she scampered to her feet. She was making a move to hurry off when Noah rose quickly and gripped her arm.

"No. You're hiding in my office today. People are out and about. They'll see you. Stay inside."

"You gonna lie if someone comes in to see you and I'm hidin' under your desk?" Ava didn't miss the way he snatched his hand back when her loose hair swept over his fingers.

He held up a palm as he sidled past her and into his office. "Just get in here and shut the door."

15

Wren

"This isn't a wise step, Arwen." Her father stared at her from across his desk. A sculpture of Gandalf perched on the end, his wizard's staff stretched out over piles of paperwork as if he could command it all into neat piles of completion.

"What am I supposed to do, Dad?" Wren fidgeted with a thread hanging from the hemline of her Milwaukee Brewers T-shirt. "She's convinced."

"Convinced that Ava Coons took her daughter? *Dead* Ava Coons." A raised thick black eyebrow contradicted Wren's coppery hair.

"That *someone* took Jasmine." She always felt small in front of her father. Ignorant. Or maybe *unschooled* was a more appropriate term. He was the professor, after all. He lived and breathed education, and his purpose for being at Deer Lake Bible Camp wasn't to lead a ministry so much as to educate future generations of the "Scriptural prowess necessary to enable them for theological pursuits." Truth be told, Wren sometimes wondered how Professor Tristan Blythe ever decided to work at a Bible camp. His passions seemed so juxtaposed to—

"Arwen." He snapped her attention back on him. "When campfire stories become someone's reality, we've crossed a line."

"WWGD," Wren muttered.

"What was that?" Her dad frowned.

"What would Gandalf do?" Wren responded sheepishly.

"Since you asked." Tristan Blythe stood, easing his six-foot-two frame from his desk chair. He reached for a thick volume from a shelf behind him and surfed through several pages until he reached whatever page he was looking for. He turned it toward her and pushed it across the desk.

Wren noted a familiar quote from Tolkien highlighted on the page, her father's scribblings marring the margins. She didn't respond. Didn't have to. She knew what it said, and she knew her father would enlighten her for the millionth time.

"Tolkien felt that reality was the fabric from which we are cut. It is who we are, and what surrounds us. Fairy tales are meant only to center us in the actual world using fictional environments. They're not an escape from reality, they're a *return to* reality."

Wren waited. As expected, he continued.

"If Meghan Riviera insists the fairy tale of Ava Coons is real, then deep inside her something is seeking to validate her reality with a story."

Something in her father's eyes made Wren question whether he was speaking *just* about Meghan. "Your point?" Wren had learned to be blunt with her father.

"She's avoiding the truth by facing it in a tale. That of Ava Coons."

"So you *don't* think there's even a possibility that Jasmine was taken?"

A glower flashed across Tristan Blythe's face. "That's not what I'm saying. I'm saying her daughter is missing. Meghan's insistence that someone took Jasmine may very likely be an avoidance of the basic truth: Her daughter has wandered off and gotten lost."

"But she'll be found," Wren concluded.

"Will she?" Her father sat back in his chair and tapped the open volume of Tolkien quotes and philosophies, along with the author's biography. "The other notable difference between reality and fantasy is that fantasy creates hope, whereas reality . . . well, one might say we're dealing with odds."

"What about faith?" Wren challenged.

"Of course. Faith. The results of faith are the parts of the story, fantasy or reality, we cannot predict. God becomes part of an equation of statistics and imagination. It changes everything. Except the root fact that fantasy is still fantasy. We must always face reality, no matter how painful."

"So you're saying, in your roundabout way, that helping Meghan Riviera pursue her theory that Ava Coons"—Wren caught sight of her father's raised eyebrow—"that *someone* abducted her daughter and made her vanish is akin to encouraging delusion?"

Her father folded his hands in front of him, resting them on the desk and leveling a resigned look on his daughter. "Precisely. And we all know the longer the clock ticks, the more likely the little girl will not be found. We don't want to foster false hopes out of mercy for the individual. It's a much shorter height to fall from when one faces reality."

"Well, I'm going to factor faith back into this equation," Wren mumbled, hating that her father's calculated philosophy was tremendously discouraging.

He tapped an index finger on his desk. "And that, Arwen, is exactly what Samwise Gamgee would do."

She wasn't sure she liked being compared to a hobbit.

"She's doing good tonight." Eddie appeared in the doorway to the living room. Wren looked up from her phone. Her eyes had fixated on its screen for far too long, scrolling through reel after reel of people dancing senselessly, playing practical jokes, and her personal favorites, cats and kittens doing funny things. They were thirty-second moments of escape. For all her dad's lecturing about the importance of re-centering on reality, Wren felt even more anxious to escape it tonight.

Jasmine was still missing.

Ben had responded to her text that said she'd meet Meghan at the Rec Barn in the morning. His response had been curt. Wren stuffed down her guilt that she was doing the wrong thing. She couldn't squelch her feeling that Meghan wasn't chasing a ghost. That maybe—maybe there was something connected here, between Wren's own dream, the woman Jasmine had seen, and even . . . even Ava Coons—as ridiculous as that sounded.

Eddie flopped onto the couch next to her, causing Wren to bounce on her cushion. He lifted the remote for the TV and flicked it on to begin an absentminded scrolling through the Netflix options.

"True crime?" He gave Wren a side-eye.

"No." The last thing she needed was more reality to invade her attempt to escape tonight.

"Ghost hunting?" Eddie was teasing her now, but she wasn't in the mood for it.

Wren gave him a small scowl. "I should go hang out with your mom."

"Not a bad idea." Eddie settled deeper into the couch, which brought his body closer to hers.

Wren could feel the warmth from his leg, his side, his arm, all of which touched her platonically. She edged away. It still affected her for some reason. She could smell the fresh scent of shampoo on his freshly showered damp hair. His deodorant was piney and strong.

Eddie flicked the channel to one of the political debate stations, but twisted to look at her. "What?"

She didn't realize she'd been studying him. "Nothing."

His brown eyes softened. "Sure. Nothing." He didn't believe her.

"Doesn't it ever get to be too much for you?"

Eddie hit the mute button and drew in a deep breath. "You mean about Mom?"

The reference to Patty, slowly dying in the other room, snagged Wren's breath. She nodded.

His honest answer was still painful, though Wren knew he didn't mean it to be without feeling. "Death is a reality of life. Dwelling on it doesn't change anything. It's a walk of faith."

"Ouch." Wren gave him a floppy snarl more laden with tears than derision. She blinked rapidly to stop the tears.

Eddie worked his jaw back and forth for a second. "Will it hurt when Mom passes? Yeah." His throat bobbed as he swallowed. "Yeah, it'll hurt, Wren." He lifted his hand as if he was going to touch her, but he didn't. Instead, Eddie dropped his hand back to the remote that balanced on his leg. "But I don't want to live in that hurt. I want to live knowing that Mom lives too. With the Lord."

"Heaven," Wren managed to say around the lump in her throat.

"Yeah."

They looked into each other's eyes for a long moment. The air between them was thick, emotion drawing links between them that would be difficult, if not impossible, to sever. For a moment, Wren couldn't breathe. Some kind of force—friendship, understanding?—moved them closer to each other. She could smell mint on Eddie's breath, could see the blond highlights in his whiskers.

Eddie pulled away and shook his head, picking up the remote and pressing the volume button so the TV sound blazed into life. He waggled his eyebrows to deflect whatever had just happened. "Time to listen to politicians argue."

Wren had to wait a few minutes to gather herself. Eddie seemed unaffected, but she was shaking. She looked down at her hands resting in her lap and linked her fingers together to steady them.

Patty.

Launching from the couch, Wren muttered, "I'm going to go see your mom."

Eddie didn't try to stop her.

~~~~~~~

The bedroom was warm. Patty lay propped at a slight angle in the hospital bed that had been brought in. The room was lit with dim lighting, the curtains drawn against the night that lurked outside.

Patty opened her eyes. They had tired, dark circles underneath. Her peppery gray hair was short like a pixie cut, but that was because it was all that had grown since her last and final chemo treatment. The blankets were pulled up to her waist, which was small now, unlike the plumper, curvier version of Patty that Wren remembered from when she was a child.

"Wren . . ." A smile fluttered across Patty's face. She patted the bed. "Come. Sit."

Wren returned the soft smile and took her place at Patty's side. The bed sank under her weight. Wren adjusted by slipping her knee onto it and propping her other foot on a stool by the bed.

"You look like death warmed over," Patty observed. Her voice was shaky. Weak from battling the disease that ravaged her body. She hadn't lost her sense of humor.

Wren smirked. "Very funny."

"Eddie said they've not found the little girl yet." It was an observation, but Patty waited for Wren's response.

"No. They found her sweatshirt."

"Yes." Patty winced. "There was blood on it?"

Wren nodded. "They said it wasn't a lot. So maybe it was just a cut or something. I hope."

There was silence for a bit. Wren picked at her fingernails but felt Patty's assessing gaze. Finally, the woman spoke again.

"What's bothering you?"

Wren smiled then, lifting her eyes. Patty could read her like no one else could. There was no hiding from her. "Just that old feeling again."

"You had another nightmare?"

Wren nodded. The effects of this nightmare had lasted longer than past ones.

Patty reached out and gripped her hand, squeezing it weakly. "You need to explore it, Wren. I've always said that even though they don't necessarily mean anything, they reflect your spirit. Your soul."

"But why?" Wren forgot about Patty's condition, and that the woman was in the process of dying. She returned Patty's hand squeeze. "I've no excuse to feel so . . . lost. Life has been—you know, *life*. I mean, outside of Mom passing away years ago, I've lived a decent life. Dad and Pippin are—well, Dad and Pippin. But I've not experienced abuse or trauma or . . . other life-altering events that should incite dramatic dreams, and this feeling of something being lost, taken, or haunting me . . . I don't know," she finished lamely.

"Have you ever asked your father?"

"Dad? No. Why?"

Patty offered a small shrug. "Maybe he could help explain or understand. Surely he knows about your nightmares."

Wren nodded. "Maybe I am like Gollum," she mumbled.

Patty's laugh was weak but musical. "Gollum? 'Precious, my precious'?" She grew serious. "If I were to ask you what you feel you've lost, what would you say?"

"My mom," Wren said without hesitation.

Patty nodded. While they both knew this was true, they also knew it wasn't the answer. Wren had reconciled with her mother's death—at least she thought she had—and this seemed associated with something different. Darker even.

Wren drew in an unsatisfied breath. "If I knew what I'd lost, then I'd know what to look for. I think that's why I have these dreams. And I cannot get Jasmine off my mind! Did she really just get lost? A little girl, wandering in the wilderness? *Thousands* of acres! Or what if she was taken, or led away, or—or misplaced?" It didn't make sense, but Wren suggested it anyway.

"Is that how you feel?"

Wren gave Patty a sharp look. "I can't compare my emotional cavity to a child's physical reality."

Patty smiled. "Now you sound like your father."

Wren opted for a change in subject. "Meghan, Jasmine's mother, is convinced Jasmine saw Ava Coons in the woods the day Jasmine disappeared."

"Ava Coons," Patty nodded, remembering. "They say she's seen now and then."

It was Wren's turn to smile. "It makes the campfire story better."

"True, but . . ." Patty shifted in the bed. The sweater she wore slipped off one of her bony shoulders. Wren reached out to help adjust it. "I thought I saw her once actually."

This snagged Wren's attention. Patty was by far not a believer in lore, superstition, or ghosts. Patty met Wren's stare. She blinked. Wren noted her eyelashes had filled out since the chemo ended.

"I was in town. You know the market at the far edge of town, near the park?"

"Spider Link Park? The one that butts up against state land?"

"Mm-hmm. They had a summer farmers' market set up. I was getting produce when I caught sight of a woman on the edge of the forest right where they stop mowing the grass. She was standing there in overalls, messy long hair, just like they always described Ava Coons. I swear it was like looking back into a time capsule, what with how she was dressed. I was with a friend, and I mentioned for her to look, but when we turned back, the woman was gone. Vanished. As though she'd never been there."

"Probably just a tourist? Shopping the market?" Wren supplied, but not failing to tense at the similarities between Patty's story and Meghan's.

"Maybe." Patty rubbed her eyes, stifling a yawn. "You know, after Eddie's dad and his buddies found Lost Lake back in the eighties, a few men from camp went diving in it to see if they could find the Coons family's bodies."

"Did they find them?" Wren knew the answer but asked anyway.

"No." Patty shook her head. "It's been decades since Ava Coons supposedly murdered her family." She closed her eyes, leaning her head back against the pillow. Wren could hear weariness and pain in her voice. "I will say, life is definitely odd sometimes."

Wren studied Patty for a long moment. The woman faded, falling asleep under the influence of her pain medication. Wren hated that death wasn't a possible *if*, but instead was a *when*. Her mother, Ava Coons, Patty, maybe even little Jasmine . . . Wren squirmed, uneasy, trying to avoid the nagging feeling that she was next. That somehow it was more than Ava Coons that haunted the woods around Lost Lake, but death itself. And everyone knew you couldn't escape death, no matter how hard you tried.

16

"Not. Funny." Wren stared at the creepy doll, who was perched on the kitchen bar, its back leaning against a napkin holder, one eye still rolled back into her head, and her real human hair sticking out all straw-like.

Eddie shot a glance over his bowl of ice cream while his dad, Gary, chuckled from the kitchen sink. "Told you she wouldn't like it."

Wren had just left Patty and made her way to the kitchen thinking of popcorn or chips or something else that was salty.

"Redneck Harriet was lonely." Eddie's banter was meant to be funny, but Wren kept staring at the doll. Any direction she moved, the doll's eye followed—or so it seemed—and Wren's name stood out starkly on the bottom of the doll's foot.

"Redneck Harriet?" Wren raised her brows.

"Eddie's nickname for the possessed creature." Gary dried a coffee mug with a red dish towel.

"She's not possessed," Eddie insisted, balancing a spoonful of Neapolitan ice cream. "She's—"

"Evil. Wicked. Demonic," Wren inserted. "I can go on." She reached for Redneck Harriet and lifted the doll, its body stuffed, porcelain legs and arms wagging. Marching to the kitchen garbage can, she stepped on the latch and the lid popped open.

"Whoa! Whoa! *Whoa!*" Eddie's chair scraped on the floor as he catapulted from it. "Don't throw her away!"

Wren dangled the doll over the garbage can, feeling as if she might take all her angst out on the worthless antique. "Convince me to save her life." She cocked an eyebrow at her friend. Eddie grabbed for Harriet, his fingers grazing her hand. Wren jerked it away. The doll's eye made a sound and rolled back down from where it had been hiding in her skull.

"She's vintage." Eddie reached for the doll again. They did a little dance around the garbage can. Eddie snatched at the doll and instead caught Wren's shirt. He tugged her toward him, and she stumbled into him. His arms came around her in a wrestling-type hold, his breath warm on her neck.

"Give me the doll," he teased.

Wren heard Gary's chuckle, but she ignored him. She twisted in Eddie's hold. "Nevah!" Her exaggerated retort was playful, and she dropped toward the floor, effectively breaking Eddie's hold on her. For a moment she felt bereft. Disappointed. Brushing it away, she lofted Redneck Harriet over the garbage once again.

"I don't like her. Flaunting her in my face will not win friends and influence me." Wren let go, and Harriet began her descent into the innards of the can. Eddie lurched forward and caught her, pulling her up.

"Don't do it. Don't end Redneck Harriet." He had a weird attachment to the doll.

"Whatever." This time Wren felt all playfulness drain away. The doll stared at her wide-eyed, questioning, the cracked face hiding stories it had no intention of telling. "Didn't you ever watch *The Waltons*?"

"Ohhhhh, good one!" Gary shook a spatula at her.

"No, it didn't take priority over *Power Rangers*." Eddie smirked.

"There was an episode where Elizabeth was supposedly being haunted by a poltergeist. She'd watch the rocking chair in her room move, the radio would turn to static when she'd walk by. It ended with Elizabeth's doll moving toward her. Like some sick creature. Elizabeth was screaming, and her parents came running, and it scared the crap out of me when I was a kid. I hate dolls."

"*The Waltons* had some weird episodes. I remember that one." Gary jammed the spatula into the utensil holder by the stove.

Eddie returned to his ice cream bowl, but he took Redneck Harriet with him. Now that he'd dubbed the doll with a moniker, Wren was even more disturbed by it. Eddie took a spoonful of ice cream and seemed to contemplate it for a moment, seriousness replacing the teasing in his expression. "She's got your name on her foot, Wren."

Gary stilled. Wren followed suit.

Eddie's spoon clanked against his bowl. Redneck Harriet lay on the counter next to it. "You should see if the Coons family had anyone in their house named that." He leveled a knowing gaze on Wren. "You will not relax until you know why your name is on her foot. I know you."

"Troy said it's not a big deal." Her response was weak.

A flicker flashed across Eddie's face. For a moment he looked irritated, but then it was gone. "Yeah. Well . . ." He stood, gathering his bowl and spoon to put them in the sink. "Troy hasn't woken you up out of a nightmare before." He set the dirty dish into the sink and hiked from the kitchen, leaving the doll faceup where she was on the kitchen bar.

"What got into him?" Wren scowled. This week the world had become even more crooked on its axis than it already was.

Gary pressed his lips together and widened his eyes, his expression one that implied she was missing something obvious.

Whatever. She needed sleep. She needed—Wren glanced at Redneck Harriet. Now both eyes had rolled back into its skull, leaving cracked white eyeballs staring into the abyss of the kitchen. Wren scurried away to the spare room. Once there, she shut the door harder than she'd intended. Dolls. Irritable Eddie. Ava Coons.

She tugged off her shirt and reached for her pajama top that was lying over a chair by the window. She pulled it over her head and then pushed back the curtain. It was supposed to be a full moon tonight. The woods behind the Markham home were the same woods Jasmine wandered. Or at least the search party wandered. How much longer would they keep it up? A week? Two? When did a rescue become a retrieval instead? A little girl could only survive so long against the elements, even if it was summer.

The trees cast arm-like shadows across the lawn, the gravel driveway splitting it into two sections. Gary's toolshed was a silhouette against the woods. Wren scanned the darkness, marveling at how light it seemed. A blue light cast from the moon that seemed to smile from its place in the sky. Somehow it didn't feel like a friendly smile. It was mocking. As though it watched them all suffering—each one of them individually writhing in their own internal and external pains of just being alive. The missing, the dying, the lost . . .

Her breath stopped. A wash of alarm coursed through Wren with such fervor that her body could only stiffen in response, her hand still holding back the curtain.

In the center of the driveway, near the end where it met the road, was the blue-black outline of a woman in what appeared to be overalls. She stood with her arms hanging at her sides. Her long hair was pulled back, but wisps still blew in the breeze, lifting toward the sky. Her face was dark, and where her eyes should be were even darker hollows. The moonlight acted as a disguise by covering her face in shadow.

"Ava Coons." Wren's whispered declaration startled herself. She dropped the curtain. Hesitating only a second, she charged from the room and rushed through the house to the back door. The Markhams never locked their doors. Why would they when the crime rate in these parts was nonexistent? Wren wrenched the door open and ran out into the yard.

She was gone. The woman who had stood at the end of the drive had vanished. Wren ran her hand over her eyes, sure she'd been seeing things. This week was getting to her. Toying with her nerves. Unsettling her and tipping her courage out of her already half-empty emotional glass and refilling it with lunacy. Sheer lunacy.

Wren had had enough. She spun on her heel to head back into the house, then stilled. There, on the doorstep, was her name. *Arwen*. Written in chalk. Even worse was the name below it. *Ava.* A lone object lay beside it. Wren bent and lifted it. The missing shoe to the doll inside the house. Holding the little shoe up to the light, Wren bit back a whimper of fear. It was old, cracked, and . . . stained with blood.

17

Ava

"Who's Emmaline?" Ava asked from her perch on the floor in Noah's church office. She leaned against the wall, chewing on the end of a pencil and staring at the door, wishing she had enough personal gumption to just get up and walk out. But walk to where was the burning question, and avoiding Tempter's Creek in its roiled-up condition was also critical.

Noah's head jerked up from his study of the Bible. The old Book was splayed in front of him on his desk. Its pages were crisp and new. It looked like he hardly read it, truth be told.

"Where'd you hear that name?" It was apparent he wasn't pleased with her question, but Ava met his stare with an innocent one of her own.

"Saw her letter on your desk." She chewed the pencil a little harder underneath his critical eye.

"And you opened it and read it?"

Ava shrugged. "Figured it was there and somethin' to do. You're the one who left it out in the open."

"Under the assumption that general etiquette protocol would be applied in the situation and . . ." Noah's words fell flat and he bent his head, then flexed his neck.

"Not going to tell me who she is, then?"

Noah ran his hand under his nose, sniffing, agitated. He dropped his palm on his Bible. "No. I'm not."

Ava nodded, bit down harder, and felt the pencil snap between her teeth. "You don't know what to do with me, do you?" Might as well call it out and be done with it. People danced around the truth too much, and if the truth was there to be had, a person best claim it. There was enough question in life as it was.

Noah grimaced at her honesty but shook his head, leaning back in his chair. "I don't. I don't know what to do about any of this."

"You get yourself into scrapes a lot, don'tcha, Preacher?" It was a simple observation she'd already found out by reading his body language. The man was as jumpy as a frog on a hot iron griddle.

"Why do you ask that?" he retorted, his dark eyes flashing.

Ava rolled the two pencil halves in her fingers. "Well, 'cause you're in one and don't seem to know how to get out. A person who doesn't get into scrapes learned a long time ago how to get outta them—or avoid them."

Noah studied her for a long moment. Ava squirmed. Finally he spoke. "You're a deep thinker, aren't you?"

"Me?" Her voice squeaked. She straightened against the wall from her spot on the floor, ignoring the chair that sat in front of Noah's desk, empty and ready if she wanted it.

"Yes," he answered.

Ava shook her head vehemently. "Don't think so. I just observe. You know? A kid learns to do that when her parents are dead and she's gotta look out for herself."

"Mmm." Noah nodded thoughtfully. He seemed to relax a bit. Maybe it was the distraction of focusing on her life instead of his. "And you don't recall your family? At all?"

Now it was her turn to squirm. "Little pieces of them, I remember," she answered, then blanched. Little pieces. Perhaps the wrong description considering what had supposedly happened to them.

"Why did you come to the church last night?"

That was the question, wasn't it? Ava knew Noah Pritchard had been waiting to ask it since he'd found her there that morning. She debated on lying and giving some silly answer, but then one didn't lie to a preacher, and certainly one didn't lie in the Lord's house. At least Ava Coons didn't.

"Thought I'd see if'n I could find records here. 'Bout my parents. Who they were. Who might've known 'em."

"Marriage records?" He raised his eyebrows.

Ava nodded. "Or baptism ones. For my brothers—for me. Can't recall much, see, and I figure I better start before I get caught for somethin' I didn't do."

Noah seemed to agree with her as he nodded slowly. "Yes." He drew in a deep sigh. "They've yet to find Jipsy. Matthew Hubbard's funeral is Saturday."

"You're doin' the funeral?"

"I am. It's my first one," he admitted.

Ava drew back in surprise. "Your first one? But I thought you were a preacher?"

Noah offered a small smile. "Even pastors have to have their firsts."

Ava accepted his response, and a companionable silence descended for a blessed moment before Noah saw fit to break it.

"How did you know Matthew Hubbard?" It was Noah's narrowed gaze that made Ava squirm again. She made a pretense of trying to fit the broken pencil back together again.

"Didn't. Didn't know him much at all." She knew Noah wouldn't be satisfied with that.

He folded his hands together as if in prayer, resting his forearms on top of the open Bible. "There has to be a connection. Why would the town think you killed him otherwise?"

"'Cause there was an ax in him?" Ava knew she should probably get all swoony like some of the ladies in town at the idea, but when one grew up hearing folks talk about how your own family was axed to death, one became numb to it.

"Folks assume that's what happened to your family, don't they?" Noah raised an eyebrow.

Ava nodded. The pencil wasn't fitting back together. She flipped it onto the floor. "Sure."

"But you've no recollection of it? They never found your family's bodies?"

Ava met his eyes then. She was sure hers looked as haunted as his usually did. There was something in Noah's voice—that gentle soft bit of something that made her melt inside. Not in a nice way either. The kind of way that made her feel little again. Scared. Needing to be protected—no, *defended*. She wondered if Noah had been around when she was thirteen and emerging from the woods covered in blood, if life might've turned out different. Maybe he would've taken her in. Avoided Widower Frisk and all his chores and hollerin', and avoided Jipsy with her shrewish face and bossy attitude.

"Ava?" Noah pressed.

She blinked, breaking their connection. "No. They didn't. Figure animals or somethin' got to them."

"There would still have been some remains." Noah fidgeted with the corner pages of his Bible. "Some evidence of their deaths."

"Oh, there was evidence!" Ava sat up straighter. "Folks went out lookin' and found our cabin by the lake. The cabin was burned up. They found blood all over outside it."

Noah slouched back in his chair, crossing his arms over his chest. "Did they search the lake?"

Ava shrugged. "Don't know."

"So then how do they know your family was killed by an ax?"

She lifted her eyes. "Guess they don't. I was just dragging one behind me and it had blood on it. Stands to reason, I s'pose."

He stood and paced back and forth behind his desk before pausing and staring down at her. "Those are all drummed-up conclusions based on nothing but circumstantial pieces to the puzzle. There's no way you, as a child, could have wielded an ax like Lizzie Borden."

The name stilled Ava. The chanting from the night before made its way through her recollection. That hissing, whispery voice that taunted her, knowing she was there in the office, but instead of seeking her out to do her harm, it toyed with her like Jipsy's cat toyed with a mouse.

"'Ava Coons took an ax and gave her mother forty whacks.'"

"What!" Noah's voice was sharp.

Ava stared up at him. "Heard that before?" She didn't like the quaver in her voice.

Noah nodded. "Yes. But about Lizzie Borden, not you."

"Who *is* Lizzie Borden?" Ava ventured, unsure she wanted to know after last night.

Whack. Whack.

Noah squatted in front of Ava, balancing on his toes. He searched her face for a long moment before answering. "Back about forty years or so, she murdered her parents. With an ax. She killed them while they slept. But they did not convict her of the crime."

"Like me?" Ava whispered.

A shadow flitted across his face. He gave an abrupt nod. "Like you. She lived out her life—a fairly good one, as far as she seemed to portray. But the little song was made up during her trial and it stuck."

"What if she didn't kill her parents?" Ava mumbled. "What if'n she was like me and just . . . couldn't remember nothin' at all?"

Noah reached out a hand in a gesture meant to encourage Ava to stand with him. She ignored his hand and stood on her own, and he quickly followed suit. "There was supposedly a lot of signs that made most people think she *did* kill her parents. There was much more evidence in that case than there is here against you. What motive would you have had as a young woman? What motive would you have now to kill Matthew Hubbard? Jipsy?"

"I can't abide Jipsy," Ava supplied matter-of-factly.

Noah frowned. "Enough to kill her? Make her body vanish like your family's did?"

Ava looked away. He kept coming back to the crux of the matter, and that was the worst part of it for her. She simply didn't know. She couldn't remember half of what she did. All she knew was that last night someone came to find her, and instead of taking her and turning her in, they left her with the echoing voice of the Borden rhyme, but with her own name inserted, and an unspoken threat that *they* knew. They knew the truth of it. And they intended on enacting their own sort of justice, but only after they finished making Ava suffer the mental torture of wallowing in the vague memory of her family's blood.

"Here it is." Noah hefted the massive tome of church records onto his desk. Dust poofed into the air. There was the distinct smell of musty paper.

Ava sidled up next to him, peering around his shoulder at the records in the hardbound ledger.

Noah held his index finger under the names of Ava's parents. "Chester and Bertha Sparks Coons, married April fifteenth, 1905."

"That can't be right." Ava bent closer to study the handwriting that had inked her parents' marriage date into the church records.

"Why not?" Noah gave her a sideways glance.

"'Cause of my older brother—I recall them sayin' he was fifteen when he got killed. If that was the case, then he was born in 1905. Ain't enough time for my parents to get hitched and have a baby before it turned 1906, if'n they got married in April."

Noah cleared his throat. Ava noticed his body tensed a bit. "Well, perhaps—perhaps he was born early."

"Doubtful." Ava tapped her parents' names. "Ma always said he was a big tub of a boy even when he was born. That's not right if'n he was early." How she recalled something like that and not something as monumental as her family's deaths, Ava couldn't explain.

Noah's face reddened.

She wondered why for a moment, and then it dawned on her. "Ohhhhhh! You think my ma might've already been with child when they up and married?"

Noah choked. Coughed. Cleared his throat. "It's a possibility."

"Well, I'll be." Nothing much shocked Ava, the least of which that her ma had gotten herself into a bit of a pickle. "Nice church to put my parents in this here record seein' as they were sinners," she observed.

Noah turned the pages toward the middle of the book where baptisms were recorded. He didn't look at her when he replied, "My guess is, the reverend wasn't aware of your mother's . . . condition." He ran his finger down the length of the page, turned it, repeated the process, and continued for the next few pages. "Ah. Here." He tapped on Ava's brother's name. "Arnold Chester Coons. Baptized . . ." His voice waned.

"Baptized Sunday, October eighth, 1905," Ava finished.

"There you have it, I suppose," Noah muttered.

"Ma was well on when they got married in April." Ava looked at Noah. "Think her dress was a tad tight?"

Noah choked again, and this time his cough increased. Ava slapped him on the back a few times before he sidestepped her hand and ran his arm over his mouth. "I'm guessing—" he coughed again—"we'll not know that detail."

"Well, it ain't a small one when you're a gal getting married." Ava rolled her eyes at the preacher. The man was a tad dumb, if she was honest. "No girl wants to be as big as a sow when she puts on her wedding dress."

"No. I would guess not." Noah accepted her argument and made pretense to investigate the records further. A few pages more and he found her second brother's name. "Richard James Coons, baptized May twelfth, 1907."

"Then there'd be a few years between Ricky and myself. So check on 1912. That's when I was born."

Noah did so. Every month. Ava's name did not appear. She felt the weight of his stare. "You're not in here."

"I was born, though, we know that." She attempted to shrug off the niggling hurt that apparently she hadn't been baptized as an infant. Maybe her parents weren't much for coming to town by then? Made their place off in the woods and didn't want to socialize? Maybe they'd lost faith, or tradition, or— "Well, guess I'm for sure goin' to hell then," Ava concluded.

Noah drew back, his expression startled and confused. "Why on earth would you make that conclusion?"

Ava tilted her head to the side and looked down her nose at him. "Think on it. Even if I didn't do a thing to my family, I wasn't baptized. My parents didn't see no good reason to save me and get me all washed up in the water, so Jesus sure ain't gonna stop when He sees me comin'."

Noah turned, that softness entering his voice again. She didn't dare look at him. "Ava."

Nope. Not lookin' at him.

"Ava."

She looked at him.

"Ava, you're not going to eternal damnation because you weren't baptized as an infant."

"I'm not?" She half challenged him and half hoped he was telling the truth.

Noah seemed to stumble for words. He wasn't an eloquent preacher-type, that much was sure. "No. Baptism is just part—I mean, well, there's an awful lot of doctrine out there about baptism and the role it plays in the condition of the soul before—"

"You're bumping gums, Preacher. I've no idea what you're tryin' to say."

"I'm saying there's more to it than baptism," Noah finished in a flurry. He seemed frustrated. Disgusted with himself.

"Oh" was all she had to offer him.

A door in the church slammed, echoing from the sanctuary down the hall. Noah's head jerked up and toward the door. "Get under my desk," he commanded.

Ava had no intention of arguing. Church might have a sanctuary, but she didn't think if the law entered she'd be any safer here than in the road outside.

Footsteps thumped.

"Reverend?" a man's voice hollered.

Ava heard Noah make his way across his office floor. He met some-one at the door, where his attempt to leave the office was thwarted.

"Ah, Mr. Sanderson."

Ava hoped Mr. Sanderson hadn't brought his wife.

"Reverend Pritchard. Pleasant morning outside, yes?"

"Most assuredly," Noah responded politely.

"I was wondering if I might have a moment of your time?"

"Of course." Noah cleared his throat. "Would you . . . like to have a seat in the sanctuary?"

"We may as well make use of your office here, Reverend. No need to bother the peace of the good Lord with our chatter in the pews on a Tuesday."

"No. Of course not."

Footsteps.

Ava squeezed back farther into the darker recesses of the desk's alcove. She saw Noah's legs as he took a seat in his chair. His foot bumped her knee. She stifled a yelp. He shifted it a bit.

"I see you're looking at old church records." Mr. Sanderson was as nosy as they came, Ava determined.

She heard the book thud shut. Noah must have closed it from Mr. Sanderson's prying eyes. "How may I help you today?" he asked instead.

Mr. Sanderson shifted in his chair. Ava heard it squeak beneath his weight. She could picture the lean but broad-shouldered man sitting there in his suit, looking dapper and for all sakes and pur-poses as though he owned Tempter's Creek and its inhabitants. He practically did. Without his company, most would be out of work and Tempter's Creek would dwindle into a ghost town.

"I wanted to ask if you've seen Ava Coons by any chance?" The man didn't mince words.

Noah's response was carefully measured. "Would I not say some-thing if I had?"

"I would like to believe so."

Noah cleared his throat. "If I may be honest?"

"Please," Sanderson welcomed.

"I find it a far leap of the town to accuse Miss Coons of anything that may have happened to Jipsy. As well as Matthew Hubbard," he added.

"Hmmm, yes." Mr. Sanderson didn't seem upset by Noah's observation. "Perhaps it is. But you know how rumors spread and people get riled up into nonsense."

"Seems to me you have enough influence to put such rumors to bed." A sternness laced Noah's words.

Ava nodded to herself in the darkness of the desk's cubby.

"Perhaps, but then I would need to be convinced myself of her innocence to make such a strong assertion, and frankly, I am not."

"You believe she murdered two people?" Noah countered.

"I believe anyone is capable of anything."

"Do you have a vendetta against Miss Coons?" Noah wasn't backing down. Ava looked at his feet. One shoe-clad foot tapped the floor repeatedly in agitation.

"I'm affronted you would imply such a thing." There was offense in Mr. Sanderson's tone. "I'm merely looking at the evidence laid before me. Ava Coons is no stranger to the ax, Reverend."

"She was thirteen when her family was killed."

"Yes?" Sanderson's word was weighted with challenge.

Noah shifted in his chair. Ava heard him sniff in aggravation. "A thirteen-year-old young woman could successfully murder her entire family and not be overpowered by her father and two older brothers?"

"Reverend Pritchard, I was not there when Miss Coons's family died, so I do not have an inkling as to what did or did not occur. What I *do* know is that she is the only surviving member of the Coons family, and, incidentally, she was covered in their blood when she was discovered."

"Circumstantial," Noah muttered.

"Or damning," Sanderson retorted. "It depends on how one looks at it. Regardless, I'm not here to debate the guilt or innocence of Ava Coons. I'm merely here to see if you have, in fact, had contact with your charge? You *were* responsible for her, you know?"

"Yes, of course I know," Noah snapped.

"And yet you do not know where Miss Coons is now?"

"No."

Ava clapped her hand over her mouth. The preacher lied with such ease.

Mr. Sanderson's chuckle showed a reluctant acceptance of Noah's lie. "Well then, I suppose I've nothing else to ask then. I've been aiding the police in the search for Jipsy and her abductor or killer, assuming she *is* dead. So, I felt stopping here to chat with you made sense."

"You've not found Jipsy, then?" Noah ventured to ask.

"No. We have not. Widower Frisk is nigh on losing his mind. Who knew the old man actually could have feelings for that woman."

"And no one has inquired as to what part the widower may have played in Jipsy's disappearance?" Noah argued.

"The man is beside himself. Inconsolable. One hardly could accuse him of such a crime."

Noah didn't reply.

"And the service for Matthew Hubbard," Mr. Sanderson continued, "preparations are going well?"

Noah must have nodded. "I need to meet with the family later this afternoon."

"Yes. Therein lies another mystery. Did Ava Coons have motive to slay Matthew?" Sanderson sounded as though he were baiting Noah.

Again, Noah didn't answer.

"Yes, well . . ." Mr. Sanderson sniffed. "Everyone in town knew that Miss Coons had a thing for Matthew. If anything spoke to her potential innocence, I would assume it would be that."

Noah remained silent.

"Well, Reverend, I will let you return to your studies of the Word." Both men stood. Mr. Sanderson's chair scraped against the floor. Noah walked him to the door and muttered a proper goodbye.

Ava waited, huddling still under the desk, sure that Noah would seek her out when it was safe. She didn't have long to wait. A few moments later, Noah ducked under the desk, his eyes boring into hers as if she were indeed guilty and he was the judge.

"You had a 'thing' for Matthew Hubbard?"

This time, Ava felt a deep flush creep up her neck and into her face. Noah reached in and yanked on her arm, gentle but insistent.

"Come, Ava Coons. Do tell the truth."

18

It wasn't that she was *trying* to be secretive, but some secrets weren't hers to tell. She might be a backwoods girl, but Ava had a sense of decency, and that meant holding to her word. Supper was a morbid affair. Hanny maintained her promised absence like a suffragette on strike. Ava could see the light in Hanny's house next door. She could even smell the roast beef. Better than the cold chicken they were eating with a little salt sprinkled on it. Pulling it from the icebox, Noah must have been too hungry to wait to heat anything up. He all but threw it on the table and then told her to sit down and eat.

Now Noah stabbed at his food like a man about to murder a pest, if not another man, and he reminded Ava of one of those sticks of dynamite that had sparks licking the tip of its fuse. One of these days, this man was going to blow, and Tempter's Creek better give him fair enough distance or they'd be blown to smithereens too.

Between Noah's pouting and her stubborn silence, they finished off the chicken just as a knock sounded on the back door. Noah shoved his chair back to answer it, and as soon as the door opened, the place was filled with the smell of hot apple pie. Hanny hustled in as Noah quickly shut the door behind the old woman.

"Brought you both a pie." She set it on the table on top of a hot pad. Eyeing them both, the old woman rested her hands on her hips. "Go get some plates and I'll dish it up."

Noah did as he was told.

Ava stayed still in her chair.

Hanny looked between them when Noah made his way back to the table with three plates.

"You two are trouble like I've never seen before." Hanny served a slice of pie onto one of the plates. "A whole two days with this kerfuffle. I'm not sure you're going to make it. Neither one of you." Hanny raised her eyes to the heavens. Or the ceiling. Ava looked at her pie as Noah took it from Hanny and set it on the table in front of Ava with a clatter.

"Did you figure out what you're going to do?" Hanny eyed Noah. He shook his head and retrieved his own slice of pie. Hanny harrumphed. "I told you, truth will find you out."

"I know that," Noah grumbled. He took a bite of his pie, standing in place as if he couldn't decide whether to sit or run and take cover. "It's not that simple."

"Well, it was until you messed it up." Hanny waved the pie-serving utensil in the air.

"They want to—"

"I know, I know what the good people of this town want to accuse Ava of!" Hanny glowered at Noah. "It's what *you* did that I'm talking about. Feeding their frenzy with your deceit—"

"Enough." Noah marched from the dining room, taking his pie with him.

Hanny and Ava stared after him, silence the only remaining companion in the room. Finally, Hanny saw fit to take her place in Noah's chair. She folded her hands and rested them on the table. "You know that man has put his entire ministry on the line for you. You realize if they find out he's hiding you in the parsonage, he's more than likely to lose his place in the church?"

A pit formed in Ava's stomach. No. She'd not considered that.

"And furthermore," Hanny added, "if you *are* guilty—or even caught and convicted—he could be arrested for helping you."

Now she felt nauseated.

Hanny stared at her for a long moment, her milky blue eyes grave.

"Are you saying it'd be best if I left?" Ava whispered. She'd been contemplating it anyway. Leave the parsonage. Leave Tempter's Creek. Just leave.

Hanny didn't answer.

"I don't know where I'd go," Ava admitted. She didn't have a home, a place, a family . . . She only had, well, if any place was home, it was Lost Lake. But going back there would be running headlong back into a nightmare. A nightmare she'd left behind in hopes she'd never have to return.

Ava tiptoed down the hallway. She had slept little and now midnight was stretching into the longest hour of the night yet. Now she had Preacher Noah Pritchard's welfare on her conscience, thanks to Hanny. Ruin his ministry? Get the man arrested? It made Ava sick to her stomach just thinking about it. Her jaunt to the church hadn't really paid off anyway. Aside from learning that her parents had indeed been married, her brothers baptized, and she herself not even mentioned, the church records had done nothing for her.

The floor creaked under Ava's weight. She halted just outside Noah's bedroom door, her right foot raised, balancing her weight on her left. Moonlight stretched across the wood floorboards from the window at the far end of the hall. She held her breath.

There was movement behind Noah's door.

He was supposed to be asleep!

"Ava?" Noah's voice filtered through the door.

Darn it. She put her foot down. "Yeah?"

"Where are you going?" His voice was muffled. He hadn't opened his door.

The air thickened around her. Ava swallowed. She could picture the preacher standing in his room, hand on the doorknob, wrestling with whether it was even decent enough to open the door or not. Alone. In the parsonage. Unmarried. A single woman accused of murder.

Oh heck, yes! Hanny was right! Ava needed to leave! For *both* their sakes.

"I'm—" she choked—"I'm leavin'."

There was a slight thud on the door, as if Noah had leaned his forehead against it in resignation.

A few long seconds passed.

"Where are you going?" he asked through the door.

"Don' know," she admitted.

More seconds.

She started to count. *Eight, nine, ten, eleven, twelve, thirteen, fourteen—*

"It's not safe."

"Not safe here either." Ava stated it as truth. A different sort of dangerous.

The knob rattled, and the door opened. Noah stood half hidden behind the door. Ava looked down at her feet. He wasn't wearin' a shirt. Pants, sure, but a shirt? No.

Not safe. Noooooot safe.

"I shouldn't have lied," he said. "I'm not sure why I did."

Ava poked the toe of her shoe against a chip in one of the floorboards. "People do crazy things when nothin' makes sense."

"I guess." He gave a sigh.

There was a long enough moment of silence that Ava risked lifting her eyes. Noah's silhouette in the darkness was chiseled. His jaw straight. His face shadowed, but his expression worried. "I can't let you go, Ava. It's not safe."

"Let's be honest," she said and managed a wobbly smile, "I ain't ever been safe."

He flinched.

"So let me go," she finished.

Noah opened the bedroom door wider and made a pretense of

147

stepping out of his room. Instead, he hesitated, then closed the door back a bit as if it were some sort of shield.

"Where are you off to?" His voice was a mix between husky and a full-on growl.

Ava wrapped her arms around herself and tilted her chin up. "Gotta find Jipsy. If I find her, and if she's livin', then I'm not in trouble no more."

"What about Hubbard?" Noah pressed his lips together. "Finding Jipsy alive changes nothing as far as your state of security in this town."

Ava squirmed. "That'd be next on my list to do."

"Jipsy is probably dead, Ava," Noah stated bluntly. "I'm not sure what, but you're hiding something about you and Hubbard."

Ava nodded. "Isn't my story to tell."

Noah squeezed his eyes shut as if he were trying to block out the very sight of her for a moment. When he opened them, he stared at her with those flickering coals of brown-and-black eyes. "I'm as invested in this as you are now, you know?"

Ava nodded. "Hanny told me so tonight. Not sure this is what God called you to Tempter's Creek for, though. I suppose I should say I'm sorry." She tried to offer him something.

Noah widened the door again. He took a step out into the hallway. "Me too." His words washed over her like a warm surprise. She hadn't expected him to apologize. "I never should've put you in this position."

"You ain't much of a preacher, are you?" It was all she could think to say.

"Not when you're around." Noah lifted his hand. He was going to touch her. She knew it. Knew it like she knew it was going to rain when all the leaves on the trees flipped upside down as if to shield themselves from the brewing storm.

The back of his fingers hovered by her cheek. Even in the shadows, Ava could see his eyes darken. She dared not drop her eyes from his. Seeing a reverend without his shirt on had to be the missing "Thou shalt not" commandment.

"If'n you just take a step back so I can leave, then I can get outta your hair."

Noah dropped his hand without touching her. Awareness seemed to take over him and he stepped away. Ava took a step past him.

Noah's voice made her hesitate. "Problem is, I don't mind having you in my hair."

Ava made quick work of leaving. It was the only safe thing to do.

19

Wren

Wren hiked down the sidewalk in downtown Tempter's Creek. She was alone, planning to meet up with Meghan Riviera at the coffee shop that was run out of a remodeled parsonage across from the old Lutheran church. The police had taken their statements, once they'd arrived after Wren had stopped screaming and Eddie had called them. An overreaction? Probably. But considering the way her nerves were on fire from the sheer creep factor of it, she felt she had a reasonable excuse. The cops had no explanation, and there were no signs of anyone in the area that might have explained the woman in the driveway or the writing on the walk. They didn't agree that the brown stains on the doll shoe were blood, and with nothing more to go on, they'd departed with a "Call if you need anything else."

Wren skirted a fire hydrant and adjusted the strap of her yellow backpack she'd slung over her shoulder. It *was* blood on that shoe. Old, gross, vintage blood.

"This is wacked." *Whacked*. Probably a poor choice of words considering the tale of Ava Coons. "And what do *I* have to do with Ava Coons anyway?"

Enough talking to herself. Wren had garnered a side-eyed glance from an older man passing her on the sidewalk. She supposed she couldn't blame him. She was muttering rather vehemently.

The coffee shop was named The Parsonage, and after another block, Wren saw it up ahead on the right. It was small, probably a six-hundred-square-foot house with a front porch, white siding, and a sign that hung from chains. The Parsonage had the distinct aura of a vintage 1930s- or '40s-style Northwoods home, and the owners had allowed the paint on the weatherworn porch to chip and crack. They'd scattered a few round tables on the porch with old ladder-back chairs painted a teal color. Each of the tables had three hardback books stacked in the center, along with a tin-can vase that held yellow, purple, and blue wildflowers. Wren cast an appreciative glance at them as she opened the screen door and stepped into the front room.

Apparently, back in the day, The Parsonage had a sitting room, a small dining area, and the kitchen, with stairs leading to the second-level bedrooms just off to the left. These areas had since been opened up to make one room with fewer walls, filled now with tables and chairs like those on the porch, and a counter divided the front from the kitchen. The mechanics of the coffee making were kept behind the counter. The stairs were open for customers to head up to lounge-type reading areas. Each former bedroom had been converted so coffee drinkers who planned to stay awhile could sit in comfort on overstuffed chairs and old couches.

On a good day, Wren enjoyed escaping the crazy summer chaos of camp and coming here with a book. On a day like today, she ignored the pull of the place in exchange for looking around to spot Meghan. She was in the far corner—which wasn't all that far away—looking desperate, haggard, a ball of nervous energy. Wren quickly asked for a black coffee, and after receiving the brew of the day in a teal pottery mug, she wound her way around a few tables and sat opposite Meghan.

Startled, Meghan jerked her head, eyes wide and red-rimmed. "Oh! I'm sorry, I was . . . thinking."

"That's okay." Wren rested her mug on the table, noting that Meghan had only a cup of water in front of her.

Meghan glanced at her mug and then offered a flimsy smile. "I can't drink caffeine right now. I'm too jittery as it is." Her eyes filled with tears, but she quickly blinked them away, mustering a stronger smile this time. "I know I'm a mess, and I know you're probably humoring me by doing this."

Wren shook her head, determination flooding her. "Listen, no stone should be left unturned when it comes to finding a missing child."

Their eyes locked, Meghan searching the depths of Wren's and seeming to assess her honesty and genuineness.

"Thank you," Meghan breathed. She ran her index finger around the rim of her mug. "Ben thinks I'm—well, I can't blame him." She laughed nervously. "I know my entire theory has more holes in it than a sieve, but I also know what my baby told me. And I know the stories of Ava Coons. I can't explain how it relates to Jasmine, but I believe there *has* to be a connection of some sort."

Wren took a sip of her coffee. "And the police have followed up on it?"

Meghan nodded. "They have. Yes. To the degree they've searched for the woman Jasmine saw. But even though Tempter's Creek is a small town, there's still five thousand or more people—not counting the summer tourists."

"We have a couple hundred at camp alone," Wren acknowledged.

"Right. So my description could fit many people."

"Can you run it by me again?" Wren was not a detective by any means, but she was curious now to see if what Meghan had to say aligned at all with the shadowy form she'd spotted last night in the Markhams' driveway.

Meghan reached for her purse that was hanging from the back of her chair. She opened the quilted number with pink tassels and tugged out a spiral notebook. Paging through it, she set it on the table and turned it for Wren to see. It was a pencil sketch of a woman's face, not unlike an FBI artist's sketch, which carried down to her shoulders. The woman was older, probably in her sixties. Her hair was parted down the middle and pulled into braids. She had overall straps over her shoulders. Her face was relatively nondescript, and outside of the overalls, there wasn't anything particular to match to the vision Wren had seen the night before.

"I know it's not much, but it's based on what Jasmine told me. She said this woman came out of the woods at the park and talked to her for a few minutes. Somehow I missed it. I was on the phone with my mom, and I—" Meghan choked up and looked away quickly.

"But that wasn't when Jasmine disappeared, was it?"

"No."

"Yet you went back to the park the following day, and then Jasmine went missing?"

Meghan inhaled a shuddering breath. "Yes. I-I didn't sense any danger. Tempter's Creek is small, and I'm familiar with it. It's not unusual for a stranger to say something to a child. Not here."

Wren understood, though she realized many wouldn't. Small northern towns were a bit like stepping back into time. "Why do you think this woman is Ava Coons?"

Meghan reached for her sketch pad and pulled it back toward herself. She rolled her eyes, either in exasperation that no one believed her or because she felt it was as irrational as it truly sounded. "Because *Jasmine* said it was Ava Coons."

"Did Jasmine know the story of Ava Coons?" Wren found it hard to believe someone would have seen fit to terrify a six-year-old with the campfire tale of an ax-murdering woman.

Meghan blanched. "Yes. Last year, my older brother and his family joined us at our cabin here for a week during the summer. He thrives on those sorts of tales, so he was telling his own kids. Jasmine overheard it. She slept with Ben and I for three nights. She was so scared that Ava Coons was going to emerge from the woods and drag her into them, making her vanish. Or worse, kill her." Meghan's voice hitched. She stifled a sob, pressing her fingertips to her mouth as if it would hold back the gale of tears brewing below the surface. The look she leveled on Wren was desperation at its worst. "When she saw this woman, she was sure of it, but she said that *this* Ava Coons was *nice* and nothing like Uncle Stone's campfire story."

"Did Jasmine say what she and the woman talked about?" Wren couldn't fathom anyone being cruel enough to *pose* as Ava Coons for a child, but then crackpots weren't as rare as they used to be these days.

Meghan's lips worked back and forth, her chin dimpling from holding back tears. She shook her head. "Just—Jasmine's shoes. They talked about her shoes."

"Her shoes?"

Meghan nodded. "Jasmine had on her new purple tennis shoes. The woman kept telling Jasmine how pretty they were. How her favorite color was green, but purple was pretty too."

Shoes.

A conversation with Jasmine about shoes. Leaving a child's doll shoe on the Markhams' stoop the night before?

No. Wren dismissed it, even though part of her didn't want to. It was too circumstantial. Farfetched and definitely overreaching. She was getting ahead of herself. Ahead of Meghan. If Wren wasn't careful, *she'd* be to blame for taking Meghan into the dark imaginations of theories and make-believe stories. It wasn't a place the mother of a missing girl belonged. It wasn't a place where Wren belonged either.

They returned to the park from which Jasmine had disappeared. Meghan and Wren got out of Wren's truck, Meghan wrapping her cardigan around her like a shield, even though it was nearing eighty degrees. Wren grabbed a baseball cap from the back seat and jammed it on her head, tugging her hair through the hole in the back. Mosquitoes swarmed the park, especially since there was so much shade here. To avoid getting eaten alive, Wren grabbed a can of bug spray and doused herself while Meghan waited.

"Want some?" She offered it to Jasmine's mom.

Meghan shook her head. "I already have lemongrass and eucalyptus on."

Essential oils. Any other time, Wren would have quipped back to the woman a few years her senior that "good luck" was in order. She'd never known any essential-oil brew to work against the Wisconsin bloodsucking vampires. One hundred percent DEET was most effective, even if it poisoned the rest of you.

Ready, Wren shut the car door and hit the locks. The seesaw was squeaking as two children kicked the ground in an opposite rhythm. The swing set was very occupied. A boy was trying the ever-so-popular attempt to swing oneself over the crossbar while his mother shouted "Too high, too high!" at him.

"It was over here." Meghan interrupted Wren's observation, pointing to a set of picnic tables underneath an oak tree. "I was there, talking to my mom on the phone. Jasmine had been on the slide there." She pointed to a slide off to the side by its lonesome. "She saw Ava Coons there." Meghan motioned to the edge of the woods, where a dirt trail appeared to be carved out of the earth and disappeared into the forest. Wren hiked toward it with Meghan on her heels.

"I don't know why there's a trail there," Meghan said.

Approaching it, Wren peered into the woods. The trail was overgrown and definitely not maintained by the park. This was the border to the national forest, which melded with the state forest. Miles upon miles of woodland and lakes stretched from here, and while some roads cut through it, or a small town was etched in here and there, overall it was forest from here until you ran into Lake Superior about one hundred miles as the crow flies.

"It's more of a deer trail," Wren stated, sensing Meghan's anticipation beside her. "Not a trail for hiking. See? It's narrow, like a walkway, and none of the branches are cleared away. A few are broken, but it's not man-made."

"So, Ava Coons came to my daughter on a deer path?"

Wren hesitated. She didn't want to entertain an all-out delusion, but then it was easier to call the mystery woman Ava Coons rather than "that strange woman."

"Maybe? If you're sure this was where Jasmine met her."

"I am." Meghan nodded vehemently.

Okay, so a lady in overalls, who seemed in Meghan's sketch to be a lot older than the Ava Coons of the campfire story, had *appeared* to Jasmine here. It wasn't a typical place for someone to emerge from the woods. Wren knew of a few hiking trails, and to her knowledge, none of them were in the near vicinity of the deer trail.

"Did the police search this area?" Wren asked, stepping into the woods, swatting at a mosquito that dodged her hand.

"No," Meghan said from the grassy line at the trees.

Wren ducked under a branch, letting it scrape the top of her baseball cap. She noted the undergrowth was thick here, a few blackberry bushes with berries forming, and a blanket of leaves, dead sticks, and saplings. She squeezed through another embrace of tree branches as they intertwined with each other. One of them caught the brim of her hat and tipped it back on her forehead. Wren straightened it. She should call Troy. He might have an idea where this deer trail led to. With all the various bodies of water in the forest, the deer might have carved a trail from one of them to the park's edge. If that were the case, maybe they'd find a camper or hiker who would fit the description. Maybe that person would be . . . not Ava Coons but the abductor. Assuming Jasmine had been taken, not just wandered off.

It returned to her then, the recollection of Patty's story. Her "sighting" of Ava Coons. The woman. In overalls. The park. If Patty had seen a woman here, fitting the same description, it was years earlier. That eliminated a vagrant passing through or a tourist. It was someone more native to the area—at least within the past few years.

Wren steadied herself with a palm against a tree trunk. The other little girl who'd gone missing in high school . . . Trina was her name. Her father had kidnapped her? They'd never reported having found her—or him. What if whoever this was in the woods had taken Trina? What if the searchers had misread the situation—as they might be doing now—and it wasn't a parental abduction? Just as Jasmine wasn't a little girl gone lost?

She turned toward Meghan to voice her thoughts, but the expression on Meghan's face stopped her. The woman was pale, her lips quivering with emotion. She stared into the abyss of trees and undergrowth and the darkening shadows of the wilderness stretching out before them. The idea of someone—*anyone*—lurking in these woods and being responsible for the disappearance of little girls . . .

Wren moved to head back toward the park, motioning for Meghan to follow. She had no intention of adding further credence to Meghan's fears when it was still only a theory in Wren's imagination.

20

"I'm telling you, this can't be a coincidence." Wren dropped the doll's shoe on the table in front of Troy, the same shoe that had been left on the Markhams' steps.

He drew back and looked up at Wren, who, admittedly, was overwrought at the moment. She'd stewed the entire way back to camp after leaving Meghan in the safe embrace of Meghan's family, who had gathered at an out-of-the-way vacation rental to avoid the news reporters who'd begun to move into the area. Inquiries about the missing girl—it all made for a good news story. It wasn't one that Meghan was up to telling. But the silence in the truck was enough for Wren to work herself into an emotional state. She'd returned to the Markham home to grab a quick lunch, only to find Redneck Harriet perched on the counter by the coffeemaker, where Eddie must have casually left her. Both shoes were on her feet now. Maybe he thought covering up her name with the errant shoe would help. It hadn't. Wren had wrenched it from the doll's foot and now stood in the middle of the camp's dining hall.

The room was packed with campers and counselors, camp staff, and a few stragglers from the SAR who had missed out on receiving a bagged lunch that morning.

"It's a shoe." Troy fingered it where it had fallen by his plate of homemade pizza.

"It's the doll's shoe." Wren plopped onto the empty chair next to her boyfriend, propping her elbow on the cream Formica-topped dining table.

"Ooooooookay?" Troy raised a dark eyebrow.

His counterpart across the table, Damion, flicked an errant green pepper at him. Damion helped Troy with leading the wilderness trips, and he appeared ready to go on a new one, with his bandanna around his forehead and his pack on the floor next to him. "Dude. Don't play stupid!" Damion warned, clutching at his chest. "Detrimental to relationships when a woman is rampaging."

Wren glared at Damion. "*The* doll's shoe." She waited.

"Oh, *that* doll." Troy winced in apology. "Sorry, Wren. I sort of forgot about it."

"He doesn't play with dolls anymore," Damion teased.

"Damion," Wren snapped, annoyed at Damion's insertion when none of this was a joking matter. The dining hall was a din of voices, and it was hard enough to hear as it was.

"Hey, give us a moment, okay?" Troy asked his counterpart. He turned a shoulder to Damion, lifting the shoe. "So, why the panic?"

Of course. Wren bit back her anxious irritation. She had texted Troy about last night at the Markhams', but they hadn't had the chance to chat. Still, he should know it was upsetting, right? This wasn't a small thing. It was . . .

"Wren." Troy's hand came down softly on hers.

She jerked it away.

"Hey." He frowned.

"Sorry." And she was. She was just—Meghan had gotten to her. This entire *week* had gotten to her. And every insecurity she'd ever had as a child feeling aimless and unaccounted for was coming to the fore in light of Jasmine's disappearance. "I'm just upset."

Damion seemed to sense the tension. He cleared his throat. "Hey, Troy, I'm gonna start loading the van."

"Yeah." Troy gave him a nod. "Thanks."

"The van?" Wren pushed her hair back. She smelled like insect repellant.

"Yeah. I've got a group headed to Black River Harbor, remember?"

Yes. She did. She'd just forgotten. In the chaos of a missing child, Deer Lake Bible Camp still needed to continue. Troy was, after all, head of wilderness trips. He had a group of eight high schoolers and five adults coming in for a camping excursion to the Upper Peninsula of Michigan. The plan was to go kayaking and explore the waterfalls and caves along Lake Superior. He'd be gone for a week.

Anxiety wrestled with a strange element of relief within her. What if she needed Troy while he was away? There'd be no contact—no cell service. Having him far away would eliminate the feeling she wasn't as invested in their relationship as he was. It would—

"Wren, listen." Troy glanced around them. There were so many people, kids throwing napkins at each other, counselors telling them to stop it, and camp staff zooming here and there on their own personal missions. In the din of it all, they were also very much alone.

Wren waited. There was a strange something in Troy's voice. She noticed he drew a deep breath and then looked around again. Leaning forward, he reached for her hands. She didn't withdraw this time but instead noted how his touch didn't make her feel any better. It was that same lost sensation she'd always had, and while she'd assumed a relationship would fill the empty places that nagged at her with no reason or explanation, Troy simply hadn't. At least not yet.

His hands squeezed hers and he looked intently into her eyes. "Please try not to take this on yourself. Jasmine's disappearance, Meghan, they're not your responsibility."

Wren drew back a bit, yet Troy held on to her hands. He was being sincere. He even winced, as if the words hadn't come out the way he wanted them to.

He tried again. "I'm not saying you shouldn't care, and shouldn't help, I'm just cautioning you not to internalize it. Like that shoe. Trying to find significance, well, it will weigh you down."

"It *should* weigh me down." Wren frowned. "It should weigh us all down." Not to mention that the shoe had been deliberately set on that step. It hadn't just materialized out of nothing for no reason!

In fact, she sort of wondered why they hadn't cleared the camp and started an all-out rescue mission in addition to allowing SAR to run their operation from their property. She knew it wasn't practical, but a little girl was missing! "A little girl is missing, Troy." She repeated her thoughts.

"I know. And I'm praying—we're *all* praying—she's found. But ministry here at camp doesn't stop, and you making this burden your own will only—"

Wren drew her hands away. "Will only what?"

A pained expression flashed in Troy's eyes. He ran his fingers through his black hair. If she could just curl up in his arms, feel safe . . . Why did she need to feel safe? At the thought, Wren stilled. She wasn't the missing Jasmine. She wasn't lost. She was right where she should be and . . .

"I just don't want to see this eat you up," Troy finished, his words low and grave.

Wren's eyes widened. "You know something, don't you?" she breathed.

Troy bit his lip and looked away, unable to meet her frank question with a direct answer.

"Troy." Wren reached for him, taking his hand, this time of her own volition. "Tell me."

He looked back at her. "I overheard the police speaking with some of the head of SAR. They're more seriously considering foul play."

"Kidnapping." Wren wasn't surprised. Not after what she'd witnessed last night, not after spending the afternoon with Meghan. Maybe the ghost of Ava Coons hadn't returned to snatch the child, but someone had. "Finally. They're listening to Meghan!"

"Or . . ." Troy let the word hang there.

Wren's head dipped forward in shock. "They think she's been—"

"It's possible."

161

She noted neither of them could say the words. *Killed. Murdered.* They were too harsh, too final. "Why would they start questioning that?" Wren looked around and leaned closer to Troy, not wanting to cause an undue panic at being overheard.

Troy dodged her question. "There was blood on her sweatshirt."

"So she cut herself or something. It wasn't *covered* in blood," Wren argued.

"They found—this morning, they found more blood."

There. Troy had finally stopped dancing around the truth. The weight in Wren's stomach thudded harder with the words. "More?"

Troy nodded. "Toward Lost Lake, actually. There was a small clearing, and they found blood there. Not—just a little."

"Did they find *her*?"

"No. But they've taken samples to be analyzed. If it's confirmed to be human—maybe matched to Jasmine—then this will change from a search and rescue to a search and recovery." Troy tilted his head forward until his forehead touched hers. "I know that will eat you alive if it does, Wren. And I'm not going to be around to help you."

"I'll be fine." Wren heard the water in her voice. She wasn't very convincing, considering she was already trying not to cry. "I have Eddie," she added to reassure Troy there was someone in his absence.

His eyes darkened. He pulled back a little. "Sure. Yeah. That's good." He offered an encouraging but tight-lipped smile. Nodding, he reached for her again, and this time Wren allowed the embrace. It was short, but it held meaning. Troy cared. So deeply.

"She's not dead, Troy," Wren whispered.

"I hope you're right," he responded, yet his tone told her he was doubtful.

"She's not." Saying it made it true. It had to.

~~~~~~~

The lone swing swept the air back and forth, its chains squeaking with the motion. A metallic resistance against the movement. It wanted to be still. The swing wanted to rest. Yet something kept it in motion, though its yellow seat was empty, the park devoid of humanity.

Wren walked toward the swing, noting how the fog curled around her ankles. Embracing her like an obsession that willed her forward. The tree line was thick, dark blue with hints of evergreen marrying with the fog.

"Jasmine!" she called. It was nighttime. The search parties had all retired, but she wouldn't. She couldn't. Wren had to keep searching. Giving up was admitting Jasmine was lost, and that was unacceptable. You never gave up searching for a child. You never gave up. Never. Gave. Up.

"Jasmine!" Wren's voice wobbled, weak from overuse and hoarse from being dry. She patted her side for a water bottle, then realized she'd not put her backpack on. She'd come to the park in the deep of night with no preparations. What if she found Jasmine? What if Jasmine was truly hurt? How would she help?

The fog cleared a bit from the deer trail, and Wren stilled. A shadow moved across the path. It didn't take any form. It just moved. In unison with the squeaking of the swing. She took a step closer until she saw it, in the depths, reaching from the woods. A white hand, long fingers, extended through the branches. Its fingertips curled as if to beckon Wren toward it.

She shivered. The hand looked dead. The skin was white, the flesh wrinkled—disintegrating—as if it had been submerged in water for days. As Wren drew closer, she noted the fingernails were blackened, and one of the fingers was missing its nail altogether.

"No." Wren's whisper was louder than she'd expected. She declined the hand's beckoning motion. "No, I-I can't."

"Baby?" The voice was a woman's. It was coming from behind her. Wren tried to turn, to twist around to see. "Come back to me." The woman was crying. Wren could tell by her voice as it drifted across the park.

The swing stopped swinging.

The hand curled into a fist and yanked backward into the darkness, disappearing.

Wren screamed.

~~~

"Hey, hey, hey."

Wren jerked forward into a sitting position in her bed. Her shirt stuck to her body. It was drenched in sweat. The sheets were also damp, and they tangled around her feet like the fog in her dream.

Eddie pulled his hand back. He must have been patting her cheek lightly. Trying to awaken her.

"Is she okay?" Gary's sleepy voice, a rough growl, came from the hallway.

"Yeah, Dad. I got her," Eddie replied over his shoulder.

"Good. I'm going to go check on Mom." Gary moved on toward Patty's room.

Wren ran her hands over her head, pushing her hair back, the coppery strands almost maroon in the dim light. A dream. Right? It'd been a dream. The hand. The woman's voice.

"You were screaming again." Eddie wasn't blaming, just informing her.

"I'm sorry to wake you up."

Eddie was sitting on the edge of her bed, fully clothed in jogging pants and a T-shirt. "S'all right. I was up anyway."

"Patty?" Wren startled, worried Patty was losing her final battle for life.

Eddie shook his head. "Mom's fine. At least—well, you know."

Wren drew in a shuddering breath and nodded. "Yeah." She knew. One of these days or nights that wouldn't be the answer. Death was a ticking bomb just waiting to go off, but it had hidden its timer from them. They had no concept of how to prepare.

"Want to talk about it?" Eddie offered. His familiar face, crooked nose, and warm eyes brought her comfort. Wren relaxed, allowing the tension to drain from her shoulders. She shivered, chilled from her sweaty clothes.

"No. No, it's okay."

"You probably should talk about it." Eddie didn't mince his words.

"I don't want to." How could she describe the hand? That horrible dead hand?

"Was she dead?" Eddie's blunt question startled Wren.

"What do you mean?"

"In your dream. Was Jasmine dead?"

Wren shook her head vehemently. "No. I didn't see her at all this time. I called for her, but I—it was—I was—missing. It was me. *I* was the one missing." Realization seeped into her. Wren turned a confused face toward Eddie. "A woman was calling for me, and evil . . . evil was in the woods."

"Evil?" Eddie frowned.

Wren realized she was clutching the sheet so tight her knuckles were white. She couldn't release it. It was as if she held on for the sake of her life.

"What do you mean 'evil'?" Eddie pressed.

Wren met his eyes. A tear slipped from hers. "There's evil at Lost Lake, Eddie. I can *feel* it."

Concern brewed on his face. For her. Eddie was concerned for her state of mind. But all Wren felt anxious about at the moment was the hand. The rotting hand of wickedness that guarded the secrets, which had begun the day Ava Coons murdered her family.

21

Ava

The woods were alive, and they were evil. Ava could sense it the deeper she went. Hidden out here with the wild creatures were the ghouls of the forest. The souls and spirits that dipped, dodged, and intertwined with the trees. They mocked her. They mocked her memories—or lack thereof.

Ava's toe hit a root buried under leaves. She lurched forward, falling to the ground, her hands outstretched to catch herself. Skinned palms stung as she rolled to a sitting position. She held them up, dawn's light stretching through the tree covering. They weren't bleeding, just scratched.

She looked around her, trying to regain her bearings. They were here, somewhere. The bones of her family. The dusky memories were so vague they taunted Ava with their elusive summons. Beckoning her to remember while playing hide-and-seek at the same time. Nothing in the woods looked familiar. It was all trees, and boulders, and an occasional stream or marshy area. A grove of poplar trees grew in the distance, mimicking birch trees with their white trunks.

Ava frowned. She remembered a small piece of poplar that sat on a rough table. The wood had been partially hollowed out, and someone had put a candle in it. The flame flickered. Licking at the air. Dipping when the air was disturbed.

"Stick yer finger in it."

Ava jerked her head up. She'd heard the voice as distinctly as if it had been in front of her. Only she was alone. It was her brother's voice. Just changing from boy to man. Ava closed her eyes to allow the memory to wash over her.

"I ain't stickin' my finger in no fire," she'd argued back.

"Promise won't hurt none. See?" Arnie swiped his index finger through the candle flame. It came out unscathed.

Intrigued, Ava squirmed to her knees on the wobbly chair she sat on. She half climbed onto the table so she could reach the poplar and its candle. Reaching out her finger, she hesitated. "I'm scared."

"Don't be." Arnie swiped his finger into the flame and back again. "See? Not even a blister."

Ava moved to drag her finger through the flame.

"But ya gotta go quicklike," Arnie added.

Ava yanked her finger back, her eyes widening. Ricky entered the room, and in a few steps her other brother had taken hold of her hand. His eyes narrowed. They were black.

"Fraidy-cat." His growl wasn't teasing. It was mean. Mean and annoyed. He shoved her finger into the flame, but unlike Arnie, he didn't sweep her finger through it. He held it there. Ava whimpered. The flame touched the nerves in the tip of her finger.

"Ricky!" Arnie yelped.

Ava whimpered again, but Ricky leaned into her, his words a demand in her ear. "Don't cry. Don't ever cry."

But she couldn't not cry. It hurt. She was a little girl. She wanted her ma. But ma wasn't there. No one was there to rescue her. No one but—

The door to their cabin flung open and hit the wall.

"Richard!" the voice yelled with authority.

Ava opened her eyes from her perch on the forest floor. A chipmunk sat opposite her on a downed oak tree. Its cheeks were full with food it had scrounged. Ava breathed. Her breath scared the critter, and he dropped to all fours and hurtled away into the woods.

Richard.

The memory of her brother unnerved her. Was it even a memory? Had it happened? And the person at the door, stopping her brother from the fiery abuse. She couldn't make out the voice in her recollection. Man. Woman. She had no idea. She couldn't see them.

"They gotta be important somehow," Ava muttered to herself, scooting to her knees before pushing herself up from the ground. Standing, she stared at the poplar grove. It wasn't unique. Not really. There were poplar groves interspersed all over in these woods. She could no more claim that bunch of trees as near her family's cabin than she could say that chipmunk knew the way.

It was time to face the facts. She had no idea where she was going. The part of her that had hoped she'd enter these woods and by instinct head to her childhood home was sorely disappointed. Ava swiped a dead leaf that stuck to her overalls. Maybe it was a good thing she had a memory, but what did a new memory about her brother wanting her to burn her finger off have to do with what happened to them all those years ago? Maybe everything. Probably nothing at all.

Ava kicked at a stick. It snapped.

Jipsy was missing—probably dead.

Matthew Hubbard was definitely dead.

Her family was more than dead, decomposed and turned back to dirt. Ava had seen the carcass of a deer once. She'd been out hunting with Widower Frisk—he always dragged her along so she could carry his burlap sack filled with squirrels he'd shot. She hated that job. Fleas jumping through the sack onto her and bitin' her. But the dead deer . . . Ava rejoined her original thought. That deer had been all skin and bones, but several hunts later it was just bones, and then even they disappeared for the most part. The skull stayed there. A few ribs. She wondered if they really had turned to dust or if other animals had made off with them. Either way, the forest wasn't friendly to the dead. It consumed them. It made them its own. Absorbed every drop of blood like a rain shower.

She started forward again. Might as well just try. Wander and try. See if her feet knew the way better than her brain. Ava wasn't sure what she'd find when she got there anyway. Folks had said years ago that when they'd gone to the Coons home, the cabin had been all burned up. If people in Tempter's Creek weren't so dang sure she was a killer, she could've just asked someone the way to her family home. She had a feeling it was quite a ways back in. Her family had been loners. Not keen on people and socializing. The farther out they could be, the better. But Ava didn't know why. Had her daddy just been mean? Maybe he'd been the one to kill them all. Tried to kill her and she'd run away with his weapon? Maybe. Then what happened to him? How'd he disappear?

All these questions and not a lick of an answer.

Ava neared the poplar grove. By now the morning sun was sending light crystals through the air. The white of poplars' trunks seemed like an oasis in the middle of the dark woods. Fairies could live in here. Fairies or angels. That gave Ava pause. Angels. Did her family turn into angels when they died? Could they even without a proper burial?

A lump—probably a fallen log—lay in the midst of the poplars. Ava wound her way toward it. It seemed out of place there. Seemed to reason if it was a downed tree, it wouldn't be all gray and lumpy, but white. Like a dead poplar.

She narrowed her eyes as she neared it. No. That wasn't no downed tree. It was too short for that. A boulder maybe? Ava picked her way through buckthorn bushes, twigs snatching at her overalls. She pushed aside a branch with her left arm and ducked under another. Once in the clearing, Ava stilled.

"Good Lord in heaven . . ." It was a dead body. Human as they came. All curled up with the head tucked in and an arm over its face.

Ava tiptoed toward the corpse as if any noise might awaken

it. Nearing it, she crouched next to the body. It was on its side, its back toward her. She looked around for something to turn it over with. She wasn't of the mind to be touchin' a dead body. No, thank you.

Finding a stick about two inches in diameter and nearing two feet long, Ava yanked it from its tangle with leaves and undergrowth. Once she gripped it in her left hand, she hooked it through the person's elbow and tugged. It was a lot harder than she'd expected. Ava tugged again, this time the motion making her balance on her heels unstable.

With a cry, Ava fell forward onto the body. It was stiff and ungiving against her weight. Ava scrambled away from it, and as she did so, her own motion pulled it toward her. She stared at the face. Eyes were vacant, gazing emptily toward the sky. The face was swollen, mouth and lips open. Ava could see that the flesh around the neck was discolored, and the skin under their chin was bloated. As the body landed on its back, a sigh erupted from the body's mouth. It was as if the dead gave up its spirit at last or somehow was still struggling to find breath through the shape of its shell. It told a tale that was gruesome in its form.

Ava pushed herself away from the body, staring at its profile. At first sight, one might've thought it to be the body of a man. But it wasn't. Jipsy appeared dreadful in death. Her chest was bloodied, crusted over, and black.

Spinning, Ava bent and retched.

Bursting into the parsonage back door might not have been the wisest of decisions. Ava hurtled inside, slamming the door and falling back against it, her chest heaving from her wild run through the woods. Well, if she was bein' honest, it was more of a run, then stop and gasp for air, run more, then walk really fast.

Noah leaped from his seat at the lunch table, his soup spoon clattering into his bowl.

"Did anyone see you?" Noah barked, hurrying to the front windows and drawing the curtains.

"Don't think so," Ava gasped. Her lungs hurt. Her legs hurt. Her *eyes* hurt after what she'd seen. She'd never been sorely fond of Jipsy, but she'd never wished the woman dead as a doornail. And what did that mean anyway? Dead as a doornail?

The preacher pushed past her and flipped the lock on the back door. He untied the curtains over the sink and let them fall into place before turning the full front of his concerned expression on to Ava.

"What in—are you all right?"

"I found Jipsy!" Ava knew her eyes couldn't be any wider if she'd propped them open with toothpicks.

"Jipsy?" He leaned back against the sink.

Ava nodded. "Dead. Deader than that deer Mr. Sanderson hit with his truck awhile back. Remember that? Lyin' in the road for two days 'fore someone moved it? All bloated-like."

Noah ignored her gruesome description. "Where is she?"

"In the woods!" Ava affirmed.

"Yes, but *where* in the woods?" Noah pressed.

"In the poplar grove." Ava furrowed her brow. "I'm guessin' about a mile or two in past the sawmill."

"You went past the sawmill?"

Ava could see Noah's mind spinning. It was one of the most populated places in Tempter's Creek. "It was still night when I went by. No one saw me. No one saw me now."

"You don't know that." Noah dared a peek out the window, his hand holding the curtain back by an inch or two. He let it fall back into place. "You're sure it was Jipsy?"

"She hasn't been dead that long," Ava nodded. "Still looks like her." She swallowed down her nausea. "What are we goin' to do?"

She hadn't intended on laying the full weight of the problem on Noah. Fact of the matter was, she hadn't intended on returning to the parsonage ever. But after she'd fallen on top of Jipsy's stiff body, all of her senses took flight like a flock of crows.

Noah was looking at her strangely.

"What is it?" She realized there were black shutters in the corners of her eyes. Noah was turning all blurry. He was reaching for her. She let him catch her. It felt good—bein' caught. He was a right bit softer than Jipsy had been.

22

The sound of someone pounding on the door woke Ava with a start.

"Shhh!" Noah pressed his hand against Ava's arm.

Ava was lying prostrate on the sofa in the front room. She vaguely remembered passing out and Noah catching her as she fell. Now that had been a silly thing to do. She'd never swooned before in her life and—

"Open up, Reverend!" Someone pounded on the door again. It was just out of sight from the front room.

"Shhhh." Noah held a finger to her lips. His finger was warm where it pressed against her sensitive skin. He stood from his place next to her and headed for the entryway. There was the sound of the front door being opened. She could picture Noah opening it only a fraction and peering out between the crack of the door and the frame, with a foot braced behind the door should someone try to push their way in.

"Sorry for the intrusion." The voice was Officer Larson's. Clear as day. It made Ava shrink into the sofa.

"What can I help you with?" Noah's voice was muffled.

"I had a report that Ava Coons was seen not far from the parsonage here. Just this afternoon."

"Oh really?" Feigned interest on Noah's part.

"Yes."

Silence. Officer Larson was waiting for Noah to offer up information. Noah apparently had no intention of initiating anything.

Officer Larson cleared his throat and asked directly, "Have you seen her?"

"I can ask Hanny if she has." Deflection seemed to be Noah's hidden talent.

"Hanny is here?"

"She brought me apple pie just last night." At least this time Noah wasn't blatantly lying.

"Has she seen Miss Coons?"

Noah's response was another evasion. "She didn't mention anything."

Larson cleared his throat. "Well, if you see Miss Coons, you *will* let me know, right?"

"Who reported having seen Miss Coons in the first place?" Noah dodged. "I thought she disappeared when Jipsy did."

Ava felt the cold from Jipsy's dead corpse all over again. She shivered.

"Probably shouldn't be sayin'," Officer Larson replied. "But, seein' as you're the reverend and all, it was Mrs. Sanderson who saw her. Mentioned it to her husband, who let me know right away."

"The Sandersons don't even live on this street." Noah's observation was astute, yet Ava could tell he was fishing for something.

"I guess she was visiting someone? I didn't ask. Figured she was credible and had no reason to lie."

"Certainly not." Noah accepted the answer as probable.

"Well then, I'll let you get back to your . . . afternoon." Officer Larson seemed reluctant to leave. Maybe it was because Noah hadn't invited him in.

"Thank you" was all Noah said.

Ava heard the door close firmly.

───────

He was gutsy.

She had to hand it to Noah. For bein' a preacher, he didn't just sit in a chair, scribbling away on paper until Sunday morning when he rained down all the judgment from heaven on his parishioners. Fact was, Ava hadn't even heard him whisper a sentence that sounded like he was preachin'. He hadn't hardly said a word about the Lord either.

"Hurry up," Noah gritted over his shoulder at her.

Here they were, the two of them, slinking through town like two criminals running from the police. She'd seen a picture in the paper of that one bad guy—John Dillinger—now he was a bit of a looker, if you asked her. In the darkness, Ava could make out Noah's profile. He was a tad more criminal in looks than most preachers, if she was bein' honest.

"C'mon!" He waved her into the shadows behind the post office and ducked down by a barrel filled with garbage. The moon was mostly behind the clouds, and it wasn't quite pitch-dark out yet. Still, Tempter's Creek had fallen asleep, or at least retired to their homes. When he yanked her down by her overall leg, Ava fell onto the ground beside him.

"Hey! You're gonna break my leg!"

"Shhh!" He glowered at her, poking his head out from behind the barrel. After a moment, his body relaxed a bit. "Thought I heard someone coming."

"We're in a heap of trouble." Her stating the obvious to Noah likely didn't help matters.

Noah glanced at her. "Don't I know it?"

"What plan do you got up your sleeve?" she pressed. Ava had rested during the afternoon, exhaustion having overcome her. When she'd awakened, it was to see Noah in the chair across from her, just watching her. He'd moved quickly on her awakening, and before she knew it, he'd snuck her out of the parsonage under cover of darkness with nary so much as an explanation.

"We're going to go get Jipsy." Noah's quiet proclamation made Ava freeze. Her eyes widened until she was sure they were about ready to pop from her skull. Not unlike what Jipsy's were probably gonna do soon if they left her out there in the woods too much longer.

"And *what* are we gonna do with her?"

Noah didn't bother to answer her but instead gave a wave with his hand and hurried back into the darkness. They ducked and dodged their way out of town—which wasn't very far—and toward the mill and the woods where Ava had been earlier that day.

She had to admit, it was a whole lot different headin' back into the dark abyss of the forest with Noah ahead of her. 'Course Ava couldn't say he was all brawn and muscles, but he was all man, and from the back she could appreciate the appearance of him—again, if she was bein' honest. He had a way about his movements that seemed to say he wasn't unused to sneaking around in the night or even wrestling another man if need be.

Ava recalled the letter from Emmaline and how Noah hadn't even bothered to explain it.

Yes sir. There was something more to Noah Pritchard than simply being a preacher.

The woods swallowed them whole. If the trees had fangs, Ava was sure they'd be mincemeat by now, and she never was a fan of mincemeat pie. She followed Noah, wondering when he was going to bother to stop and ask her in which direction they should go. But he seemed more focused on just getting into the woods deep enough so they weren't seen. Or followed. Or arrested. Or—

"You gonna stop anytime soon?" Ava huffed for breath. They were practically running, and aside from tripping a few times on sticks or viny stems that reached up from the earth like demons, she couldn't say as if she'd had anything else try to deter them from the mission.

Noah waited for her to catch up. It was pitch-black in the woods now, and she couldn't see his face, let alone his eyes. But she could feel them. Yes. She could feel them. They were intent. Focused. Most definitely not engaged in any sense of humor at all.

"Which way?" Even Noah sounded short of breath.

"To the body?"

"Yes," he snapped.

"You know, for a preacher, you're short on patience," Ava quipped in return.

Noah tugged her toward him so he could see her more clearly. Now she could make out his eyes in the darkness.

"Listen, Ava. Listen closely. We need to get Jipsy's body back into town and make sure we don't leave a thing behind that could tie it to you—or me. And then we're going to hurry back to the parsonage and go to bed and pretend this didn't happen."

"Why not just leave her in the woods?" Ava wasn't fond of the way he held her. Well, that wasn't true. She was fond of it. She wasn't fond of *being* fond of it. There was coiled strength in his fingers.

"Jipsy deserves a Christian burial." There was that war between a man and his inner religious parts.

"So where're you plannin' on dropping her body? In front of the police station?"

"No. At Widower Frisk's place. He can answer for her."

"Widower Frisk would never hurt Jipsy," Ava argued.

"I never said he did. But the town needs to start looking at other folk than just you."

"So you're trying to get Widower Frisk into trouble?" Ava's voice rose. "Have you plumb lost your Christian senses?"

"It has nothing to do with that," Noah hissed. He pulled her closer. Ava felt his breath on her nose. "I just—Frisk will get her taken care of. The town can try and figure out what happened, and maybe it'll deflect all this attention away from you."

"I'm not going to bed at the parsonage," Ava said.

Noah stepped back. He cleared his throat. "Of course. Well. We'll figure that out later. Now, which way do we need to go?"

Ava pointed. "Thataway."

Noah dropped her arm. She'd never wanted to be manhandled by a man before, but the way Preacher Pritchard held her wasn't mean. It was firm. Decisive. A bit like he was saying, I need you to help me so that I can help you. Sort of like a linking of arms if they'd been on the same team and he just needed to get her attention.

Well, Preacher Pritchard had her full attention. She could still feel the heat from his hand on her arm, and he was already several paces ahead of her.

23

Wren

Wren could feel Meghan's eyes on her as she drove her pickup toward their destination. She could read the woman's mind and she waited, knowing the question on the tip of Meghan's tongue.

"You believe me, don't you?"

And there it was. The question Wren was terrified to answer. If she answered no, she would crush this already fragile woman. If she said said yes, then she opened a much larger can of worms. And Meghan was already shaky as it was since the discovery in the woods and the shift in tone for the search for Jasmine.

Meghan accepted Wren's silence. She sighed and turned back to look out the windshield. "Ben told me that Search and Rescue is getting nowhere. They've covered so much land already. But if Jasmine moved—if she's running—Wren, what if she hears them and she won't come because she's afraid? Afraid of Ava Coons?"

Wren still couldn't find words.

Meghan filled the silence. "I know they found blood, but I refuse . . ." Her voice caught, and she held her fingers to her lips. "I won't go there. Not yet."

"There's no reason to. Results haven't come in yet, and it may be nothing." That might have been the lamest thing she'd ever said.

Blood was never nothing. Wren winced and adjusted her grip on the steering wheel. Distract. They needed to distract from the idea of death.

"This is why we need to go chat with Wayne Sanderson. His family has been in Tempter's Creek for over a hundred years. If anyone knows the true story of the Coons family, I'd think it would be him."

Meghan was rustling through her purse. She found her Chap-Stick and uncapped it, swiping it across her lips. Wren noticed the mother's hand had a definitive tremor to it. Suppressed nerves, emotion, and terror. She pushed the cap back on. "Is he a historian for the town?"

Wren shook her head. "No. But Gary—my friend Eddie's dad—told me this morning that Wayne used to help at the camp years ago. He's one who has invested himself into the people of this area—the town's history and such."

"Why does his name, Sanderson, sound so familiar to me?" Meghan dropped the ChapStick back into her purse.

Wren steered her truck onto a side road. "Because the Sanderson name is what Tempter's Creek is built on. Logging. They owned the sawmill that used to run this town."

"They don't anymore?" Meghan zipped her purse shut.

Wren shrugged. "Logging isn't as big around here as it was back then, especially with so much of the forest being state or federal land now. A lot of folks work outside of Tempter's Creek. At the medical facilities in the bigger surrounding towns, or there's a plastic manufacturing plant about forty-five minutes from here that many work at."

The street was lined with oak and maple. Little boxy houses with well-maintained flower beds dotted the neighborhood, their badly cracked walks evidence the people here lived on low-to-moderate incomes. Wren strained to see the house numbers, and when she spotted Wayne Sanderson's house, she parked on the street alongside it and killed the engine.

"Ready?"

Meghan nodded, and they both exited the truck. Wren led the way to the front door. She had called Wayne earlier, dropped Gary Markham's name for a mutual tie, and received an invitation from the older man.

Wayne answered the door looking every bit the part of a North-woodsman. His buffalo plaid flannel shirt seemed far too warm for the late-spring sun, but the sleeves were rolled up and it was un-buttoned at the neckline to reveal a clean white undershirt. Wire-framed glasses were propped on his nose, his gray hair parted on the side and combed neatly into place. He was clean-shaven. For a man who was sixty-something, he showed the remnants of being quite handsome in his younger years.

"Wren? Mrs. Riviera? Come in! Come in!" His smile warmed Wren's insides and made her instantly feel like she could ask the man anything. He also seemed very aware of Meghan's delicate mental state, muttering immediately that he'd been praying for Jasmine and offering her a beverage.

They walked through the front room, the kitchen, and to a back door that led onto a small deck. An umbrella table was waiting, with four cushioned patio chairs positioned around it. On the table were a pitcher of ice water and mismatched glasses, even a plate of cookies. Nutter Butters, if Wren's guess was accurate.

"Have a seat!" Wayne's smile reached his eyes. He pulled out a chair for Meghan, who took the offer graciously. "There're cookies and some ice water, if you like?"

Wren nodded. She never turned down a cookie.

Once they were settled, Wayne leaned back in his chair and hooked his ankle over his opposite leg. "So, you're wanting to learn about Ava Coons?" He smiled. "I haven't told that story for some time."

Wren returned his smile politely. "We're actually less interested in the campfire story than what really happened to the Coons fam-ily. Where they ended up. Did Ava marry, have children? That sort of thing." She didn't explain—nor did she intend to—the notion that little Jasmine had seen Ava Coons in the woods.

"Yes, well, so much of the history gets shrouded with story and lore. It's sometimes hard to know what is accurate and what's not."

"I guess we're more interested in the Coons family after the story."

"Ahhh." Wayne nodded and took a sip of his water. "Well, that is a bit of a question." He leaned forward and set the glass on the table with a *clink* of glass on glass. "You see, the story goes that Ava Coons vanished in the woods, and no one saw her again after the murders."

Wren glanced at Meghan, praying this would not upset her more than help her.

Wayne continued. "Her family's murders, of course, when Ava was a child, but then there were also two killings in Tempter's Creek in the 1930s. Similar fashion to how they assume her family was killed."

"By an ax?" Meghan inserted.

It relieved Wren to hear Meghan's investment in the conversation and that she wasn't going to melt down. Yet anyway.

"That's what they say. A man named Hubbard and then some other woman. Folks felt Ava Coons was to blame for it—I suppose 'cause the M.O. was like her own family's passing. But shortly after, that's when she disappeared, and no one ever saw her again."

"So, no one knows if she ever married, or had children, or—?" Wren wasn't even sure where she was going with that theory.

Wayne lifted his shoulders in an apologetic shrug. "Don't know. If she did, I suppose her offspring moved far away from Tempter's Creek. She probably did too. This wasn't a place where Ava Coons was going to settle and get any peace. And if she married, we've no idea what her last name changed to."

Wren took a bite of her cookie.

Meghan fiddled with hers.

Wayne rapped his fingers on the arm of the chair before inquiring, "Why is it important to find out about Ava Coons's offspring—if there were any?"

It was a good question. Wren hadn't even tied all her thoughts together. But if Ava had offspring in the area, maybe there was an explanation for Jasmine having seen Ava Coons. A misunderstanding. Someone posing as Ava Coons. It was easier to accept than that a ghost had led Jasmine off.

"I'm just curious," Wren replied, avoiding a more honest answer.

Wayne's eyes were sharp, and she could feel him assessing her.

Meghan shifted in her seat. She shot Wren an anxious look before speaking. So much for flying under the radar. "Mr. Sanderson, my daughter saw Ava Coons. The day before she disappeared. I need to know if this is even possible."

He didn't answer for a long, loaded moment. When he did, he seemed to choose his words carefully. "You mean, if Ava Coons took off with your child?"

"Yes." Meghan nodded vehemently. "Only Wren believes me."

Well, she'd never actually *said* she believed Meghan. "Or someone who appears to be Ava Coons—someone who's *alive*, but . . ." Saying it aloud made it sound even crazier.

Meghan continued, "What happened to Ava? Where did she disappear to? It's the only way I'm going to find my baby."

Wayne worked his jaw back and forth. Meghan Riviera was literally chasing a ghost. Wren was trying to add flesh and bones to it—for her sake as well, though she didn't want to admit that aloud. Wayne's responses would either make Ava Coons vanish again or come back to life.

"Mrs. Riviera—"

"Meghan."

"Meghan, then." Wayne bent forward, resting his forearms on his knees and looking intently at her. "Ava Coons is an age-old legend about a murder, throwing bodies into Lost Lake, and disappearing. There have been folks who go into the national forest and state lands here who never return. They just disappear. Now,

I don't know what happened to them. Is it probable that it's Ava Coons's ghost luring people into the woods so she can do to them what she did to her family?"

Wren held her breath. Wayne was going to demolish Meghan's theory. Which was good—at least the ghostly part of it. But then, once it was humanized, it became more terrifying, didn't it? That someone had actually *taken* Jasmine?

"Ava Coons is a ghost story. Plain and simple." Wayne's conclusion took the air from the moment.

Meghan paled. "My daughter said she saw Ava Coons. How do you explain that? Where do I go to look for her?" Meghan shot a desperate look to Wren, then back to Wayne. "Wren said you *knew* about Ava Coons—that you could help us!"

Wayne shifted uncomfortably in his chair. He rubbed his palms together as if considering his answer.

"Tell me something—*anything!*" Meghan was growing agitated.

Wren started to reach for her, but Wayne interrupted by clearing his throat.

"*If* someone took your child, they'd go farther toward Lost Lake—not in the search grid based on how a child would travel alone."

"Lost Lake?" Meghan's voice trembled.

"Why Lost Lake?" Wren interjected.

"Because—" Wayne paused and leaned back in his chair, his face strained—"it's obscure. Murky. The bottom of the lake is all muck."

"Why is that important?" Meghan's faint but wobbling question chilled Wren from the inside out.

"Mr. Sanderson—" Wren tried to interrupt.

Wayne's voice shook, and he ignored Wren's attempt to temper his honest opinion. "A little girl disappeared years ago too. Trina. Police say her daddy took her. But I've said all along that the authorities need to dredge Lost Lake. They'll find her body. They'll find others too." He offered a sad smile.

Wren lurched to her feet. "Mr. Sanderson—"

"I hate to be so blunt." Wayne shrugged. "But if there's anything true about Ava Coons, it's that she knew the best place to get rid of a body in these parts. That's at Lost Lake." His stare burned into Wren's. "Best you tell that to the search team."

24

Wayne Sanderson needed to be tarred and feathered. Wren pumped the brakes as she pulled her truck into the lot by the Rec Barn. Meghan had been weeping the entire way back to camp. Could she blame her? Wren wanted to swear, but she tempered her thoughts. The idea that Wayne could help shed light on who the mysterious Ava Coons lookalike in the park might be, well, they'd never actually gotten to that, had they? *Dredge Lost Lake for bodies? Tell that to the search team!* Not to the woman whose daughter was missing! And bringing up Trina from years ago? Tasteless.

Yet Wren was just as annoyed with herself as she was with Wayne. She didn't know what she'd expected. What she'd hoped to gain by going there. In retrospect, all it had done was prove she was lacking in her judgment calls.

She startled when the pickup's passenger door yanked open. Ben reached up for Meghan and, without a glance at Wren, whisked her away.

"Ben!" Wren shouted after him.

Eddie was beelining it for the truck and gave Ben's arm a slap as he walked by. The kind of *I'm here for you* guy slap that boded no good news.

"What happened?" Wren jumped from the truck and slammed the door. She rounded the hood.

A cry rent the air, and she saw Meghan collapse into Ben's arms. Wren froze, her knees threatening to give out. She met Eddie's eyes as he jogged toward her.

"Eddie?"

He grabbed her arms to help steady her.

"Tell me she's okay," Wren demanded of him. Eddie rubbed her upper arms.

"Let's sit down." Eddie steered her toward the side of the Rec Barn. They rounded the corner away from the crowd that was fast gathering and the ruckus of tears and conversation.

"Is it Jasmine?" Wren begged Eddie to tell her. "They found her?"

Eddie shook his head. "No. But they found another . . ." He swallowed hard. "You remember ten years ago? The girl who went missing?"

A pit formed in her stomach. Only moments before she'd been discussing her with Wayne Sanderson. "Trina Nesbitt?"

Eddie nodded. "They found her."

"Trina?" Wren's knees weakened. She leaned against the barn. Struggling to compose herself, she swiped the backs of her eyes with her bare arm.

Eddie's hand on her arm did little to reassure her. "One of the volunteers on the search party found the remains. It wasn't far from Lost Lake."

"Then how do they know it's Trina?" Wren hated the thrill of hope that shot through her that it wasn't Jasmine. But if not Jasmine, it was another little girl—whose father had *not* whisked her out of state in a child custody battle.

"They'll need to examine the remains to know for sure." Eddie squeezed her arm. "There wasn't much left. It's been ten years. They found a necklace, though. Trina's name was engraved on it, and it matches the necklace she was wearing in the photo on the missing person flyer that was circulated at the time."

Wren didn't try to stop the burning tears as they trailed down her face. It was close—too close to what was happening now with Jasmine. And right after what Wayne had stated?

"At least it's not Jasmine, but the entire search team is shook. Ben didn't take it well at all. The police are shifting their emphasis and . . ." Eddie let his words hang as he watched her. "You okay?"

Apparently she wasn't. Her knees gave out, and Eddie caught her. "Hey, hey." He helped her slide down the wall to sit on the ground. Wren pulled her knees up to her chest and looked helplessly at her friend.

"Something's not right—about any of this. Wayne—" Her voice caught.

"What about Wayne?" Eddie leaned forward. "Wayne Sanderson?"

Wren blathered the details of her visit with Wayne, and she didn't even notice when Eddie had reached for her as he sat next to her. She realized she was talking into his shoulder, her words muffled against his shirt, when she got to the part where Wayne had suggested they dredge Lost Lake.

Eddie pulled back. "Did you tell this to the police?"

Wren cast a look of utter desperation at him. "I haven't had the chance." Her face crumpled, her eyes so flooded she could barely make out Eddie's features. "We came back to *this*! It's as if Wayne isn't nuts at all! Who is in these woods, Eddie? Who is *hunting* people?" Wren was afraid. Every ounce of her soul was bleeding with the possibilities of more impending grief, but this time with Jasmine. And then there was the . . .

"Why is *my* name on Redneck Harriet's foot?" Wren blurted out the question they'd asked before. "Am I a target? Is someone watching *me*? Ava Coons wrote our names on *your* doorstep. The doll shoe! Do people really disappear in these woods? Am I next?"

"Stop. Just stop," Eddie interjected sternly. His hand ran across her cheek as he pushed back her hair and held her face with his palms. "Listen to me. You need to calm down."

"Sure. Dead body. Calm. I'm calm." Her voice was high-pitched and squeaky.

"We need to get the facts. There's nothing saying someone murdered or harmed Trina, not yet. Maybe she got lost. It *is* Lost Lake, remember? It was off the map for decades, and even with GPS now it takes effort to get to it."

"I know, but—"

"And they didn't find Jasmine. She is still out there, and as far as any of us are concerned, she is still alive."

"But—"

"As for the doll?" Eddie's gaze bored into hers. Good ol' Eddie and his boring brown eyes and plain crooked nose. "We'll figure it out."

Well, that was concerning! She wanted him to say something bland, like *It's just a doll, and the name is from Tolkien.* Or *You're overreacting. Is it that time of the month?* Yes, she'd even take that awful excuse of a male faux pas and then, after she pummeled him for being sexist, they could go get a cherry smoothie at the canteen and—

"Wren." Eddie snapped his fingers in front of her face. "Back to earth, Wren."

She blinked.

He stared.

She blinked again.

Suddenly the air between them was thick. In a way she didn't understand. Wren realized she was holding him. Around the waist, no less, in a death grip. She didn't want to let go. He was strong. Lithe. She could feel his abdomen through his shirt. She could feel the warmth from his body. But more than all that, Wren sensed his strength oozing into her spirit. As it always had. Since the day they'd first met at the camp's horse stables.

"Wren?" Eddie's question snapped her out of her mental fog.

She dropped her arms.

He cocked an eyebrow. "I need to get you home."

Yes. She nodded. Home. It was a good first place to start.

"Come here." Patty beckoned weakly from her bed. Today her rose-pink blouse brought out a touch of blush in her cheeks. It was good to see. For Patty, it was a good day.

Wren glanced at Eddie, who tipped his chin up. "Go." She squeezed his hand gently as she left his side. He knew. He knew Patty was her calming agent, her voice of reason, her . . . God help her when Patty left them forever.

"Sit." Patty tapped the arm of the chair next to her bed. Her eyes danced with a familiar joy that was unique to Patty. Even through the pain, she carried that element of peace that Wren envied. She sought it too. But prayer and Scripture reading and all the church fellowship in the world hadn't taught Wren what Patty had learned through trial. Some things couldn't be captured *but* through the experience of pain. It was a wicked but essential way to understand the depths of perfection, the depths of God, more intensely. Pain either magnified faith or disabled it. For Patty, it only confirmed her belief that this world was broken, and her Lord was the One who brought beautiful redemption.

Wren breathed in the essence of Patty as she sank into the stuffed chair and pulled her legs up beneath her. Curling up next to Patty felt like curling up next to her mom. The memories of Mom were foggy. Pleasant but distant. Patty was now.

She studied Wren for a long moment and then smiled again. "Eddie texted and said you were, and I quote, 'an absolute wreck.'"

They both laughed, Patty's weak and Wren's watery.

"Your son has such a way with words." Wren wiped at her eyes again. "I don't know what's wrong with me."

"What do you mean?" Patty offered another small laugh. "You've experienced a lot of heavy stuff this week."

"Has it only been a week?" Wren curled her lip at what felt like a month.

"Not even." Patty reached for Wren's hand.

"I don't know why I'm internalizing everything," Wren admitted. "It feels selfish. She's not my daughter, she's Meghan's."

"Eddie said you had another nightmare?"

"Yes." Wren nodded. "Last night. And it was . . ." She pulled her hand away from Patty so she could fidget with a thread hanging from the seam on her *Sarcasm Is How I Hug* T-shirt. "The dream was about me. *I* was the one missing, and *I* was in the woods where Jasmine was supposed to be, and it was all so amplified!"

"Eddie told me about the doll you two found at the old Coons cabin."

"Troy was there too," Wren said, feeling like she shouldn't forget about him.

"Yes," Patty acknowledged. "Eddie said the doll has your name on its foot?"

"Creepy, huh?" Wren lifted her eyes. "And that's the thing! Why *my* name? Now they're pretty sure they found Trina Nesbitt's remains. I'm scared, Patty. She was just a child!"

Patty's face furrowed into concern. "Do you feel that maybe this *does* include you?"

"I do." Wren hated to admit it. Hated to make all the trauma about herself, but she couldn't address it if she couldn't be honest about it. And who better to be honest with than Patty? She would take Wren's emotional secrets to the grave—literally.

"Why?"

Wren shook her head at Patty's simple question. "I keep asking myself the same thing. Why? Why me? You want to know what's really weird?"

Patty nodded.

"I feel like I relate," Wren admitted, epiphany taking over the urge to cry. "I feel like I relate to Jasmine. Lost and everyone's looking for me, but no one is finding me. I feel like I relate to Trina. I'm just—out here. Lying here. Alone. Dead."

"You're not dead."

"I know that, but—" Wren squeezed her eyes shut and wrinkled her nose in frustration. "Why do I feel lost?"

A knowing covered Patty's face. She offered a soft smile. The kind that Wren wanted to somehow bottle up and preserve. "Do you realize the first day Eddie brought you home to play when you both were, what, ten? Eleven? I took one look at you and thought you reminded me of a lost little girl."

Wren sighed. "My mom hadn't even died yet."

"No." Patty shook her head. "She hadn't."

"Did you—did you and Mom ever talk? You know, about me?"

Patty winced as she adjusted her position against her pillows. "All moms talk about their kids. Yours was no different. She went on and on about Pippin, how smart he was. She was so proud of him."

"Wonder if she still would be, considering he lives in the basement and is almost forty."

Patty's laugh was muted but filled with humor. "Well, knowing your mom, she would've enjoyed having her boy with her. Being his top girl was always her pride and joy."

Wren noticed Patty hadn't mentioned her. "And me?"

Patty's expression grew soft. "Your mom loved you, Wren, you know that. She treasured you. Having lost a few pregnancies between you and your brother, I think when you finally arrived, you were, for all sakes and purposes, her miracle. At least that's what she told me."

"So, my feelings of being misplaced wouldn't be from her." Wren's musing wasn't meant to criticize her family or shed doubts. But she couldn't place it. A quality, albeit a tad too Tolkien-obsessed, family unit should not leave a person feeling dysfunctional.

Patty hesitated, but Wren couldn't tell if it was because of the conversation or the cancer. She waited while Patty closed her eyes for a long moment. Finally they opened, a sadness in them that Wren hadn't seen before.

"I'm going to be honest with you, honey."

Those were never the opening words to something good. Wren grabbed the blanket that hung over the back of the chair and covered her lap with it. Like a shield, the blanket made her feel protected against whatever Patty was going to share.

"A few times, when your mom and I were together, she—she alluded to your father in a way that made me wonder."

"Wonder what?" Dread coiled in Wren's stomach.

Patty winced, then admitted, "Wonder if he was your biological father."

The words were out. They'd been spoken, and Wren knew Patty couldn't take them back if she'd tried.

"You think my mom had an affair?" Wren's voice shook. She wasn't angry or hurt, just confused and, frankly, terrified.

Patty pulled her own blanket up so that it covered her chest. "I don't want to speculate. I never *did* want to. But you—"

"I don't fit," Wren finished for her.

Patty turned her head on her pillow a bit to look more directly at Wren. "You don't. More so after your mother died. It's been just Tristan and Pippin and you, and even Gary's noticed. All these years, you've gravitated to us. To *our* home. I know you and Eddie are remarkably close, but it's more than that."

"Well, I missed Mom," Wren said. "You were the next best thing." Or better. But she didn't add that.

Patty's sigh was an acknowledgment of Wren's explanation. "But it wasn't just because of me either. You're not—*bonded* with them. With your father. Pippin, I can understand more. He's your brother, but he's twelve years older and . . ." Patty hesitated.

"Unique?" Wren inserted.

They shared a laugh.

Patty smiled. "Well, sure. We'll use that word. But your father? I would have thought after so many miscarriages, you'd be his little princess."

"He did name me Arwen." Wren thought of *The Lord of the Rings*, of the elves. Arwen was a much-loved cinematic character, if not more of a bit character in the novel itself. That had to account for something in her father's world.

"I might be wrong," Patty said and waved it off weakly. "I hope I am. I've said nothing because I didn't want to plant ideas in your mind that were simply not true. It's not a pleasant thing to insinuate that anyone had an affair or that your parentage isn't what you thought. I don't mean this to be a reflection on your mother's faithfulness or—"

"Patty." Wren leaned forward, resting her palm on Patty's bone-thin shoulder. "It's okay. I asked. I need to figure out what is going on and you're helping me. It's not your fault to have suspicions, and suspicions aren't necessarily an accusation of guilt. It just confirms that my questioning isn't—well, that I'm not isolated in my thinking."

"You're not." Patty shook her head.

"I need to see my birth certificate."

"Your father probably adopted you—if my theory has any merit," Patty added quickly.

"I'm sure." Wren narrowed her eyes as more thoughts grew in her mind. "But I always found it odd that my scholarly dad would want to work at camp instead of a campus. Didn't you? What if—what if we're all tied to this place for some reason? To the Lost Lake region. What if the doll with my name on its foot actually *does* have something to do with me?"

Patty stifled a yawn. "I'm sorry," she apologized.

"No. You rest now." Wren pushed herself up from the chair and bent over, dropping a kiss on Patty's cheek. "Don't wear yourself out." Even though that was inevitable. "I need to do some family history digging."

"Be careful." Patty's eyes filled. It was her turn to be weepy. "I love you. I don't want you hurt."

"I have Eddie," Wren said flippantly, meaning to make Patty feel secure at the thought of her son.

Patty's smile was different this time. It was filled with undefinable meaning, even though it maintained its soft demure ambience. "Yes," Patty answered. "You have Eddie."

25

Ava

"Where are we?" Noah's whisper was more of a hiss, and completely unnecessary.

"In the woods." Ava's response was sassy, but she took pride in that she wasn't whispering. Who was there to hear them? Owls? Coyotes? Maybe a black bear, but then even a footstep would spook that furry beast into a full-on escape from them.

Noah was sure hard to see in the dark, the branches casting shadows over his face. She was certain he was annoyed, but also attempting that preacher-thing he did where he summoned patience from the Lord above. "I meant"—his response was evenly measured, this time in a voice louder than a whisper—"where *in* the woods are we? We need to find Jipsy's body and get her back before sunrise."

Well, that might be a problem. Ava wasn't sure how to break it to the man that they were utterly lost in the forest. She did not know where that poplar grove was—leastways not in the dark. She had *thought* she could find it, but now Ava was pretty certain finding Jipsy was going to be more like finding Widower Frisk's hidden whiskey that everyone knew existed but never saw.

"You don't know, do you?" Noah pushed a branch out of his way as he walked the few paces back to Ava.

She looked up at him, trying to see his eyes but instead making out just the vague shadows of his face. "I'm sorry." Ava couldn't think of anything else to say. But somehow it satisfied him.

"Then where'n heck are we?" Noah's hands were at his hips, and he twisted, peering into the night as if he had some special ability to see in the dark.

"You didn't bring a flashlight?" she asked.

"I don't own one."

"Even Widower Frisk owns one."

"Well, I don't." It was said with enough emphasis that Ava could take the clue Noah was shutting down the conversation. "Listen." He leaned close enough that she could see the whites of his eyes. "Do you have any sense of where Jipsy's body is from here? Any sense at all?"

Ava looked around, eyeing the depths and recesses of the forest. It was haunting here. All the crevices and sheltered places were hiding spots for all that couldn't be explained. It brought unheralded the fact that the woods resembled her memories. Her life. Filled with places that were unseen and unexplained.

A chill passed through her. She squinted, staring into the blackness. If a spirit could call to her, beckon her, it would be now. A specter weaving among the trees until it drifted into her, merging with her.

Come.

Ava could hear it. Noah dissipated into nothingness, his body becoming a vapor that bled into the trees like a fog.

Come home.

"Jipsy?" Ava called. The night was not a friendly place. The voice was unfamiliar to her. Neither male nor female. Simply a murmur.

Ava moved toward the voice, straining to see, to make out a person, a form, but she saw nothing. The void beyond was unending. It was a maze of twisted trees and branches, bushes and undergrowth. She pushed her way through, ignoring everything but the mystical beckoning that Ava could not disregard.

We're waiting for you.

Ava moved faster now. Stumbling over roots and rocks underfoot. They were waiting for her. She needed to come. To hurry. More than one voice joined the soloist now. It was a chorus. A chorus of unremembered souls. Those who had perished here. She knew that now. It was the dead. The dead were calling to her. From a place deep in the fathomless recesses of the forest.

Ava tripped, her toe hooking on a vine that ate at her foot and sent her catapulting forward. With a cry, she skidded on the ground, her knees colliding with the earth and her palms scraping on the underbrush. It was a decline. Her body rolled forward, the blanket of wet leaves beneath her adding momentum as she tried to stop.

The woods opened up as she slid to a halt against a rotted fallen log. Bark splintered off, the smell of mold and dead tree assaulting her senses. Ava breathed heavily, grappling to catch her breath, but feeling as if someone had wrapped skeletal fingers around her throat and was squeezing. Blackness invaded the corners of her eyes, then cleared, then formed again.

Ava shook her head. "No. No, please," she muttered, clawing at her throat to disengage the ghoulish hands from her skin. "Leave me alone." Her breath caught on a sob. Another sob. "Leave me—alone."

She lifted her eyes. The sky opened up above her. The trees thinned out and parted as if they were a crowd of onlookers making way for something larger, more powerful, and more intimidating. Ava scraped at her throat. The hands. They wouldn't loosen. She could feel her eyes widening as she gasped for breath. For air.

There. It was there. Ava saw the lake. It undulated with navy-blue waves that licked the shoreline like a beast tasting its prey. Stars reflected off its water, shimmering spirits of souls long forgotten. Ava twisted onto her hands and knees, crawling toward the shoreline.

Come. Find us.

The voices were louder now. More distinct.

"Ma?" Ava cried, lifting her right hand and reaching for the waters.

Ava?

"Ma!" Her hands submerged in the wet silty bottom of the lake as Ava reached the edge of the water. She crawled into the lake, determined. A fierce protectiveness rose in her. She would fight for them. Their souls lay entombed here. She could feel it. Sense it. The souls of her family. Butchered and left to bleed into the lake, the very essence that made up their lives.

The lake pulled her under. She would go. To find them. For the first time in forever, Ava could see their faces. Ma, Pa, Arnie, and Ricky. Water sucked at her ankles. She opened her eyes in the murky depths and saw the lake weeds waving to her from the bottom. A hand and arm stretched from the depths, fingers wrapping around her ankle. In the silt on the lake bed, a face emerged. Eyes open. Long hair floating and waving like the weeds that beckoned her to come to them.

Ava's arms cut through the water, directing her body to go downward. To join—

A force jerked on her neck. Under her arms.

Ava fought, clawing at the restraints that tugged on her, taking her away from her family. She watched the hand release her ankle, the face disappearing as the lake water washed over it.

"Nooo!" Her voice was warbled. Muffled. Water filled her throat, gagging her protest.

Air pummeled her face as Ava broke through the surface. She screamed, but the water in her mouth and lungs prohibited the sound. Water splashed as she was hauled from the lake. Ava pried at the arms that hooked under her shoulders and locked her against a body not much larger than hers but possessing a strength she couldn't fight against.

She couldn't breathe. Ava was half thrown onto the shore, her back scraping against small pebbles. Now breath seemed essential. She sucked at the air, but it wouldn't come, barred by a watery wall in her lungs. She was pushed onto her side. Her chest heaved, choking, and water pushed up her throat, through her nose, choking and relieving her simultaneously.

"That's it." He sprawled next to her on the shore, pulling her into his lap so she lay over his arm. He pounded her back.

Ava vomited more water this time, the blessed sensation of air kissing her lungs and bringing awareness to her. Noah held her, but he too was dripping with lake water, his shirt clinging to his chest. Ava was limp in his lap. All her strength ebbed from her body. She coughed. Choked. Spit up more water.

Eventually, Ava's coughing ceased, and she lay across Noah, her head in the crook of his elbow. He pushed wet hair from her face. Ava closed her eyes at the sensation. It comforted her. It was warm and safe and—

"What'n heck were you thinking?" Noah's sudden deviation from anything tender startled Ava into further awareness that she was sprawled in the arms of the preacher after her surreal experience that bordered on suicidal.

Ava shoved Noah, and he fell backward as she scrambled from her place in his lap. "What'd you do that for?" she shouted. She was angry and couldn't comprehend why. It filled her. Every pore of her. She'd been thwarted. Canceled from completing what she'd been so close to accomplishing.

"*Saving* you? I was *saving* you?" Noah matched her tone.

They sat a few feet apart, water dripping down their faces. The forest bordering the lake was silent. The sky had gone dark as clouds passed over, blocking out the stars.

Noah moved to his knees. "I asked you if you knew where we were, and the next thing I know, you're hauling off into the woods in some catatonic state. I could hardly keep up with you!"

Ava's breaths still hurt. Her lungs were sore. Her throat throbbed. She breathed like she had just finished running for miles.

"Then you're crawling into the lake like a madwoman! Have you lost your mind?" Noah spat the last unfriendly word at her.

Ava didn't answer. She looked beyond him. Around them. Her eyes assessed all the shadows, all the bulges and formations that jutted from the darkness. She stiffened. Straightened. Starting to her feet, she tripped forward. Her shoes were heavy with water, her overalls weighing each step down as they dripped water onto the gravelly shore.

"Ava?" Noah was gentler now. He was concerned. She could hear it in his voice, and yet he sounded distant. Behind her.

She increased her pace, stumbling as she moved from the shoreline into the brush. It was overgrown. So thick. Ava swiped at buckthorn bushes and shoved her way through blackberry bushes that grabbed and hooked on her clothes.

"Ava!" Noah cried again.

Ava could hear him crashing behind her. But it was coming clearer now. The tree. A big looming oak tree. Its trunk was massive, wide enough that if it was hollowed, she could fit her entire person inside it. Smaller oak and saplings branched under its canopy. She remembered the tree. Its oak branch Pa had hung a swing from. The swing wasn't there. At least she couldn't see it in the dark.

The remains of home grew out of the agonizing night. What was left of the Coons cabin rose from the undergrowth like the memories in her heart tangled with the brush of today. She could make out the edges of fieldstone. The foundation. Charred support beams rose into the air several feet before breaking off into upright spikes. But she remembered it—remembered it as it had been. A cabin, on the lake, its windows glowing—as if it had been alive.

A sob crowded Ava's already sore throat. She grappled her way to the foundation, reaching to grasp one of the corner posts, ignoring how it broke off into a decade's-old bits of coal.

"Ava!" Noah puffed from his rush to catch up to her.

She ignored him and instead lowered to her backside, balancing on the fieldstone and then sliding into the abyss below. Her feet crunched on stone, and her ankle twisted, a sharp pang sending thrills of pain up her leg. Ava crumpled to the floor of the cabin, her body mashing into the debris. A dead tree had fallen into it, its branches breaking off and scratching her arm.

"Ma." Her whisper was an ache that grew in her soul. Ava connected with the remembrance of her. Rough hands from the labor of living in seclusion, churning her own butter, helping stack wood, and doing laundry without the modern benefits of a washing machine. "Ma." This time her word was a choked sob. A cry for a family she'd lost, for a woman she could barely recall, and a nurturing she had been cheated out of.

Noah dropped beside her, his landing far more secure than hers had been. Water squished from his shoes as he crouched beside her. Ava felt his hand on her shoulder. She shrugged it away. She didn't want to be touched. Didn't want to be aware of any other presence than the elusive memories of her family. There was a horror growing inside her. A dread. She could hear it. A scream. Shouting.

Whack

Ava slapped her hands over her face, unconcerned by the sting of flesh against flesh. She wanted to erase the sound from her mind.

Another scream.

She hit her face again.

Heavy footsteps on a wood floor.

The heels of her hands pounded her temples repeatedly.

Whack, whack . . .

The echo of Arnie's yell.

Ava's fingers tore at her hair. She curled into herself, rocking back and forth. "Stop. Stop. Stop." They were coming. Small, captured moments from a time she had anchored herself far away from, never to drift back into those troubled waters.

She saw it then. In her memory. The cavern. The hole in the ground. Ava pushed off Noah, who was attempting to grapple her into stillness. Slugging at him with her forearm, she shoved him aside, scraping her body across the remains of the cabin floor until she reached it.

The cellar. The door was still intact but covered over with vines and branches. Ava clawed at them, tearing them away from their secure grip on the past. Here. It was here. Safety. In the cellar. Her fingertips edged under the trapdoor and lifted. Dust blew into her face. Old familiarity beckoned Ava to twist her body around and settle her feet on the ladder rungs.

Two hands landed on hers. Startled, Ava looked up from her position on the ladder as she descended into the gloomy depths.

Noah leaned over her. Worry was etched into what she could see of his face. Ava shook herself free of his touch, staring into his eyes as she lowered herself down. The ground swallowed her. A blessed beckoning into the bowels of the earth. To the place she had huddled. The place she had wept as a thirteen-year-old girl, as she listened to the screams of her family in their last moments of life.

26

Wren

Wren tugged open the bottom file drawer in her mother's filing cabinet. The metal-on-metal scraping sound announced her intention to snoop. She wasn't trying to be sneaky, but at the moment, Wren preferred not to be confronted by her dad. What if he didn't know? Didn't suspect? What if Patty was right and Wren truly was an accidental pregnancy because of an affair? And if Tristan Blythe didn't know . . . Wren didn't want to be the one to break the possibility to him. Either way it was spun, it felt as if she would be betraying her mother and her memory, or else betraying her father and his current day perception of their life with Mom back when she was with them.

She fingered through the manila files, thankful her mom had been organized and that her dad hadn't done much with her things beyond clearing out her clothes and daily belongings.

Appliance Warranties

Insurance Policies

Car Loan

"What are you doing?"

Wren shrieked and jerked her knee, connecting with the metal edge of the filing drawer. "Pippin!" She scowled at her brother, rubbing her sore knee.

He looked around the doorframe, his hand braced on the wall. His hair was ruffled per usual, and he wore his blue-light glasses. He'd been programming in his basement office.

"I'm looking for my birth certificate." She pushed the filing drawer shut. The folders were not giving up anything beyond standard household records.

"In a filing cabinet?" Pippin raised his eyebrows.

"Where else?"

"Safe-deposit box?" he tossed back. "Mom never kept important records like that in a filing cabinet."

"She has a safe-deposit box?" Wren stood from her place on the chair, rubbing the small of her back.

Pippin nodded. "She did when I was a kid."

"Eons ago."

"Funny." Pippin spun and left her alone in the room. Wren chased after her brother as he wandered into the kitchen. He opened the refrigerator and reached for a Pepsi.

"When you were a kid, we didn't even live in Tempter's Creek. Did Mom get a new deposit box here?"

Pippin popped the can top, and fizz cut through the air. He shrugged his T-shirt-clad shoulders. The face of the Tenth Doctor of *Doctor Who* stared back at Wren from Pippin's chest. "I didn't pay attention, Arwen."

"How would I find out?" She wasn't willing to give up that easily.

"Ask Dad."

"Thanks. That's helpful." Wren tossed him an annoyed glare.

"What?"

"Can't you look that stuff up online now?" She crossed her arms over her chest.

Pippin took a swig of his soda. "Probably."

Wren waited.

Pippin eyed her from the rim of his can. "No."

"Why not?" She couldn't deny the little sister wail that infiltrated her voice.

"Contrary to popular belief," Pippin said as he lowered the Pepsi, "I actually *do* have a job. I'm under contract right now and I need to get this app finished. I don't have time to dig into ancestral files."

"I don't need a family tree, Pip. I need my birth certificate."

"Ask Dad."

"No."

"Why not?"

"Because!"

"Arwen!"

"Pippin!"

They were at a standoff. Pippin wasn't easy as an older brother. She'd tried to establish a friendship with him since she was little. The age gap between them hadn't helped, and his preference for virtual friendships over face-to-face relationships had long been established. Outside of Mom, Pippin had never been close to either their dad or Wren.

She tried again. "Pip, I know you. It'll take you all of thirty minutes to dig it up online."

"Maybe." He mashed his lips into a thoughtful scowl. "Never done it before."

"You created a digital map of *The Lord of the Rings* geographic layout in a day."

"That's different."

"It's *harder*."

"Yeah, well . . ." He took another swig and skirted past her as he headed toward the basement stairs. "From what I know, you can find birth records, but to get a certificate you need to request it from the state you were born in."

Wren trailed behind him, her feet padding on the carpeted stairs. "A certificate isn't necessarily important—not at the moment anyway. I just need to see my birth records, and if they're online, that's all I need."

Pippin plopped onto his leather gamer chair with its bright orange edging. He set his Pepsi on a cork coaster. "Why? What do you need them for anyway?"

"I'm curious." Wren sat on his wall-length desk, her hip balancing on the edge.

Pippin hit a key on his keyboard. His six monitors powered back to life, three mounted on top with three on the bottom. A Netflix show was paused on the bottom right corner. A *Pokémon* cartoon. Of course. "About what?" Pippin reached for his headphones.

It wouldn't necessarily upset Pippin, but she wasn't ready to share her suspicions, even if her brother's emotional reactions were practically nonexistent. Would he even be upset if he found out that Dad *wasn't* her biological father?

Pippin broke into her thoughts after he typed a string of code. "I'll help. Just not now. I've got to get this coding done."

Accepting that this was as far as she was going to get with Pippin, Wren slid off his desk and tried not to stomp her way to the stairs like an irritated middle-school girl.

"Hey." Pippin's voice stopped her.

She looked over her shoulder.

"I heard they found that missing girl."

"Trina Nesbitt?"

"Yeah. No sign of Jasmine yet?" At least he was concerned about her, if nothing else.

"No." Maybe she should confide in him. If Pippin knew she thought maybe she was in danger, then he'd be more inclined to help. She opened her mouth to say something, then snapped it shut. Pippin had turned back to his monitors, his fingers flying across the keyboard as a silent Pikachu battled against some other huge-eyed *Pokémon* character.

"You're serious about this, aren't you?" Eddie straddled a chair as Wren tapped the screen of her tablet. A camper sidled by, hitting Wren's elbow.

"Sorry," the person mumbled around a long Jolly Rancher stick.

"I signed up for a membership on this site. I should be able to access the general information about my birth records."

Eddie nodded. Wren could sense him studying her. It made her squirm. She looked up. "What?"

He was frowning. "I'm just trying to figure out the connection. If there even is one."

Wren nodded. He meant between her, Jasmine, and Trina. And the only reason she was thrown into the mix of unfortunates was that stupid doll they'd found in the cellar of the old burned-out Coons cabin.

"Look up Trina Nesbitt. See if you can find any info on her disappearance." Eddie stood, spun the chair around, and hunched next to Wren.

She opened another tab on her browser, pushing off her own personal history for a moment. Searching, a litany of links popped up with Trina's name.

"That one." Eddie pointed to a local news source.

Wren clicked on it, waited for the page to load, then silently scanned the beginning paragraphs. "Trina Nesbitt went missing ten years ago. So we'd have been . . ." She tried to do the simple math in her head. Her brain was frazzled.

"Sixteen, and I was eighteen."

"It wasn't long after my mom died." Wren shot a quick glance at Eddie. The comment about a mother passing didn't seem to affect him. "I didn't pay a whole lot of attention to it."

"No surprise." Eddie gave her an empathetic smile. "Especially since they pretty quickly came to the conclusion that her dad had absconded with her."

Wren studied the online article. The words blurred, then came back into focus as she shoved back a sudden onslaught of tears that wanted to surface. Tears for herself and her own loss, tears for Eddie and his impending loss. And Gary! The man was going to lose his *wife*! Patty was a link for them all, and without her . . .

"See?" Eddie pointed at the screen. "There was a search ongoing for Trina and her father. She was last seen with him, and he was last seen in northern Minnesota shortly after Trina disappeared."

"I wonder why they never found him?" Wren mused. She scrolled down the article.

"If Nesbitt took Trina to Canada, then that would have explained a lot." Eddie shrugged. "I know that's what a lot of people concluded."

Wren nodded in agreement. "Her parents were divorced." She typed the Nesbitt family name into the search engine next to *Tempter's Creek* as a search criteria. Another link popped up to a news article a few years after Trina's disappearance.

"The Nesbitt home was sold after Trina's mom moved out of Wisconsin. There was an auction on their house."

Eddie grimaced. "All this time, the dad's desertion was a distraction from the fact that Trina was still here."

"By Lost Lake." Wren leaned her head on her palm, elbow propped on the canteen table. "Wayne was right."

Eddie's eyes sharpened. "About?"

"That Lost Lake needed to be searched. He insinuated that Trina had gone missing and he'd thought it needed further searching back then."

"Why does Wayne Sanderson care about Trina Nesbitt?"

Their eyes met as Eddie's question sank in. Wren scrunched her face in a struggle to piece it together. "An amateur sleuth?"

Eddie frowned. "Hard to believe." He shifted the laptop toward him. "Let me check . . ." He waited, then opened a page that popped up. "Okay . . . Sanderson, Wayne. Tempter's Creek."

Wren realized they were studying a rudimentary Sanderson family tree. "There's been a Sanderson here since before Ava Coons was ever born."

"Yeah." Eddie scrolled, narrowing his eyes as he studied the screen. Finally he shook his head. "Huh. I don't see any connection to the Nesbitts."

"Why would there be?" Wren was trying to follow Eddie's line of reasoning.

"I thought maybe they were related, which would explain why Wayne Sanderson would have a vested interest in Trina—enough to bring her up in front of Meghan Riviera."

"There can't be a coincidence that two six-year-old girls disappeared ten years apart. A decade. It's kind of a landmark," Wren noted.

"True." Eddie leaned away from the computer. "Still, I don't understand Wayne's tying a situation from ten years ago to the current one. And it's a bit suspicious he'd bring it up the same day we find Trina's body. Don't you think?"

"I agree." Wren tapped the table with her finger. "But it's not like Wayne knew she'd be found while we were talking to him."

"Even so, outside of some similarities, Trina and Jasmine are unrelated and separated by ten years. To be super picky, all three of you are unrelated." Eddie sighed. "I'm not trying to be insensitive, but I don't see any connections—unless you're a conspiracy theorist trying to create one."

"My name on Redneck Harriet's foot?"

"What do we have then?" Eddie appeared open to considering it all. "Ten-year segments, a doll with your name on it, two missing girls with one of them now deceased . . . someone Ava Coons had nothing to do with."

"But the doll was at the Coons cabin, and Trina wasn't found far from Lost Lake."

Eddie blew out a breath, running his hand over his mouth. "Man. I don't know."

"Lost Lake *is* a connection." Her insistence was met with a chocolate-eyed look of doubt.

"All we can do is share Wayne's story with the police."

Wren opened her mouth to argue.

Eddie held up a hand. "If the cops think they need to look into Wayne Sanderson, they can. I think you're better served helping with the search party as it stands and looking up your birth records."

Wren bit back a sigh, alt-tabbing back to the original screen she'd been working on. Wisconsin's database. Birth records. She blew out a puff of air, and a napkin on the table skipped across the top.

"'Cause that will explain why I feel so misplaced?" Wren asked, but it was rhetorical, and Eddie knew it. Being misplaced as a child—whether lost or taken, whichever way it was spun left dark and unsettled shock waves in the life of an adult who'd lived it. If Tristan Blythe wasn't Wren's father, then who was? And was she making a ludicrous jump of logic to assume it really was *her* name that was written on the doll from the Coons cabin? Right now it didn't feel much different from if she'd been putting a puzzle together and someone came along and swept their arm across the table, sending the pieces flying in all directions, mixing them with pieces from other puzzles. Puzzles that had nothing to do with each other, and yet they seemed as if they were supposed to fit together.

27

Ava

She cowered in the cellar's corner. It smelled dank, and the ground was cold. Damp earth clung to her already wet clothes, and Ava shivered uncontrollably. Her knees pulled up to her chin, she wrapped her arms around her legs, holding them tightly to her chest. She couldn't see much. The cellar was darker—if that were possible—than the night sky. It had to be nearing dawn. Had to be! But then she wasn't sure she was concerned that morning ever came. Here, in the corner of the cellar, glimpses of horror and grisly remembrances came back to her. They were things the morning light would not evaporate. The sun could not erase a nightmare.

"Ava." Noah's voice was soft. Coaxing. Not unlike someone who had cornered a petrified kitten and hoped to earn its trust.

She sensed him nearing her. Smelled him. Lake water. Night air. Something distinctly Noah. His fingertips touched her knee. Ava jerked back, squeezing closer to the hard-packed dirt wall of the cellar.

"What is this place, Ava?" he asked, but Ava knew he had already surmised the answer.

It was her home. The place she had lived until the day she'd wandered into Tempter's Creek.

"Do you remember? What happened here?"

Another pressing question she had no desire to answer.

Noah moved, his body making shifting noises in the darkness. Ava felt his shoulder as he settled in next to her, his back also against the wall. "We're going to have to find our way back home. I'm afraid we're not going to find Jipsy's body, and we're both sopping wet."

"I don't care." And she didn't. Not about Jipsy. Not about being wet. Not about a potential chill setting in. Nothing.

"I know." His two-word acceptance made Ava's heart still. She turned her head to look at him but could barely make out his form in the darkness. It felt safer that way. Having Noah faceless. Just a person in the dark with her, sharing in the hovering gloom of wickedness that lived here.

"This is your home?"

"Sure is." Her entire chest ached. It hurt with the weight of it.

"I'm sorry."

"Ain't your fault." And it wasn't. It never made sense to Ava, people apologizing for things they didn't have a hand in.

"I know. I'm empathizing with you."

"What's that?" She was thankful for the distraction.

His chuckle met her ears. "Never mind."

They didn't say anything more. Ava unfolded her arms from around her knees and stretched her hand toward the wall. It connected with the shelves she knew would be there. A glass jar met her fingertips. She felt it, wondering if it were canned carrots, or canned venison, or what type of food remained behind. Evidence of her mother's existence.

"I used to hide down here," she mumbled. Noah was silent. Ava dropped her hand back to her lap. "Arnie and Ricky always knew I did. But when I was little, they pretended they didn't."

She remembered that. Remembered Ricky's solid footsteps as he tromped down the ladder. Remembered the anxiety that would well up inside her when Ricky drew closer to finding her. She liked it better when Arnie found her. He'd just tap her. Ricky would slug her and holler "You're it!" with a voice that made her think he wanted to do more than just bruise her. "My brother Ricky had a mean streak," Ava admitted out loud.

"He did?" Noah's question encouraged her to talk. He was trying to be all preacher on her. Share her soul. Then he'd set to work on seein' it healed up and drawing nigh to Jesus.

She'd entertain him, for no other reason than her tongue wanted to speak even when her spirit wanted to withdraw. "Mm-hmm. Maybe it runs in the family. I don't know. Can't recall much about my family, to be truthful." No. That wasn't truthful. She was remembering more just being here. But she didn't want to.

"Do you think—?"

"Think Ricky killed my folks?" Ava interrupted. "No. Not when he wound up dead too. Don't make no sense, that way of reasonin'."

Noah cleared his throat as though he had a larger question on his mind.

"Spit it out, Preacher." He might as well, Ava determined. Sitting here wallowing in her personal horror was just going to get worse if she didn't get her mind a bit distanced from the emotion.

"Well, I was just going to ask—how do you know *who* died?"

Ava twisted her head in Noah's direction. "What do you mean?"

"If their bodies were never found, how do you know . . . ?"

"The blood. I was covered in it." And she remembered that. The screamin' too. She remembered the whacking. A gag rose in Ava's throat, and she swallowed it back. Best if the preacher stopped asking questions now.

"Did the folks in town come and look for your family?"

Ava swallowed the sour taste in her mouth. "That's what I recall. Councilman Pitford once told me it was akin to butcherin' at the meat market." And why Councilman Pitford had ever seen it right to tell her that, she'd never know!

Noah coughed. Maybe he was trying not to puke too. "But they never found your family, so how would he know to compare it to such?"

"I don't know." Ava worked her lips back and forth. She sniffed. Dang it, if she cried she'd be mad at herself! Cryin' in front of the preacher. 'Course, she'd already made a fool of herself. One of those blackouts. Where she'd wandered and didn't know what she did.

"Sorry I got all funny-like and took off on you." Ava diverted Noah from further questions.

He was quiet for a moment, and then, "Do you know why you do that?"

Ava stilled. Now she felt all weepy again. Weepy and helpless. "No." Her voice was small. Watery. She could hear it, so she bet he could too.

"They say when someone experiences trauma, each person reacts differently. Some go into a depression. Others pretend it never happened. Then there are those who drift off in their minds and—"

"So, I'm crazy?"

"I didn't say that."

"Sure ya didn't." Ava swiped at a tear on her cheek. God bless the darkness now.

"I didn't." He shifted and was even closer now. She could feel his shoulder press against hers. Part of Ava wanted to move away, but then another part held her there.

"I'm just saying, I think when the remembering becomes strong in you, your mind tries to blank it out. You go to places inside yourself that no one can get to."

"And then I try'n drown myself?"

"Were you? Drowning yourself?" Noah posed the question so poignantly, so directly, and with so much forgiveness in his tone, Ava felt another tear escaping her other eye.

She brushed it away. "No, I wasn't." Yet she didn't want to tell him how her mind had played tricks on her. Images of her dead mother floating at the bottom of the lake, her white face, her wide eyes. Her brother's hand reaching up toward her, trying to pull her down to be with them.

"I shouldn't be here." Her whisper was raw.

Noah didn't respond.

"I should be dead just like them."

"Why?"

The simple question made the tears flow harder. Ava made sure not to sniff, so that in the darkness of the cellar, Noah wouldn't be aware of the tears.

"I remember"—her voice shook—"climbing down here to hide, 'cause that's what I did when I needed to hide. I squished behind a barrel of potatoes. Me and my doll, and I held her, even though I was thirteen I held my doll like she was the last thing I had left. I nigh on squeezed the stuffing out of her, and I hid. I just—hid."

Noah's hand rested on hers, the shadows covering his movement. His fingers threaded through hers, his skin warm and real. Strength was in his hand, and sure, he probably meant nothing by it, but the way his fingers slid between hers left Ava breathless in a way she was not prepared for. She should move her hand away. But she didn't. She couldn't.

"Do you remember who was here that day?" Noah asked softly.

It was the question she wanted to answer. More than anything, Ava wanted to answer it. But all she could see in her memory was a pair of brown shoes as they clomped across the cellar floor toward her. And she'd looked up, up, and then . . . it was all blank. Just a murky image of someone who had left her here that day. Her and her doll.

Ava pulled her hand away from Noah's. She wrestled to her knees and began patting the floor.

"What are you doing?"

"Looking for my doll." Ava ran her hands over the earth, connected with a barrel. "My doll. I left her here. I left her behind." Sure enough, in the darkness behind the barrel, Ava's hand connected with the soft body of a doll. Pulling it toward her, she cradled it against her chest, her chin coming to rest on the doll's hard porcelain head, the hair feeling like straw against Ava's skin. "I left her behind," she murmured again, feeling not so different from her doll and from the empty cellar that was the last remnant of the Coons family's lives. "I left her behind."

That's what this place did, after all. It stole things. Abandoned innocence. In its trail, it left a bloody path of broken bodies and broken hearts.

28

The parsonage that had been more like a prison was now a respite, a place of hidden safety. They snuck back into the parsonage before daylight cast its full attention to the earth and before the lumbermen and wagons broke the stillness with the first hints of a busy day to come. Noah had closed the door behind them and locked it. He'd gone from window to window and made sure the curtains were pulled. Worry etched the corners of his eyes, as did defeat. His plan to bring a measure of dignity to Jipsy's death had fallen dismally shy of whatever resolution he'd figured would come of retrieving the woman's body.

They stood in the kitchen shivering in their wet clothes, both of them at an impasse, although Ava wasn't sure why.

"Best get into dry things," she said.

Noah's eyes trailed down her body and then he swiftly looked away. Toward the coffeepot, cold on the stove. "Good idea."

Ava glanced down at herself. For a second, she wondered why Noah had looked away so fast. Must be she was as ugly as a bug's ear. Then she noted, with some embarrassment, that her shirt had unbuttoned the top few buttons, and skin was peeking out in places that made sure anyone who saw knew she wasn't a girl anymore, but a full-fledged woman.

She clutched her shirt closed. "I'll go change."

"You do that." Noah made a pretense of checking the firebox of the woodstove. Darned if his own damp shirt wasn't stickin' to the muscles in his back. Ava stared for a long moment, lost in the ticklish feeling that traveled through her. A preacher shouldn't have muscles, should he? Not like those.

Noah lifted his head. His eyes locked with hers. "You'd best go, Ava."

"Yes." She scurried away. Blushin' like a schoolgirl probably. Once in her room, she shrugged out of her blouse, her overalls, her wet underthings. There weren't many options for other clothes other'n the two dresses Hanny had brought for her. Probably scoured from the mission bin at church. Probably castoffs—with her luck—from prissy Mrs. Sanderson.

Regardless, Ava slipped the navy-blue dress over her head, making sure the pearl buttons on the pleated front were securely buttoned. Once she'd finished, she wrestled her hair into a braid. A look in the mirror reminded her of the shadows in her heart, as they were reflected under her eyes. She should just collapse on the bed. Drift away into dreamland and try to forget the horrifying memories that once again began to crowd into her thoughts.

Desperate to escape them, Ava hurried from her room and back down the stairs.

"Slow down or you'll break a leg, child." Hanny's voice floated from the sitting room.

Ava ducked into the room, looking around for Noah. Hanny was quick to notice. She was already seated on the sofa, embroidery in her lap. "Noah has already left. Places to go, people to see, I expect."

"Why are you here?" Ava didn't mean to sound rude; it was just confused curiosity as to the quick shift of Noah's presence to Hanny's.

"Why, I brought over some cinnamon rolls." Hanny gave Ava a meaningful look filled with censure and grandmotherly sternness. "A good excuse to come over to the parsonage. Check in on you two."

"We're fine," Ava answered quickly. She flopped onto a chair, then popped back up and fidgeted with the curtain at the window.

"Mm-hmm" was all Hanny said.

Ava walked the length of the sitting room—which wasn't that far—and back to the window. She wanted to look out, to see if she could spot Noah across the street at the church. Or maybe to take in normal life outside. It would be nice to witness a day of sunshine, to be able to leave the parsonage without worry of the ramifications of those actions. She'd give just about anything to perch on a barrel of bootleg whiskey outside the general store and shoot the breeze with Ned.

"You cannot keep pacing, child. You'll be the death of me!" Hanny exclaimed. "There's no need to rush that any sooner than it's already coming."

Ava stopped pacing, and it landed her in front of Noah's desk. The corner of Emmaline's letter stuck out from beneath a few other envelopes. Ava fingered it, recalling the words of remorse the woman had penned Noah. Who was she? What was her story? And why did she owe Noah an apology?

"I wouldn't if I were you."

Did Hanny have eyes on the top of her head? She was still bent over her embroidery.

Ava jerked her hand back. "Do you know who she is?"

"Who *who* is?"

"Emmaline."

Hanny paused and lifted her head. "You read his letter?"

"No," Ava lied.

"You did or you wouldn't know her name. It's not on the envelope."

"Do you know who she is?"

"*She* is none of your business. And no, I really don't. The reverend is quite private, you know."

Ava dropped onto a chair, the air from the cushion poofing from her weight. She couldn't figure why it bothered her, but there was a little pit in her stomach. She jumped up again. "I can't just sit here and do nothin'."

Hanny sighed, hooked her needle through the embroidery, and set it aside. "You've not much choice."

"I do. I can march down to Officer Larson and let him know he's plumb wrong about it all. I didn't kill Matthew, and I didn't kill Jipsy. You can't blame a person just 'cause they were a victim of something unsolved."

"No. You *shouldn't*, but people do. They talk and conspire and wheedle gossip until it sounds like the truth."

"No matter how it hurts someone? It's all right to discuss another's life and hang them with no sort of proof?"

Hanny offered her a sad smile. "Sometimes they believe they have proof." She struggled to her feet, pushing off the sofa arm with her hand. "Here. If you need something to occupy your time . . ." She neared Noah's desk and pulled a few sheets of stationery from the center drawer. "Write a letter to the missionaries. They'll appreciate the correspondence, and you'll be doing something generous with your time."

Ava took the proffered paper, looking at it as though it were going to disintegrate in her hand.

Hanny limped toward the doorway. "No time is wasted when used for others. I'm going to make tea before I head home and cause more questions by being here too long."

Ava watched Hanny disappear around the corner. All right then. Write a letter. It might get her mind off last night. Off the ruins of her home. Off Lost Lake. Off Noah . . .

She moved to the desk and sat in Noah's chair, reaching for a pencil. What did one write to a missionary?

Dear person of God,
   Most people think I'm a murderer, but I figured I'd write you anyway.

Ava closed her eyes against the dark humor. Only one name reverberated in her mind, and she didn't know why. She didn't understand the repetitive nature of why she kept thinking of this person, considering she didn't know her at all. But it was eating at Ava's insides. The not knowing. It pretty much seemed like every part of her life was touched by not knowing.

She set her pencil to the paper.

It was time to figure out something. However small, it was at least a distraction from her problems.

Dear Emmaline . . .

The front door burst open. Noah hustled inside like a man being chased—'course, he more'n likely was. Ava sat on her hands, primly as she could, in the chair in the front room. She avoided looking at Noah's desk. Her letter to Emmaline was long gone. Hanny had taken it with her when she'd left, after Ava slipped it between two other letters Noah had addressed and stamped. Hanny offered to go to the post office. Ava hoped the woman didn't thumb through the envelopes and discard Ava's letter to Emmaline.

Noah dropped a pile of books, including his Bible, on his desk. He raked his hand through his hair, and with it all disheveled, Ava couldn't stop staring at him. Her stomach did funny things. Especially when she saw the cords on his forearms where he'd rolled up his sleeves.

"Listen to me." He crossed the room and kneeled in front of her. Eye to eye, she was distracted by the sincerity in the brown fathomless depths. "Ava."

She blinked, then met his eyes. His narrowed for a moment, and then he seemed to shake himself out of whatever thought had crossed his mind.

"The town's going to be all riled up in a bit. They found Jipsy's body."

"How?" Ava scooted to the edge of the chair, leaning forward.

Noah's smile was lopsided and confessionary. "I tried a similar tactic, only in the daylight. I took a walk."

"A walk," Ava repeated.

He nodded. "Yeah. A long one. One of prayer and supplication that led me to an out-of-the-way poplar grove and Jipsy's body. No one is questioning me, especially since you're supposedly not under my care anymore."

"They wouldn't. You're the preacher." Ava cocked an eyebrow. "But how'd you find the poplar grove?"

"It's a lot easier to find in the morning."

"Seems like that was a simpler solution all the way around," Ava acknowledged.

Noah rocked back on his heels and stood. "Yes, well. Regardless, I reported it to Officer Larson, who took a team out to retrieve Jipsy."

Noah seemed a bit more hopeful. "But from what I could tell, Jipsy wasn't—it didn't look like it was consistent with how Hubbard was killed. I'm hoping Larson will see reason and be able to communicate that more effectively to the rabble-rousers like Chuck Weber who are so convinced you're somehow behind this mess."

"They'll see what they want to see. They always have."

Noah rolled down his shirtsleeves. He buttoned them at the cuffs. "I'm going to put on a tie and clean myself up a bit. Then I will head back to the police station. I'll be able to get a feel for how the dice will roll, and how it will affect you."

"Be careful." She whispered it, not as a backward, backwoods girl, but as a woman. She'd known the preacher for a short time really, but he was laying himself out on the line for her in a way no one ever had before. It only seemed fair someone worry about his welfare too.

Noah gave her a platonic tip of the head that didn't match the rush of affection Ava had felt only moments before. "I will."

And then he was off to his room upstairs. Ava could hear his footsteps. She could picture him tying his tie and shrugging into a jacket and makin' himself look all preacher-like. But she could tell something else about Noah Pritchard in their short but tumultuous time together. He wasn't a natural-born preacher, and those coals in his eyes? They darn sure were because he was a man. Very much a man.

29

Wren

The SAR teams had dwindled. It was the disgusting truth about tragedy, alive or dead, missing or taken. Eventually, life's demands called even its most well-meaning people back, until all that remained were the specifically assigned lot.

Wren sought to rescue Meghan from the heavy atmosphere of the Rec Barn. Ben had reluctantly agreed. "Thanks for taking Meghan. Go shopping. Get coffee. It's Tuesday—get tacos. But no more looking for Ava Coons—or seeing that *man* who puts ideas in her head. You'll both go *loca*, and it doesn't help anyone."

Wren looked over her taco at Meghan, who had taken one bite out of a nacho chip. Her taco remained cooling on her plate.

Meghan's eyes were red-rimmed, her skin pale. She picked at a chip on her plate, breaking it into smaller pieces. "You heard what they're saying now that it's been a week?"

Wren nodded. She had. It was turning into a retrieval. Since they'd confirmed they were Trina Nesbitt's remains, the writing was bold on the wall. The odds of finding Jasmine alive in the woods were slim. Now that the authorities were factoring in the possibility of abduction, the investigation and search took remarkably different turns.

"They've found no evidence that Jasmine was taken?" Wren

asked outright. She hated being so blunt. Hated the pain that stretched across Meghan's face and hated how Meghan simply accepted it.

"Nothing strong enough to give them any direction." Meghan snorted in disgust. "And they thought I was nuts. I *told* them someone took my daughter!"

Actually, she'd told them *Ava Coons* had taken Jasmine, but Wren didn't correct her.

"And the sweatshirt they found? The other blood in the woods?" She hated to ask, but there was no skirting the facts.

Meghan shrugged. "There was nothing on the sweatshirt that belonged to anyone other than Jasmine."

Wren shifted uncomfortably in her seat. Of course they would have run a DNA test on it to see if it belonged to Jasmine.

Meghan smiled weakly. "Ben said the blood they found in the woods came back as animal."

"Thank God," Wren breathed.

"Good afternoon, ladies." A male voice broke into their lunch, and Wren looked up to meet the friendly but unwelcome features of Wayne Sanderson.

Wren gave him a startled glance, mentally running through a zillion frantic ideas as to how to avoid further conversation. This was exactly what Ben had *not* wanted. A run-in with Wayne Sanderson, who only fed Meghan's fears of abduction and death. Apparently lifting a chip to her mouth was not a subtle enough hint that they were eating and didn't want to chat.

"I want to apologize for the other day," Wayne said, seeming sincere. He turned to Wren. "The story of Ava Coons has always been strong with me. Then with Trina having gone missing . . ." He choked up and looked away for a long moment. "I was insensitive."

Wren studied him. "Thank you."

Wayne didn't leave. He shifted his weight on his other foot as he stood at the end of their booth table. "With the . . . uh, recent developments, I sat down with the police and told them my suspicions."

Meghan's head jerked up.

Oh no. Wren bit down on the chip in her mouth.

Tears shone in Wayne's eyes again. He blinked rapidly, and they cleared. "I had to stand by my recommendation. I've begged them for *years* to dredge up Lost Lake. I'm not saying your daughter . . ." He held up his hand and gulped. "I'm simply saying I thought it should be explored when Trina disappeared, and they wouldn't do it. They were so sure of themselves." Bitterness laced his words. Wayne shook his head. "Now they've found Trina . . . but your daughter is still missing."

Wren gripped the edge of the table. Was he insinuating that Jasmine was at the bottom of Lost Lake? Because it was what he'd believed about Trina Nesbitt?

Meghan sucked in a breath. A sob? Wren wasn't sure. She reached across the table to rest her hand on Meghan's. Looking up at Wayne, she half growled, "Mr. Sanderson, what is your interest in Trina Nesbitt?"

Wayne pressed his lips together as he weighed his words. "The chief of police and I go way back, to high school. He knows I wouldn't suggest a small town like Tempter's Creek squander its resources on a theory that has little probability of producing results."

Wren waited. He hadn't answered her question.

Wayne continued, taking her lack of response as an opening. "I've been doing research for years . . ."

Wren startled as Meghan drew her hand away and scooted to the far end of their booth. "Please," she said and patted the brown seat. "I want to hear more." Meghan met Wren's eyes and held them. "I do, Wren. Anything to find Jasmine." Her voice broke. "Even—searching Lost Lake."

Wayne sat down and then reached for a chip, crunching on it without bothering to ask if he could have one. "Lost Lake was central to the murders of the Coons family. The conclusion was that Ava disposed of them in Lost Lake. Years later, they said she had little guardianship or constraints, and she began killing again. It wasn't until a local preacher apparently took her in that the killings waned. But then Ava disappeared. There is speculation she lived the rest of her years in the forest and around Lost Lake, although no one ever proved that."

"That has nothing to do with Jasmine—or Trina," Wren argued, for the sake of logic, reason, and sort of hoping it might shake some sense into her own addled mind.

Wayne reached for another chip. He picked it up and broke it into a few pieces. "Look at Ava Coons like this chip." Wayne gave Meghan a sideways glance to make sure he had her attention. He did. "You break it into pieces, and most would say you don't have a chip anymore. But really you do. You just have bits that spread out and touch other parts of your plate. But the chip—or in this case, Ava Coons—started as a whole. The remnants of someone who has infiltrated Tempter's Creek and still does."

"And Jasmine saw her," Meghan affirmed.

Wayne pushed the chip pieces together into a pile.

Wren interjected, "Just because the Coons family became a ghost story doesn't mean Ava is still haunting the woods." It couldn't. But the image of the woman in the Markhams' driveway made Wren's insistence lack conviction.

"Doesn't it?" Wayne's gaze was direct. "History has a way of repeating itself. People prey off old superstitions."

Wren eyed Wayne. "So you're saying the Coons story could be a cover for someone else's deviousness?"

Wayne nodded. "A diversion. Like a fog to confuse the reality of the situation. Which is that someone took Trina ten years ago. Someone has taken Jasmine."

"But I thought you believed Ava Coons haunted the woods?" Meghan's voice was small and unsteady.

Wayne smiled patiently. "Everything in the woods is infused with Ava Coons. It started when she was a child and murdered her family. No one ever truly resolved that case. It went cold. Ava disappeared. Since then, others have too—or they've died—with zero explanation."

"How many others?" Wren asked.

Wayne raised his brows as he considered and drew in a deep breath. "The Coons family, two murders after them, Trina . . ." His voice wobbled. "Others."

"Others?"

Wayne tapped his fingers on the table. "A hunter went missing in the sixties. His body *was* found, and a gunshot wound apparently killed him. But he was missing for quite some time, and no one could ever figure out how he shot himself. It was an awkward angle and didn't suit a suicide or an accident."

"Murder?"

Wayne met her eyes. He was daring her to argue with his theories. "Who knows."

"So, one hunter?" Wren attempted to grasp at reason. "And his story has nothing to do with Trina—or Ava Coons."

Wayne scowled. "So you say."

"Jasmine *saw* her," Meghan insisted quietly from her corner in the booth. "She *saw* Ava Coons."

Wayne reached over and patted Meghan's hand. "I believe you."

Of course Wayne would say that. Wren glared at him. But while she glared, she hated the parts of her that believed Meghan too. The irrational parts that told her, before Ava Coons murdered her family, these woods had been a peaceful place. A place of respite. Of nature. Of God's creation. Now they were acres upon acres of land still overshadowed by a murderous Ava Coons.

30

Wren parked her truck and shut off the engine. Here she was. Back at the town park, staring at the small playground, her eyes scanning the woods where Jasmine had supposedly seen "Ava Coons"—or some rendition of the ghostly murderess. An actual abductor? Perhaps. Sitting in her truck, Wren forced herself to take some deep breaths. Pray. Attempting to calm herself after Wayne Sanderson. Perhaps the man had ideas that might help, but telling them to the mother of the missing child? There was something intense about Wayne. Wren couldn't put her finger on it. There were amateur sleuths interested in cold cases and legends, and then there were obsessed individuals who inserted themselves into actual crimes for the thrill of it . . . or because they were invested in it personally for some reason.

And now Wren was here. At the park. Indulging her own questions, insecurities, and conspiracies. She had reluctantly dropped Meghan off at the library. Meghan wanted to be alone, but Wren knew better. She was going to research. Search for clues. Do what the police were already doing—and with better resources. When Wren offered to stay, Meghan had been adamant that she needed time alone. Since the library was public, Wren wasn't too concerned about Meghan, but she still didn't like the way Meghan urged her to be off.

Wren drew in a deep breath, counting. *One, two, three, four, five, annnnnnnnd blow out. One, two, three, four—*

Wren froze.

There she was. The woman. Standing just inside the edge of the woods. Her body was partially hidden by the branches and bush in front of her.

"Ava Coons," Wren whispered. She jerked the door open. Leaping from her truck, she shouted, "No!" when Ava spun and disappeared into the woods.

Wren broke into a sprint, crossing the park yard in a few seconds. She pushed her way into the woods, her tennis shoes connecting with the deer trail she'd first visited with Meghan.

"Ava!" she called after the figure that was fast retreating into the woods. Wren felt silly calling after a woman who had died decades ago. A branch scraped her face. "Ava!"

The woman ahead of her was fast, and she knew the terrain. Wren glimpsed her overall-clad form before she ducked to the right and disappeared again.

"No, no, no!" Wren muttered, picking up speed. Her foot landed on a root that jutted up from the trail. It bruised the ball of her foot, but she kept moving. The trees were thicker the deeper Wren went. Saplings threaded through the low branches of cedar and pine, and oak trees lent their own version of shadows, making the forest floor dark even in the afternoon.

She shoved aside the scraggly arms of a cedar and froze. Up ahead, on the trail, the woman stilled. Yards away, Wren could make out her face. It was older—not the youthful version of Ava Coons that Wren had in her mind. A braid hung over one shoulder. Peppery gray. Wrinkles lined the woman's face. Her eyes were wide. Fear. Concern. She reminded Wren of a spooked deer.

Wren held up her hand in peace. "Ava?" The name came naturally as if it were the truth. "Ava, please." She tested the woman's courage and took another step toward her. "I need to talk to you."

An expression spread across the woman's face. Wren stilled. There was a viciousness in it, mixed with a darkness that overtook the woman's eyes. Obsession of the worst sort, the kind that stole a person's soul, held them captive. She was a woman who would not be thwarted, deterred, or questioned. This Wren could assess by the narrowing of the woman's already intense eyes.

Wren reached for the trunk of the tree next to her, and she braced her hand on it to stabilize her suddenly unsteady legs. Instead of fleeing, Wren took yet another step. She had to. She was getting lost in the woman's black eyes. They were speaking to her, telling her something, even as the ominous darkness reached the corners of the woman's eyes and drew them into slits.

The theme song to *The Lord of the Rings* blared from Wren's pocket. The woman's eyes flew open. She spun and fled deeper into the woods, sticks and twigs snapping as she ran. Wren's legs became like jelly, and she sank to the forest floor. She should follow. No. She shouldn't.

What had just happened?

Her phone continued its peal. Wren dug it from her jeans pocket and answered, "Hello?" Her voice was breathless.

"Where are you?" It was Eddie.

"Umm . . . at the park?" She didn't sound convincing. *Oh, hey! Yeah, I was just chasing Ava Coons through the forest.* That would go over like ketchup on pancakes.

"I need you."

The words shocked Wren from her own current circumstances. Eddie never said things like that. Never. The lump of fear from her encounter with the woman turned into a different sort of dread. "What is it?"

"It's Mom." Eddie choked. Was he crying? "You need to get here fast, Wren."

Gravel spun from her tires as Wren gunned her truck up the Markham driveway. She slammed the brakes as she pulled up in front of the garage. Putting the truck in park, Wren wrenched the door open, slamming it behind her as she sprinted for the house. No one was in the kitchen, so she hurried through the living room toward the back hall and Patty's room. As she rushed around the corner into the hall, she collided with Gary. His hands grabbed her upper arms and stabilized her. Wren looked up into his face. Drawn and haggard, his eyes reflected that moment right before your soul was ripped from you.

"Patty?" Wren asked, breathless.

Gary's face contorted as he tried to control his emotion. He coughed, clearing his throat. "She's still with us, but . . . going downhill fast. The hospice nurse said we should gather."

"Oh, Gary!" Wren didn't bother to ask permission. She wrapped her arms around him. Gary and Patty were soulmates. They were everything Wren wanted someday in a relationship—with Troy?—maybe. But she could feel the grief in Gary, in the way he hugged her in return. He was in disbelief. Shock even. While it wasn't a surprise this moment had come, was it any less traumatic?

Gary pulled back and patted Wren's upper arm. He sniffed, but a tear traveled down his cheek, burying itself in his beard. "Come."

Wren couldn't speak. The burning in her face was every ounce of internal angst spreading through her blood, her pores, her muscles. She couldn't do this. She couldn't. She couldn't say goodbye.

Gary rubbed her arm. "Kiddo, we can do this."

Wren felt awful, shaking her head at the man whose wife was being torn from him in the name of cancer. "Gary . . ." Tears dripped from her cheeks and ran down her neck.

Gary's own fell. "She's ready to go. She is. It's time for her to go Home."

Wren nodded. "Okay." The empty hollow inside her pressed out any other concerns. It was a resignation to the inevitable. The inevitable stealing away what was most precious and leaving behind only whispers to accompany them into the future.

Every footstep toward Patty's room was weighted. Time slowed to an almost imperceptible movement. Wren entered the doorway, Gary just ahead of her. Sunlight splayed across the room, the filmy white curtains creating a quiet glow of beauty. Patty lay on the bed, her eyes closed. Wren could see her breathing. Labored . . . a long pause . . . slowly releasing. She was frail—more frail-looking than she'd ever been. If she could have seen the other world that hovered just beyond the veil of spirituality, Wren was certain she would see Patty's soul reaching from the shell of a body that had betrayed her life here on earth.

Eddie sat by his mom, his frame curled as close to her as he could be. He held her hand so gently against his cheek. His eyes lifted and met Wren's. Her breath caught at the helpless pain in them. A lost, stricken look that knew he could do nothing to keep his beloved mother here. A willingness to relinquish her to her Heavenly Father. A brokenness that in that relinquishment came separation. A tearing, a stripping away of who Patty was—to all of them. Eddie was her son, a little boy, a man . . .

Wren approached the bed, dropping to her knees beside Eddie. Gary lay down next to his wife. The moment was intimate, desperate, and yet somehow peace entered the room as Patty wrestled for breath. Her eyelids flickered. Gary took Patty's other hand, holding it. She squeezed his fingers. Wren bit her lip hard. She laid her hand on Patty's blanket-covered leg. It was warm. Soft. She was alive . . . but she was leaving.

Wren tried to summon strength from deep inside her soul, only there was none to find. She couldn't still the stream of grief as it rolled quietly down her face. Gary settled his forehead against Patty's shoulder, his eyes closed.

"Mama . . ." Eddie reached out and brushed his hand across Patty's forehead.

Her eyes fluttered. She opened them, but it seemed as though she barely focused. Then came a brief respite—an awareness. Wren could see the acceptance in Patty's expression. Even so, in every crevice of her face, she was a mother. No matter when a person held hands with death, they reached with their other to hold on to those they loved.

"Buddy . . ." she rasped. Her fingers moved against Eddie's face, her fingertips memorizing the man he'd become, yet her eyes seemed to see the boy he had been.

"It's okay, Mama." Eddie turned his face into her hand. He closed his eyes. "Go in peace," he whispered. He was crying. Wren had never seen Eddie cry. Not like this. Not the letting-go type of tears that left a person with a gentle, empty ache.

Wren bit her lip, not noticing the pain.

Patty turned her head toward Wren. "You're never lost," she whispered. A tear trailed down her cheek. "His eyes are on the sparrows—" a pause, a small smile—"on my Wren."

Wren's face crumpled. She sucked in a sob.

Patty turned back to Eddie. "My Buddy." There were no words. There didn't need to be. Everything a mother needed to express to her boy was in her eyes. The cherished love and years. The moments she treasured she now passed on to Eddie to hold.

Gary stroked his wife's cheek. Patty closed her eyes, but her words were now for him. "Don't you cry now." Her hand released Gary's. "I'll see you soon."

Eddie's chin shook. His chest heaved, and he laid his head on Patty's shoulder. Gently. So gently, a soft hum filtered through her lips. Their song.

Good night.

Eddie hummed with her.

"*Au revoir*," Patty whispered, and then there was silence.

None of them moved. Gary lay against Patty, his eyes closed, tears staining his cheeks. Eddie mirrored his father.

Wren felt an ache spread through every crevice of her spirit. An ache that held hands with an inexplicable peace.

Patty had gone Home.

31

Ava

She'd heard Noah return to the parsonage late last night. She'd heard him sigh too. And it didn't help this morning when they met at the breakfast table with each of them avoiding the other's eyes. Noah looked downright guiltier than a man who'd spent the night gambling away his life savings, only Ava was sure the guilt had nothing to do with that. It was the fact that she was there. Sitting at the table, eating a piece of toast and fried egg with the same combination on a plate for him. Like an old married couple. But they weren't married. There was the problem—leastways how Noah saw it.

The truth was, Ava had thought less of their unmarried predicament than she had of the predicament of Jipsy's body and Matthew Hubbard's death. In light of that, the parsonage pairing of the two of them seemed trivial at best. Either way, it did make for awkward eye contact in the morning, and Hanny hadn't bustled in with some excuse to make the situation any less awkward.

"You find out anythin'?" Ava had finally broached the subject of Jipsy and the police.

"Just that Weber still has folks around town antsy, hoping you don't show back up. There's talk you've escaped justice and are already miles away from here." Noah lifted his eyes for a brief second as he took a sip of coffee. "Others think you're hiding out, waiting to get your next victim."

The idea was ironic. It also didn't help nothing. She was stuck here at the parsonage, in hiding. Noah was stuck having her here in hiding. He was bearing the brunt of her life on his shoulders. It just wasn't fair. And that he was carryin' it without complaint? Wasn't right. Just wasn't.

The more she sat, the more she dwelt on Jipsy's death, on Matthew Hubbard's death, and the more she knew she could not leave it all to rest on Noah's shoulders. After Noah had withdrawn to the church to work on pastoral things, Ava made quick work of preparing. Her overalls were dry, but they were soiled and in sore need of washing. She kept on her navy-blue dress she'd worn to breakfast, tied her hair back with a ribbon, and slipped her feet into her shoes. They were still wet. She opted for bare feet, and within minutes she'd snuck from the parsonage.

Ava dodged the main street, slinking behind the buildings in the shaded alleyways. Now, a noise sent Ava sprawling against the brick wall of the general store. No one should be back here, but then that didn't account for the fact that sometimes they stored goods on the back dock. But a quick survey assured Ava the doors to the dock were closed, and there wasn't anyone around Ava could see. She just needed to get to the station—to the police.

Maybe it was suicide of a sort that didn't take her life but took her hopes of a future. Still, she needed to get Noah off the hook. He was bait just dangling, and some big-toothed fish was going to bite. Noah would be eaten alive, and it wouldn't save her any more than if he was completely out of the picture. Ava figured if she could get to the station without being seen by the people of Tempter's Creek, she could bank on the slim hope that Officer Larson would listen to her. Give her some benefit of the doubt. He had, after all, put up a fight for her the first night the town had grouped together after Matthew had died. He could find a different solution for protecting her until this was all sorted. Or, if he wanted, he could just throw her in jail. Either way.

Ava stilled and leaned against the back wall of the general store.

She wasn't a silly girl. She knew she was beginning to carry a torch for the preacher. Fact was, it worried her. That she cared about anyone at all.

"Where'n heck have you been?" The voice behind her whispered loudly, and Ava bit back a shriek, ducking down by the corner of the store behind a sumac bush. She leveled wide eyes at the person who had spotted her. Ava's shoulders lowered. She blew out a breath of relief.

"Ned."

His hair seemed grayer on the sides since the last time she'd seen him . . . what was it, just a week ago? Time was going too slow, and this mess was like a slow-spreading barrel of spilled maple syrup.

The lean, older man looked in all directions before squatting down next to Ava, pushing a sumac branch from his face. "Town's gonna be right mad if they see you lurkin' in the shrubs!" he stated.

Ava did her own quick surveyal of the area. "Don't I know it!"

"Where've you been?" Ned batted the branch again as it sprang back and scratched his cheek.

"Don't matter." Ava trusted Ned, but she had no intention of incriminating Noah to anyone. "I need to talk to Officer Larson."

"Whatever for?" Ned reared back. "He'd be the one to arrest you!"

"I know, but he also said there wasn't proof I did anything to Hubbard, and it's gotta be the same with Jipsy."

Ned grimaced. "Jipsy. Who'da thought!"

"I bet Widower Frisk is fit to be tied." Ava could only imagine the old man. He'd either be moanin' in his liquor or fuming at the world.

"He's a wrong number any way you spin it. Jipsy coulda done better than him." Ned affirmed. "But he swears up and down he'd never have hurt her—he ever lift a hand to Jipsy when you were there?"

Ava shot Ned a quick look. "No." No, Widower Frisk had only been rough with her. Jipsy had stood between them, and Widower

Frisk never crossed Jipsy. She had some sort of magic hold on the man. He worshiped her as much as he still had a wandering eye.

Ned scooted closer to her. Ava could smell cigarette on his clothes. He whispered conspiratorially, "I was thinkin'—if Jipsy is dead, it might be Mrs. Sanderson's fault."

Ava swiped at a black fly that landed on her neck. "Mrs. Sanderson? Why on earth would she have any reason to off Jipsy?"

"Jipsy wasn't no friend of hers. You know, Mrs. Snooty-Pants thinkin' she's better than everyone else. I heard tell Jipsy was planning on letting out some secrets about her. Scandal. All that."

"Like what?" Ava had not heard of this.

"Don't know for sure. Somethin' about Mrs. Sanderson and Matthew Hubbard."

Ava tried to silence her snort of laughter. "Mrs. Sanderson and Matthew Hubbard?" she repeated. "You've lost your ever-lovin' mind, Ned."

He looked offended. "Have not. You saw how upset she was the other night at the town meeting."

"Upset with *me*!" Ava retorted. "Not Jipsy. Mrs. Sanderson thinks *I* killed Matthew."

"That's my point. Why'd she care one way or another who did it unless she cared about Matthew?"

Ava contemplated this for a moment. Matthew Hubbard. In all the hoopla of Jipsy and being accused of murder and blacking out, Ava hadn't allowed herself to dwell on him. He was in his early forties, twice Mrs. Sanderson's senior and a bit more Ava's senior. But he'd been a decent man. Nothing special. But—

"He worked for Sanderson," Ned said, interrupting her thoughts. "Stands to reason the missus would've met him."

Ava waved Ned into silence. She looked around them again, afraid someone else was going to round the back of the mercantile or open the loading dock doors. When she was reassured they were still alone, she responded, "If Mrs. Sanderson was goin' to kill anyone, she'd use arsenic or somethin' fancy. She wouldn't use an ax or—" Ava caught herself. She wasn't about to admit to Ned that she had laid eyes on Jipsy's body. That the woman had enough blood on her clothes that whoever had done it had been up close and angry. Not with an ax either. Ava guessed it was a knife, which meant someone had stabbed Jipsy several times. She couldn't fathom pinch-faced Mrs. Sanderson in all her delicate femininity driving a knife into Jipsy once, let alone more than once.

"Be that as it may . . ." Ned rose from his crouch and glanced around. "I'd put money on it."

"And what is your point, then? What am I s'posed to do about it?"

Ned eyed Ava as if she were dumb. Maybe she was. He was only a tad older than Matthew Hubbard. Maybe years added some reason and figurin' into a man's mind that she simply didn't have yet.

"You want to clear your name, right?" Ned asked.

"Of course."

"Then you'd best get that woman alone and get her to tell you everything. Or find some sort of proof she did it."

"But what about Hubbard?"

"What about him? He's dead and gone. There isn't a thing you can do about that."

"I know, but if Mrs. Sanderson offed Jipsy 'cause she was jealous, who killed Hubbard?"

Ned stopped. Frowned. "Dunno. One murder at a time, Ava, one murder at a time."

———

Slinking around town like a bandit was one thing, but doing it in the daylight was a whole other lot of talents Ava was pretty certain she'd run out of real quick. Ned sauntered off to avoid looking suspicious, leaving Ava to scurry from the bushes and head into the woods that trailed along the border of town. She diverted from her intention to find Larson, to beg for his leniency and bank on his ability to reason based on evidence and not emotion. Darn if Ned's suspicion hadn't gotten under her skin now. And it didn't make a lick of sense! No more than the wild assumption that Ava herself had killed Hubbard and Jipsy. 'Course talkin' never hurt anyone, and it mayhap was a better idea than bustin' into the police station and blabberin' out a self-defense.

Ava squirmed as she eyed the Sanderson house. Here she was in the Sandersons' woods at the border where the tree line met the lawn. Ava was lost as to what to do next, so she made practice of breaking sticks into one-inch sections while waiting for some sort of brilliance to invade her mind and resolve this entire mess she was in. She couldn't rightly go up and knock on the door! Mrs. Sanderson had never been one for conversing kindly. There was a way about Mrs. Sanderson. An education, an etiquette maybe, that made her feel ages older than Ava, even though they truly were mere years apart.

The screen door on the back porch swung open, and Ava ducked down so she wasn't seen. Mrs. Sanderson stepped out, looking all pretty in a green polka-dot dress that flowed midway down her shapely legs. Her blond hair was cut chin-length and waved perfectly. The woman made her way to a chair and table, took a seat, and primly opened a small book. Probably poetry. Ava couldn't picture Mrs. Sanderson wasting her time on fiction. She was too good for stories.

It was now or never. Ned had said she should just ask. But who in their right mind would up and respond, *Oh yes, I did murder Jipsy. I took a knife and buried it in her multiple times. She was so vexing.*

Ava rolled her eyes at her own thoughts. No. She'd have to be smarter than asking outright. Maybe if she—

A rough hand clapped over her mouth. The motion jerked her head back against a man's chest. She grabbed at the hand, but his other arm came up around her midsection, pinning her to him. As he dragged her backward, Ava tried to scream into the callused palm. Instead, all that released were whimpers and squeals. She kicked at the ground, but he was too strong for her.

He clasped her head against him. Ava couldn't move it to make out who had snatched her.

"Sneaky little chit." The words growled in her ear, the man's breath hot against her skin.

Ava squirmed. His grip tightened.

"Goin' to go to Sanderson, eh? Think they'll help ya?"

Ava strained to recognize the voice. It was the same hoarse whisper as in the church the other night. A whisper that seemed purposefully disguised. Speaking an octave lower than their normal pitch maybe? His mouth brushed her temple as he held his cheek and jaw against her head.

"Murdering witch. It's in your blood. You *feed* off the killin'. Forty whacks and all that nonsense is as much about you as anyone!"

Ava grunted. She tried to kick with her feet, but he'd pulled her back far enough to where she was stretched out at an angle against the earth, her head and shoulders braced against his body. She twisted, trying to identify him. All she could see was an unfamiliar hat pulled down over eyes and tilted enough that the only parts of the face Ava could see were a mouth and a chin.

"I should snap your neck right here an' now and be done with you."

But he didn't. Ava twisted. He rammed his knuckles into her cheek. Ava's scream was garbled, the violent act shocking her into submission. The throbbing of her face was equal only to the heat of pain the blow had caused.

"Breaking into the church. Sneaking off with the reverend."

Ava wrestled against him. He jerked her tighter to his chest. The chin that pressed against her shoulder was clean-shaven. Whiskered, but no beard. Ava racked her memory trying to place who she knew in Tempter's Creek—aside from Noah—that was clean-shaven. Seemed like every man from Widower Frisk to Officer Larson had a full beard.

"No. I'm not gonna end you. Not yet." He squeezed her until

Ava was gasping for air, her chest constricting beneath his clutch. "Too much fun watchin' you squirm and hide. You deserve to, you know. And I'm goin' to *hunt* you. How does it feel to be the prey, my pet? *My* prey? How does it feel?"

He launched her forward with a shove. Ava cried out, her body smashing into the forest floor, twigs stabbing at her bare arms and legs. She rolled over and tried to sit up to see who had accosted her. Crashing reverberated through the forest as he ran. The snapping of branches. Ava glimpsed blue denim. An arm clad in brown wool. But he was soon gone.

Ava clapped a hand to her bruised face, and this time her breaths came in short sobs. She swallowed them back. Cryin' wasn't goin' to solve nothin'. Crawling to her feet, she raised her shoulder and tilted her head so her dress would soak up some of the blood welling up in the corner of her lip. He had split it when he'd struck her cheek. As she brought her arm away from her mouth, Ava felt the warmth of the blood smear against her cheek.

"Good Lord in heaven!" A feminine voice trilled from the forest edge.

Ava met the shocked and horrified blue-eyed gaze of Mrs. Sanderson.

"Ava Coons, you little devil."

32

"This might sting."

Ava eyed Mrs. Sanderson as she squeezed water from a wash-cloth and lifted it to Ava's lip. She sat at the Sandersons' kitchen table, which was already finer than any table Ava had ever sat her bottom at before. Lace covered it, a vase of wildflowers perched in the middle, and a long slab of polished wood was on the far end, on which rested what appeared to be a freshly made blackberry pie.

Mrs. Sanderson dabbed at the blood. Ava winced, the warm water seeping into the split on her lip.

"Who did this?"

Ava didn't answer. If she was bein' honest, Mrs. Sanderson scared her now. If Ned was right—if she really killed Jipsy—Ava needed to be on her guard.

"You're not going to speak?" Another dab with the wet cloth.

Ava tightened her lips.

Mrs. Sanderson submerged the cloth into the bowl of water she'd brought to the table. Ava noticed a few wet spots dotting her dress front. "You are aware all of Tempter's Creek is looking for you?"

Ava nodded.

Mrs. Sanderson opened a drawer below the kitchen counter and pulled out a metal box. Returning to the table, she raised the lid. Inside were bandage supplies and various ointments. She set to work on Ava's lip, the silence growing between them. Ava could hear Mrs. Sanderson's quiet breathing. Her perfume was flowery—rose maybe, or gardenia?—Ava couldn't tell between the two.

When Mrs. Sanderson finished, she packed away the medicine kit and returned it to its drawer. She opened the icebox and wrapped a chunk of ice in a cotton dish towel.

"For your cheek." Mrs. Sanderson handed the ice to Ava. "Hold it against it. It will help ease the bruising and swelling." She took a chair opposite Ava and sat down, folding her hands primly in front of her. It was an act of kindness. Ava wavered between concern over Mrs. Sanderson's trustworthiness, and gratefulness for the tender care the woman had given her.

"So, Ava Coons, you've become quite the hassle for Tempter's Creek."

Ava didn't reply but instead lifted the ice and held it against her cheek. Even with the cloth wrapped around it, it chilled her skin almost instantly and seeped through to cause her hand to sting with cold.

Mrs. Sanderson smiled thinly. "Did you know we aren't that far apart in age? In another life and another world, we might have been friends."

Now that was a lark. Ava smiled at the irony. Mrs. Sanderson did as well. Their smiles weren't friendly so much as wary.

"It appears there's more to you than meets the eye. Or else you have involved yourself with someone who finds bruising a woman not to be off-limits. You're blessed that whoever did this to you missed your eye. Regardless, since I've now played your nursemaid, you may call me Sarah." When Ava didn't respond, Sarah continued, "I suppose that makes me more relatable, yes? Being on a first-name basis?"

Ava didn't think it meant a hill of beans difference really. Relating to Sarah Sanderson would never be on her list of things to do, and if Sarah believed that somehow they shared a hobby of killin' people, well, she wouldn't find a kindred spirit in this room.

"You were always quite mouthy, Ava. Why stay silent now?

Especially now? Silence will do nothing to plead your case." Sarah's lips pursed for a moment, rosy and full. She raised a thin eyebrow. "And you are well aware of my opinion regarding you."

Ava adjusted the ice, pressing her lips together. Best to keep her mouth shut than say something Sarah could turn against her.

"Tea perhaps? Might that loosen your tongue?" Sarah eased herself out of her chair with the grace of a princess. She filled a kettle with water at the sink and then set it with a clatter on the stovetop. "I believe I should call the police."

"No!" Ava yelped.

Sarah's eyes narrowed in a smirk of satisfaction. "Well, that got you to talk. But truly, we need to report this attack. In no way should any heinous man be attacking women in the daytime. Not at nighttime, either, but the daylight speaks to his audacity. Tell me who did this to you, and I'll be sure he receives his due punishment."

"No police." Ava shook her head. She wanted to go into the station on her own terms, if she was going to go at all. Having the cops called on her would set her off on a worse foot than she was already standing on. Quite at Mrs. Sanderson's—no, *Sarah's*—mercy. It was an awful place to be in. How was she supposed to get any truth out of the woman now?

"Hmm . . ." Sarah crossed her arms over her chest in thought and tapped her fingers on her elbow. "You won't reveal the man who attacked you? Or is it a ruse to divert our attention to your absence after poor Jipsy's death? Paint yourself as a victim as well?"

"No." Ava lowered her hand that held the ice pack.

"Really?" Sarah nodded. "What a pity if poor Ava Coons herself was injured by a vagrant roaming Tempter's Creek with an affinity for violence."

"I'm not doing no such thing." Ava bit her tongue. Her resistance wasn't helping.

Sarah sniffed. "You murdered Matthew Hubbard in cold blood."

Ava narrowed her eyes.

"Then Jipsy."

Ava tilted her chin up. She wouldn't answer.

"And your poor, poor family . . ."

Sarah Sanderson prodded Ava's weakness.

Ava bristled, stiffening in her chair. "Go get me one of your man's axes. I'll show ya I can hardly hoist it over my head now, let alone as a thirteen-year-old girl!" Ava protested, bringing her hand down on the table with a slap. "Chuck Weber an' people like you got folks around here to forget to put their thinkin' caps on!"

Sarah clicked her tongue. "My, my."

"Perhaps *you* killed Jipsy." It wasn't the smartest way of going about it. Ava knew that the moment she whipped the question out.

"Me?" The surprise in Sarah's posture seemed genuine enough. "Whyever—where on *earth* would you come up with that addle-brained idea?"

"Doesn't matter where," Ava argued. Her lip was beginning to throb, almost worse than her cheek. "Everyone knows you and Hubbard had a little thing going on the side." Might as well bait the highfalutin prissy and see if she got mad enough to blurt out something true.

"The gall!" Sarah stiffened as her kettle whistled. She jerked it off the burner with a hot pad. "How *dare* you imply I am anything but faithful to my husband!"

"Jipsy knew, didn't she? She was goin' to out you, so you had to shut her up." Ava was all but copying Ned word for word. It was self-preservation if nothing else.

Sarah paced the kitchen, looked out the back window, then spun to face Ava. Her eyes were shooting darts of anger. "Gossip such as that can ruin a woman. Where did you hear of it?"

Ava tilted her chin up. "Gossip such as someone killin' her family can ruin a woman too. Where did you come up with that?"

"Everyone knows it," Sarah spat.

"Then everyone knows you were sneakin' off with Matthew."

"Matthew, is it?" Sarah's eyes narrowed.

Ava colored. Drat. She lifted her hands to her cheeks. She'd not told a soul, had no intentions of tellin', even if Jipsy was dead and gone.

The two women eyed each other. The room became thick with their unspoken accusations and defenses. Both breathed a mite heavier than when Ava had first come in. Finally, she dropped her gaze from Sarah's penetrating one. Water droplets were soaking into her dress from the ice melting through the dish towel she still clutched in her hand.

"Since we both *know* so much about the other's sins"—Sarah's words were laced with sarcasm—"perhaps we should just leave the other alone and be done with it."

Leave each other alone? It was like a small gift in the turmoil for Sarah Sanderson to imply she'd stop stirring the pot alongside of Chuck Weber. But to offer that sure seemed like maybe she'd hit a sore spot and Sarah *was* hiding something she didn't want found out. Maybe Ned was right. It was possible, Ava supposed, and if Sarah didn't want Tempter's Creek to know her secrets, then . . .

Pushing up from her chair, Ava determined it was a good time to take her leave before Sarah Sanderson used that kitchen knife on the counter—or maybe that meat cleaver over by the stove—to resolve this conversation in an entirely different fashion.

"You're leaving?" Sarah's hand was on the kitchen counter. A few inches away lay a paring knife.

Ava mustered her blandest face. "I think you're right." She offered an olive branch. "We'll just call it even 'tween us."

Sarah's fingers twitched.

Ava eyed the paring knife.

"Hardly even, Ava Coons. You've accused me of adultery."

"You've accused me of murder," Ava retorted.

Sarah tilted her head to the side, staring down her nose at Ava. "Humankind *does* have an affinity for breaking the Ten Commandments, don't they? However, *I* am not one of them."

Silence.

A bird warbled outside the window.

The paring knife remained where it was.

"Off with you then," Sarah commanded. "And stay away from me, you hear?"

Ava darted out the back door. No need to test Sarah Sanderson and her paring knife any further than she already had.

33

"Now's not the time," Wren muttered to herself, swiping to ignore Pippin's call. Her brother could leave a message. He was never great at empathy, and trying to talk through tears was hard enough as it was.

Today drained every ounce of energy from Wren—from the Markham home. She curled at the end of the sofa, a fuzzy blanket over her lap, a wad of tissues in her hand.

"He may need something," Tristan Blythe said from across the room. Having her own father here helped—a little—but she wondered if he was more capable of being a moral support for Gary than for her. The two widowers would relate in their own way. Patty's passing had reopened the wounds of Wren's mother's passing. Both left voids behind that were unfathomable.

"Pippin can wait," Wren responded belatedly to her father. And she was right. He could. Still, she swiped to her voicemail screen and read the voice-to-text composition.

Searched for your birth records. Didn't find
anything. You'll probably want to . . . Dad knows
. . . or at the safe deposit box. Talk later. Bye.

It was a half-translated message but enough to give her pause. So Pippin *had* pulled through for her, but his powers with technology had come up short. The knowledge gnawed at her already raw stomach. Wren set her phone on the arm of the sofa, eyed her dad who was chatting quietly with Gary, and pushed the knowledge to the back of her mind.

Her gaze connected with Eddie's form as he worked in the kitchen. It was his comfort place. He knew what to do in the kitchen. His aide, Esther, was manning the camp's kitchen for the rest of the week due to Patty's passing, yet Eddie needed to stay busy.

Wren eased off the couch, tugged her socks on straight, and headed for the kitchen. Dishes clanked together as Eddie pulled them from the dishwasher, clean and ready to put away.

"Need help?" Wren's question sliced through the emotionally ladened air.

Eddie shook his head. "Nah. I'm just goin' to make some cookies."

"Chocolate chip?"

"Butterscotch," he responded. He threw a pile of forks into the silverware drawer.

"Oh." That was odd. Eddie didn't even like butterscotch. Her heart plummeted further. They were Patty's favorite. "Eddie?"

He began stacking glasses into the cupboard, his back to her. "Yeah?"

"Do you want to go for a walk?" It was a paltry offer considering butterscotch cookies, but the truth of the matter was, Wren knew no one was hungry.

Eddie shook his head as he kneed the dishwasher door shut. "No thanks." He tugged off the quilted mixer cover that Patty had sewn, pulling the appliance toward him on the counter.

Wren hesitated, searching desperately for words. Maybe there were none. Maybe this was the right thing for Eddie to do. The people from the funeral home had left an hour ago with Patty. Wren was certain she'd never forget the sound of the stretcher and its wheels traveling across the floor. She'd closed her eyes quickly as it had exited Patty's room, but she'd caught sight of the black bag that embraced Patty's body. It was the gruesome side of death. The vacancy of everything. Her body, her room, their lives. Eddie's life. Gary's. All of it was empty. And yet there were little reminders of Patty everywhere they looked. A vase she'd bought at a garage sale sitting in the windowsill. A watercolor she'd painted before Eddie was born, hanging by the calendar on the wall. Her shoes were by the door, along with her favorite baseball cap she wore when she was out in the sun.

The hospice staff had been helpful, but Patty had been gone no more than forty minutes and they were collecting the morphine pills, checking off boxes on an end-of-life task sheet, and calling for someone to come retrieve the larger items like the walker and bedside toilet. Life was already moving ahead at a pace far faster than should be allowed. A hospice aide had just broken down the hospital bed and hauled it out in pieces. The back door had closed. The van driven away. The house left in a stone-cold silence that caused them all to question what had just happened.

Tristan Blythe came.

They'd gathered.

Eddie had gone to the kitchen.

Now here they were. Baking butterscotch cookies. The most mundane homelife activity.

But Patty was gone. And yet . . . Wren fingered a devotional book Patty always kept on the kitchen bar . . . she wasn't.

Wren glanced at the clock. It was ticking. It needed to stop. Time needed to freeze.

"Do you want help?" Lame. She wanted to race after the undertaker's car and make them unzip the bag and give Patty resuscitation. It was a cruel prank. Patty was still alive. In fact, Wren was almost sure if she returned to Patty's bedroom, she would be there, tucked in and with a ready smile.

"I got it." Eddie pulled two sticks of butter from the fridge. He unwrapped them and dropped them in a glass bowl, popping it into the microwave.

"Want me to get the eggs?" Wren offered. Anything to pretend life was as it should be. That she didn't hear Gary's voice cracking with tears in the other room, and the low grumble of her father's voice attempting to comfort him.

"Wren, I've got it!" Eddie snapped.

Tears sprang to her eyes. Which was dumb. *She* was dumb. It wasn't personal. Eddie was hurting. Broken. Like the eggs.

Eddie tossed the eggshell in the garbage and broke another egg into the mixer's bowl. He froze, then leaned against the counter, his head bent. "Sorry," he mumbled.

"It's okay." Wren stood there. She'd never felt so helpless before.

Eddie cracked another egg. The shell exploded in his hand, shards of it dropping into the bowl. He swore under his breath, startling Wren. Eddie never swore.

Digging into the goop, Eddie attempted to swipe out the egg-shell. The microwave beeped, indicating the butter was ready. He abandoned the shell and popped open the microwave. The butter had completely melted and boiled over onto the glass plate. Eddie swore again. This time louder.

"Eddie?" Wren took a step toward him.

He slammed the microwave door shut. He swore again.

"Eddie." She opted for stern this time.

"Knock it off, Wren." Eddie's bite was harsh.

Wren backed up the step she had taken. Eddie reached into the mixer bowl and tried to fish out more shell but succeeded only in completely slopping egg all over his hand. With a roar, he flung the egg white into the sink. His curse filled the kitchen, silenced their fathers in the living room, and made Wren sink onto a barstool.

Eddie stopped. Met her stunned expression, then growled again and made for the back door.

"Eddie!" Gary hurried into the kitchen, Tristan Blythe behind him.

Wren held up a hand. "I'll go."

"He needs to grieve," Tristan observed.

"He will, Dad." Wren glowered at him. Sometimes he was obtuse for an educated professor. "Patty just died. Give him time."

Gary met Wren's gaze with a look of lost helplessness. She eased off the barstool and made her way in the direction Eddie had fled. As she reached for the back door, the thought hit her. They were both motherless now. All they had left were their fathers, extended family . . . Wren's breath caught as she closed the door behind her. That was assuming she even *had* a family. Pippin's voicemail reverberated in her mind. No birth records. None. How was that even possible in this digital age of impeccable records?

⁂

Eddie was trudging down the gravel road, flanked on both sides by woods. Woods that, if traversed deeply enough, would wind their way to Lost Lake. The site of another tragedy, past and possibly present. Wren hurried after her childhood friend. Now wasn't the time to be thinking about Jasmine.

"Eddie!" Wren shouted.

He slowed his pace but didn't look back at her. His hands were stuffed into the pockets of his army-green shorts. His blue-and-green plaid shirt hung loosely, only emphasizing his bowed shoulders. Wren broke into a jog, regretting that she'd slipped on a pair of moccasins instead of tennis shoes. But in a few moments she caught up with him. Her shoulder brushed his as Wren slowed her pace.

"There's nothing to say, Wren." Eddie was trying to get out ahead of her in conversation.

"I know." She matched his steps. Matched his hands by shoving her own into her jean shorts pockets. A black fly buzzed her head. Wren swatted it away.

They hiked for a few minutes before Eddie paused. The woods had cleared way for a small pond, the road becoming a bridge as it spanned it. The water was covered in a thick moss of green algae with some lily pads interspersed, their white flowers staring up at the sun.

Eddie looked down into the water.

A sparrow flew overhead, reminding Wren of Patty's last words to her. *"His eye is on the sparrow . . ."* Tears sprang to her eyes.

"Today is the first day of a long time to come," she stated. Eddie needed to know she shared in his grief. In the absence of Patty. That she wouldn't be just carrying on with life in a week as if Patty had never happened.

"Yeah." He nodded.

Wren could tell Eddie was swallowing back emotion. A muscle in his jaw twitched.

"Sorry about back at the kitchen." Eddie sniffed. "I was just—"

"It's okay." Wren reached for his hand. Eddie glanced down at them when she curled her fingers around his. Funny. For all the years they'd known each other, she couldn't remember ever holding Eddie's hand. It was callused. Strong. But she felt the tremor in it.

A frog leaped from the pond's shoreline and splashed into the water. It stretched its front and hind legs out as it swam a path beneath the surface, then disappeared beneath the algae.

"I just—" Eddie blew out a big breath and shook his head. "Yeah. I dunno."

"You don't have to say anything," Wren offered.

Eddie stared at the spot where the frog had disappeared. "Mom loved walking to this pond. She used to say if it were legal, she'd pick every lily pad flower and make a bouquet out of them."

"Stupid state regulations," Wren commiserated.

They shared a small laugh.

Eddie kicked at the gravel. "Yeah. When I was eight, I picked one for her. I had no idea they were a protected plant."

"Oops." Wren smiled.

Eddie offered her a crooked one in return. He adjusted his fingers around hers but didn't pull away. "Yeah. Mom didn't miss a beat, though. She spent the next few minutes telling me about environmental protection, and then she put the lily in a glass yogurt jar. She said it was too late to put it back, so she considered it God's gift to her that day. Me and God. We always watched out for Mom."

"I know you did." A lump grew in Wren's throat.

Eddie took a few breaths, then looked at Wren as he chewed on the inside of his bottom lip. "I can't do life without her."

His eyes filled with a type of lostness that was hollow and lonesome. His mouth twisted as Eddie pushed back emotion. "I know all the God things to say to myself, but it doesn't change that she's gone."

"No, it doesn't." No son should ever lose his mama. It was inevitable, but it was unforgiveable at the same time.

Eddie choked, coughed, cleared his throat. He tugged his hand from Wren's and coughed again. "One more day . . . I'd kill for just one. One. More. Day." Eddie's hand flew to his mouth, and he sucked in a chesty sob. A boy that wanted to cry for his mom but was wrapped in a man's body where weeping was foreign.

Wren did the only thing she knew to do. She reached for him. Eddie's arms enveloped her. Wren could feel his pain through the shuddering in his chest. His head bent and hid in the crook of her neck as his hands kneaded into her shoulders.

"I could tell by the way she held me yesterday. It wasn't the same, Wren. She was leaving, and she knew it."

"I know." Wren didn't resist as Eddie held her tighter.

"I didn't know what to say," he confessed, this time tears choking his voice, his breath warm on her neck.

Wren threaded her hand through Eddie's hair on the back of his head. "She loved you so much."

"Yeah." Eddie nodded against her neck. "I just had to watch her fade . . . I asked God for just one more day. Every day I prayed for one more. Just one. But yesterday she told me no. She said 'no more.' So I didn't ask for another day. I just—I told myself I'd be fine." Eddie drew back, burying himself in their shared brokenness. "I'm not." He shook his head. "Wren, I'm not fine."

She held him. Quieted Eddie with a nurturing "Shhhh." Eddie was right. In grief, a person was never *fine*, they were just *there*. Standing there. Alone. In the memory of the one who had taken their heart and flown away.

34

Ava

She'd been right. In the past. When she'd thought there were coals in Noah Pritchard's eyes. They'd just burst into flames, and by the way he was pacing the sitting room floor, the entire parsonage might go up in smoke.

"Who was it?" he demanded, pausing long enough to rest his hand on his Bible. Drawing on some supernatural strength. The coals dimmed a bit. But just a bit.

Ava sat on the sofa, Hanny next to her as she dabbed at the lip that was now crusted with blood from where it'd continued to bleed after Mrs. Sanderson had dressed it.

Ava shrugged. "I don't know."

"How do you not know?" Noah demanded.

"I-I don't. His voice—he was all growly—and he wore a hat. He didn't have no beard, though." Ava berated herself for not knowing. Seemed she should. Seemed downright crazy that she didn't.

"She was scared, Noah." Hanny pressed a warm compress to the lip. "When you're scared, your mind shuts down."

Ava whimpered.

Noah stilled. Leveled his gaze on them both, as if Hanny and Ava were mutually in trouble. More'n likely, they were all in trouble. "We need to report this. To Larson."

Ava pushed Hanny's hand away from her mouth. "I was goin' there. To the police. When all this happened."

"Why?" Hanny's intake of breath went against her assertion that truth be told.

Ava offered her a weak smile of appreciation for the elderly woman's protectiveness. "'Cause this has gotten way outta hand. No reason Noah needs to get wrapped up in my troubles."

Noah stilled.

Ava avoided looking at him, directing her attention instead to Hanny. "It's my lot to deal with. You both have been more than generous to me. I know I've done nothin' wrong. Larson seemed open-minded—"

"Larson had the men bring Jipsy's body in," Noah interrupted. "She was stabbed fourteen times. Your name has *not* been taken off the table as a potential, Ava."

"Gracious!" Hanny gasped.

"I should still go in. It'd clear up this mess."

Noah shook his head. "It won't clear up anything. Larson said Jipsy's death doesn't seem like your work, Ava, but that doesn't clear you of Hubbard's. With Chuck Weber breathing in Larson's ear . . ." Noah blew out a massive pent-up sigh. "But we can't have this lunatic attacking you now. We need to report it."

Ava moved to rise from beside Hanny. Now or never.

"Wait." Noah sagged onto the worn chair across from them, leaned forward, and rested his elbows on his knees. "I need to know—who was Hubbard to you?"

"Who's Emmaline to *you*?" Ava deflected the only way she could think of. She instantly regretted it.

"Ava." Hanny's soft voice held warning.

Noah clenched his teeth. "Emmaline has nothing to do with this. Hubbard does. Hanny and I are both out on a limb for you here, and—"

"I know that," Ava said. She picked at a burr that stuck to her dress from her jaunt in the woods. It was a burdock burr, round and sticky.

"All right then." Noah slapped his knees and pointed toward the door. "Go. Convince Larson some loony is out in the woods attacking people, boxing in your face, and God knows what else! Face Tempter's Creek on your own and see how long it is before Larson throws you behind bars and you stand trial for murder."

"You just told me I needed to report this!" Ava could throttle the preacher if she didn't owe him so much already. She pointed to her cheek. It still throbbed. She could tell her words were getting thicker too, along with her lip.

Noah glowered. "I'm trying to understand—as much as I can, Ava. The fact is, a select number of folks in Tempter's Creek are working on making what little evidence they have fit their narrative. If you want to know from my firsthand experience, once there's a narrative of guilt, it really doesn't matter how innocent you are."

"You two are like a couple dancing in a circle at a waltz and you can't hold hands," Hanny interjected. "Either hold hands and work together or find a new dance partner." The woman rose to her wobbly feet and reached for her cane. "I've had it up to here with the two of you making not one lick of sense." That Hanny was irritated was clear, but Ava didn't understand what had gotten in her craw, and a glance at Noah told Ava he was perplexed by it too.

Hanny clicked her tongue and looked at them both as though they were wayward school children before toddling out of the room toward the kitchen.

"Well, she told you," Ava muttered.

Noah tilted his head, and the embers flamed to life again. "Who is Matthew Hubbard to you?"

Ava looked away. The preacher couldn't mind his own business if Jesus himself told him to. She glanced up at the painting. Sure enough. Jesus was staring off and away—almost looking like He was rolling His eyes at them too.

"Did Jesus ever do anythin' wrong?"

Noah's head jerked up. "What?"

Ava gave him a nonplussed stare. "Just answer the question."

"No, He did not." Noah frowned. "Why on earth would you ask that?"

"Well, if He never did nothin' wrong, then how come He even bothers with us who have?"

Noah stared back at her as if to assess if she was serious or not. He chose his words carefully in response. "That's the significance of who He is. We don't deserve His grace—He gives it freely."

"That's a mighty fine answer."

Noah took it as sarcasm. "It's the truth, Ava."

"Never said it wasn't."

"You meant it," he stated glumly.

"'Course I did. Figured you of all people would be happy. I'd be an easy convert if you even tried just a little bit."

Noah reddened.

Ava had to be honest. A big part of her had always wished God might smile at her instead of glare at her from the sky, ready to rain down hellfire and brimstone. Fact was, she had a feeling she deserved it, even if she didn't murder her parents.

"Who is Hubbard to you?"

"Gosh darn it, Preacher!" Ava blew out a breath of exasperation. "You don't give up, do you?"

Noah's lips flattened together. "I'm nothing if not consistent."

Ava squirmed. "Why's it important?"

"Because it might give *me* a clue as to whether we even have an argument to spare toward proving your innocence. Not that there's much we can do about it anyway. I'm at a loss."

"I didn't kill him," Ava asserted.

"So you've said. Many times." Noah drummed his fingers on his knees. "But we've also well established that you *do* have a connection to him. Sanderson knows this and will use it against you to make his point."

She hadn't told Noah about Sarah Sanderson. About their truce. About how suspicious she was herself, or Ned's theory regarding

Sarah's guilt. But there was no question Hubbard was a link. Between them all.

"If'n I tell you, you can't judge me."

Noah considered it for a long moment. Longer than Ava was comfortable with. Preachers should be quick to forgive. Or so she thought anyway.

"I won't judge you," he replied at last. There was something in his voice, though. Not resignation so much as recognition. As if he'd judged before and preferred not to revisit it.

"I told her I'd not tell a soul."

"Told who?"

"Jipsy." Ava had never cried loyalty toward Jipsy, but the woman *had* taken her in as a child. Taken her in along with Widower Frisk. Fed her. Housed her. Kept Widower Frisk away from her . . .

"Jipsy," Noah repeated.

Ava nodded, finally meeting his yes. "Jipsy and Matthew Hubbard . . . well, they had a little thing goin' on the side." Not unlike what Ned had accused Sarah Sanderson of. That irony wasn't lost on Ava.

"Oh." Apparently that wasn't what Noah had expected. She had an idea that he thought she had one of her own personal confessions, but she didn't.

"And now I'm questionin' whether he had somethin' going on with Mrs. Sanderson too."

Noah choked. Held his fist to his mouth and coughed. "Mrs. Sanderson and Matthew Hubbard?"

"Ned seems to think so. Maybe Mrs. Sanderson was jealous of Jipsy and so took her out."

"But Hubbard was already dead. What difference would it make by then?" Noah raised a brow.

Ava shrugged. "Jealous is jealous, Preacher, you should know that. Sin don't always follow logic."

"No. No, it doesn't." Noah shook his head. "None of this is helpful, Ava. I don't see how we're going to clear your name. Going in to report your attack today—it's just going to look like a smoke screen. A tactic to get their attention off of you. My guess is, they won't take it seriously."

"So then. Here we sit." Ava sagged back into the sofa. She adjusted the skirt of her dress, as it'd ridden up past her knees. She noticed Noah watched her hands. Her legs. Then he shifted his gaze quickly to the floor. For a long moment, they were both quiet, lost in their own thoughts. Ava had a feeling her thoughts were far different from Noah's.

He was in fix-it mode. She'd spent a day or two watching Mo Jackson at the machine shop fixing things, so she could recognize it in a man. There was a deep concentration when something needed set to rights. Whether it was a car engine or wagon wheel or a person's life. Only, Ava figured it was right easier to fix an engine than a heart.

She studied Noah. He looked downright exhausted. His chiseled face might be handsome, but Ava didn't disregard the droop of his shoulders, the defeat in his expression, and his overall approach to pretty much everything. *Resigned.* That was the word. He was resigned. Like he owed it. To others. To God. The more it cost of himself, the better off it'd be. Like a loan. Widower Frisk had a loan once, Ava recalled. Took him nigh on two years to pay it back, and though she was sure he paid most of it back with goods from his hidden whiskey stash, it definitely cost him. He wasn't happy till it was paid in full.

"What are you payin' back, Noah Pritchard?"

Noah's head came up, and his eyes locked with hers.

Well, darn it. She hadn't meant to ask that out loud.

They both stared at each other, the air thick with unspoken words.

"She break your heart?" Ava suddenly knew—not *who* Emmaline was so much as *what* Emmaline did.

Noah's expression changed little. It couldn't. Resignation was a part of him now. He took in a deep breath, his chest rising, and then released it. "No, *I* broke our hearts. It was all me."

Ava wasn't sure what he meant by that, but it made those embers in Noah's eyes make more sense. He was a man created to feel, but one who was forcin' himself not to. And one of these days, he was gonna lose his well-honed control. Would she be able to handle whatever those flickers of emotion in his eyes meant? A part of her wanted to try.

———

The doll's eyes were empty. Staring out from her cracked porcelain skull like hollow voids. The trauma she'd witnessed was buried behind them, tormenting and killing. Ava reached for her doll, her fingertips connecting with the hair. Human hair, Ma had said, 'cause it was all special and expensive-like on a doll. Ava's fingers grazed the hair as she tried to grab it, but the doll rolled away.

Fog rolled in, from the sides. A strange thing, seeing as she was back in the cellar—somehow. Dreamin'. She had to be. Another look at her doll and Ava left her behind, climbing the ladder. Her scream caught in her throat, choking her and stealing breath from her lungs. The fog parted across the cabin's wood floor, leaving her face-to-face with a dead man.

Her pa's eyes mimicked her doll's. Open. Blue. Reflecting a horror that froze the moment death had stolen breath from him.

"Pa. Pa." Ava crawled across the floor. Her hand jostled his shoulder. He was a mess, so she turned her face from the sight. She was scared. She needed someone.

"Ricky? Arnie?"

Ava scurried past her pa. He was scary, lyin' there like that. Strength had been conquered and defeated, and now he lay there dead. He couldn't do a thing to help her. The hemline of her calico dress that was too small and hung just past her knees dragged through his blood. It painted a swath across the cabin floor.

Something smelled like smoke. Maybe that hadn't been fog. A dream? Could a person smell things in a dream?

She couldn't figure it out. Ava looked at the woodstove, then her crawl turned into a mad rush to get past her pa. It was Ma that Ava was scraping her knees on the floor to get to.

Ma lay by the stove. Facedown. But her fingers were moving. Blood was under her nails.

"Ma!" Ava reached her side. She pushed on her ma until the woman's head lolled to lie on her right ear. Her eyes were rolling back in her head.

Ma mumbled something.

"Mama!" Ava cried. Tears hurt, and no one could ever tell her differently.

"Ava Marie . . ." Ma's voice gargled. Her eyes grew big.

"Can't hear ya, Mama." Ava leaned closer. Her ma's whisper was an icy breath on her ear. A name. Just a name . . . it wasn't her name . . . but she couldn't understand, couldn't— "Mama!"

Just like that, she was gone.

Smoke rolled across the cabin floor and up the sides of the wall. Startled, Ava sat back on her heels. "Pa?" she shouted, but she knew he would not answer. In fact, she hoped he didn't 'cause it'd scare her more if he ever looked at her with that wide-eyed haunted gaze again.

Ava tripped as she pushed herself to her feet. She looked wildly around. Where'd her doll go? The cellar! Ava hurried to the opening and saw the ladder leading down, and it was then she saw the flickering of orange flames licking at the cabin outside the window. The front door stood open. She could see the clearing outside the cabin, the roots in the dirt, Pa's log pile, the wheelbarrow, the lake just beyond.

She staggered from the cabin.

Where was he? She'd seen his shoes. He'd been in the cellar lookin' straight at her not long before. But now he'd vanished. Ava noticed two prostrate forms by the edge of the clearing where the oak and cherry trees met up with the dirt line Pa had carved out of the woods.

It was them. Ricky. Arnie. A thousand dollars wouldn't make

her go over and see to 'em. Didn't take a doctor to figure out they were dead too. Dead as doornails. The flames behind her grew. They were going to eat the cabin like a delicious final meal. Pa once said demons were real, and Ma had followed it up with a "Yeah, demon liquor and the like." She'd thrown a bottle out the front door, and Pa had hollered, but then he'd stormed out, not touchin' any of them. Pa never hurt them. Never. Ricky was the hot-tempered one. From what Ava could see from where she was standing, it looked like Ricky had put up the biggest fight too.

She gagged.

Retched into the dirt.

That man was coming back. She knew it. Could sense it. Ava's head jerked up, and she stared at the lake. Without a second thought, she raced back into the cabin. She couldn't let Ma and Pa burn up. She couldn't! But dragging them to the safety of the lake's water meant she had to hurry. Fire waited for no one, and neither would the man with the ax.

35

"No. No, I need to save them." Ava grappled for her mother's body. Her hands found the blanket in the dark, but then slid downward until they hit the floor. The blanket didn't cover her mother. She was gone. "Ma!" Ava's cry was garbled, horror-filled. Ma's body was missing now. Ava pounded the blanket and floor, feeling her way across the room, unable to see much of anything. She realized her eyes were closed. Sealed tight. And they burned, not from smoke but from tears.

"Ava."

A hand closed around her shoulder as she crawled across the floor. She flung her arm up, batting it away, a scream catching in her throat.

"Let me go!" She flailed at the man who'd returned. Come back to finish what he had started. "Let go of me!" Ava raked at the man's face with her fingernails. He grabbed her by her wrists, and they wrestled, her on her back and him looming over her. Ava's eyes were still closed. She couldn't open them. Couldn't see. Couldn't—

His full weight fell on top of her as she scraped at his face. His body took her breath away, his chest smashing against hers. He brought his knee over her legs to hinder Ava from kicking. His hands pinned her arms over her head, his fingers gripping her wrists with an impenetrable force.

She squirmed beneath him, her attempt at screaming sounding

more like a whimper filled with the hint of weeping. Ava's breaths came in quick gasps.

"Ava."

She struggled to open her eyes, but even as she did, Ava didn't stop trying to lash out. She lifted her legs as best as she could and bucked her body to throw him off.

"Ava!" This time his voice was sharp. Startling.

Her eyes flew open.

He was close. So very close.

"Let me go!" She twisted under his body.

"Ava, it's me. Noah." He emphasized his declaration with an added press to her wrists.

She stilled. Stared. Moonlight filtered in through the curtains drawn over her bedroom window. Ava could make out the outline of the dresser across the room. She felt the coarse rub of the carpet beneath her and heard the creak of the wood flooring it covered.

Noah's grasp loosened as awareness returned to her.

"I thought—" she gasped. Cryin' wasn't going to help a thing. Not a thing. Yet in her mind's eye Ava could still see her mother's vacant stare. She could see the flames, the bodies of her brothers. Her throat felt sore from the screams she had released that day so many years before. "I remember." Ava's whisper was hoarse. "I remember."

Noah braced his hands against the floor, lifting his weight from her chest. He hovered over her, his chocolate gaze black in the night. "What do you remember?" he whispered.

Ava turned her head away from him. There were tears, and then there were torrents. Hers were becoming the latter, and she didn't want Noah to be a witness to them.

"Leave me alone," she begged.

Noah shook his head. "I can't do that."

"Please."

Noah's hand rested against her cheek, turning her face to look up at him. She could tell, even with the shadows dancing across his features, that his expression was one of concern.

"I remember *them*. I remember them dyin'."

"Do you remember who it was that killed them?"

Of course. *That* was the critical question. Ava shook her head, struggling to sit up. Noah pushed himself away from her, offering his hand. She drew into a sitting position on the floor, leaning her back against the bed. Ava swiped her arm across her face, sniffing into the sleeve of her nightgown. Her legs were bare, her knees sticking out as she sat cross-legged.

Noah adjusted to sit next to her. They both stared forward, eyes fixated somewhere along the opposite wall. The window behind them lurked above the bed, and the moon attempted to crack the midnight.

"Ava?" Noah's pressure to tell him what she knew was gentle, yet there was an urgency in his tone to find a key that might bring resolution to their situation.

"They were all dead. All of 'em." Ava noted the mirror on her dresser. The window's reflection in it. She saw the outline of the windowpanes through the curtains. "My pa, my ma, my brothers . . ."

Noah's arm moved. His hand settled on the floor next to hers. He didn't touch her, but Ava could feel the warmth generating from his nearness.

"The cabin was on fire. Like hell had risen from the pit and was lickin' it." Ava knew she'd experienced another one of her blackouts. "I drug them toward the lake." It was an admission. Of guilt. Of regret. Of sorrow.

"You were just a girl."

"I didn't go get help," Ava retorted. The clouds covered the moon, and the curtain shifted in tone from gray to dark blue. "But I had to get them away from the fire."

"They must have been very heavy when you dragged them."

She turned to look at Noah. "Funny when you're scared how

strong a person gets. I just pulled them out of the cabin and into the lake. Deep as I could get 'em. The fire was awful hot."

"What else do you remember?"

His eyes locked with hers. The moon had come out from behind the clouds again. Its glow reflected off the mirror, casting a bluish light across them. Ava could see the shadow of whiskers on Noah's jaw. His hair lay on his forehead. His nightshirt was open, revealing a broad naked chest. It'd been hastily tucked into his trousers.

"You shouldn't be in here," Ava whispered, the air thick between them.

"I know," he whispered back.

She froze when Noah's finger rose and swept a tear from her cheek.

"You're not as strong as you think you are," he observed.

"Strong enough." Ava tilted her chin up in quiet defiance.

"You survived." Noah's little finger brushed against hers from their position on the floor.

Ava was breathless for quite a different reason.

His finger stroked her hand. A gentle rhythmic sweep that both soothed and stoked something inside her.

"Everyone survives in their own way." Ava's words drifted between them. "You're surviving too."

Noah's eyes flared to life. His chest rose and fell. Ava could hear his breathing. Could feel his full hand now as it crept slowly to cover her own.

"You don't know the half of it," he mumbled. His forehead tilted toward hers.

Ava stared into the depths of his eyes. Reading between the little flames that sparked there. A line of hurt threaded through them, of regret.

"You're a piece of work for a preacher," she muttered, not knowing what else to say.

Noah's hand lightly massaged hers.

Ava couldn't move away. Didn't want to. There was a wistful

magic in the night. A wishing. A wishing for a sweet release from the pain that had drafted its way into their very different souls and claimed them for a lifetime of wondering. The asking of *why?* The secrets harbored deep within, stunting even the flicker of hope.

"I'd best get back to bed," Noah said. But he didn't move. Didn't even twitch. His fingers continued to caress hers.

Hypnotized by his presence, Ava turned her hand over so their fingers could link. Noah's eyes slid shut. He was warring against something. Warring against himself, against this moment. Ava shifted to her knees. She reached out, tentative, pushing back a loose strand of dark hair from his forehead.

"Ava?" Noah's eyes were still closed. He leaned into her hand.

"Yes?" she answered.

"Please." His voice shook a bit. "Don't."

She should listen. But she'd never taken direction well. Ava trailed her fingertips down the side of Noah's face, feeling the stubble beneath her skin, the flex of his jaw, and the corded strength of his neck.

"You're going to be the death of me." Noah's eyes popped open, and the intensity in them startled her.

Ava withdrew, pulling her hand back.

His eyes half begged her to obey him, while the other half dared her to defy the truth of the moment.

Ava struggled to her feet, her bare toes catching on the hemline of her nightgown. She stumbled, reaching for Noah's shoulder. He swept upward, his hands settling on her waist to steady her. The warmth from his hands burned through the thin cotton of her nightgown.

"I didn't kill 'em." She stated it more to bring herself back to the reality of the night. The cold, stark truth of it.

Noah's hand drifted to the small of her back, urging her toward him. He drew himself to his feet. Her chest brushed his. Ava's eyes widened. Noah leaned into her, his lips against her ear.

"I believe you. Now let me go."

Ava made quick work of obeying this time. She backed away, as did the preacher. He exited her room quickly, shutting the door, the latch clicking loudly in the stillness. Ava's skin tingled. Her heart pounded. Every part of her was awakened, and this time it was less of a nightmare and more like a murky daydream.

36

Wren

"They're doing *what* when?" Wren straightened from her slump at the Blythe kitchen table. She watched her dad lift his head at the announcement as Pippin entered the family kitchen. For the hundredth time that morning, she regretted the complimentary night's stay at her family's house instead of remaining at the Markhams'. She'd wanted to give Eddie and his dad time together—especially since, per Patty's request, the memorial service wouldn't be held until the end of the camp's summer program. Praise and worship, she requested, along with a camp family cookout. Typical Patty. But it made closure difficult, with the event looming weeks away still.

Tristan Blythe removed his reading glasses and rubbed the bridge of his nose. "Today?"

Wren ping-ponged her attention between her dad and her brother.

Pippin poured a bowl of cereal while nodding. "Yeah, I heard it on the camp's scanner. Troy's group just got back from their trip to Black River Harbor. They're taking him and a couple other guys from camp to help since they're certified divers."

"They're really going to search Lost Lake?" Wren hadn't forgotten Wayne's declaration and his influence on the local police. But it made her already nauseated and grief-laden stomach wrench harder after her own breakfast of her dad's dry, homemade carrot muffins.

"Yep." Pippin chewed a spoonful of cereal. *The Prancing Pony* sign hung on the wall just beyond him. A remnant of their mother's attempt to turn the house into a literal-looking setting of *The Lord of the Rings*.

Wren pushed away from the table. Resolution weighed heavily. "I need to go."

"Where?" Tristan looked up at his daughter. His morning devotions splayed on the table beside him. Her dad's meditations were another's study in Greek, a thick theology textbook with fine print.

"Lost Lake." Wren tugged her sweatshirt over her shorts and went to the cupboard to fish out a water bottle from the array of odds and ends jammed into it.

"I don't think that's wise." Tristan leaned back in his chair. "After losing Patty? Arwen, you don't know what they'll find, and I'm not sure your constitution can handle it at the moment."

"I can handle it." She lifted the faucet handle to let the water rush into the bottle. Besides, she needed to see Troy. Things were weighing on her. Lots of things. She avoided letting her mind drift in that direction.

Pippin eyed her, chewing his cereal as he leaned against the counter. She cast him a sideways glance. He was growing a mustache. She rolled her eyes and turned her attention back to the water bottle. Her older brother was going to turn into a walking hairy hobbit.

"Want me to come with you?" Pippin preferred his basement and screens to the woods and mosquitoes. From most, it would have seemed a generous offer. To Wren, she heard the critical tone in his voice. He expected her to break. To collapse. Some sort of emotional demise. Pippin was a conundrum to her. Never the protective older brother, he was more a lurker in her shadows. Rarely did they find camaraderie. Instead it was a truce between two vastly different people who were siblings in a house that never quite felt like home.

"No, that's fine."

"I'm serious. I'll come with you."

Maybe she'd misread his intentions. "Just—" she hesitated—"do some more digging on my behalf, okay?"

"On your behalf?" Tristan interjected. He looked between his adult children. "What's this about?"

Wren screwed the lid on her water bottle. "Nothing, Dad."

"She can't find her birth certificate," Pippin provided.

Wren shot him an irritated look.

"What?" He shrugged. "I told you it was better to ask Dad, anyway."

"Your birth certificate?" Tristan's voice boomed into her thoughts.

Wren waved her hand in dismissal. "Never mind about that." She really didn't want to question Tristan Blythe about it now. Not when Jasmine and Lost Lake were calling to her. She couldn't deal with the idea of casting suspicion over her mother's memory and faithfulness. What would Dad do if he found out she thought Mom had an affair and she resulted from it?

"Your mom kept your certificate in a metal file box under our bed," Tristan offered blandly. He reached for his coffee and took a sip as though it were nothing to have a missing birth certificate.

"She did?" It was too late to back out now. Wren set her water bottle on the granite counter with a metal *clank*.

Tristan dismissed her with a tip of his mug in her direction. "Mm-hmm. It was easy to grab when she needed it for things like your driver's license test. Pippin's is in there too."

"Then I can just—go get it from there? Is there a key for the box?"

Tristan pushed his glasses up his nose, his attention directed at his textbook. He tapped a pencil against his notepad. "You can look, but I don't think it's there anymore. Last time your mom used it, though, I recall it got torn. Something about getting caught in the car door or something? I don't know. She was going to get you a replacement." He scribbled something on his notepad. "I'm not sure if she ever did."

Back to square one. "Then I'll go online and request a new one."

"You can't. No one has records of you." Pippin's interruption brought Wren's stare swinging back to him. She remembered his voicemail. She just didn't think he'd offer it up so passively. There was a tremendous impact in that statement. Aside from the implications of infidelity, even the most practical was affected.

"I have to be able to get one. What if I need a passport? What if I get married? What if I switch jobs?"

"You'll never switch jobs." Pippin stated it as a fact. She really didn't like the mustache shadow on his upper lip. He pushed past her. "I've gotta get to work."

"Yeah, enjoy your pit of darkness!" Wren called after him as Pippin disappeared down the stairs. She turned to her dad. "Listen, I need to figure out my birth certificate thing. But for now, I'm going to head to Lost Lake. It'll take me a bit to get out there. I need to see if they find anything."

"There's too much fuss being made of all this." Tristan shook his head.

"Dad, a little girl is missing." He wasn't that callous. He couldn't be.

Tristan lifted his eyes. "Oh, I didn't mean about Jasmine Riviera! I meant this whole idea there are bodies in that lake. People take the story of Ava Coons too far."

"Says the man who names his bathroom after Mordor," Wren muttered.

"Uncalled for," her father retorted.

"See shoe. See shoe fit, Dad." Wren snatched the water bottle from the counter. "We'll talk later." And they would. They had to. As of right now, Wren didn't have an identity. Apparently, she was the only person that fact even bothered—which made it all so much worse.

The area around Lost Lake was more populated this afternoon than since the Coons family had lived here back in the 1920s. A quick survey as she entered the area told her that neither Meghan nor Ben were in attendance—which was good. The people milling around seemed official. She recognized two guys from camp. Eddie's officer friend, Bruce. The SAR organizer, John. Scanning, Wren didn't see Troy.

The lake was smaller than Deer Lake. Its surface covered over a hundred acres, with most of the land surrounding the lake heavily wooded. This afternoon the sun was high, and the warmth saturated the area, sending rivulets of sweat down Wren's back. She'd appreciated the long hike back to the lake for the time it offered to clear her mind. There were so many pieces rattling in there, it reminded her of a box of puzzle pieces that if one could just sit down long enough to piece together, the entire picture would make sense.

"Hey."

Wren saw Troy approaching. His smile was ladened with sympathy, and he searched her face quickly before pulling her in for a hug. She accepted it but noticed how she didn't feel like wrapping herself around him like she had with Eddie. That made sense, though, didn't it? They shared their grief. Troy was an outsider looking in.

"How was your trip?" she asked.

Troy tugged at the brim of his baseball cap. "It was good. One kid sprained his ankle on the falls. We ended up at Lake Superior for an afternoon instead of spending another day at Black River Harbor."

"Sounds like fun." Her words sounded stilted even to her own ears.

"You doing okay? I wish I'd been here for you when Patty passed away."

"I'm fine." Wren wrapped her thumbs around her backpack straps that spanned her shoulders. She offered Troy a smile that was both assuring and intended to shut down the conversation before emotion crowded in. "I mean, we'll be okay."

"We?"

"Gary. Eddie. Me." She stumbled over her proclamation.

Troy's brow furrowed a bit, but then he nodded. "Yeah. That's gotta be rough for the guys."

"It is."

"So, do you know why I was corralled into helping at Lost Lake today?"

Wren shot a sideways glance at Troy. No wonder he sounded weary. There were bags under his eyes, and he looked like he hadn't showered yet from his weeklong excursion with the campers.

"Wayne Sanderson apparently pulled strings with the authorities. He's convinced they'll find someone at the bottom."

Troy frowned. "I didn't hear there was any evidence that they thought Jasmine Riviera was actually . . . well, dead."

Wren lifted her hands in acquiescence. "I don't know what Wayne might have provided to convince them. But they did find little Trina Nesbitt not too far from the lake. The stories of Lost Lake, you know . . . Jasmine is still missing."

Troy blanched. "The last thing I want to find at the bottom of Lost Lake is a kid."

"I know." Wren eased out of her backpack. They watched the leaders of the search party as they gathered their supplies and set up for the quest to explore the bottom of Lost Lake. "I don't get how they plan to dredge it. The lake isn't exactly small or shallow like a pond."

"Lost Lake is a little over twenty feet deep," Troy supplied, "so it's doable. But I'm not sure how mucky the bottom will be. Muck and silt would suck a body deeper and bury them. If that's the case, I can't imagine visibility will be great."

Wren supposed there was a lot more science involved in searching the bottom of a lake than she understood. She eyed the red inflatable boat with its small outboard motor. A man sat in the middle of the boat, fiddling with what looked like sonar equipment. That had to have been a pain to haul back here. Logging roads only went so far in; the rest would've had to have been hauled in on foot or maybe by ATV.

Troy pointed. "They'll monitor the lake bed with the sonar and look for anomalies. If they find anything, they'll send one of us down to check it out."

"I thought dragging a lake meant sweeping a net across the bottom or something," Wren said.

Troy offered a sad chuckle. "If only it were that simple."

"Do you think they'll find the bodies of the long-lost Coons family?" It was easier to focus on the lore of the place than picture little Jasmine sinking to the depths of the lake all alone. Innocent. Wren shivered.

Troy shook his head. "Ninety-year-old skeletons can only survive so long underwater."

"I thought it took bones forever to decompose." Wren shuddered at the gory topic.

Troy nodded. "Well, yeah, but think about it. Almost a century underwater? You might have a mandible left."

Wren waved her hand. "Stop, okay? No more."

Troy leaned toward her. "You all right—?"

"I'm fine," she snapped. Then she quickly met his hurt eyes. "I'm sorry. It's all so much, Troy. I don't know . . ."

"Why'd you even come out here? It's going to be hours, maybe even days. This isn't a place for you to find any sort of resolution to Jasmine's disappearance."

"I know that." She ran her hand over her forehead, wiping beads of sweat from it, then drying her hand on the side of her navy-blue trekking pants. "I just . . ." Wren searched for the words. She just what? Creepy woman in the woods had her convinced Ava Coons really did still exist somehow? Jasmine's disappearance was linked to the Redneck Harriet doll with Wren's name on her foot?

"I think I may be losing my mind," she muttered.

Troy rubbed his hand on her arm. Wren stepped away. He dropped it, directed his eyes to the ground, and kicked at a rock. "You're not losing your mind." His affirmation seemed weak considering he didn't know the concoction of a story swirling in her head.

"Do you know where your birth certificate is?" Wren asked suddenly.

Troy gave her a confused look at the abrupt subject change. "Um, sure. Yeah. I have it in my files at home."

"Home as in . . . ?"

"As in Iowa. Where I was born. My parents' place. I wouldn't bring those types of records here to camp."

"But you've seen it?"

"Sure. Haven't you seen yours?"

"No." Wren met his questioning stare. "No, I haven't."

"Is that a problem?"

"Yeah. My dad seems to think my mom accidentally damaged it and needed to get a replacement. Pippin ran a search online and tried to reorder it. The state came back saying there's no record of my birth."

This time Troy's expression darkened. "No record?"

Someone on the lake shouted. They both redirected their attention for a moment, then realized it was routine and nothing had been spotted. Wren turned back to Troy.

"None. That's weird, right? I mean, I'm not overreacting by thinking it's really odd."

"Did you call your grandparents?" Troy asked.

Wren hadn't thought of that. Mom's parents lived in Oklahoma, but they might be able to shed some light on her birth. Maybe she hadn't been born in Wisconsin like she'd thought. But then she would have thought her dad would've said something right away to clear up that misunderstanding.

"Diver!" someone shouted.

They both stilled.

With Troy as a backup diver, he would not be first in the water. They watched as a few men and women scurried along the shoreline. A diver flipped backward into the water from another inflatable boat. In the distance, a loon popped up from under the surface of the water, saw the group of searchers, then disappeared back under. Wren imagined the waterfowl speeding along underwater, well acquainted with the lake bed, having already seen long before whatever it was the dive team was going down to identify.

It seemed like it took hours. Wren lost track of time, and even as she and Troy made their way closer to the lake and to the controlled chaos, a mounting dread welled up inside her. Jasmine. Little Jasmine. The only sign of her had been the hoodie sweatshirt with some blood on it. Not a shoe. Nothing.

Wren prayed repeatedly in the quietness of her soul. *Not here, God. Not here. Please don't let them find her here.*

A diver broke through the surface. They hauled him up into the boat. From the shoreline, Wren saw the diver remove his regulator from his mouth.

Walkie-talkie static filled the air. One of the SAR workers onshore lifted hers to her mouth. "Come again?"

"Nothing. Just an old trunk or something."

"Were they able to open it?"

"Didn't need to." More static. "Top rotted through. It was empty."

Thank God. Murmurs of gratitude rippled through the crew.

Wren sagged against Troy. She had been certain it was going to be Jasmine. Why she had felt so sure, she didn't know. Maybe it was the expression on the woman's face in the woods near the park as she'd stared at Wren the day Patty had died. No, it wasn't evil that was in the woman's face. It was the look of knowing. She *knew.* She knew what had happened to Jasmine. Perhaps to Trina Nesbitt as well.

But then wasn't that how the old campfire story went? Ava Coons always knew. She saw, she took, and she didn't return.

37

"Did they find anything?" Meghan floundered as she leaped from the picnic table outside the canteen. Wren hadn't expected to be accosted by the desperate mother on her return to camp. Being at Lost Lake and watching the slow-going process left her feeling more defeated than if they had actually found something—someone. It just seemed no matter what avenue they took to find Jasmine, they came up short. Even a shoe. Couldn't a diver have at least found a shoe? In no way, shape, or form was Wren wishing Jasmine's body would be located, but any clue to help urge the search onward would sure be a positive next step.

"They haven't found anything." Wren shrugged off her backpack and dropped it on the wooden deck of the canteen.

Meghan collapsed back onto the bench next to Ben. His black hair stuck up in various directions, outing his nervous habit of running his hands through it. His bronzed skin and dark eyes were a sharp contrast to Meghan's blond hair. Wren had seen pictures of little Jasmine. She looked a lot like Ben, only she had her mama's fine bone structure.

"They're using all the tools they have on hand," Wren assured the bereft parents.

"But not finding anything is good, yes?" Meghan looked between them.

Ben nodded. "*Sí*. If they find nothing, then we pray Jasmine isn't there."

After a few comforting but likely empty words, Wren moved away from their table, fumbling in the front pocket of her pack for her phone. Her shoes crunched on the gravel as she crossed the camp's main drive toward the lodge and the offices. Thumbing through her contacts, she found her grandmother's number. She hadn't seen her grandparents in years. They lived on a small ranch, and traveling wasn't in their budget, nor was it practical to leave the animals they boarded to pay her family a visit. Mom had never been that close to her parents, Wren recalled, yet she also remembered the two times they had spent a winter vacation in Oklahoma visiting the ranch. Pleasant memories. Her grandparents had been warm. Friendly. In comparison to her highly educated and bookish father, her grandfather seemed *normal*.

Wren paused on the walk outside the lodge building. She wanted to check in with her dad one more time about her birth records. But first . . .

"Hello?"

Her grandmother's voice broke through, and Wren smiled in spite of herself and the circumstances.

"Grandma!"

"Arwen, is that you?"

"It is."

"Well, land's sake, honey! We haven't heard from you or your brother in months!"

"I know." Wren bent and fished a candy bar wrapper from its tangle in the grassy edge of a flower garden. "Sorry about that." She stuffed the wrapper into an outdoor garbage receptacle.

"How is everyone? Your dad?"

"Oh, we're fine," she lied. Pleasantries were easy fibs, and Wren didn't want to relive the raw agony of loss with her grandmother over the phone. She didn't want to revisit the stark reality of Jasmine's disappearance.

"Good. Your grandpa's dog just had pups the other day. Blue heeler puppies are the darndest little devils."

"Are you keeping them?" Wren fought her way through the pleasantries.

"Oh no. No, we'll sell them once they're weaned. Of course, there is a wee little one your grandpa has his eye on. She's wrapping herself around his little finger. So I wouldn't doubt if one of them escapes being sold."

Wren laughed.

So did her grandma.

There was a moment of silence. Wren paced in front of the lodge's entrance. She shot another staffer a smile as the person passed by and lifted a hand in a wave. She toed a dandelion in the grass.

"Arwen, what's going on? What do you need?"

Her grandmother was perceptive.

Wren squatted down to finger the dandelion. "So, I had a few questions. About my birth."

"Your birth?" There was honest confusion in the older woman's voice. "All right. I'm not sure what I can offer. We weren't around when you were born."

"Well, Mom had me here in Wisconsin, right?"

"No, they were living in California. Your father was teaching at the university. They moved to Wisconsin . . . ohhhhh, I think about a month after you were born?"

"Oh." That was news to her. She'd known about California in her parents' past, and even that Pippin had attended his early years of school there. But she'd not known it was where she'd been born. "My birth records would be in California, then."

"What do you need your birth records for? Getting married?" There was a teasing lilt to her grandmother's voice.

"Funny." Wren mustered a smile, even though her grandmother couldn't see her.

"Well, honey, just submit a request to the California Department of Health. They can reissue a certified copy, and then you'll be all set. I'm sure things were lost or forgotten after your mom passed away." Grandma's voice broke for a moment. She collected herself. "I wish I could help you more. We just weren't that close to your father and so . . . things were distant then, as they are now."

"Were you around when Pippin was born?" The twelve-year gap between them made Wren wonder if things had ever been different before she'd been born and before her mom had experienced miscarriages.

Grandma was quiet a moment and then, "We were. Your parents met here in Oklahoma, you know, where your mother was raised. But shortly after Pippin was born, your father earned his position at the university. It was his dream. I knew their move to California would put distance between us, but I didn't expect it to be distance in more than just miles."

Wren picked the dandelion and spun it between her finger and thumb. "Did they just get busy?"

"Yes?" Grandma responded as if she were questioning her own memories. "Tristan never wanted anything as much as he wanted to become a professor at a place of higher education. Your mother— she simply wanted to be a mother. With Pippin, she completely lost herself in him, but then came the miscarriages . . . and I was far enough away. I wasn't there for her."

Wren waited, sensing there was more.

Grandma cleared her throat over the phone. Wren heard water running in the background, then the sound of a glass being filled. "I wanted to fly out to California after the sixth miscarriage. Well, I wanted to after the first, but your mom insisted it wasn't necessary. By the sixth, Pippin was already eleven, and I think your mom was afraid I'd try to talk her out of trying again. She was probably right. Six? Six miscarriages take their toll on a woman's body. Her hormones, her mental capabilities, all of it. And people don't understand how traumatic one miscarriage is, let alone sequential ones."

"But then I came along and saved the day." Wren heard the lackluster humor in her voice.

Grandma chuckled. "When your mother called me to let me know about you, you were already four days old! A total surprise to your grandfather and I! We had no idea, but she told us she didn't want us to worry and be burdened anymore, so she and your father had agreed to keep the pregnancy quiet until a child was born healthy. Pippin even got on the phone and told us all about you. He was excited—well, as excited as Pippin ever gets."

"And then they moved a month after?" Wren studied the dandelion. She'd read somewhere that dandelions weren't actually weeds but flowers. It was a random thought. Maybe a deflection against the growing wariness in her gut.

"Yes. They did. Your father took a new position at a smaller private college there in Wisconsin and then, as you know, when you were in grade school, he moved you all to the Bible camp."

So her father had downgraded. Each position he took held a lesser educational integrity—or at least according to how Wren knew her father would interpret them. "Why did Dad want to leave his dream position at a California university for a private school in Wisconsin?"

Grandma half snorted into the phone. "Now you're asking the million-dollar question we've asked for years. It doesn't matter, though. In spite of not seeing you all nearly as often as we wanted to while you were growing up, Tristan has done well."

Wren snapped the flower off the dandelion's stem. Unlike Grandma's generous impression of Wren's father, Wren knew him better. Her father wouldn't simply forgo the prestige of a position without the draw of another equal or better opportunity. He might be in charge of an entire camp's biblical education department, but that wasn't even his PhD wheelhouse. He prided himself in his intellectual prowess of English literature, his specialized expertise of Tolkien . . . but a Bible camp in the sequestered Northwoods of Wisconsin? It didn't lend itself to his own natural interests.

"Thanks, Grandma," Wren concluded as suspicions danced in her mind.

"You bet. Oh, and honey?"

"Yeah?"

"Don't be too hard on your parents for not keeping things straight with your birth certificate. Times were tough back then, and your mom—she wasn't in the frame of mind to be organized. Even when you were in grade school . . . you probably never knew, but she struggled. With depression and the like. I always wanted her to be seen by someone. I suggested once to your father that maybe she was bipolar. She had such mood swings. But neither of them would have anything to do with it. She said she had Pippin, and she had you, and that was all she needed."

"Mom often seemed just out of reach," Wren admitted. It was why she'd gravitated so toward Patty.

Grandma was silent for a long moment, and then Wren heard her sigh. "I know she was. Something in those years after Pippin was born and before you came along . . . well, it changed her. She wasn't ever the same again. But I always figured that's what the loss of six babies will do to a woman."

38

Ava

She hadn't been the same since the night Noah had awakened her from her nightmare. But then neither had he. Looking each other in the eyes was simply not going to happen. But it wasn't just the brewing between her and Noah, it was the remembering. The remembering had left Ava huddled in the parsonage like a scared little girl all over again. She was both petrified and angry simultaneously. How she could recall her parents' and her brothers' mutilated bodies, but not their killer, was infuriating. Remembering the terror that soaked into the marrow of her bones as a child and settled there was another factor that left Ava paralyzed.

She sat on her bed, her back against the wall, her knees pulled up to her chest. Across the room, perched on her dresser, was the doll. *Her* doll. Retrieving it from the cellar, Ava had expected to be comforted in its return. The girl doll in the purple dress with the head of human hair twisted into a little tail at the back of its head. But what once had been an imaginary friend in a reclusive life was now a demon taunting her.

> *Dead, dead, they're all dead.*
> *Came today and chopped off their heads.*
> *Put them in pieces, in bits and in blood.*
> *Laid them in death in a pile in the mud.*

The limericks played over and over in Ava's mind. Subliminal. Traveling the space between them in the bedroom. Floating across the air, over the whitewashed wood floors, brushing the patchwork quilt on the bed, and settling in every nerve of Ava's body. She swore the doll smiled. The corner of its porcelain lips twisting into an evil mockery.

> *There is the lake, so bury them there.*
> *Keep it a secret, your personal terror.*
> *But I will know, and I will hide,*
> *the fact that as a child you lied.*

Ava grabbed her pillow and launched it at the doll. It hit her, sending it toppling to the floor. Yet she remained unshattered. Her face only cracked into more thin spidery lines. Her eyes stared vacantly at the ceiling, much like Ava's mother's had, and the doll's mouth remained turned in its tiny contorted smile.

Lied. She hadn't lied. She just couldn't remember. Not when she was thirteen, and not now. Ava slid off the bed and retrieved the pillow, tossing it back in its place. She bent to pick up the doll, then paused. Something in her mind was hiding from her. Just in the shadows. Of course, it was the owner of those boots. The ones that had clomped down the cellar ladder. The body that had stood there, contemplating. Debating whether to kill Ava? In retrospect, Ava knew she couldn't have truly been hidden out of sight from the killer. He had spared her. Why?

She retrieved the doll, its body soft under her grasp. They stared at each other. One questioning, the other accusing.

There was a knock, then the doorknob on her bedroom door rattled. She spun toward it, holding the doll against her chest as if it would protect her while simultaneously imagining the doll gnawing at her flesh with its wicked face.

"Ava?"

It was Noah.

Ava crossed the room, doll still against her, pressed into the pleated front of her green dress. She missed her overalls. Hanny had whisked them off to her house on the pretense of washing them. She'd not returned them but instead had brought the green dress. Ava supposed washing heavier denim was difficult for the old woman. She should help Hanny . . .

Ava pulled the door open. She directed her gaze to the tip of his nose. Avoiding his eyes. She didn't really know what she felt. Not with him. Not with her memories. Not with anything.

Noah shifted his weight on his feet. "Jipsy's funeral is this afternoon."

"I know."

"I figured you may entertain thoughts of trying to attend in the shadows, but I wanted to request that you don't. I know you're not keen on how things are right now, but—"

"I'm not comin'." Ava put Noah's fears to rest. She wasn't planning on doing anything today that made her susceptible to that creeper hiding in the forest. Her fingers touched her cheek. Noah's eyes followed her movement.

He nodded. "Good. I'm hoping, once she's laid to rest, things will settle down a bit."

Ava scoffed at him with a laugh. "Tempter's Creek will never let nothin' rest."

Noah looked down at his feet. The man was a bottled-up jar of nitroglycerin waiting to explode, but dressed under the guise of a preacher.

He lifted his eyes.

Ava refused to look at him.

"Ava," Noah began, "we're going to need to come up with a plan. You can't stay here, not forever—not . . . like this." Alone. That was what he meant. Alone with the potential of more moments like the other night. Where the warmth in the room was caused by more than just a summer's night.

She knew that. But today she was afraid. Her confidence, her reckless nature, was squashed by the potency of her memories.

Noah cleared his throat. "I think if you go back—"

Ava snapped her head up. "I'm not goin' back to that lake."

Noah weighed his words. "Now that you remember so much . . ." He hesitated. "Well, going back to your family's home—to the lake—it might look different to you now. Maybe you'll see something that helps you remember who killed your family."

"I'm not going back." Ava half hid behind her door, holding on to it for support. She had been so disassociated from her family's deaths. But with the memories came the emotions, along with the fear and the horror of it all.

"I'd go with you," he offered.

Ava glared at him. "You think it's 'cause I'm afraid to go alone? No. I'm afraid to go, period." She cursed the tears that burned her eyes. "I don't need to see—I don't need to see nothin' to remember more'n what I already do." Least of which, the killer's face. God help her if she remembered his face. Ava was terrified it would imprint on her mind and never go away. For the rest of her life, she would see the killer's eyes, watch in a replay his fingers adjust on the handle of the ax . . . the contemplation . . . kill the teenage girl?

"You'll never be free of this." Noah's declaration was harsh to Ava's ears, even if his tone was gentle.

Ava grimaced and looked away. She adjusted her hold on her doll, feeling the doll's hair tickle the back of her hand. Turning back to Noah, she nodded in agreement. "I'll never be free of it if I remember more. It'll haunt me." Ava swallowed as anxiety crept up her throat with its stranglehold. "An' I don't like ghosts. Never did. Never will."

"Come away from the window, child." Hanny's calming voice made Ava allow the curtain to fall back into place. The old woman had visited shortly before Noah departed that morning. She'd brought a pan of baked goods in case she was spotted, and so no one would ask questions about the amount of visits to the parsonage. But that she stayed and Noah left? Well, Hanny said she was banking on the fact that people were preoccupied with Jipsy's funeral. She was right. They were. It seemed as if all of Tempter's Creek had turned out.

Ava covertly hid behind the curtain, observing. The little cemetery behind Noah's church would become the resting place for Jipsy. "I wonder if they're really comin' 'cause they care about Jipsy, or if'n they're snooping around in business that ain't theirs?"

"Probably both." Hanny patted the sofa. "Come. Sit."

Ava paced across the front room to the picture of Jesus. She stared at Him. He looked busy today. Probably preoccupied trying to make sure Noah did a good job with the eulogy and trying to withhold His fiery judgment on Widower Frisk. Ava knew the old man would smuggle a bottle of whiskey in his inside coat pocket. Drinking at Jipsy's funeral? It was just something the widower would do. He had to survive somehow. Him without Jipsy was like a saloon without patrons.

"Funerals are a miserable thing," Hanny observed. "When my Kendrick passed away, I was utterly beside myself. Of course, that was thirty years ago now, but still. I prefer to avoid funerals. Sorrow is a bitter memory and a dreadful companion."

Ava glanced down at Hanny. The woman was embroidering. Her stitches were small and impressively delicate for someone whose hand had the tremor of old age in it.

"I never had a funeral for my family." Ava stated it as a realization. There was a vague recollection of the lake. Smoke hovering over the earth, making young Ava choke. The lake had been the place she'd hefted, and pulled, and tugged, and labored four times over to bring her family to an illusion of safety. Safety from the fire meant the lake became their coffin. How long had their bodies floated in the lake before sinking to its depths? Ava knew she couldn't have possibly gotten any of her family very far into the lake. The wind and the waves would have had them drifting into the deep, but eventually death would've made them float slowly back to the surface.

"How long does a body float?" Ava voiced her morbid thought to avoid the swift violence of her own sorrow. Distance. She needed to distance herself from the *feeling*. Shocking herself with black, offensive facts about death brought her family's murders into a clinical perspective.

Hanny clucked her tongue. "What an awful thing to consider."

Ava met Jesus' eyes. "A few hours? Days? Once I saw a bloated dead dog floatin' in old Nipper's pond. He told me the dog had been dead quite a while, disappeared under, then came back on top all puffy. Guess somethin' inside him made him float."

"You do beat all, child." Hanny bit the embroidery thread after tying it off.

Ava thought about the dog. Considered the way it had almost doubled in size, it seemed. "'Course, Nipper left him out in the middle, and not long after the dog sank again. Never did come back up."

Hanny brushed her hand across her embroidery. "Praise be," she mumbled.

"Do you think that's what happened to my folks?" Ava asked Jesus more than she asked Hanny. But neither of them answered her. It was that awful silence where no one really wanted to say anything. Only the clock ticked. A hypnotic *ticktock, ticktock* that made Ava's eyes heavy. But she didn't want to close them. Didn't want to think anymore. No more. No more thoughts of bodies, of the lake, of her family . . .

"I'm goin' to go take a nap," Ava announced, though she wasn't sure she'd ever napped a day in her life before. It was the only way she could think of to make the thoughts go away. To still the whirling in her mind, the awful sensation in her gut that this time she wasn't going to be able to forget. That her family's murders were following her with a vengeance that required restitution.

"You do that, dear."

Ava took Hanny's encouragement, and with a last glance at

Jesus, she hurried from the room. Jesus had looked, for a moment, as if He shared her sorrow. Her pain. But it was just a painting.

She took a quick detour into the kitchen. A glass of water would be good. Quench her thirst. Still her spirit. Do something to—

The back door was ajar. Ava stared at it as if the door were going to open further. But it didn't. Its gap was wide enough for a cat to squeeze through. A ray of sunshine followed the path of the imaginary cat, stretching across the floor and resting on the leg of the kitchen table. Ava looked around the kitchen in a swift gesture. Stove. Icebox. Sink. Table. Nothing was moved or upset. A dish towel hung over the back of one of the chairs. The curtains over the sink were still drawn.

Ava made quick work of crossing the kitchen. She grasped the doorknob with her left hand and moved to shut the door. But something kept it from closing. Ava looked down and noticed a shiny object leaning against the doorframe. Cautiously, Ava bent, daring a peek out the door to see if anyone stood there. There was no one. Nothing. Only the backyard that stretched into the woods. A honeybee buzzing across the back step. A crack in the cement boasting one lonely violet.

She turned her attention to the item wedged in the doorway. Reaching for it, Ava realized what it was, and she snatched her hand back.

I will hunt you.

The hissing voice of her attacker filled her. Ava could feel his arms around her again. This time she could smell his raunchy breath. Her ear throbbed. He had made that vow, that promise. He was playing a deadly, wicked hunting game.

Ava pulled the heavy iron ax-head into the parsonage and slammed the door shut. Staring at the offensive item, she could no longer stifle the growing terror and agony inside her. She reached for what resembled the weapon that had been used to murder her parents—to kill Matthew Hubbard—and with a wild scream, Ava launched it through the kitchen window.

39

Wren

Eddie edged past Wren as she entered the camp kitchen. His white canvas apron was stained with water droplets from his position at the industrial-sized sink. It was piled with stainless-steel pans that needed a good hot scrub to get off the baked-on remnants of cookie bars.

"Eddie." Wren tried to capture his attention, but he was focused. He'd been this way since Patty had died. An intensity surrounded him with an air of standoffishness. She couldn't be frustrated with him, but she ached for him to let her in. It seemed ever since his moment of vulnerability, he'd withdrawn. Selfishly, she wanted to bounce off her conversation with her grandma and get Eddie's opinion. She wanted to draw him into the unsettled trepidation that was growing within her. She wanted his opinion on the search of Lost Lake—whether he thought they'd ever find anything there. Not that he would know more than the experts, but . . . well, it was Eddie. They'd always shared everything. Now, in the wake of his mother's death, it seemed to be driving them apart.

He lifted the sprayer from its holder and sent scalding water splashing against the dirty pans. The spray misted into the air. A few of the kitchen staff remained, high schoolers volunteering their time at the camp for the week. They hovered behind Eddie. He seemed aware of them if he wasn't aware of her.

"You guys can head out if all the dishes are being run through the dishwasher," he called over his shoulder.

"Yeah, they are!" one of the guys responded. He glanced at Wren, who offered him a smile.

"Thanks, guys. Good job on getting the place cleaned up." Eddie's consistent encouragement kept these teenagers engaged in menial work. Getting a few hundred campers and staff through one meal could be strenuous work, but three meals a day was nothing short of monumental.

The kids scampered from the kitchen, tossing their aprons into a five-gallon bucket that housekeeping would later snatch, take to the laundry, and return.

Eddie grabbed a scrub pad and put some serious elbow grease into cleaning a pan.

"Eddie," Wren tried again. She was only a few feet away from him in the doorway. There were four big sinks, and he was at the third farthest from her.

He gave her a quick glance. "Hey."

Wren hesitated. He wasn't unfriendly. He was just . . . she'd never experienced awkwardness with Eddie before. Ever.

"What's up?" He hefted the scrubbed pan into sink number four, which was filled with sudsy water.

"Do you want help?" she offered.

"Sure." He managed a lopsided smile that didn't reach his eyes.

Wren rolled up her sleeves and headed for the last sink. Plunging her hands into the hot water, she fished around for a dishrag. "I missed you at lunch today," she managed. She intended to follow it up with a comment about how she'd been at her dad's house, and Pippin was helping her look up her birth records in California. But that would require filling Eddie in on a lot more details than just that. He didn't seem ready for that type of conversation.

"I was working in the kitchen," he explained.

Of course he was. Wren wasn't surprised, just—well, often he'd come out and eat with her while the rest of the experienced staff managed the trail of hungry campers.

"Are you okay?" She gripped the edge of the sink and went in for the jugular. Eddie was never one to mince words, and Wren wasn't sure she could take this continued distance between them. This undefined arm's-length thing.

Eddie nodded. "Sure." He continued to scrub at an especially black part of the burnt batter.

Wren cocked her head. "Really?"

Eddie scrubbed harder. "What do you want me to say, Wren? Mom just died a few days ago. Sure. I'm ready for Disney World. When do we leave?"

"That's not fair." Wren instantly battled tears of hurt.

Eddie dropped the scrub pad in the dirty water and turned to her, his hands dripping. "Wren. Just—I need space."

"Why are you withdrawing from me? Now of all times." She couldn't help the tear that rolled down her cheek. It betrayed her. Betrayed how much reliance she had on Eddie and had never really realized.

He closed his eyes as if to gather his own emotions. When he opened them, he worked his jaw back and forth. "I'm not withdrawing, Wren, I'm just—we both are hurting and—"

"And we could help each other through this!"

"No. Wren . . ." Eddie held up his hands. "Just let it go."

"Let what go? The fact that we both lost someone we loved? That the last several days have been traumatic?"

"That *you* can't keep coming to *me*," Eddie snapped. He grabbed the towel from over his shoulder and wiped his hands on it. His sandals squeaked on the wet tile floor as he brushed past her and tossed the towel onto the stainless-steel counter.

"What are you talking about?" Wren demanded. Now her tears were because she was frustrated. Hurt. Angry. "That's the dumbest thing I—"

"No," Eddie interrupted, his hands at his waist. "It's not. You have a boyfriend, Wren. If you need something, you need to go to him. Not me. I can't always be there to pick you up. I have my own—Mom is *gone*. She's not here anymore. I have to deal with that. I have to figure out how to let God walk me through it and get me out to the other side. The fact is, you have to do that too, but *without* me."

Wren stared at him.

Eddie stared back.

The impasse between them was cavernous.

"So, after all these years of being best friends, I'm supposed to just—not talk to you?" She was confused. Bewildered really.

"Talk to me. Hang out. Yeah, fine. But if you *need* me, if you need support, a shoulder—go to Troy. That's what he's there for."

An emptiness grew in Wren's stomach. A wicked, painful hollow that spread quickly and was stark in its honesty. "I-I don't—"

"I'm not your other half, Wren. I won't be. I *can't* be." Eddie's voice cracked. He cursed softly, shocking Wren even more. "I'm sorry."

She backed away from the sink. Water dripped down her arms. Whirling, Wren raced from the kitchen before she made a fool of herself. It was clear. Very clear. The hesitation from both Eddie and Troy when she mentioned the other. The thin line of tension between two nice stand-up guys. She thought of Patty's comments about Eddie. Her own comments about Eddie. Troy . . .

Wren burst into the outside air, the double doors of the dining hall slamming open and then shutting behind her. She took in a few deep, shuddering gasps. It was awful how someone could be surrounded by people they loved and still be as misplaced as someone who had vanished without a trace.

She needed to find Troy. She didn't *want* to find him, but she needed to. It was as clear as the fact her red hair was natural that she needed to talk to him. Wren was annoyed that, by the time she reached the main lodge, she was a complete wreck. A few campers passing by had given her the side-eye as she wiped an unending stream of tears from her eyes as she charged ahead. One staffer had asked if she was okay. Wren had gasped out "Patty," only to receive an empathetic nod. Everyone knew Wren was grieving too. They didn't know it was a convoluted mess of personal displacement, loss of a second mother, fitful exhaustion from searching for the missing child, and now this—this relationship bomb that had dropped from the sky. It had probably screamed at her as it was falling, but she'd been blind to it. Eddie was just there. He'd always been there. He'd always *be* there.

Now, as she sprinted up the stairs in the lodge toward the camp offices, she wondered how she had ever been so ignorant. Troy was a saint. He'd tolerated—no, he'd *accepted*—her and Eddie's comradeship like a flipping hero! The problem was, it wasn't Troy she ached for when she was hurting. It wasn't Troy she found herself seeking out for advice. It wasn't Troy who filled her with a sense of calm when everything else spun out of control.

Wren collided with another staff member. He stumbled backward, his shaved bald head glowing with the light of the inset ceiling bulb. He laughed. "Whoa, you're on a mission."

"Sorry, Kyle." Wren liked the older man. He was about her dad's age, but he had a genuine warmth about him that wasn't inhibited by any type of self-importance. "I'm looking for Troy."

"In the offices?" Kyle raised an eyebrow.

"Well, I thought he may have to spend some time up here to work on his next trip's roster."

Kyle laughed again. "I'm just teasing. It's funny to even see Troy inside. The man belongs in the woods with the wolves."

"Yeah." Wren chucked nervously.

"He was just getting ready to pack up for the day, I think. They want him to help with SAR tomorrow."

"I know." Wren nodded. Boy, did she know. "And they're not finding anything in Lost Lake either."

Kyle startled. "You didn't hear?"

Dread seeped into Wren's gut. "Hear what?"

"They found a few bones. Human. Part of a skull, a hip bone. Definitely not anything related to Jasmine, but they're speculating it may actually be part of one of the Coons family members who was killed years ago."

The idea sickened Wren. Everything sickened Wren. Ava Coons's family had never been found, but if these remains were theirs, then that part of the story would actually be true. The Coons family *had* been buried at the bottom of Lost Lake.

"I'll catch you later." Kyle waved and carried on his way. He was too happy. The search team had found bones. *Bones.*

Wren shuddered and hurried toward Troy's office, which was more of a closet than anything else. She drew to a stop outside his door. Her stomach rolled. Her breathing grew shallow. She had come here knowing nothing other than she needed to see Troy. But now? This was only going to initiate more pain. Leave her—and Troy—more displaced.

"Wren!" Troy opened his door, his backpack slung over his shoulder. His grin brightened his face, but he must have read something on hers because it dissipated just as fast. "What's wrong?"

"Can we talk?" Wren mustered up the will to at least ask that.

Troy's teeth clenched for a moment before he ducked his head. "Yeah. Yeah, sure. Come in."

She sidled past him. The office had a small desk with a chair, and one extra chair just under an open window. There wasn't room for any other furniture.

Troy let his backpack drop to the floor.

Wren sat down on the extra chair and twisted her fingers together.

Troy reached out and rested his hand over hers. "Hey."

She looked up.

His eyes were understanding—too understanding.

"Troy, I—"

"It's okay, Wren." He gave a small laugh. "It doesn't take a rocket scientist to know what's on your mind."

"It doesn't?"

"Wren, you've gone through a lifetime's worth of crud in the last week and a half. Anyone helping with the search for Jasmine has been affected. It's unnerving, not to mention—you probably shouldn't have gone to watch them search Lost Lake when you'd just lost Patty."

It made it all so much worse. Troy's understanding.

"Troy—"

"I know." There was gravity in his voice. He drummed his fingers on his desk, the palm of his other hand scraping against his three days' worth of whiskers.

"I don't know what's wrong with me." Wren bit her lip, sucking back the wateriness in her voice.

"Nothing's wrong with you." Troy's eyes darkened with understanding. "You've been through a lot here in a short period of time, and I'm—not your rock."

Wren lifted her eyes.

Troy continued, his expression pained. "Eddie is. He always has been. I can't compete with that."

"I didn't realize," she admitted. Wren picked at a fingernail. It was hard to look at Troy. She despised causing anyone pain.

"No. You didn't. Neither did I when we first started dating a few months ago. But it's clear. Neither of you have acted on it because—well, I think 'cause you've just always been in each other's lives. You took each other for granted."

"Eddie never said anything."

Troy gave a small laugh. "Oh, he did. In his way. He doesn't *say* things, but . . . it was pretty clear to me. Eddie gave you space. He's not going to risk losing your friendship, and once we were dating, he's too good of a guy."

Wren brushed a tear from her cheek. "Patty knew."

"I'm sure she did." Troy reached for a quarter on his desk and started flipping it between his fingers. "Listen, I'm not going to lie, this isn't how I'd hoped things would develop between us. But I get it. Right now, you both need each other more than you probably ever have."

"I'm sorry." Wren dared to look at Troy. The handsome features. Girls clamored for his attention. It wasn't often someone came around with such handsome, outdoorsy guy looks with a character of good values and faith to match. But Eddie was that too—maybe more average-looking, but he had a solid character and . . . "I need him." Wren sucked in a sob. She looked over Troy's shoulder to avoid seeing any potential pain on his face.

She heard the quarter hit the desktop.

Troy was holding out a tissue. "And I'm not stopping you."

40

She hadn't seen Eddie since their interlude in the kitchen. Wren had wanted to find him for the last two days. It wasn't as though Deer Lake Bible Camp was *that* huge that she couldn't find a staff member after a bit of trying. She'd ended up at the Markham house a few hours after breaking things off with Troy, only to have Gary inform her that Eddie had taken the rest of the week off and had left to get some time alone. Gary also let Wren know he was locking up the Markham house and heading to his brother's place in Michigan for a week or two.

They were raw, the Markham men, in the wake of Patty's passing. Wren understood, but their absence created a chasm. A painful, deep chasm. Her entire support system was crumbling. The SAR base camp had greatly reduced in size. People were still searching for Jasmine, but the amount of people invested had dwindled. Two weeks and already the authorities were beginning to speak of Jasmine in the past tense. Ben and Meghan had averted their efforts to arguing with authorities not to disband the search teams that remained. The dive teams had scoured the bottom of Lost Lake. Aside from the old human bones, they'd found nothing.

"They sent the bones to a lab to be tested and dated," Troy had told Wren. At least they were still on speaking terms. But now he was off on another wilderness trip with a busload of canoeists. The Flambeau River was calling their name, with its Class II rapids that were strong enough to make novices nervous, but boring enough that Troy would go down them wearing only a life jacket and lying on his back.

Wren flung open the screen door on the back deck of her family's house. Nestled in the woods like every other home in this area, the mosquitoes were kept at bay tonight with lit citronella candles and three massive pots of lemongrass. Dusk was settling, the air still and calm. There was Wi-Fi here, so Wren sank onto a patio chair and pulled out her phone. She set her mug of hot peach tea on the table and rested her feet on a patio chair opposite her.

Thumbing through the apps, she opened the search engine and typed in *Ava Coons*. A litany of randomness came up, and she had to narrow her search to *Ava Coons campfire story* to get any specific results.

"What are you looking at?"

Wren jumped as Pippin opened the screen door and stepped onto the deck. He had a blueberry scone in his hand, and his other clutched a glass of milk.

"I'm reading about Ava Coons." Wren ignored her brother as she continued scrolling through the few articles online.

Pippin sat down in a chair and yawned. "That old story is over-done."

"Not if they found their bones in the lake."

Pippin rubbed his eyes, tired after a long day of staring at his herd of computer monitors. "Yeah, *if.*"

"I'm trying to find news articles about the murders. All I can find is just the stories and exaggerated legends."

"The records probably aren't digitized," Pippin informed her. "Tempter's Creek Courthouse just got on Wi-Fi ten years ago. We live in the boondocks, Wren."

"No one would believe you if you told them that." Wren mustered a laugh.

Pippin didn't laugh. He didn't have much of an expression beyond boredom. "That's the difference between living in Chicago or L.A. versus Podunk, Wisconsin."

The screen door opened a third time, and their father stepped onto the deck. His loafers and pressed pants seemed out of place here in the woods. His glasses were academic, his features lined but handsome in a dignified, standoffish sort of way. Wren eyed him as he occupied the fourth and final remaining chair.

There was a graveness in his expression. His brows were pulled together as he set an envelope on the table.

"What's that?" Pippin leaned over to look at it.

"That's what I'd like to know." Tristan Blythe leveled his fatherly stare on Wren. "Arwen?"

She tilted her chin up and looked down her nose, trying to see what it was. "What is it?"

"A letter from the State of California."

"The Department of Health?" She'd applied online for a copy of her birth certificate. She hadn't expected a response by mail in just a few short days.

"Yes." Tristan's index finger tapped the envelope. "Why are you contacting the California DOH?"

"I needed a copy of my birth certificate." It was a simple answer. Wren wondered why she felt guilty under her father's assessment.

Pippin took a drink of his milk. His mustache was tipped in white when he drew the glass away. "You're in trouble."

Wren took the envelope from her father's proffered hand and ripped it open. Skimming it, she released a breath of defeat. "What in the world?"

Neither man responded.

Wren looked up at them both. "There's a whole form to fill out. They need more information."

Pippin chewed his scone. "You can probably fill it out online. Did they include a web address or just a paper form?"

Her father made no comment.

"Is there something I should know?" Wren skewered them both with a look. Remembering Patty's words, she'd wanted to avoid unnecessary hurt for her father's sake, but now? "Did Mom have an affair?"

Tristan Blythe erupted into a fit of shocked coughs.

Pippin stared at her as their father collected himself. "I'll leave you two alone." With that, he retreated into the house with his glass of milk and half-eaten scone.

Wren watched him depart. It felt like a one-hundred-pound weight had settled on her chest. "I'm sorry, Dad, but what am I supposed to think when my records are so difficult to come by?"

Tristan cleared his throat. "Your mother did not have an affair, Arwen. She could barely get out of the house to socialize."

"She was depressed," Wren ventured. "Grandma said Mom struggled mentally. She wasn't stable. Maybe she found comfort elsewhere."

"Enough!" Tristan's hand came down on the glass table.

"Dad—"

"No." Tristan stood, scraping his chair backward on the deck's floorboards. He bit back an oath, strode toward the door, then stopped. Looking over his shoulder, he softened his expression. "Arwen, your mother was—I know she wasn't a Patty Markham to you, but she was a *good* woman. A *good* mother."

Wren nodded. She didn't know how else to respond.

Wren wasn't sure what awakened her, and she was so accustomed to crashing at the Markhams' that she was disoriented when she opened her eyes. The window was to the right of her. Its blinds pulled, lavender curtains appearing dark blue in the dim light. She lay in a full-size bed instead of the narrower twin type. She rolled over to face the door. A framed poster from *The Lord of the Rings* movie hung on one of the walls, with another poster of actress Liv Tyler as Arwen beside it.

Home. She was in the Blythe home, in her old bedroom. Wren reached for her phone. Almost two o'clock in the morning. She checked her text messages. Nothing from Eddie. She knew him well enough to know he wasn't on social media, so she didn't bother to check.

A thump on the back deck outside her window grabbed her attention. That must have been what had awakened her. Wren tossed back the covers and swung her legs over the side of the bed. Wild animals were no strangers to their deck, but raccoons caused issues, as did skunks. She pushed back the curtain and stuck her fingers between the blinds to peek out.

Nothing.

Uneasiness spread within her. Immediately, the image of Ava Coons standing in the Markhams' driveway came to mind. The creepy message. Ava Coons near the park, her face tainted with what felt like evil.

Wren stepped back, allowing the blinds to snap together and the curtains to fall into place. She had the sudden urge to jump into bed and pull the covers over her head. But if it really was a raccoon, it could get into the garbage cans and then they'd have a mess in the morning.

Mustering courage, Wren snuck into the hall. Her father's bedroom door was shut. Pippin slept downstairs. She hopped over the one spot beneath the carpet that creaked and tiptoed into the kitchen. Peering out the window above the sink, Wren scanned the deck. The motion sensor hadn't made the light go off. From this vantage point, the deck still looked empty. But she noticed a citronella candle had fallen from the deck's rail. Something had definitely knocked it over.

"Fine," Wren muttered to herself. She went to the back door and moved to unlock it, then noticed it was already unlocked. It didn't alarm her. Many people in this area never locked their doors. But a chill still ran down her spine.

She tugged the door open, leaving the screen door as the only barrier between herself and the back deck. Crickets' chirrups met her ears. An uninterrupted cadence that made her feel slightly more comforted that no one or thing was lurking on the deck and waiting to spring. Expecting a raccoon felt a lot better than planning for an assault from a supposed-to-be-dead Ava Coons.

The deck was empty. Barefooted, Wren crossed it and bent to retrieve the fallen candle. Lifting it, she placed the pot back on the deck rail, staring into the deep shadows of the forest. A few coyotes yipped in the far distance. The breeze picked up and blew its breath across Wren's face. Peaceful really. Nothing to alarm her.

Was Jasmine out there yet? Alone? Wren leaned against the deck rail, crossing her arms and resting there. For the first time, she entertained the probability that Jasmine was gone for good. Wandered too far into the woods to be found, or worse, abducted and had never been in the woods to begin with. Meghan's theory of Ava Coons, Wayne Sanderson's obsession with Lost Lake . . . it was too much.

She needed to go back to bed. She wasn't thinking clearly and trying to reconcile everything was only making her more awake and less likely to fall back asleep. Wren turned to go back into the house when her gaze landed on something propped by the back door.

The doll—or as Eddie had nicknamed it, Redneck Harriet— glared up at Wren from its crouched position. Its shoulder hung low on the left side, making its head tilt at an awkward angle. In the moonlight, the cracks that webbed across Harriet's face looked like wispy spider legs all going in tangents. Uncontrolled and mad.

Wren and the doll stared at each other. The doll unblinking, and Wren holding her breath as though any second Redneck Harriet would launch herself from her spot by the door and go all horror-film on Wren's face. The doll had been at the Markham home. Not here. Not at the Blythe house. Someone had placed it there, by the door, and it hadn't been there earlier in the night when Wren had confronted her father.

Wren spun and cast wary glances into all the corners she could see into. Tree branches waved in the summer night breeze, their arms stretching up and out like clawed hands wanting to grab her. The crickets had gone still. The coyotes had ceased their howls.

Wren faced the doll again and forced herself to approach.

It's just a doll. It's just a doll.

But the doll had a moving part. Someone behind it, someone who had placed it at Wren's back door. Something was pinned to the doll's dress. Wren squatted in front of it, not breaking her gaze on Harriet's glass eyes. She quickly unpinned it, and the movement made Harriet slide over and fall on her side. Her eyes rolled into her head.

Wren scooted away from it. The paper in her hand was small, crinkled, and thin. It felt like a napkin. She wrenched her gaze from the doll and squinted in the dim light. Handwriting scrawled across it. She already knew what the first two words would be.

Arwen.

Ava.

The same as the print on the back steps of the Markhams'. The violation made Wren shudder. She brought the napkin closer to her face. There were more words this time.

October 9, 1996
Find her in the paper.
She is not dead.

41

Ava

Ava wrenched her arm away from Noah's attempt to grab on to her.

"Do *not* touch me!" she seethed between clenched teeth. Recently she had wondered what it would be like to cope with the embers that brewed inside Noah Pritchard, but today her own had flared to life. By fear. By an instinctual and primal knowledge that death was nipping at her heels. She had witnessed it before. Seen it, felt it, breathed it. The ax-head in the doorway was evidence that Ava had merely been surviving these past years, and now death had returned.

Noah sprinted after her. Ava could hear his feet pounding on the ground. She could also make out the shouts and clamor of the gathering for Jipsy's funeral. Tempter's Creek was awakened to her presence in the parsonage the moment she'd hurled the ax-head through the kitchen window.

Ava ducked around the corner of the pharmacy, glancing in the windows at the soda bar. It was mostly empty.

"Ava!"

She ignored Noah's call. Ax-heads were everywhere in Tempter's Creek. A logging community had no shortage of them. But the stark memory of dragging a logger's ax behind her as a girl verging on womanhood had come rushing back. The weight of the ax.

The injustice of anyone thinking she was strong enough to swing it multiple times and overpower her entire family. The cruelty that rumors and falsities would land on her shoulders for Hubbard's death—for Jipsy's.

Ava hurtled into an alley, intent on reaching the back of the blacksmith's shop. From there, she had an inkling of how to make it through the woods toward her homeplace. They didn't want her in Tempter's Creek? Someone wanted to threaten her. Hunt her? Then she would take them back to where it all began. There was no avoiding it. No running from it. No hiding from it. Noah had been right. She needed to go back—and now she'd lead the entire town back there too. Where it all began.

She collided with something solid. Knocking the breath from her, Ava stumbled back, but Noah grappled for her arms to save her from connecting with the earth. He hauled her up and against him, spinning around the corner of the blacksmith's shop and pressing his back against the wall. Ava smelled cedar and cinnamon on his shirt, her cheek pressed into his chest as he palmed her head against him. She could hear the pounding of his heartbeat and feel the warmth of his skin through his saturated shirt. His necktie scratched her cheek.

"Don't say anything," Noah hissed.

Ava heard the voices of various town members. Following them. Looking for her. They weren't a mob—yet—but there were numerous intent inhabitants of the small population who believed it their civic duty to find Ava now that she had made her presence clear. And find . . .

Her head shot up to investigate Noah's face. "They're looking for you too?"

"Of course. You were in the parsonage—living there with me, alone." His eyes widened in resigned acceptance. "It's twice the scandal. Now shush." Releasing her, Noah's hand slid down her arm and gripped hers. There was no emotion in it, no feelings to tingle her heart. It was a necessity.

"Come on." He tugged her toward the woods, and they scurried across a small clearing as fast as they could. Thornbushes scraped at Ava's bare legs. Curse this dress. God knew she craved her overalls. Noah didn't stop pulling her into the brush and the shelter of the trees. For several minutes they pushed and dodged their way through the brambles and growth of the forest, until finally they reached what must have made Noah feel was shelter for the moment.

Oak trees rose above them, mixed with pine and a few poplars. Saplings tried to reach for the sky, scattered across the forest floor, but their demise was inevitable with the thick overgrowth from the mature trees that shut out the sunlight.

"What'n heck were you thinking?" Noah paced the area, agitated. He kicked his foot at a rotten log on the ground. A few bones from a deer carcass were scattered near it. The spine, a few ribs . . . it was gruesome, but it was reality. Life met with death. Always.

Noah's glare was a mixture of frustration, worry, and something else Ava couldn't place. But he was upset, that much was clear, and she didn't think any amount of waterlogged words would douse the fire that emoted from his expression.

"You threw an ax-head through my window?" Noah was incredulous. His shoes crunched on the forest floor as he paced again. His suit coattails were pushed out behind him, as his hands never wavered from their place at his waist. His tie was crooked.

"I did." Ava stood still, staring down her nose at him. He didn't understand. Wouldn't understand. He hadn't even asked why she'd made such a ruckus. "I'm done with it all. Don't rightly care if they take me—put me in jail. I can't do this no more!"

"You determine this now—when it's more than apparent we've been living together? I put my entire reputation on the line for you!" Noah's arms waved in exasperation. "Not a soul will believe we—"

"Well, I never asked you to!" Ava spat.

"My ministry here is shot to heck." He skewered her with a look, striding a few paces toward her.

"Then move to another church. Doesn't seem like you're happy here anyway." Ava tilted her head and glowered at him.

Noah stilled. "And why would you say that?"

"Doubtful I've ever seen you smile," Ava challenged.

"You've been in my house all of a couple weeks."

"Most people smile at least once in fourteen days," Ava retorted.

Noah glared.

Ava raised her brows. "'Sides, it's clear as the nose on your face that *Emmaline* has caused you problems. Seems like I ain't the only one with ghosts in my closet."

"I never *killed* her."

"I never *killed* my family."

They stared each other down. Both of them breathing heavier. Angry. Hurt. It was thick between them. As thick as the air that swirled but with something entirely different. Something that made Ava distinctly aware of the way Noah clenched his square jaw. Of the way his hair fell over his forehead. Of the way his eyes burrowed so deep into her soul that she was afraid he could read every part of it and know every nook and cranny.

"Emmaline isn't my issue," Noah responded finally, his voice a bit softer.

"Then what is?" Ava held up her hands. "No. I don't need to know. Wanna know why? 'Cause I've had my face bruised in and bloodied. Someone left an ax-head in the back door for me to find. People think I'm a bloodthirsty murderer. Seems like I've got enough on my plate to be considerin' than worryin' about what your problem is."

Noah's eyes darkened. "Ava."

"Don't *Ava* me. You don't have the slightest clue what it's like to be afraid all your life." Ava could hear herself ranting, like a dam of pent-up emotion she didn't even realize she had. "You don't know what it's like to be lost. To grow up never knowin' why your family died. To live with a crotchety old widower who thought your only worth was to do his chores and watch his traplines and rap at your door at night till Jipsy intervened. Ain't no one ever cared enough to love me. To want me. Only thinkin' I'm some mystery and then bein' quick to judge when they needed someone to blame. Now I'm runnin', but to where? Only home I got is deep in these woods, and it's all burned down. I drug my family into the lake to save 'em from burnin', but they was already dead. Dead and bloody. So don't talk to me about your *issues*! Your problems. I'm sooooooo sorry I added to your troubles!" Ava was trying to shout, but her throat was clogged with tears, and her words came out more of a croak than anything.

"Ava—"

"You can move on. You prob'ly got family, and well, if'n Tempter's Creek wants to make a mess of you 'cause you were helpin' me, an' they want to make up lies 'bout you, then it ain't like you can't pick up and go start new somewhere else."

"Reputation and sin follow you."

"So you're gonna make this about sin now?"

"No," Noah growled in exasperation. "That's not my point."

"Just let me go, *Preacher* Pritchard. It's time we go our separate ways. I never asked you to look out for me. I never asked you to defend me. I never asked you to *care*!" Now she was crying, and that made Ava more frustrated. She wrapped her arms around herself.

"Maybe caring is just what I do best."

"Ain't no one ever cared before." Ava choked on her tears.

"Maybe you should *let* someone care."

Ava tightened her embrace on herself, her fingers curling into the material of her dress. "Anyone who cares about me dies. Then I'm all alone. That there's the hard cold truth of it, Preacher."

Noah cleared the distance between them in a few quick strides. His hand threaded through her hair at the back of her head and he hauled her toward him. His mouth closed over hers, needing, searching, communicating something—something Ava wasn't sure how to understand. But she responded anyway. She released her embrace on herself and clutched at his necktie, his shirtfront.

Noah's free arm slid around her waist and pulled her close to him. Ava could feel the breadth of his chest. She could taste him as he kissed her. Over and over, until she couldn't breathe. *He* couldn't breathe. They broke apart, and Noah leaned his forehead against hers, his hand still holding the back of her head.

His eyes were fully on fire. There was a passion in them that went beyond the kiss, went beyond any physical need. It was longing for closeness, a soul seeking oneness. The pain in Noah's expression mirrored her own, and Ava couldn't understand. Couldn't fathom how he knew her ache without experiencing it.

They breathed in unison, staring into each other's eyes. Oh, she'd been wrong. She wasn't capable of handling the flames in this man. It was powerful. It held promise of things Ava longed for, but it was dangerous. A different sort of dangerous than what lurked in the woods—in her past and present—but dangerous nonetheless.

He kissed her again. This time, Noah was gentler. His lips held hers. Then he pulled back. "I'm not sorry."

It wasn't what she'd expected.

Noah ran his finger down her cheek. It left a fiery trail on her skin, traversed over her tears, and left Ava feeling alone when he pulled it away.

"You're not alone."

Ava shook her head. "I am."

"You *were*. You're not anymore."

Ava backed away from him. His words filled a hollow in Ava. A chasm that had formed in her that day she huddled in the cellar and listened as her family died. But it also terrified her. With aloneness came the security of only fending for oneself. With togetherness, she would have to care, have to listen, have to put down roots. And while that was everything she wanted, it was everything she was afraid of.

Ava did the only thing she knew how to do.

She ran.

42

Wren

She'd texted Eddie but had heard nothing. A quick jaunt to the Markham house confirmed it was intact, with no damage or evidence of a break-in. But there had to have been, considering Redneck Harriet had last been in Eddie's possession in the house. Wren looked for the hidden key under the garden gnome. It was there. She noticed the imprint of a foot near the gnome, and it was smaller than a male foot. Immediately, the image of Ava Coons was blazing in Wren's mind. She'd been here. The woman in the woods. Smart enough to find the hidden key.

Wren snatched the key from its hiding place and hurried to the front door, inserting it in the lock. Sure enough, there were two muddy footprints just inside the door. A quick call to Gary, who thankfully answered, confirmed he wasn't aware of anyone who would have accessed the house. An hour later, the police met her there, surveyed the area, filed a report, and shrugged a little since there was no evidence of anything broken or stolen. Wren showed them the doll that was lying facedown on the passenger seat of her truck. After she explained it had been taken, the police pointed out that it had also been found and now returned. There really wasn't much they could do.

Annoyed, Wren sped a bit too fast on the gravel back roads,

clattering over the wooden bridge that spanned Lily Pond, and headed for Tempter's Creek city limits. Once there, she pulled through a corner coffee shack and ordered a strong quadruple-shot hazelnut latte and was perturbed enough she didn't even ask for almond milk but instead upped it to a breve. Sipping it, she headed for the library. A little brick building with a selection of pre-2010 books and a limited selection of more current releases. But they had free Wi-Fi, and no one would look over her shoulder. She hadn't said a word about the previous night and the doll to either her father or Pippin. This morning, Wren hated to admit, there was an even wider chasm between her father and herself. He'd poured his coffee in silence, hefted his laptop bag to his shoulder, and driven off to camp to welcome a new speaker for the upcoming week's family camp.

It didn't take long for Wren to get settled at a table near a shelf full of large-print Danielle Steel novels. She tugged the paper that had been pinned to Redneck Harriet's dress from her bag.

October 9, 1996

It had to mean something, regardless of who had broken into the Markham home and who had left the doll at the back door of the Blythe home.

She started by punching the date into Google. As figured, the results were general and generic. Everything from zodiac signs to "what happened on this day." Wren took a long sip from her latte. It was thick and milky and strong. She swallowed, glanced up at a mother and child passing by the table, then redirected her attention to her laptop.

Think, Arwen. Think.

She looked back at the note.

Look in the paper.

Wren considered it for a moment. *The paper* probably meant newspaper. Okay. She typed in the website address for the Tempter's Creek newspaper and checked to see if archives were available online. Surprisingly, there were. Rather good for a Podunk town paper. Wren jabbed in the date, and an image of that day's paper appeared. Skimming it, she noted the weather report, an article about a local high-school athlete who was on their way to earning state in wrestling, and a story about the tavern league.

Disheartened, Wren sagged in her chair. Of course, that was too easy, too simple. She racked her brain trying to place any semblance of meaning onto the date. Something that she would recognize. Aside from it being the year she was born, there wasn't anything . . .

Wren straightened. The year she was born. Ava. Arwen. Whoever the woods-woman was, she was trying to communicate that there was some connection between Ava Coons and Wren. She'd tied it back to Redneck Harriet, who bore Arwen's name on her foot and had been found in Ava Coons's cellar.

October 9, 1996.

Two months after Wren had been born.

According to her grandmother, Wren was born in California, where her dad had been a professor. She bent over her laptop.

Stanford, California.

She added the date.

Several pages pulled up about a university, some economics . . . Wren refined her search to seek the title of the local newspaper. Once she found it, she pulled up its website and clicked on their archives.

"Wren?"

Wren jumped. She jerked around to meet Meghan Riviera's eyes. "Oh! Meghan. Hi." It was a lame greeting. Meghan appeared gaunt. Her eyes were pulled downward, her skin pasty enough that all color had disappeared. Her eyes shifted back and forth, looking over Wren's shoulder, then back to Wren. She adjusted the strap of her purse over her shoulder.

"Are you okay?" Wren asked.

Meghan tugged out a chair and sat down, leaning into Wren. "I need your help." Her whisper gave Wren chills.

Wren shot a glance at the laptop. One click and she'd bring up the newspaper from Stanford, California, in 1996. She looked back at Meghan.

"What's wrong?" The mother needed Wren's prioritization. She was trembling. "Have you eaten anything?" She was worried Meghan was about to pass out.

"No," Meghan whispered. She tossed a look over her shoulder toward the front door, then back to Wren. "I got this, this morning." Shoving a piece of paper into Wren's hand, she waited. "I needed you to see it."

"How'd you know I was here?" Wren asked as she unfolded the crumpled piece of paper that wasn't unlike the one she'd salvaged from Redneck Harriet.

"I saw your truck."

Small-town problems. Privacy was hard to come by.

Wren opened the paper. Her breath caught. She met Meghan's eyes. "Where'd you find this?"

Meghan gave Wren an almost panicked look. "Outside our RV. Taped to Jasmine's bike."

"What!" Wren straightened in her chair.

Meghan nodded. "I'm going crazy. Wren, I'm losing it." Her breath quivered. "I can't do this any longer, and everyone thinks I'm nuts already."

Wren looked down at the note, so similar to the one she was just researching. "What does April second, 2016, mean to you?" She had a gut feeling but had to ask anyway.

"It's Jasmine's birthday." Meghan's eyes welled with tears. "Who would do this?"

"I don't know." But she did. The woman in the woods. It was all her.

"And your name." Meghan jabbed at the paper in Wren's hand. "Your name is by Jasmine's birthday. Why?"

Wren spun to her computer and quickly opened another tab. She typed in Trina Nesbitt's name and Tempter's Creek. A report came up instantly, discussing the disappearance of Trina, naming Trina's mother and others searching for her.

"Why are you looking at that?" Meghan leaned over Wren's shoulder.

"There's something connecting all of us. But I can't figure it out." She eyed Trina's birth date. It didn't hold any special significance to her. She skimmed the article.

"Wayne Sanderson." Wren tapped the computer screen.

Meghan looked confused. "What about him?"

"He helped with Trina's search."

"So?"

Wren turned to Meghan. "He's inserted himself into Jasmine's search too. His stories of Lost Lake. What if they're a deflection? Something to keep him involved so he can watch and—"

"You think he's a psychopath who takes kids?" Meghan breathed. Her fingertips met her lips, which were in a shocked O.

Wren hated voicing her suspicions out loud, but they were there nonetheless. "It makes me wonder. Look. They even interviewed him about Trina's disappearance, and there—he mentions Ava Coons. Right there."

"But how do *you* fit into this? Why would Wayne Sanderson leave a random note on Jasmine's bike with *your* name on it?"

"I don't know." Wren hesitated. Her fingers alt-tabbed back to the screen where the Stanford, California, news archives waited. Without putting further thought into it, Wren slammed her index finger down on the enter key. The newspaper pulled up.

A black-and-white picture of a baby stared back at them. The headline sent a wave of horror through Wren.

Missing: Taken from park, 2-month-old baby girl. Search continues with no leads.

"What is that?" Meghan's inquiry was natural.

Wren drew in a carefully controlled breath. If she wasn't cautious, she could go into a tailspin like Meghan, and take Meghan right along with her.

"Wren?" Meghan's hand came down on Wren's forearm.

Wren stared at the familiar baby. The eyes. The cheeks. The hair that, while a shade of newspaper gray in the picture, was a brilliant red in real life. She'd seen this baby in other pictures. There was even one hanging in the hallway of the Blythe home.

"It's me," Wren whispered.

"What?" Meghan frowned.

Wren tapped the black-and-white photo of the baby. "That baby is me."

Meghan stared intently at the headlines, at the picture, then back to Wren. "You are—you're the—you're the missing baby?"

Wren couldn't breathe. She couldn't speak. White dots filled her vision. She heard Meghan calling her name, a distant echo. Her eyes could barely filter the words below the headline.

Authorities say the window of time making it probable to find the missing baby has expired. The FBI is cautioning parents to monitor their children in the Stanford area, as the kidnapper is still at large. If anyone has any information, please call the Stanford Police Department.

43

Ava

Ava plunged into the clearing. The lake stretched in front of her, its dark waters the grave marking of her family. She knew. She sensed in her gut it would not be long before those of Tempter's Creek who were sure she was guilty would descend on this place. This time not to learn what had happened to the Coons family, but to string her up. If not by her neck, then by her soul. They'd haul her in with no evidence but their own concocted realism. She'd be at the mercy of a judge, a court, and God knew what would happen then. Fine. Let it be. She was tired. Exhausted. Shaken.

Ava waded into the water, allowing the cold to wash over her legs, soak through her shoes, and saturate the hemline of her dress. She reached forward, fingers outstretched, as if by doing so her family's bodies would rise from the watery depths. Their cold gray corpses reaching back to her just as they had in her vision. Covered with weeds and silt from the bottom of the lake, but family all the same. Ma, Pa, Ricky, and Arnie . . .

She fell to her knees, the water splashing up and dotting her face, matching her tears. Ava was surprised Noah hadn't followed her. She'd expected to hear him crashing through the woods behind her. But with that kiss and promising hope had come the shattering reality of their demons that dogged their steps. Hers, the Coons family's demise. His, Emmaline? Who was Emmaline? Had she received Ava's letter?

Ava ran her wet hands through her hair, loosening it from her braid. "God, you may as well take me. Just throw me in the water and hold me under." It was a challenge to a God who was supposed to make sense in a place of confusion. The only sense Ava could make of anything was death. There was finality in it. An ending. This living thing? It was nigh on exhausting. Heartbreaking.

She tried again. "Don't you have an angel up there what could come down and just make me die?"

Ava looked up to the sky. Clouds. Fluffy. Blue sky. It was really beautiful here. She could understand why her family had home-steaded in this place so far out from Tempter's Creek. She could see why someone would want to disappear into these woods—to vanish, to never be seen again. There was a peace here, in spite of the echoes of violence that had bled into its very soil.

"You up there listenin' or are you asleep?" Ava raised her voice.

No face of God shone down and fulfilled her expectation. No angel of death came to meet her request. She wasn't brave enough to do nothin' that dramatic herself.

"I don't want to die anyway," Ava muttered. Her mouth twisted as she grew aggravated at the tears that were just plumb set on coming today. "I just want your help. You know?" She thought of the painting of Jesus in the parsonage sitting room. So nice-looking, really. Peaceful. A bit like Noah, if she was honest. That gentle softness that hid an underlying passionate protection of fierceness. "Maybe just—do *something*?" Ava prayed.

She heard him before she saw him. Not God, but Widower Frisk. When she saw him, she stiffened. He'd shaved his beard. But this time he didn't wear a floppy hat pulled down to his nose. She could see his eyes. Small, narrowed. She knew those eyes. But she didn't recognize his face without his bushy beard that had covered three-quarters of it since the day she'd met him. He stood on the shoreline behind her. Hunched shoulders. Wearing overalls, not unlike the ones Ava was accustomed to wearing.

She struggled to her feet in the water and faced him.

"What do you want?"

"Whack, whack, whack," Widower Frisk cackled. He didn't try to disguise his voice, didn't hiss or whisper. His words were bolder than that night in the church or the day he'd landed his fist against the side of her face.

Ava pushed through the water and back to shore. She hated the widower in this moment. "You killed 'em. Jipsy. Matthew Hubbard. Didn't you?" Anger sucked away Ava's fear.

Widower Frisk rocked back and forth on his feet. He rubbed wrinkled, callused hands together. "You'd like to pin that on me, wouldn't you, you little witch?"

Ava's feet cleared the water.

Widower Frisk waved his arms around. "Here's the damage that begun it all, huh, missy? You an' that bloody ax. Then you traipsed into town like a special kind of poison. Right into my house. 'Course, I didn't know it then." His yellowed eyes scaled her body from top to bottom and then up again. It made her skin crawl. "Had other ideas for you and no plans to let a little chit like you take an ax to me or Jipsy."

"I don't know what you're talking about." Ava skirted around him until she was firmly on the shore.

"Wheedlin' your way in. That's right." Widower Frisk was spry. Even in his older years, he was wiry and strong. His eyes were wide, tinged with crazy, and not at all kind. "Got my years' worth of work outta ya, but then Jipsy. You an' Jipsy and your little *secrets*." He spat a stream of tobacco.

Widower Frisk knew. About Jipsy and Matthew Hubbard. Somehow he knew.

Ava's nerves settled in a ball in the pit of her stomach. Jipsy had started messin' around with Matthew Hubbard a year ago. When Ava caught them, they'd sworn her to secrecy. Jipsy with threats of a whippin', and Matthew with a much kinder approach of bribery. Chocolates. Candies. The like. She'd taken it. What girl wouldn't be bribed by chocolate? 'Sides, Matthew Hubbard might be a bit sleazy, but he was a keen sight better to look at than Widower Frisk. She'd always wondered why on earth Jipsy had any common-law marriage or commitment to the old geezer.

"It wasn't my doin'." Ava tried to convince Widower Frisk of her innocence. Seemed like that was her life's calling.

"Sure it was." Widower Frisk smiled again. He gave a broad sweep of his arm. "Fine place you got here." His cackle was cruel.

Ava narrowed her eyes. "Did you kill my family? So you could have me for free labor? A kid you could use to do all your chores?"

Widower Frisk scowled in disbelief. He hiked toward the burned-out ruin of the cabin. Ava dogged his steps from a safe distance.

"You think I did this." It was a statement, not a question. He bent and picked up a charred piece of wood that had once been part of a wall. He tossed it into the ruins. "I didn't do this." When Widower Frisk turned toward her, his expression was bitter. "But you did this to me. You let Jipsy get away. You an' your secrets. S'why I hunted you down. Scared ya too, didn't I? The church? The woods? That ax-head? Folks in town are stupid. Wharn't hard to figure out the preacher was hidin' you in his room. Little hussy that you are."

"It wasn't like that!" Ava hurried to Noah's defense.

Widower Frisk's eyes narrowed. He stepped toward her. Ava took a step backward. "'Forty whacks' . . . you ain't the first female to kill her parents."

"You honestly think I could have hacked my parents to death? I was a child!"

"Ya came outta the woods draggin' an ax and covered in blood. This place was burned down, blood in the grass, ax marks in the soil and wood. Your family was missin'. I came and looked myself."

"You did?" Ava paused. She hadn't known Widower Frisk had inserted himself into the search for what had happened here so many years before.

The widower walked a circle around Ava, eyeing her up and down as if determining what to do with her. "Sure did. I was the one what found the drag marks in the mud. Finger marks like someone was clawing at the mud."

"They were dead." Ava's voice was weak. Her legs were trembling.

"'Course they were." Widower Frisk patronized her. "You didn't do nothin' to them. So's you said for years. An' everyone believed you until Hubbard done showed up dead."

"You killed him," Ava accused. "You were jealous and murdered him."

"Me?" Widower Frisk slapped his hand to his heart. He continued to circle her, his eyes wild. "Never. Killin' ain't my thing. Well," he added and tipped his head, "it wasn't. Not him no ways."

"*I* didn't kill Hubbard," she argued. Ava looked around for a way to escape. He was older. She would have the advantage over him for speed. But she also knew the widower. He knew these woods better than she did. He was sprightly. Odds were he'd find her again before anyone from Tempter's Creek actually made their way to the Coons homestead.

"'Course you didn't. Neither did I."

"Who—who did then?"

"Ava!" The shout came from deep in the woods. It didn't sound like Noah, but it snagged Ava's attention.

Widower Frisk leapt forward and grappled her to the ground. Ava screamed, kicking out at the man, his springy body straddling her. His hands pressed her shoulders to the ground. Ava bucked and kicked her heels. Widower Frisk sat on her legs and leaned close to her face, the heels of his hands digging into her shoulders, tobacco juice dripping from his mouth onto her cheek.

"Little witch. All you had to do was tell me about Jipsy an' you wouldn't be here." His hands snaked to her neck. Ava twisted her head away, trying to sit up against him. Arms pinned at her sides, she opened her mouth to shout. Widower Frisk's thumbs dug into her throat. His eyes were wide, blue staring into hers with the gleam of the devil in them. "You shoulda told me. Had to find out from Jipsy. Found her cryin' in the woodshed like a little girl. Blubberin'. All a mess."

Ava choked. Coughed. She dug her fingers into the dirt. She heard her name again. "Someone's—comin'," she choked out, hoping it would send Widower Frisk running and release her to find her breath.

The man ignored her. Ignored the shout. He had lost his mind with purpose, and his purpose was only her.

Widower Frisk's breath was rancid. "Ohhhh Matthewwwww!" He made a mockery of Jipsy crying. "Matthew's dead, an' the town's blamin' poor Ava."

Stars danced in Ava's vision. In the distance she heard her name again.

"Funny whatcha can do when you're mad as a hornet. Next thing I knew, Jipsy was dead too." Widower Frisk sniffed as if he might cry. "What'd I do to make her run off an' be with Hubbard? Huh? I didn't mean to hurt her. Not stabbin' her like I did. But she wouldn't listen. An' you? After all I done for you? Givin' you a place to live? Feedin' ya?"

Black shutters closed over Ava's eyes.

The pressure released on her throat. Widower Frisk's weight was thrown off her. Ava gasped, choked, her throat throbbing as she attempted to suck in air. Her vision cleared. A man tackled the widower. They tussled in the dirt, shoes kicking up stones and patches of earth as they grunted.

Ava rolled onto her hands and knees. Saliva dripped from her mouth onto the ground. She retched, her throat working to clear itself. Air sucked into her lungs. She drew in deep breaths, coughing as she did so. So close to dyin'. She'd come so close.

The sound of a fist connecting with Widower Frisk yanked Ava's attention. She saw the man who'd pulled Frisk off her rise to his feet. He took a few steps and hefted something into his hands.

Ava tried to clear her vision.

The item was long. Thick. Circular at the bottom where one powerful hand gripped the shaft, but the top was a dull metal color, held just below by the man's other hand. He sauntered toward the widower, whose eyes were now turned on the man. Widower Frisk backed away on his backside, then lifted his arms to shield his head.

"No! Don't do this!" he screamed.

Ava's eyes cleared. She watched as Ned lifted the logger's ax over his head.

Ava's screams combined with the widower's as the ax came down with a vicious stroke.

44

Wren

Gravel spit from her rear tires as Wren backed out from the parking spot outside the camp's lodge. Tristan Blythe wasn't in his office. Anger and hurt boiled inside her. Missing? A missing child? Wren fumbled with her phone as she drove, ignoring all previous cautions not to be on a phone while commandeering a vehicle. She pulled up another article and skimmed it, her eyesight bouncing between the phone's screen and the road ahead that wound through the forest land.

The missing daughter of Phillip and Sue Johnson has not yet been found. A week after the baby went missing at the local park, authorities state they have no further suspects and refrain to comment whether the child is believed to be alive.

"Phillip and Sue Johnson." Wren said the names aloud. It was unreal. The names of two individuals that only an hour or two before, she'd never heard of. Never had a remote thought that someone other than Tristan Blythe and his blathering obsession with Tolkien and literature could be her parent.

How?

How was she a missing child? Wren turned the steering wheel as she rounded a corner. She'd heard stories of people who'd adopted, not realizing the child they received had been stolen. Was that it?

But then wouldn't there still be some sort of adoption records? Black market? Maybe her parents had *bought* her. A private off-the-records adoption. That would make sense. It kept them justifiably innocent—sort of.

She'd left Meghan at the library. Wren knew Meghan was going to call Ben. Maybe Ben would start believing her now. Maybe the police would. *The police . . .*

Wren wrenched the steering wheel the other direction as a rabbit streaked across the road. She should contact the police. No. The can of worms that would open! She needed more answers before she called the authorities on her own father—or adoptive father—or whatever he was. And it still didn't explain what her past had to do with Jasmine Riviera's disappearance, or Trina Nesbitt's dead body, or Ava Coons. Right now she wanted answers.

Finding her father was step number one, and she knew if he wasn't in his office, he had probably driven to the camp's off-site property, where they had a staff cabin reserved for those needing to get away. He liked to put together educational materials for the camp, and he preferred to do it in solitude.

Wren turned onto a side road, the overhanging branch of a tree scraping the roof of her pickup. She glanced down at her phone.

Emily Ann Johnson was last seen on October 9, 1996. She is two months and three days old with red hair and dark blue eyes. She weighs approximately eleven pounds and was last seen wearing a pink sleeper with a white hat.

Emily Ann. That was her name? What if she was horribly and awfully mistaken? The baby's picture *was* black-and-white, it *was* an older newspaper, pixelated and on the computer. Babies sometimes looked alike. There was a chance she was just plain wrong.

No. No, there wasn't.

Wren dialed Eddie's number. When the call didn't go through, she looked at her phone. There was a signal, but it hadn't connected.

The problem wasn't uncommon for cell service in this area. She tried again, only to have it connect and go to his voicemail. Panic was rising in her. She hadn't seen him since the night in the camp kitchen. Hadn't seen Troy either, but at least he'd answered her platonic texts. Eddie was simply off the grid—right when she needed him most. Right when *he* needed her, but she'd been too blind to realize, too dumb to know what Patty had alluded to all along. She and Eddie needed each other. Were meant for each other. They weren't just buddies, pals, old friends. They were—

The truck bounced over a pothole, and Wren's phone flipped onto the passenger seat. Growling, she left it there and turned into the short drive of the cabin. Jumping from the cab, she strode toward the cabin.

"Dad?" she called. She'd give him a chance to explain. Wren determined that as she hopped up the three steps onto the porch. "Dad?" It was only right. He wasn't an evil man. He wasn't bad. He was her *father*, for pity's sake! There had to be an explanation.

"Dad?" Wren wrenched the cabin door open. She ducked inside and looked around. There wasn't any sign of her father. No academic books splayed on the small table. No papers. His reading glasses weren't there. Neither was his pivotal thermos of coffee that gave him the courage of Aragon, if not the personality of an Orc.

"Crud," Wren muttered. She spun on her heel and hurried from the cabin, shutting the door behind her. She headed for her truck. It wouldn't hurt to try calling his cell again. Maybe he'd pick up.

"Wren?"

She skidded to a halt as Pippin rounded the cabin. A fishing pole was in his hand. Wren sucked in a breath of relief. That's right. He liked to fish at the small pond just yards into the woods from here. His brow was furrowed, his barely there mustache lifted to the right as he scrunched his mouth in question.

"What are you doing here?" he asked.

"Where's Dad?" she demanded. Wren opened the passenger

side door and grabbed her phone. Turning, she slammed the door. Pippin leaned his pole against the porch.

"I've been trying to find Dad," she continued, "and he's not answering my calls. He wasn't in his office. He isn't at home. He isn't here."

"He is probably in town having coffee over his weekly Tuesday Zoom calls with the university."

Oh. Pippin was right. Their father always did that. Zoom calls in the coffee shop on Tuesdays.

"I have a question." Wren leveled her attention on her brother.

Pippin leaned against the hood of her truck. He didn't appear to welcome the question, but he didn't stop her either.

"Do you remember when I was born?"

He shrugged.

"Tell me about it." Wren waited.

"What do you want to know? You were born. Mom and Dad brought you home from the hospital. You cried—a lot."

"Did I?" Wren couldn't help but laugh.

"It was annoying."

Wren ignored that, and her brother's frank, unemotional stare that offered no apology for it. "Do you remember Mom being pregnant?"

Pippin rubbed his mustache. "Sure."

Wren flicked on her phone and showed the article to Pippin. He skimmed it.

"And?" Pippin raised his eyes.

"You don't recognize it?"

"The baby?"

"Yes."

Pippin's expression was placid. "It's a baby."

"It's me." Wren watched his face. It was so blank. So empty. It told her nothing.

Pippin handed her back her phone. "It's a baby," he repeated.

Wren slipped her phone into her pocket. He was no help. If

anything, he was more detached than usual. "Fine, Pippin. I'm going to head into town. See if I can find Dad." She rounded the truck and opened the driver's door to climb in.

Pippin's arm stretched out beside her and slammed the door shut.

"Hey!" Wren leveled a glare at him.

Pippin was inches from her, his arm still extended, holding her door shut.

"What are you doing?" An uneasiness she'd never felt around Pippin made her shift away from him.

"You don't need to find Dad." He was still expressionless. "Dad's in a meeting, and this type of thing would just upset him."

"Pippin, I need to figure out—"

"You don't need to figure anything out." He offered a small sideways smile. It didn't reach his eyes.

"Pippin, you're freaking me out."

"And you are asking too many questions." He grabbed her arm. His fingers bit into her skin.

"Hey!" Wren scowled and wrenched her arm away.

"Come with me." Pippin tipped his head toward the cabin.

"No." Wren curled her lip at him.

"Yes." Pippin took a step nearer to her. "I'm not asking."

Wren stared at him, then pushed against him, reaching for her truck door. "Get out of my way, Pippin."

It startled her when her brother's hand clamped onto her wrist, his grip a vise. "We need to talk."

"I don't *want* to talk." Wren twisted her wrist, but Pippin only gripped it harder. She whimpered, "Pippin?"

He yanked her away from her truck. Wren fell against him, and he curled his arm around her throat, tugging her back against his chest. Leaning into her ear, he clicked his tongue. "I won't let you hurt Dad."

Wren wriggled under his hold.

Pippin shoved her forward, and she careened onto the ground.

The skin on her palms scraped across the gravel. She looked incredulously at Pippin while crawling backward. "What are you talking about?"

He stood over her. "I'm talking about protecting my father's name—and my mother's memory." Reaching down, he yanked her up. Wren's neck cracked as her head whipped forward. Her brother had become a villain.

―――――

"Where are you taking me?" Wren wriggled her wrists, but the plastic zip tie her brother had tightened around them bit into her skin.

Her truck jolted over a pothole. Pippin shifted gears, ignoring her.

"Pippin!" she snapped, but fear was crowding her throat. Her phone had fallen out of her pocket in the tussle with him on the ground outside the cabin. He'd overpowered her quickly, and in an irrational moment of random thought, she regretted ever quitting her martial arts lessons in fifth grade.

Pippin tapped the steering wheel, ducking to look out the windshield and up toward the sky. "Looks like it might rain."

"Pippin!" Wren struggled with her wrists. Her ankles, also bound with a zip tie, were bleeding. "The ties are too tight," she whimpered. There had to be mercy in him somewhere.

"You know," Pippin said as he turned the truck onto an old logging road, which was mostly grass and ruts with two narrow trails for tires, the middle grown over by long weeds, "the more you struggle, the worse it'll get. Zip ties are a beast."

Wren stared at him in exasperation. He was so unaffected. Like they were out for a sibling afternoon jaunt in the woods. The truck hit a rut, and she bounced on the seat, her shoulder banging into the door.

Pippin pulled the truck off the trail, driving into an alcove surrounded by trees. He shifted the truck into park and shut off the ignition. Saying nothing, Pippin hopped out of the truck, rounded it, and opened Wren's door.

"Come on."

"Where are we?"

He didn't answer.

"You need to let me go."

Pippin gave a cynical snort of laughter. "That request never works. You should know that."

Wren stiffened as Pippin reached for her and tugged her from the truck. She fell against him. "What did you mean you're protecting Dad's name? Mom's memory? What do you know, Pippin?" She jerked away from him, but Pippin pushed her ahead. Tree branches scraped her face as she fell to the ground. Her knee cracked against a tree root, and she cried out.

"Oh. Sorry." Pippin leaned over and flicked open a knife. "Forgot your ankles were tied." He laughed. "Stupid of me." He slipped the blade between her ankles and the zip tie, slicing through the plastic.

Wren limped to her feet as Pippin hauled her up.

"Please . . ." She opted for begging. Maybe that would anchor itself somewhere in the cold tundra of her brother's glacial soul.

"Nice try." He shoved her forward again. This time she could move her feet, so she followed his direction.

She ducked under another branch. Thornbushes jabbed at her shorts, snagging them. Wren ripped through them, Pippin behind her. She noticed he still held his knife. It was more than a pocket-knife. As a kid she'd seen one of the camp staff gut a deer with a knife just like it.

"You know the baby in that article was me, don't you?" Wren hated where her mind was taking her. Down narrow, dark alleyways of suspicion threaded with unclear theories.

"Arwen Blythe, what are you insinuating?" Pippin snapped a twig off a tree as he passed.

"I don't know." She grunted as her toe tripped over a rock that jutted up in the trail. "I haven't pieced it together." She didn't want to either. Wren had suspected her father, suspected something not legitimate. But Pippin? He'd been twelve—*twelve* back then.

Pippin's arm pushed in front of Wren, holding back a large leafy branch that blocked the trail. She glared at him as she squeezed through. The branch snapped back into place.

Pippin followed Wren. "It really upset Mom after she miscarried the babies." His voice was monotone. Stating a simple fact that wound its way around Wren's heart with a squeezing sensation that threatened to make it stop beating.

"I know." Wren raised her bound hands to push the hair from her eyes.

"She didn't deserve to suffer like that."

"So what happened? They bought a baby from the black market?" Wren asked.

Pippin grabbed her shirt and yanked her back. Wren stumbled, reaching for her brother to keep from falling again. Her knee already throbbed, and a thin line of blood was running down her ankle into her sock.

Pippin was irritated. At least he showed emotion now, but Wren shrank away from his intensity.

"Black market?" He snorted in disbelief. "Is that what you think?"

"What else is there?"

"Who do you think took care of Mom all those years?"

Confused, Wren drew back. "Dad?"

"*Me.*" Pippin jabbed at his chest with his finger. "Dad all but lived on campus."

"So? What does that have to do with anything?"

Pippin stared at her as if she were the one who'd lost her mind. "She lost babies."

"I know she did."

"She needed a baby."

There was a nagging intuition in her gut, yet Wren refused to entertain it. "And?"

"I found her one."

Wren stilled. It was what she had feared, ignored, avoided. "You can't be serious."

Pippin smiled grimly. "I found you. In the park. There in a stroller. Alone. You needed a mother."

Wren choked. It felt as though fingers were closing around her throat, except Pippin wasn't touching her. "You *took* me?"

Pippin shrugged. "The woman watching you was chatting it up with a few other ladies. You were asleep. When I brought you home"—his gaze grew distant—"Mom fell in love with you. Immediately."

"That *woman* in the park was my . . . my *mother!*" Wren sputtered.

"No!" Pippin exploded, his index finger in her face. His expression darkened. "No. *Mom* was your mother. And Dad saw it too. He was going to take you—return you—but Mom knew what I was trying to do for her. She understood. She begged. Pleaded. Dad knew you were the only thing that was going to keep Mom alive. She was wasting away before I brought you home to her."

"Pippin, you *stole* me." Wren stumbled back into a tree. She leaned against it. Her breaths came in short incredulous gasps. "You literally stole me."

"I re-homed you." Pippin was sincere. She could tell he honestly believed his good intentions. "And Dad, after a week or two, accepted that. It was touch and go for a bit, but then Mom persuaded him until Dad did what needed to be done. He resigned from the university, and we got the heck out of Dodge. With you."

"You all kidnapped me." When she stated it out loud, it sounded so trite. So simplistic. But the complications that were intertwined among it were monumental.

Pippin waved her ahead. Wren didn't bother to resist. She continued to reason through the stunning admission from Pippin. Mosquitoes landed on her arm. Wren couldn't swat them away. She could feel the itching sting as they bit into her skin, leaving red welts in their wake.

Minutes later, Pippin urged her to the left. The trail had disappeared, and now they ducked and wove through the undergrowth. Sweat trickled down the sides of her face onto her neck. A black fly dodged at her nose. Wren lifted her hands and tossed her head to discourage it. It surprised her when Pippin noticed and batted it away.

"What?" He responded to her look of shock. "I'm not a monster."

Wren had no reply. Her mind swirled with possibilities. With questions. She was the baby in the California newspaper. She was the reason her father had downgraded his position to move to Wisconsin, far away from questions.

"My birth certificate that Dad said Mom used?" Wren asked.

"Faked." Pippin gave her a small shove forward.

Her mother was most definitely unstable, that had been clear, but this? And her father complying? The charade of caring for and raising an abducted child? It blew Wren's mind.

Wren stumbled to a stop, her chest heaving, out of breath and parched. "I need water," she gasped.

"Soon." Pippin gave her shoulder a nudge.

They ducked under more growth and wriggled around a sapling. Wren's bare legs were burning from scratches and cuts. Her wrists were throbbing from the zip tie.

"There." Pippin pointed ahead.

She saw nothing but trees. Lots of trees. What looked to be a downed pine tree was crossed over a long-dead oak. Wren started to walk around it when Pippin stopped her.

"Here."

"Here what?" She surveyed the area. There was nothing.

Pippin pointed at the pine tree. Wren let her eyes focus on the area, and slowly realization dawned as she noted that some of the brush wasn't brush at all, but a camouflaged pattern on canvas with branches covering the majority. Pippin approached it and bent low, fumbling for something. Wren heard a zipper like on a tent as Pippin opened the flap. He looked over his shoulder at her and smiled as if she'd be interested in what he had to say.

"It's a deer blind. I bought it a few years ago. Works great out here. Waterproof and everything."

Wren stood, refusing to approach it. She did not know Pippin's intentions, but hers were to stay far away from that blind. From the covering of the surrounding trees.

"Come on." Pippin waggled his fingers at her.

"Heck no." Wren shook her head and took a step backward.

He launched from his crouch, reading her mind and thwarting her instinctual plan to flee. Gripping her arm, Pippin pulled her toward the blind.

"No!" Wren dug in her heels and pulled against him.

"You'll be safe in there."

"I'm *not* going in that thing!" Wren kicked at him.

Pippin pressed his lips together and shook his head in irritation. Before Wren could react, Pippin's hand smacked her across the face, cutting into her lip. She tasted blood. She felt her tears. He shoved his face into hers.

"Look what you made me do. Mom would be upset."

"Mom's dead," Wren cried, the salt of her tears mixing with the iron of her blood.

Pippin's eyes darkened. "Shut up!" he growled. Shoving her, Wren fell to the ground. With his foot against her backside, he pushed her forward into the camouflaged blind. She crumpled inside its dark interior. It smelled dank. Musty. Like urine mixed with earth.

Pippin glared at her as he whipped out another zip tie. He wrestled her ankles together and bound them with it. He tightened the tie before fumbling on the ground for something. Wren heard the metal *clink* of chain. It snaked underneath the bottom of the blind, having been bolted into the dead oak tree just outside. Pippin zip-tied her to the chain and then sat back on his heels. Wren tried to get her eyes adjusted to the darkness in the blind. Light seeped in from a few tiny tears, but otherwise it was well hidden under the brush.

"I'll be back." His voice had leveled again. "I've got some work I need to get done. I need to figure out what to do with you." It was so matter-of-fact that it stunned Wren for a second. Then reality rushed in as she realized he planned to leave her here in the woods.

"Pippin!" she yelled. "Don't leave me in here!"

He backed away and dropped the tent flap into place, zipping it closed. His voice from outside sent a chill through her. "You can scream if you need to. It might make you feel better. In the back of the blind there's a gallon of water. I'll be back in the morning."

And then it was just his footsteps she heard, cracking twigs as he hiked away.

Wren sat in a huddled heap on the ground in the blind. She sucked in a terrified sob. Confusion, hurt, the shock of what had happened to her as a baby made her numb. But fear of Pippin's instability terrified her. How she hadn't seen it or put two and two together. His emotional distance. His social withdrawal. The way he isolated himself in the basement of his parents' house as a grown man. It wasn't normal. It wasn't typical. Yet there had been no reason to suspect anything other than he was . . . well, Pippin.

"Hello?"

Wren screamed. The voice had come from the far back of the blind. In the darkest corner. It was small. Alone. Wren stopped her wild and irrational scream. She steadied her breathing as claustrophobia warred with reason.

"Who's there?" she breathed.

Silence.

"Who said 'hello'?" Wren insisted.

A faint voice answered, "I'm Jasmine."

45

Ava

Birds clamored from the treetops, crows and blackbirds cawing and a hawk screeching its way overhead. The thud of the ax was dull as it planted deep into the earth just shy of Widower Frisk as he rolled away from Ned. Ned tugged at the embedded ax, and it released easily from the dirt. Fury was etched into every crevice of his face.

"Ned!" Ava screamed, her throat raw.

He hesitated as he moved to draw the ax over his head again.

Their eyes met, and in that moment, Ava remembered.

She huddled behind the potato barrel as the man descended the ladder. Heavy shoes—work boots—landed on the cellar's dirt floor.

"Ava?" the man's voice cooed gently. Coaxing. Laced with comfort and friendliness but cloaked with the horror of her family's screams. All was silent now. "Ava, come out. You're gonna be fine."

She peeked around the barrel, her gaze traveling up the man's body as she clutched the doll to her chest. The eyes were familiar. He was young. Not much older than Arnie, but still a full-grown man. His chest heaved with breathing, as if he'd been working hard. There were specks of red on his face, on his shirt, his pants. It was Ned.

Ned had always been safe before. Maybe he'd saved her family. Maybe he'd come along and gotten rid of whoever had made them scream.

Ava hesitated behind the barrel.

Ned smiled. He reached out a hand. "That's it, Ava. Come here."

She remembered Ned well. Many times when Pa was gone with the boys to cut wood or go into town, Ned would show up. Ma always seemed to like Ned. They were friendly. She'd caught them hugging once and it'd dawned on her then that maybe they were too familiar with each other. Ma was pretty, but she was older'n Ned. Ned didn't seem to care. It bothered Ava. She'd almost asked Pa about it, but something had held her back.

Last time Ned had been here, he and Ma had argued. Somethin' fierce. Ava didn't know why. She remembered Ma saying somethin' about "Not doing this anymore," and Ned getting all huffy. He'd left, but he gave her a peppermint stick before going.

Finally, Ava stood from her crouch behind the barrel. "Is Ma okay?" she asked.

Ned winced, then smiled. "Y-yeah. Ava, your ma, she's—there's been a bit of an accident."

And Ned had led her up the cellar stairs. She'd seen her pa, and then her ma, lyin' on the floor. And she'd screamed. Ned had reached for her, but she bit him. She'd crawled to her mother, tried to make sense of her mother's last words, and then she'd smelled the smoke. When she turned, Ned was gone. But the cabin was on fire. She had to get her family to water where they wouldn't burn . . .

"What did you do!" Ava cried. Her face crumpled as she hollered at her friend. The one person in Tempter's Creek she could truly abide. The one who'd always looked out for her from a distance and had her back. "What did you *do?*" she accused with her hoarse throat.

Widower Frisk took the opportunity to roll into a standing position. He sprinted for the woods, making his getaway. Ned looked torn between chasing after him or staying with Ava. He lowered the ax, letting it land with a *thump* onto the earth.

"It just happened. He was goin' to kill you, Ava!"

"Widower Frisk?" she cried. "I'm s'posed to say 'thank you' for that?" Ava was spittin' fire, and she was okay with that. Fear of the widower had replaced timidity and then horror of dying, and now it was outright fury. "You killed my family!"

Ned paled. His face shifted from hurt to shock. His eyes widened. He shook his head. "It wasn't supposed to happen like that."

"Yes. Yes, I remember. I remember it all now!" Ava was still on her knees. She didn't have the strength to stand.

Ned hurried toward her, but Ava reared back, and he stopped. "Ava. Listen to me."

"No." She shook her head vehemently.

"I saw red, Ava, *red!*" Ned dropped to his knees across from her. "I met your ma in town one day. Sure she was older'n me, but she was so pretty. An' we hit it off."

Ava could barely breathe, and when she did, it raked against the rawness in her throat.

"Then she broke it off, after I'd come out here sometimes. Just her and me."

"Why did you come back then? If she broke it off, why'd you come back here?" She hauled off and slapped him. Hard. Across the face with a stinging whack that left an imprint of her hand.

Ned's head jerked to the side, but he swung it back around as if he hadn't felt it. "I know. I shouldn't have. But I wanted your mama. I wanted to fix things 'tween us. But your pa, he came back from loggin' early. Was madder than a wet hornet, and *he* came after *me*, Ava!" Ned's eyes widened. Pleading with her to listen, to forgive. "He came after me!"

Ava gagged and retched onto the ground. Ned stumbled toward her, patting her back. He took a handkerchief from his Levi's pocket and dabbed at her mouth. Ava twisted away from him.

"Don't. Touch. Me." She glared. "You won't blame my pa for this. You're the one who went after my family with an ax. Why'd you let me live, huh? You couldn't have known I'd forget you? Forget you killed my family?"

"Ava, please. I just plumb lost my mind." Ava saw some of the crazy that had been in Ned that day reflected in his eyes. "Your mama and I, we were meant to be with each other. You all—you were in the way."

"Then why kill Ma? Why not kill me?" It was the trying to make sense of it that kept Ava still and not racing to be free of Ned.

"She got in the way!" Ned was crying now. Weak and shaking, his eyes growing wilder. "She tried to save your pa, and when I . . . when I hit her, and then your brothers came runnin', and well, I don't remember much after that myself. But I've watched over ya. Helped make penance for what I did. I didn't expect you to not remember. Once I came to my senses, I ran off. Left you there. I figured you'd turn me in. I'd planned to leave town, but then you didn't remember nothin', and—" he paused, his expression pleading with Ava for mercy and understanding—"and I took care of ya as best I could. For your mama."

"Get away from me," Ava snarled. "All these years I've wondered— tried to remember. I trailed from the woods draggin' that ax! The entire town thinks I'm a killer. You killed Hubbard too, didn't you? Whatever for?"

"I *had* to!" Tears stained Ned's dirty face and ran down into his whiskers. "He was comin' on to ya."

"He was *not*!"

"He *was*! He was givin' you candy and presents, an'—"

"He was buying my silence so I wouldn't out him and Jipsy to Widower Frisk!" Ava's concluding cry was shrill and tore from her throat. She hurtled toward the unready Ned and rammed her palms into his shoulders. He fell backward, his head hitting the ground.

Ava brought her arm down, hauling off and hitting the side of his face. "You killed my ma!" she screamed. Then she hit him again. "You murderin', lyin', son of a—" Ava slapped him with every ounce of her pent-up anger and grief and loss.

When arms grabbed her by the waist to pull her off him, she wrestled and kicked and fought. Her hands came up and clawed at the one behind her. She connected with Mr. Sanderson's face. He dragged her away from Ned. Ava continued to scream at Ned, who lay still.

Officer Larson rolled Ned onto his stomach and straddled him, yanking Ned's arms behind his back and cuffing him. Ned stared at Ava and kept mouthing "I'm sorry, I'm sorry," while she continued to scream and wrestle against Sanderson's hold.

"I'm gonna *kill him!*" Ava shouted.

"Stop it, you little tiger." Sanderson's command wasn't based in care or concern but out of sheer self-preservation as she raked her nails over his face.

"Ava!"

Noah's voice split through her consciousness.

"Ava, stop!"

His hands reached for her face, palming her cheeks. Ava shook her head from side to side as furious, broken sobs shuddered through her. Her eyes locked with Noah's as Sanderson continued to hold her back against him.

"He killed 'em," Ava sobbed.

Noah nodded, not releasing his hands from her face. "I know. *We* know. We heard everything."

"Widower—"

"They got him. He ran into me and the others from town as he tried to get away."

Ava's knees buckled. Sanderson lost his grip, but Noah caught her. There was an exchange of some sort between the men. Sanderson gave Noah a slap on his back, then left them alone. Ava clung to Noah's shoulders as he drew her into him. A primal agony took over her, a wailing sob from deep within her soul as she saw the ruins of the Coons cabin, the ruins of her family, and the ruins of her life.

Wren

Wren scurried the short distance between herself and Jasmine. Her eyes were finally adjusting to the darkness. The little girl huddled in the far corner, her own foot chained by a similar contraption. A box of crackers, a bottle of water, and a blanket were beside her. She was filthy. Her dark hair hung in matted strands about her face, and her thick dark lashes were wet with tears.

"Oh, sweetie . . ." Wren reached her and, without thinking, planted a kiss on the little girl's forehead. "Jasmine, it's okay. You're okay."

Jasmine buried herself against Wren. "I'm scared."

"Yes, I know, I know." Wren stroked Jasmine's hair as best as she could with her hands bound together. She pulled back to look down into the child's face. "I know your mama and your daddy."

"*Papi?*" Jasmine's chin quivered and dimpled. "I need my papi."

"I know, sweetie. We'll find him. We'll figure this out."

Wren couldn't fathom what Pippin had done. Or why. So his story about her own abduction made sense—well, it at least followed a logical progression—but Jasmine? What did Pippin want with harboring a little girl in a deer blind deep in the wilderness?

"Have you been here a long time?" Wren checked Jasmine's face and hands for wounds.

Jasmine nodded. "First, I was in a dark hole in some old burned-up place by a lake."

Wren jerked her head up from inspecting a scabbing-over cut on Jasmine's bare arm. "You were in the cellar of the Coons cabin?"

Jasmine shrugged. "It was dark. There were old things down there and spiders. That man used to come down, and he'd read me stories, but I just wanted to go home. He found a doll, and he told me all about his sister when she was little and how she made his mommy happy. That when his sister came, his mommy didn't cry anymore. He wrote her name on the doll's foot 'cause he said it's hard to remember if you can't see it now and then."

"Arwen. Yes," Wren nodded. "That's me."

"You're Arwen?" Jasmine's eyes welled with tears.

Wren wiped them away with her thumbs. "Yes, sweetie. That's me." Pippin had used the Coons cabin for his lair! It sickened Wren. She squeezed her eyes shut against the questions, then opened them and had to ask, "Did he hurt you?"

Jasmine shook her head. "No. Not really. I cut myself in the woods and got blood on my sweatshirt. He was mad when he realized I'd taken it off and dropped it somewhere. But it was an accident. He told me it'd be okay. He told me his mother was sad a lot, and then . . . she went to heaven. But that he got sad like she did now. He needed me to help make him happy again. When his mom died, there was another little girl—he said she was going to make him happy like you'd made his mom happy, only she did something so he said he had to leave her behind in the woods. And that she went to sleep and didn't wake up."

"Trina . . ." Wren breathed. It had to be. Mom dying must have triggered something in Pippin. Instead of showing his depression and regression, he'd secluded himself. Developed a persona that fit the thirty-something adult who lived at home with his remaining parent. He was odd because—he was a nerd. But his hours of aloneness, secreting himself away in the basement . . . he must have the same mental illness—undiagnosed—that Mom had! His response was to attempt what had helped Mom. A child, a companion. Trina had failed. He'd waited ten more years? What had triggered him to act now, and with Jasmine?

Wren shook her head. "But why you?" she muttered, more to herself than to the girl.

"What?" Jasmine asked.

"Nothing." Wren smoothed the hair back from Jasmine's face. "He didn't hurt you? Touch you?" She had to check to be sure.

"No, he just told me stories. Brought me food. Sometimes he

talked as though his mama were here with us, but I never saw her. He'd just talk to the air. Say things like 'See, Mama? Isn't she what you dreamed of?' Maybe she talked back? I didn't hear her or anything, but he'd get a big smile on his face." Jasmine pulled away and felt around until she found what she was looking for. She lifted another doll, this one a current doll with long blond hair and blue eyes. "He brought me a doll. To replace the one from the hole in the ground."

Wren sagged onto her heels. She fiddled with the tie at her foot, the chain. There had to be a way out of here. "Okay, Jasmine. Here's what we're going to do, all right? I'm going to see if I can find a way out of here."

Jasmine shook her head. "There isn't one."

"There is, sweetie," Wren assured her. There had to be.

46

Ava

Huddling on the sofa in the front room of the parsonage, Ava looked from person to person. Three of them sat across from her. Four, if she included Noah, who sat beside her.

Councilman Pitford swiped his derby from his head. Cleared his throat nervously. "We'd like to offer apologies from the town of Tempter's Creek. Things got out of sorts, what with Mr. Hubbard's death, and then Jipsy. It was uncouth to let the town run rampant with rumor and unfounded accusations."

Ava's gaze trailed to the next man, who also swiped his hat from his head. Mr. Sanderson. His expression was far less humble but not unkind. He ran his finger under his nose, over his mustache and beard, and gave a curt nod. "Sanderson Lumber would like to assist the town in making amends to you by rebuilding your cabin on the lake."

That was unexpected. Ava shot a glance at Noah. He was staring down at his hands. She turned back, feeling the soreness in her throat after yesterday's events. "I don't know what to say."

"You don't owe us anything," Officer Larson interjected. "We're just thankful you weren't hurt worse in the process."

Ava rubbed her throat. The town representatives were groveling at her feet now. She'd feel better if'n they just left. Left her alone.

"Don't rebuild nothin'," she finally said.

Sanderson's brows flew up to meet his hairline.

"I don't want to live there." Live in the shadows of such violent memories? No. No, thank you. Her entire world here at Tempter's Creek was splintered beyond recognition.

She sensed Noah shift on the sofa.

"Reverend Pritchard"—Sanderson's tone became graver—"we would like a word with you."

"I understand," Noah nodded.

Ava studied him for a moment. He looked beaten. Haggard. He'd also sacrificed for her, in a way no one ever had before. She straightened and leveled a defensive stare at Mr. Sanderson. "What you got to say to him, you can say in front of me."

Mr. Sanderson cocked his head to the right, giving her a skeptical look. "Miss Coons—"

"She can stay," Noah interrupted.

Officer Larson exchanged glances with the councilman. Sanderson seemed unaffected in his self-assured way. He agreed with a slight shrug.

"Well," Sanderson continued, "there is the issue of your living situation. Hardly conducive to the lifestyle of a man of the cloth. You were advised it likely would become an issue, and you saw fit to disregard it. We simply cannot—"

Ava swept to her feet, thankful to be garbed back in her old familiar overalls. "Now you just wait a second."

Sanderson held up a hand. "Miss Coons—"

"Don't be 'Miss Coons-in' me," she shot back, shaking her head. "Seems to me it's all *your* fault—yours and the town's—that Preacher Pritchard is in this position. He was the *only* one who wanted to help me out, and the *only* one who believed me when I said I was innocent. Now here tell you're goin' to punish him for doin' what the good Lord asks? To love thy neighbor?" Ava tilted her chin up. "Uh-huh. I know me some Scripture and"—she thumbed over her shoulder toward the picture of Jesus—"I know He wouldn't see this as somethin' to punish. Preacher Pritchard done nothin' wrong. *We* done nothin' wrong, and you know what else?"

Officer Larson choked. "What?"

"Ava . . ." Noah put a hand on her arm from where he sat on the couch. She shook it off.

"What else is, there's a lot of lost people in this here town. I've been one of the most lost. Don't pretend that any of you really care about me. You just want to take care of a problem and make yourselves feel better now'n you got Widower Frisk and Ned behind bars. But I've spent most of my life here, and Noah was the first person to give somethin' of himself for me that would hurt him by givin' it. His reputation. But he gave it to—to show that what he preaches ain't nothin' but the truth. I'd say if'n you want anyone watchin' over your church, it'd be a man like Noah Pritchard." Ava colored. "Like Mr. . . . uh, Reverend Pritchard."

"Well said, young lady," Councilman Pitford acknowledged with a slow handclap.

Sanderson didn't seem convinced. "There's still the fact that the congregation questions the morality of this situation. It's apparent there is something between the two of you and—"

Noah launched to his feet. His eyes sparked. Ava noticed it and wondered if anyone else did too. 'Cause she knew what it was to mess with them embers!

"Ava and I have remained pure and honorable. If you choose to believe otherwise, then it is on your conscience, not ours."

"So you're admitting there *is* something between the two of you?" Sanderson smiled smugly.

Noah set his jaw and glared down his nose at the man. "A man's personal life is between him and God alone."

"But you set the example for the pulpit, Reverend, and the community," Sanderson barked. "*This* arrangement is *not* setting the example."

"No." Noah's eyes were lit now. "*We* set the example. All of us who say we are men of faith. And you know, Sanderson? That's the beauty of God's grace. It's understanding, it's choosing to show grace. It's holding each other accountable, yes, but it's also not creating our own narrative and forcing others' stories into it. Finding the *truth* which is nonnegotiable. That is our purpose."

Ava stared at Noah. He'd taken a step toward Sanderson. Sanderson's mouth set in a thin line. Officer Larson was fidgeting with the brim of his hat. Councilman Pitford was smiling openly.

Noah continued as if he were preaching from the pulpit and had the entire congregation eating out of his hand. "If I want to pursue Ava Coons, then I've a right to. I also have a responsibility to my congregation and to God to make sure I do it in a way that's pure. Not held to man-made standards and precepts. I've no intention of her remaining here at the parsonage. Fact is, she's already moved in with Hanny. So, you go right ahead and hold your lofty, pharisaical head up high, Sanderson, and tell me all the ways you're superior in righteousness, and then—*then*—I'll listen to your accusations based on pure judgment alone."

Councilman Pitford clapped slowly once again. "Hear, hear!"

Sanderson glowered at the councilman.

Councilman Pitford offered Sanderson a nonplussed look. "He's right! And we all were sure Miss Coons was ax-murdering people, and how wrong we were about that."

"I'm not saying," Noah concluded, his body relaxing a bit, "to ignore wrongdoing—or even the appearance of it—I'm just saying be sure before you ostracize people for what you assume to be some wrongdoing, to find out the truth. Like Ava said, so many are wandering the edges of community, wanting in, wanting fellowship, wanting to be part of a family, and we push them out."

"He's right," Officer Larson said.

"You can't be serious!" Sanderson swept his arm through the air. "They've been living here together for weeks."

"I'm sure Hanny was checking in on them," the councilman interjected.

Sanderson skewered him with a look. "As if that is enough to cease any carousing when she wasn't here. Not to mention she's half blind as a bat last I heard."

"Oh, really?" Hanny's wobbly, aged voice broke the tension. She leaned on her cane in the doorway, but Ava was sure she looked about as fierce as Noah. She waddled a few steps into the room. "I'm ashamed of you boys." She wagged a finger at the men. "After all you put Miss Coons through. And for Pete's sake and Moses' sanity, have you even looked at yourselves? What gives you a place in this town and not Ava? Not Noah? *Mr.* Sanderson, have you even kept accounts of your own wife's recent tête-à-têtes?"

"What does Sarah have to do with this?"

Yes. Ava waited, holding her breath. She'd been wondering the same thing. Ned's accusation that she'd been involved with Matthew Hubbard seemed farfetched now. And considering it'd come from Ned, also unbelievable.

Hanny shook her head in disbelief. She clucked her tongue. "Ohhhh, Jason, Jason." She smiled in pity at Sanderson, and her use of his first name reminded Ava of how much older and how grandmotherly Hanny truly was. "I can tell stories about your wife. How she snivels behind other women's backs and embellishes such delicious stories about them. You know how Widower Frisk found out about Jipsy and Mr. Hubbard, don't you?"

Sanderson's face was red.

Hanny smiled patronizingly. "Of course you don't. It was a rumor your wife was circulating for quite a while. That, and about Hubbard and Ava too." She tapped her index finger to her chin. "I wonder . . . if your Sarah had kept her wagging tongue quiet, would Ned have even killed Mr. Hubbard?" Hanny gave an exaggerated intake of breath. "Fact is, maybe Sarah is morally responsible for the murders!"

"That is nonsense!" Mr. Sanderson exploded.

"And so are your unfounded accusations against Noah and Ava," Hanny snapped. She pounded her cane on the floor. "I rest my case."

Councilman Pitford snorted, as if Hanny were truly in a court of law and defending the reverend and Ava from false accusations.

Sanderson smashed his hat on his head. He opened his mouth to retort, but apparently, upon hearing how Sarah's slanderous rumormongering had set into motion the recent horrible events, he changed his mind. Snapping his mouth shut, he gave them all a curt nod. "Good day." With that, Sanderson let himself out of the parsonage.

Officer Larson and Councilman Pitford both offered small smiles.

"I believe we've concluded this conversation," Officer Larson stated.

"Thank you," Noah said.

"However," the officer added, "unfortunately, I've no say over what the church decides regarding your pulpit."

"I understand," Noah nodded.

"Good day, then." Officer Larson replaced his hat on his head, as did Councilman Pitford.

The front door closed behind them.

Noah, Hanny, and Ava all stood in silence. Until Hanny laughed and waved the tip of her cane toward the door where the men had exited.

"Bunch of goons, they are." She leveled her hazy eyes on Ava. "With Councilman Pitford head of the church board, you'll be fine. I can see he isn't taken in by all the lies. Good man, he is. Now. There's the issue of you two. All swoony-eyed and—"

"We're not—"

"Pshaw, Noah Pritchard!" Hanny waved him off. "It's plain as the nose on your face you have a thing for this girl. Backwoods country girl meets preacher from back east. It's quite the match, I'd say." Hanny moved to leave, then paused. "Oh, and I think you'd best tell the girl about Emmaline before you find yourself in another hot mess."

Pippin hadn't compensated for the fact that what could hold a six-year-old child captive was not something that could hold her. Wren pulled the canvas side of the deer blind off the ground enough to slide through. Sitting outside, she followed the chain she was tied to until she reached the bolt that was twisted into the base of a tree.

"Jasmine?" Wren called softly.

"Yes?" The little girl sniffled. She was frightened, and rightfully so. Wren wished they could see each other for the sake of Jasmine, but they couldn't with Wren outside the blind.

"It's going to be a bit, but I'm right here, honey. I'm not leaving you."

"Okay," the watery voice replied.

Wren set to work trying to twist the screwed-in bolt from the trunk. It was tight, rusted, and the trunk was already swollen over it. Her ankle was bleeding again from the zip ties she'd worn earlier. Her wrists zip-tied together didn't help much either. For the next hour or so—she'd lost track of the time—Wren grunted and cajoled the circular steel bolt to turn. She moved it a few millimeters, but then it became harder to budge again.

"Arwen?" Jasmine's voice called from the blind. "Are you still here?"

"Yes. I'm here," she reassured her. Wren's fingers were bleeding where they'd scraped the bark on the tree. She readjusted and tried again, and again, then gave a small "whoop!" when it turned. This time it was easier. "Jasmine, I think I've got it!"

A few minutes later, the bolt finally came free from the trunk, and the chain dropped to the ground. There was no way to detach herself from the chain without cutting the zip tie, so Wren hefted it into loops around her arms.

She hurried around to the front of the blind, dropping the chain and using her bound hands to unzip the door. She pushed her way in. "Jasmine, I'm free." She wanted to run now, but she couldn't. She couldn't leave the little girl behind. "I'm going to find where your chain is bolted and work on that. Okay? We'll get out of here."

Jasmine's eyes were enormous, frightened, and the dark circles under them told Wren she was dehydrated, malnourished, and exhausted. Still, the brave little girl nodded, and Wren set to work on Jasmine's chain.

It was turning dusk by the time Wren wrestled the second bolt from the tree. Her fingernails were broken, her fingers bloodied and burning. Her neck muscles had cramped from her position, and the ties had bitten into the skin on her wrists, leaving them raw.

A sense of euphoric elation stabbed through Wren as she stumbled back to the blind. "Jasmine! I got it! You're free!"

The girl hurtled toward Wren at the door, the chain around Jasmine's foot clanking. She threw her arms around Wren's neck, knocking Wren backward. She wanted to hold Jasmine, but with her hands still bound, that was impossible.

"Okay." Wren leveled her gaze on Jasmine. "I need you to help loop the chain over my hands, and then you're going to need to carry yours. It'll be heavy, but we can do this."

Jasmine was eager. Both filled with a sense of hope.

Soon Wren and Jasmine were pushing their way through the woods and into the brush. She was a little trouper, but Wren kept an eye open for Pippin. She had the nervous feeling of being watched, the hairs prickling on the back of her neck. Where they were in relation to the Coons home ruins and Lost Lake, she had no idea, yet Wren couldn't help the uneasiness she felt growing as darkness set in. She couldn't still the vision that Ava Coons would come raging from the trees, ax in hand.

~~~~~

A large crash ahead of them sent Wren ducking behind some trees. Jasmine followed, pressing against Wren for security. Balancing her chain around her exhausted, cramped arms, Wren huddled with the child.

"Shhh," she whispered.

Jasmine nodded wordlessly. The chain she was holding clanked as Jasmine inadvertently dropped it to the ground. Probably to relieve her arms, but the noise made Wren wince.

The night sky was no friend in spotting what had made the crash. Wren hoped it was a coyote. Even a black bear would be more welcome than Pippin returning to the blind. What was his end goal? He had to know people would miss her sooner rather than later?

Just as Wren was about to call it safe, a lone shaft of light from a flashlight bobbed through the woods. She crouched lower, drawing Jasmine to her side. Every prayer, every ounce of faith was poured into this moment. The light lifted, disappeared, then flicked back on. It was joined by a second shaft. Wren closed her eyes, willing her breathing to stay steady. If it was Pippin, would she be able to fight her own brother to escape? Jasmine's little hand slipped into hers. She was reminded of a day that she'd never recall, but a day that had happened when Pippin had picked her up as a newborn and hustled her away from her birth mother. An innocent. Taken. From that day forward, she had been displaced. Lost.

A shout filtered through the trees. Wren shrank farther into the bushes, thorns snagging in her hair. She drew Jasmine into the shelter of her side. The warmth of the trembling girl awakened in Wren something she'd never felt before. A sense of protectiveness. Of nurturing. She would fight for this little girl with everything she could muster. Just like Patty had, in her own quiet way, fought for her.

47

She heard her name floating through the woods. Like a breeze, it brushed across her face. Wren stiffened.

"Wren!"

Hope shot through her. A search party? How would they know to come here? This area was far from the search grid originally combed for Jasmine. There would be no reason for anyone to know to search here.

Wren remained hunkered low, thankful that Jasmine sensed the need for utter silence.

"Wren!"

The voice called again. Another joined. "Wren!"

Now a chorus of voices. Lights streaming through the woods.

"It's a search party," Wren breathed. She sensed Jasmine look up at her. Whispering in Jasmine's ear, she gave instructions. "I think it's a search party. I'm going to find out. You stay here and *do not move*. Don't come out until it's me calling for you. Do you understand?"

Jasmine nodded.

Wren could see the wide-eyed whites of Jasmine's eyes. She planted a kiss on the top of Jasmine's dirty hair, then moved from her position. "Stay," she directed again. The last thing she needed was to find out these people were not safe and drag Jasmine deeper into something.

"Wren!"

The light was closer now. It swept the forest floor.

Wren stepped from behind the tree, holding her arms up as the light shone into her face. "It's me! Please! Lower the light!"

"Oh my gosh!" the person responded, dropping the light beam. "I found her!" It wasn't a voice she recognized. Wren stumbled toward them cautiously, her chain still looped around her tied wrists and dragging to where it connected with her ankle.

"Please help me," she begged.

The light came nearer as the person rushed toward her. It illuminated his face, his gray hair.

"Mr. Sanderson!" Wren collapsed to the forest floor.

Wayne raced to her, dropping to his knees beside her. Concern was etched into the crags of his face. The flashlight lay on the ground beside him, casting its beam up. "Are you all right?"

"I'm fine. I'm fine." Wren's reassurance made him relax until he noticed the chain.

"You've got to be kidding me!" He whipped a jackknife from his pocket and in two clean strokes sliced through the zip ties. The chain fell to the earth.

Wren whimpered as she moved her arms back into a more normal position. Her muscles were sore and cramping.

A few more people joined them, charging through the forest in anticipation.

Wren lifted her eyes to meet Troy's. A smile split his face, but he turned as another person surged past him. Eddie dropped beside Wayne, and without a word he was holding her.

"Thank God! I thought I'd lost you too."

Tears came then. Happy ones, scared ones, and the ones that said everything a person could feel but not put into words. She buried her face in Eddie's shoulder before remembering Jasmine. Drawing back quickly, she met his questioning expression. Troy reached out and rubbed her shoulder. She knew he needed the physical connection to be assured she was okay. Wren wouldn't cheat him of that.

"Let's get you on your feet," Wayne instructed.

Eddie helped Wren stand.

"Wait." Wren stopped them.

Eddie was studying the raw skin at her wrists as Troy kicked at the chain in a pile on the forest floor.

A few more searchers joined them. She was about to mention Jasmine when her eyes attached to Ben. Ben. He'd joined the search for *her*? Even in the pain of his own missing daughter!

"Oh my gosh! Oh no!" Wren cried, excitement flooding her. She spun away from Eddie, hustling past Troy.

"Wren!" Eddie shouted.

She ignored him and dodged behind the cluster of trees, where Jasmine was still huddling. Obedient. Shaking. Jasmine stared up at her.

"Honey." Wren reached out a hand. "Come with me."

"I'm scared," Jasmine whispered.

"Don't be. It's time to go home."

Wren wasn't sure she would ever forget the impact of the moment when they entered the hospital emergency room and Meghan's cries echoed through the halls as she held her baby girl. The Rivieras huddled together, embracing each other, Jasmine held in Ben's arms and Meghan wrapped around them both. Her eyes briefly met Wren's with a sincere and tearful look of gratitude.

A nurse urged Wren past them. She followed, reaching behind her for Eddie's hand. The nurse opened a room and motioned for the bed.

"In here. The doctor will see you shortly. We'll get your wounds cleaned and treated. The police have questions for you as well. The doctor may want to do an X-ray on your wrists to make sure there're no fractures."

She wouldn't argue. Wren had wondered that herself. Ever since the adrenaline of being found had worn off, her wrists throbbed exponentially. She slid herself onto the hospital bed, swinging her legs onto the mattress. Eddie stood off to the side as the nurse laid a warm blanket over her.

"You can leave your shoes on," she said. "If you get cold, the button to call us is right there. But we won't be long."

"Thank you," Wren sighed as her head lowered to the pillow. She wasn't sure she'd ever experienced such luxury as a hospital bed and pillow. She almost laughed at the idea, but then exhaustion was fast seeping into the marrow of her bones.

Eddie sank into a chair, his arms resting on his bare knees. His gray shorts were frayed at the hem. His shirt was a camp T-shirt, and he'd jammed a baseball cap onto his head. He had a small growth of whiskers. His eyes were tired. Sorrowful. Yet he stared at her with such an encompassing hunger that Wren almost felt nervous. Eddie had never looked at her with such rawness, so openly, so undisguised.

"I'm okay," she assured him.

Eddie smiled a little. "I got back today, and no one could find you. The police called Dad about the break-in at our place."

"Redneck Harriet." Wren would be happy never to see that awful doll again. To think that Pippin had written her name on its foot and given it to Jasmine as a play toy! The poor kid would probably have nightmares the rest of her life about creepy old dolls with human hair.

"How did you find us? How'd you know to look in that region of the forest?"

Eddie blew out a huge breath. "Man, you'll never believe it."

Wren closed her eyes for a moment. "Nothing would surprise me." She'd already told the police about Pippin's involvement. But she hadn't even broached the full depth of his motives, and she was still perplexed as to what had caused him to take Jasmine so many years after their mom's death.

She did know, thanks to an update from Troy, that the police had apprehended Pippin. They'd found him in the basement of the Blythe home—apparently he'd been putting together a pack of items. It hadn't appeared his intention was to leave with Wren and Jasmine. Rather, he'd been intending something far less palatable.

Eddie's upcoming explanation was halted as another person knocked lightly on the glass door. Wayne Sanderson. He poked his head in.

"I'm so sorry. I had to sneak in past the nurses. They're like bull-dogs."

"What do you need?" Eddie asked for Wren. He must have felt protective, even against Wayne, who was remarkably harmless in the whole thing. Eddie rose to his feet anyway and positioned himself beside Wren's bed.

Wayne hesitated. He looked past Eddie to Wren. "I—this is probably a bad time, but . . ."

Wren waited. Wayne was pretty much the king of bad timing, so she might as well give him that allowance.

Wayne hefted a deep breath. "I need to apologize. Profusely."

"Why?" Wren felt another wave of exhaustion make the room spin. She noticed Eddie roll his wrist in a motion for Wayne to hurry up and explain.

"The woman in the woods."

"Ava Coons?" Wren asked.

"No. Her name is Isla." The admission was quiet, followed by, "Isla Nesbitt."

"Nesbitt?" Eddie interrupted. "Like Trina Nesbitt?"

Wayne looked between them, shoving his hands in his pock-ets. "Isla is my sister. She's Trina's grandmother. She's not been the same since Trina disappeared. She knew—*knew* her son-in-law didn't take Trina, not like her daughter and the police were convinced. Especially when she got word four years ago that he'd died and there was no trace of Trina."

"Next you'll tell me she's related to Ava Coons." Wren was having difficulty keeping up. She was getting chilled again as the blanket was losing its warmth.

Wayne laughed hesitantly. "No. No, she's not. In fact, Ava Coons left these parts decades ago. Story says she either vanished into the woods or moved. Most of us like to opt for the vanishing part because it's . . . well, it's more interesting. Anyway, Isla has spent years—*years*—looking for Trina in those woods. Near Lost Lake. That the search party found Trina, well, it crushed her."

"She never came forward with any of this." Eddie's observation echoed Wren's thoughts.

"No." Wayne shook his head and sighed. "And that's been my error in judgment, I'm afraid. Isla—she's gone downhill since Trina disappeared. I-I needed to protect her—or felt like I did. So I tried to be her liaison of sorts. With the police. Keeping her uninvolved and being her voice. Until I found out—well, I'm sorry, I had no idea what Isla was doing. Today, she told me that she'd seen where Jasmine was, and that she'd left you information in hopes you'd link Jasmine to Ava Coons's place, since that's where Jasmine was first being held."

"Before Pippin moved her because of the search party?" Eddie asked.

Wayne nodded. "Exactly. Then she started researching on her own. At the library. About Pippin."

"So she knew all along it was Pippin who had Jasmine?" Eddie's question was barbed.

Wren reached out and touched his arm.

"No, no, it's okay." Wayne shook his head. "She was suspicious of him. She'd seen him in the woods. She'd seen evidence of Jasmine being at the cabin, but hadn't seen Jasmine herself. So Isla was putting pieces together, but you know how it is. The police hadn't done anything—at least in Isla's mind—to find Trina. Why would they believe her theories about Pippin—without proof?"

"She must have been desperate." Wren remembered her standing in the Markhams' driveway. Chasing her in the forest. "Why didn't she just *talk* to me? Why the cryptic notes at night—or running away?"

"She doesn't trust many people anymore." Regret etched itself across Wayne's face. "When people get lost, taken, or just disappear—when there's no answers—we all respond differently.

Some of us can't process things but through our own muddled ways. And she's not . . . she struggles with mental illness. It comes and goes, and she's, well—" Wayne cleared his throat—"earlier today, she told me what she'd done. How she tried to help you connect it all together. That she'd found the newspaper article about you as a missing child when she was running searches on Pippin—the Blythes—and found out they'd come from Stanford, California. She started putting pieces together and thought—wasn't sure—but she thought that baby might be you. Then Jasmine was tied to Pippin. You were tied to Pippin. Trina was tied to Pippin. That's when I called the police."

Wren's eyes slid shut.

Wayne hesitated. "For what it's worth," he explained honestly, "Isla didn't know where Pippin was keeping Jasmine. She was searching—all this time too. He had Jasmine well-hidden after he moved her from Lost Lake."

"So it was Pippin who told you all where to look for us?" Wren opened her eyes to meet Wayne's direct gaze. She looked to Eddie.

"Yes." It was Eddie who answered then. "Pippin didn't bother to try to hide anything once the police arrested him."

"Why Jasmine?" Wren whispered, tears crowding her throat.

Eddie's reaction was empathetic. "It's been ten years." Eddie rubbed his palm over her arm, careful to avoid the wounds on her wrists. "Ten years since your mom passed. It must have revived his need to take care of her. With a girl—to make everything okay. It's why he took Trina. When she didn't survive . . . well, a decade anniversary of her death acted as a trigger."

Wren laid her head back on the pillow. "Mom. He always looked out for Mom."

Eddie and Wayne exchanged looks, but it was Wayne who responded. "We're all lost in our own ways. Some of us just hide when we shouldn't. We hide in our grief, in our minds, in our pain . . . in the woods, like Isla . . . or in a story, like Ava Coons."

48

Ava

He hadn't explained who Emmaline was. It had been apparent that Noah wasn't ready. A few days later, with her body having caught up with rest, and her throat showing green-and-yellow bruising from Widower Frisk's attempt to strangle her, Ava was back in front of the general store, perched on a barrel. She sucked on a peppermint stick, only this time she stared into the distance at the white steeple of the church. Living with Hanny had been a blessing, sure, but it didn't feel like home. The parsonage didn't feel like home. The old Coons cabin ruins? Even home didn't feel like home.

A few townsfolk skirted by her, eyeing her out of the corners of their eyes. Yep. She was still that questionable Coons girl, prob'ly up to no good. Takin' a shine to the preacher, now that didn't sit well either. 'Course, they didn't know that Noah had hardly seen her of late, and truth be told, sitting on top of the barrel sucking that peppermint stick, Ava was hurtin'.

Sarah Sanderson had come and gone into the general store. She'd walked past Ava with her chin tilted so high, if it rained, she'd drown. Lofty princess. She knew she'd started the gossip that had wound up with two folks dead. She'd known it that day Ava had sat at her kitchen table. Prob'ly felt some guilt, which was why she'd been willing to stay out of things. Ava wondered if Sarah had been right. If, in another life, they could've been friends. But then Ava'd figured that most women weren't friendly. Not really. They all spat and hissed behind each other's backs instead of being a place each other could find warm welcome and belonging. Seemed like the world was a cow pie short of an all-out mess. People just makin' up stories to suit themselves while ruining lives along the way.

"Ava Coons." The store owner stuck his head out. "Got a letter for you." His brother was the mail carrier, so Ava assumed that in small-town fashion, her letter had been dropped inside the mercantile when the mail carrier had seen her perched on the barrel.

She took it. Turned it over.

Emmaline.

Ava ripped into it with a vengeance. She'd not expected the woman to write to her.

Dear Miss Coons,

Your letter came as quite the surprise to me. Indeed, it spawned hope within me. I had thought it likely my brother Noah never spoke of me, nor received my letter.

Brother? Ava stopped, looked up as someone walked past, then dropped her gaze to the letter again.

We had a falling-out a few years ago. It was my doing, I'm afraid, and while I am happy now, I was a miserable wretch of a girl then. Noah raised me after our parents died. I expressed my gratitude to him by falling in love with a questionable young man and, to my shame, became with child. While I gave the child birth, I'm afraid I broke my brother's heart when, in secret, I gave my baby to be adopted by a couple to whom we have no alliance or knowledge. The agency assures me the child is safe, but Noah—sweet brother of mine—blames himself as well as me. You see, shortly after I became with child, he banished me from our home. He would not speak to me. When he finally reached out to offer forgiveness, I'd already given my baby into another's care. Noah could not forgive himself, I'm afraid. Perhaps he cannot forgive me either.

Miss Coons, Noah is a good man who takes others as his personal responsibility. He shows grace where none is found and yet gives none upon himself. If you could be the healing balm of Christ to his soul, reassure him I am well and happily married now. I would love to embrace him again one day.

With much regard,

Emmaline

Ava plumb near fell off the barrel.

Wren

Wren sat in an overstuffed chair in the corner of Patty Markham's bedroom. Her knees pulled up to her chest, a red down comforter wrapped around her, she balanced a mug of coffee and stared at the empty spot where Patty's hospital bed had been. Movement in the doorway snagged her attention.

"Hey." It was Eddie.

"Hey," she responded.

He moved into the room, hands in his pockets, and stared at the same spot. "Hard to believe she's been gone a month already."

"You okay?" Wren wasn't, but she would not put herself before Eddie.

"Yeah." His nod was reassuring. "Yeah, I'm good." A soft smile. "Mom wouldn't have wanted me to focus on her not being with us. That's why she wanted that big celebration of life later this summer. Worship music. You know Mom."

Wren nodded. Yes. It was just like Patty. She'd always belonged.

366

Always been confident. Always been sure of her place in the world, but also in eternity. But oh, she ached—Wren *ached*—to confide in her.

The police had arrested Pippin the night they'd found Wren and Jasmine. The following day, after word broke about Wren's kidnapping, they'd arrested Tristan Blythe as well. She was going to have to confront her dad one of these days. See her brother again. There were going to be investigations, trials, and then there was the whole other nuance to think about. The Johnson family. *Her* family. People she'd never met, never known, who had suffered for twenty-six years in fear their baby girl was dead. But Wren wasn't their baby girl. She wasn't Emily Johnson. She was Arwen Blythe. Regardless of how it'd developed. Worse than a sordid classic tale of rings and Orcs. She *was* Tristan Blythe's "precious." She was the ring that had held her family together—all for the sake of saving her mother and, in keeping her, inadvertently protecting Pippin's psychopathic traits.

Eddie approached her, sitting down on the arm of the chair. He knew she and Troy had ended their relationship, but he'd said nothing, *done* nothing, to change theirs. But Wren knew she couldn't face the next few months if Eddie wasn't with her. She might not have the murderous background tale of Ava Coons, but she could relate to what Wayne had said that night in the hospital. There were many lost people in the world. Wren wanted to be found.

"So," Eddie began, perched beside her, "I'm thinking we take Redneck Harriet back to the Coons cabin."

Wren eyed him. "You can put her in the trash compactor."

"Well, actually the police still have her, but someday it would be nice to return her to Ava."

"You're still sentimental over that ugly thing?" Wren stared incredulously at Eddie.

He smiled. In his way, he was handsome. His crooked nose, blond ombré hair, whiskers, and average brown eyes. No, he wasn't handsome. He was striking. He was . . . she wanted him to be hers.

"Listen . . ." Eddie twisted on the arm of the chair. His eyes bored into hers with an intensity she wasn't accustomed to. "I know we've always been pals—friends—like family."

Wren waited, afraid even a single blink would ruin the moment.

"Mom loved you like her own daughter."

Wren's eyes burned.

"And Dad—he thinks you're great."

Wren smiled.

Eddie cleared his throat. "I've gotten used to you, Wren."

The most romantic words she'd ever heard. Wren's eyes filled.

Eddie reached out and flicked a tendril of her hair from her cheek. "I've gotten so used to you, it just about drove me crazy when you were with Troy. I realized if that went somewhere, we'd be . . . well, over. At least the Eddie and Wren I'm used to."

Wren couldn't say anything.

"I've just . . . gotten used to you," Eddie stumbled to explain. He wasn't a man of words.

"I've gotten used to you too," Wren whispered.

The air was threaded with sparks. She'd never had sparks with Eddie before. Her mind quickly replayed the days when they were kids and came running into Patty's kitchen with muddy shoes. She'd half holler at them to get out, all while setting fresh cookies on a plate for them. She remembered the time Eddie had told her to "suck it up" when one of her high-school boyfriends had broken up with her—probably for the same reason as Troy had—seeing what she and Eddie couldn't see about themselves. She recalled the nights Eddie would help her recover from her nightmares. The ones that haunted her—the ones that made more sense now.

He leaned toward her, and Wren stilled. Her heart had stopped. She knew it had. She was surprised she was still conscious. Eddie paused a few inches away.

"I'd like to keep getting used to you," he mumbled.

"Me too" was all she could manage.

He kissed her then. It was different. It was new. A thousand

butterflies took flight inside Wren. She had never once—never ever—never—okay, she had to be honest, deep down she'd always dreamed of this. She'd just never admitted it to herself, let alone to the rest of the world who already knew it.

Eddie slid from the chair arm, and they squeezed together on the seat. Wren shifted until she half sat on his lap. She swung the comforter out and over him, and they snuggled there for a long moment. Quiet. Together. In the legacy of Patty, of her faith, and of the home she had nurtured.

Wren couldn't extinguish her smile or keep herself from looking toward the ceiling as if she could see through to heaven. She'd been found. In so many ways, Arwen Blythe had been found.

Someone cleared his throat in the doorway. Eddie and Wren both looked up to see Gary. His grin was reflective, and he chuckled. "It's about time."

Ava

"Your sister?" Ava rounded the corner into Noah's church office.

Startled, he looked up from his studies, glasses perched on the tip of his nose. Glasses? When did he ever wear glasses before?

"What?" He was bewildered. Well, sure he was!

Ava planted her hands at her waist. "When were you goin' to tell me Emmaline is your sister?"

Noah dropped his gaze to the Bible splayed on his desk.

Ava stomped forward and laid her palm on it, making Noah look up at her. She raised an eyebrow. "She wrote me, you know. Sent me a letter."

"What!" Noah's eyes widened, and sparked, and . . . shucks, they were already ablaze.

"Sure. And she said you give everyone grace but yourself."

"You don't understand, Ava." Noah pushed her hand off his Bible.

She slapped it back. "Don't 'You don't understand' me, Preacher Pritchard of Tempter's Creek Church. You and your sermons and your righteous indignation that no one should blame me for nothin', and you sit here blamin' yourself over what happened to Emmaline?"

"Ava—"

"No. I'm not allowin' it." Ava pulled her hand back and rounded the desk.

Bewildered, Noah drew back as she approached. Brazenly, she grabbed his tie and yanked on it, forcing Noah to stumble to his feet. She pulled his face down until it was almost touching hers.

"I may not have killed no one in my lifetime, but I sure as shootin' was never all that shy either. And I can tell you what you're goin' to do, Preacher. You're goin' to write that sister of yours you've been pinin' after and fix that. Once that's done, you're goin' to get a train ticket home and get yourself out of Tempter's Creek back to where you belong. With your family."

She released his tie, flipping it so its ends lay over his shoulder.

"You've no right to—"

"I've every right!" Ava slapped him lightly on his shoulder. "You saved me, Noah. You did what no one ever did before. You saw me, for me. You cared. You fought for me. It's time someone does that for you. An' it won't be all that hard, 'cause Emmaline is pretty plumb set on getting things worked out."

Hope fluttered across Noah's face. "She is?"

Ava rolled her eyes. "Men can be so dumb." She spun to march away, but Noah reached out and stopped her with a hand on her shoulder.

"Where are you going?"

"Dunno." And she didn't. She'd only had thoughts to set Noah to rights, but after she'd made her proclamation that he needed to go back home, back east, a huge part of her went into a panic.

She'd no right to him. He'd no right to her. They were as different as a wagon was to an automobile. Redneck to a city boy. Heathen to a believer. Well, she believed, she just wasn't a super-educated churchgoer. She'd told that to Jesus, though, and she swore He smiled at her from the painting. Seemed like someone had to believe to belong, and if you did, it didn't matter where you went, you just . . . belonged.

"Come with me," Noah stated boldly.

Ava's heart flipped. Maybe. She wasn't sure if a heart could flip.

Noah stepped closer. Dang those eyes!

"Let's take all your things—what little you have—like that doll, and we'll take it back to your old place and put it back where we found it. Like a burial. We'll bury your family as they should have been, at least in spirit. And then we'll just go."

"Go where?" He was toyin' with her hair, and his fingers brushed her neck, and she knew she could be as ugly as a bug's ear, but the way he was looking at her, she might as well just melt all over into a beautiful puddle of princess mush.

"Home." Noah didn't smile. He barely breathed. He just . . . smoldered.

"I'll have to think about it," Ava replied. He couldn't just tell her what she was goin' to do. She'd spent too much time on her own—

He kissed her. Gentle-like. The kind of kiss where she could taste just a little bit of him, and it was sweet with a bit of spice just waiting to happen.

When he pulled away, Ava cleared her throat. "All right then, I guess I've thought about it."

"Ready to go home?" Noah held out his hand.

It only took Ava a second to take hold of it. *Home*, a word she could make fresh memories on. Leave Tempter's Creek behind. Over time, no one here would ever remember her, or the Coonses, or Noah Pritchard the preacher. Over time, it would just be a lake, lost in the woods, hiding the souls of those who'd made Ava Coons who she was. Just Ava Coons. And she was all right with bein' Ava Coons.

QUESTIONS FOR DISCUSSION

1. Why do you think the author chose *The Souls of Lost Lake* as the novel's title?

2. Briefly tell about a camping experience or an experience in the woods during which you were afraid. Then share a camping experience that was a great adventure for you.

3. If you were to uncover the ruins of an old cabin, what vintage item would you find spooky to discover with your name scrawled on it? Why that particular item?

4. Why was Ava reluctant to trust Noah and others with her fragmented memories?

5. When Wren joins the search for Jasmine, what do you think, besides a desire to help, might have driven Wren?

6. Both Ava and Wren have suppressed memories that affect how they interact with others. What movies or television shows can you recall that depicted a character suppressing memories? How did those past events impact the character?

7. In what ways do you relate to how Wren grieved over the passing of her mother figure, Patty?

8. How does faith and hope in eternity influence how you grieve or how you have seen others grieve?

ACKNOWLEDGMENTS

All campfire ghost stories deserve to be told around smoldering coals. Bringing that element into Noah's eyes was about the best I could do, but I hope that the tale of Ava Coons revives in all of you some remembrance of childhood days, marshmallows, and ghost stories.

This book lands square in the lap of Cap'n Hook, the master of campfire tales and stories. And for a guy who doesn't do fiction, I'd say he did pretty well inspiring this novel. He is really the Markham men in this book—he did discover a lost lake, he did report it to the DNR, he did first tell me a somewhat different tale that soon became the murderous rampage of Ava Coons and Lost Lake. Other than that, it's all tales and pure fiction—or is it?

Just remember, the next time you're cuddling around a campfire, the crickets singing in the background, the woods casting their long shadows over the earth, that Ava Coons still roams the woods. Some say she's just trying to help you find your way home, but others still talk about the sounds they hear, long after the fire has dulled and the campers are almost asleep in their tents. A sound not unlike a logger's ax hurtling through the air, before it descends on yet another of Ava Coons's unwitting victims . . .

375

Jaime Jo Wright is a winner of the Christy, Daphne du Maurier, and INSPY Awards and is a Carol Award finalist. She's also the *Publishers Weekly* and ECPA bestselling author of three novellas. Jaime lives in Wisconsin with her cat named Foo; her husband, Cap'n Hook; and their littles, Peter Pan and CoCo.

Visit her at jaimewrightbooks.com.

More from Bethany House

More than a century apart, two women search for the lost. Despite her father's Confederate leanings, Clara is determined to help an enslaved woman reunite with her daughter; Alice can't stop wondering what happened to her mother in the aftermath of Hurricane Katrina. Faced with the unknown, both women will have to dig deep to let their courage bloom.

To Treasure an Heiress by Roseanna M. White
THE SECRETS OF THE ISLES #2
roseannamwhite.com

Cassie George has stayed away from her small hometown ever since her unplanned pregnancy. But when she hears that her aunt suffered a stroke and has been hiding a Parkinson's diagnosis, she must return. Greeted by a mysterious package, Cassie will discover that who she thought she was, and who she wants to become, are all about to change.

Shaped by the Waves by Christina Suzann Nelson
christinasuzannnelson.com

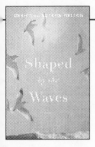

After moving cross-country with her son and accepting a filmmaker's mentorship, Val Locklier is caught between her insecurities and new possibilities. Miles McKenzie returns home to find a new tenant is living upstairs and he's been banished to a ministry on life support. As sparks fly, they discover that authentic love and sacrifice must go hand in hand.

All That It Takes by Nicole Deese
nicoledeese.com

BETHANYHOUSE

Sign Up for Jaime's Newsletter

Keep up to date with Jaime's news on book releases and events by signing up for her email list at jaimewrightbooks.com.

More from Jaime Jo Wright

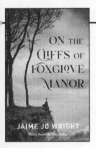

In search of her father's lost goods, Adria encounters an eccentric old woman who has filled Foxglove Manor with dangerous secrets that may cost Adria her life. Centuries later, when the senior residents of Foxglove under her care start sharing chilling stories of the past, Kailey will have to risk it all to banish the past's demons, including her own.

On the Cliffs of Foxglove Manor

BETHANYHOUSE

You May Also Like . . .

In 1928, Bonaventure Circus outcast Pippa Ripley must decide if uncovering her roots is worth putting herself directly in the path of a killer preying on the troupe. Decades later, while determining if an old circus train depot will be torn down or preserved, Chandler Faulk is pulled into a story far darker and more haunting than she imagined.

The Haunting of Bonaventure Circus by Jaime Jo Wright
jaimewrightbooks.com

Mystery begins to follow Aggie Dunkirk when she exhumes the past's secrets and uncovers a crime her eccentric grandmother has been obsessing over. Decades earlier, after discovering her sister's body in the attic, Imogene Grayson is determined to obtain justice. Two women, separated by time, vow to find answers . . . no matter the cost.

Echoes among the Stones by Jaime Jo Wright
jaimewrightbooks.com

More than a century apart, two women search for the lost. Despite her father's Confederate leanings, Clara is determined to help an enslaved woman reunite with her daughter; Alice can't stop wondering what happened to her mother in the aftermath of Hurricane Katrina. Faced with the unknown, both women will have to dig deep to let their courage bloom.

Where the Last Rose Blooms by Ashley Clark
HEIRLOOM SECRETS
ashleyclarkbooks.com